CHAOS

GUARDS OF THE SHADOWLANDS

Book 3

AOS

SARAH FINE

This is a work of fiction. Names, characters, organizations, places, events, and incidents are either products of the author's imagination or are used fictitiously.

Published by Skyscape, New York

www.apub.com

ISBN-13: 9781477847817 (hardcover)
ISBN-10: 1477847812 (hardcover)
ISBN-13: 9781477847909 (paperback)
ISBN-10: 1477847901 (paperback)

Book design by Tony Sahara

Library of Congress Cataloging-in-Publication Data available upon request.

Printed in the United States of America

First edition

For Kathleen:
We started this journey with "Let's do this!"
Well, we did it. This one's for you.

ONE

I HAD CHOSEN TO die. So as I plummeted toward jagged rocks and crashing waves, I closed my eyes and let myself dream.

A sunny day. A warm breeze lifted my unruly curls. The boy who meant more to me than my own life laughed as he pulled me close and smoothed the hair out of my eyes. His easy smile softened the harshly beautiful lines of his face.

I love you, I said to him.

I know you do, he replied.

That was the way it should have been.

But I'd never gotten to say it, and he'd never gotten to hear it.

Not yet, at least. With every cell in my body, with every scrap of my soul, I would fight for that moment. The battle had already begun.

"Really, Lela, the drama is unnecessary." Raphael's voice sounded like it was coming from inside my head. Fire blasted up my arms, and I didn't have time to scream or even breathe. The cool ocean breeze, the night, the roar of water, my dream of Malachi's face—all of it disappeared, deafening me with silence, blinding me with blankness. I hit smooth stone and slid several feet before crashing into what felt like a brick wall. Splinters of pain pierced their way along my limbs as I rolled into a crouch, bracing my palms against cold marble. Blinking, gasping, I raised my head to see Raphael, wings unfurled, skin giving off a brutal light.

He looked . . . annoyed.

I smiled bitterly. "I thought you might do something like that."

He rolled his eyes. "You really shouldn't test me."

"Jumping off the cliff seemed like the quick-and-easy way to cut through the bullshit. I want something. The Judge wants something. You just proved that. You could've let me hit those rocks. I'd be stumbling my way through the Suicide Gates right now."

"And you could have discussed it with me instead of having a tantrum."

I got to my feet, my muscles aching, the bite wound on my neck buzzing with sharp prickles of agony. A gift from Juri, the vicious Mazikin who was now wearing the most beautiful disguise imaginable: Malachi's body. He had all of Malachi's strength and knowledge. All of his memories. Now he was on the loose and wreaking havoc in the land of the living. I knew I should care about that. It was, after all, my job to stop him, to protect innocent people whose lives he'd be happy to end. But I only had room in my bruised brain to care about one thing: Malachi himself. His soul. Which, as far as I knew, was now imprisoned in the hellish Mazikin realm. The Mazikin had made it completely clear on several occasions that they wanted nothing more than to make him suffer. Nothing mattered more to me than getting him out.

"Sorry for being so emotional," I snapped. "I kind of like Malachi."

Raphael's expression softened. "I know." The light around him faded, his golden wings dimming then disappearing completely. "Well, here we are."

There we were. The Sanctum. Above me, the sun trickled through intricate stained glass, which I now recognized was portraying images of the Countryside. Mountains, oceans, fields. Angels. And just at the edges, their barrel-chested bodies covered in brown fur with black spots, their fangs dripping inside their grinning mouths . . . two hyenas, of all things. I shuddered and looked away. "Will the Judge see me?"

I whirled around at the sound of massive doors swinging wide. Raphael chuckled. "There's your answer."

My heart sped. I could feel her power flowing out through the gaping entryway, swirling around me. Cold and deadly. As I took a step toward the Judge's chambers, my legs buckled beneath me, and I threw my arms around the nearest pillar to keep myself from falling.

"I'll fix you up after she decides what to do with you," Raphael said.

I glanced at the pillar, at the smear of blood I'd left on its gleaming marble surface. "Sounds fair."

With awkward, halting steps, I crossed the threshold and started up the aisle of her chambers, letting my eyes adjust to the permanent brightness of the place. A row of massive inhuman Guards stood at attention on either side of me. Last time, their glowing jewel-colored eyes hadn't strayed to me, but this time, some of them looked right at me with suspicion. Smugness, too. But also something like respect. I focused everything I had on not falling flat on my face. It was difficult, because after being bitten by Juri I had lost most of the feeling in my left leg, and the same numbness had now crept its way down both my arms. I must have looked like a zombie, lurching my way along, my left boot squeaking as I dragged my foot behind me. As soon as I saw the figure waiting for me at the front of the room, though, my steps became a little steadier. This was why I had come—to make a deal with the Judge.

Again.

Her eyes were as black as her robes, but her skin was a warm, rich brown. She looked so much like my foster mother, Diane, that I couldn't keep my thoughts from straying to her, the only family I had. I hoped I hadn't seen her for the last time. And I hoped she was safe for the moment. If Juri got to Diane, I would never forgive myself.

The Judge smiled, revealing glistening white teeth. "Welcome back, Lela. I see that you and Malachi share a love for the dramatic entrance."

I sucked in a breath, then dove right in. No sense wasting time when she could probably read my mind. "You have to send me after him."

Her grin grew wider. "And what will you give me in return for this opportunity? Technically, you're a deserter. You abandoned your field unit at the most critical time."

"I'll give you anything you want. *Please.*" I closed my eyes as images of Malachi flooded my head, but instead of my dream of him in the sunlight, I saw a nightmare. His body arching, his muscles tight enough to snap, his eyes squeezed shut as he fought to keep his body and soul united.

An electric sensation zipped along my skin as the Judge tipped my chin up with one of her long purple fingernails. Her gaze bored into mine. "Once again, you have no idea who you're dealing with," she said quietly.

I nearly choked on my fear. "You wanted this, didn't you? This was your plan all along."

Her eyes glinted with that predatory spark. "You made the choices that brought you here. And Malachi made his."

Rage flared inside me, the heat temporarily burning away the numbness. "He has only ever served you. He was doing his duty."

"Was he? I was under the impression he was serving *you*."

I sagged, and suddenly it seemed like the only thing that was holding me up was that curved purple fingernail hooked under my chin. Juri himself had said as much, that Malachi had been so focused on protecting me that he'd forgotten to protect himself. It had enabled the Mazikin to obtain the best weapon ever—the body and mind of one of the most dangerous and successful Guards in existence. "Then if this is my fault, let me fix it," I said.

She laughed, a harsh melody that vibrated along my bones. "It's not that easy. Have a seat." She pulled her hand back, leaving me to fall.

A chair appeared behind me, which was the only thing that prevented my ass from hitting the floor.

"As it happens," she said slowly, gliding back from me, her velvety dark robes swirling around her, "there is something I want you to do."

Relief washed over me; she was willing to bargain. But at the same time, bitterness welled up in my mouth. Malachi had been right—we were just pawns in a game. It wasn't worth fighting it now, though, because he mattered more. "I'll do anything."

"I'll allow you to take a leave from your post in the realm of the living. You can journey to the Mazikin city and attempt to rescue your Lieutenant. You will be outfitted and armed for the task by Raphael and Michael, to give you the best possible chance of success. But even if you survive and are able to get to Malachi, you will not be able to leave the city until you have performed a secondary mission."

My fingers clamped over the edges of the chair.

The Judge pointed at the far wall of her chambers, and a desert appeared. A vast gray sea of sand. The only thing that interrupted the barren landscape was an enormous reflective dome, beneath which I could make out a row of smokestacks and buildings, sticking up like crooked teeth and ringed by a dark wall.

"I want you to go in there," she said, her finger trembling as she glared at the distant city with absolute loathing, "and destroy the portal. It's what enables them to leave their realm and possess human bodies. They never should have gotten access to it in the first place."

The Mazikin city didn't look as big as the dark city, and the buildings weren't as tall, but it was still huge. "Where is the portal?"

She lowered her hand but not her gaze. "The Mazikin are not under my authority."

I guessed that was her way of telling me she didn't know. "So I have to destroy the portal, and then I'm free to leave?"

"And kill the Queen. She'll only rebuild it if you don't." The Judge stared at the distant dome. "She was one of the first. She carries the knowledge in her head."

I clenched my teeth. "Okay. Destroy the portal. Kill the Queen. Anything else?"

Her eyes slid from the city to me, and her lips curled with amusement. "Isn't that enough?"

I looked up at the ceiling, because the sight of her face made me want to cry and laugh and scream all at the same time. "So if I succeed, you'll get us out?"

"No." She sounded surprised I'd even asked. "If you succeed, you'll have the *chance* to get out. I told you—the Mazikin are not under my authority. My angels cannot deal with them directly."

"What *can* Raphael and Michael do, then?"

"They can prepare you, and they can let you in to the dome, and perhaps out—if you complete the mission. The rest is up to you. That's my offer, baby."

I lowered my head and met her eyes; they were black voids, like a shark's. She was giving me a choice, but it didn't feel like much of one. My chances of success were slim. I might go in there and trap myself right alongside Malachi. And even if I freed him, we'd still have to destroy this portal thing and kill the Queen. But what was I supposed to do? Walk away? If Malachi were standing here, if he were making this deal for a chance to rescue me, he wouldn't even hesitate. "Sign me up," I said.

The Judge smiled. "Wonderful. Your new Captain is already waiting for you."

"Captain?"

She arched an eyebrow. "Are you questioning my decision in this matter?"

I wanted to—I'd expected to be in charge or to be going in alone. Who could possibly care more about saving Malachi than I did? But I was afraid the Judge would decide to revoke her offer completely if I argued, especially since she already seemed to have someone else in mind to complete the mission.

"When will we leave?" I didn't want to think about what the Mazikin might be doing to Malachi right at that moment. I just wanted to get to him.

"You need to prepare first. Unless you want to go in there as is?" Her gaze drifted down to my torn, blood-soaked clothing, then lingered on the bite wound on my neck. Juri. Heat coursed up my spine as I tried to imagine slitting his throat, but my stomach turned, because all I could picture was standing over him, looking down at Malachi's beautiful face. I lurched to my feet, only to have my world tilt as a sick dizziness overwhelmed me. I grabbed for the chair, but it had disappeared, as had the Judge.

"Good luck, baby," her voice said in my ear.

Raphael's hands kept me from falling. "Time to patch you up," he murmured, wrapping an incredibly warm arm around my back. He led me down the aisle, past the Guards. This time, they were keenly interested; all of them watched me pass. But the suspicion was gone from their faces, replaced with pity.

We entered the soaring lobby, and the doors to the Judge's chambers swung shut with an echoing click. "Where to?" I mumbled, my lips almost too numb to push the words over my tongue. Any strength I'd pulled together to face the Judge was gone. My heart beat sluggishly, forcing Juri's venom through my veins. I allowed my heavy eyelids to close for a moment, and opened them to see we were now making our way down a wallpapered hallway lined with wooden doors. "Are we in the dark city?"

"Not quite," answered Raphael. "We're still in the Sanctum. It's the connection between all of the realms, but not really *in* any of them, even though it looks that way. You'll stay here until you're ready to leave."

I opened my mouth to ask when I would meet my new Captain, but at that moment, a door up ahead opened, and a woman stepped into the hallway. Tears sprang to my eyes. She wore the navy-blue shirt and fatigue-style pants I recognized as part of the human Guard uniform. Her gleaming black hair was pulled into a high ponytail, and her skin, a coppery umber, was far less pale than the last time I'd seen her, when I'd held her hand as she died. "Ana?"

Her dark cat's eyes drifted over me and then lit on Raphael. "Have you healed her yet?"

"Not yet," he replied.

"Good."

She drew a knife, twirled it in her fingers, and threw it right at my chest.

TWO

RAPHAEL PULLED ME TO the side at the last millisecond, but the knife hit right below my collarbone, wrenching an airless scream from my throat. I coughed, choking, as blood from my lungs burbled up my windpipe.

"That was truly uncalled for," Raphael said sharply as he scooped me into his arms. "Awake or asleep, Lela?" he asked. "Decide quickly."

"Asleep," I mouthed, knowing I couldn't cope with the pain without Malachi there to hold me together.

"Wise choice," Raphael replied. "I'll work as quickly as I can."

My head lolled as I tried to look at Ana, attempting to make sense of what had just happened. Despite my fogging vision, her cold glare was easy to see.

"When you wake up, we have a few things to talk about," she said.

With that fun-filled promise, a thick black wave of nothing rolled over me, shielding me from dreams and love and light, and, for a moment, protecting me from the searing loss of all three.

When I opened my eyes, Raphael was nowhere in sight. Ana, however, was sitting next to my bed, twirling another knife in her fingers. I'd always liked Ana, looked up to her, but I hadn't forgotten how dangerous she was. Especially because, for some reason, she appeared to want to kill me. Beneath the sheet draped over me, my hands traveled slowly to my waist, looking for the blades I usually carried there. I found only pajama bottoms.

"How did it happen?" Ana asked quietly.

"How did you get here?" I blurted at nearly the same time. "The last time I saw you, you were—"

"Dead. Yeah. The Judge let me out of the dark city." Ana's knife spun along her fingers like it was an extension of her body. The blade flashed under the light of an oil lamp.

"And it put you in a really bad mood?"

She tilted her head. "It wasn't quite what I expected."

"She didn't release you into the Countryside?"

"She did." Ana's smile was a bitter twist of her lips. "I was so certain Takeshi would be waiting for me . . ."

"But he wasn't." I closed my eyes.

Takeshi had been Malachi and Ana's Captain, but to Ana, he'd been much more than that. He'd loved her, too, enough to stay in the dark city with her, long after he was ready to be released. Long enough to grow too weak to fight off the Mazikin that took him. When Malachi killed Takeshi's possessed body all those years ago, he and Ana had believed that would liberate Takeshi's soul from the Mazikin realm. But it had been a beautiful lie, one the Mazikin were eager for the Guards to believe, because it made us more likely to kill the possessed instead of imprisoning them in the dark tower, an eternal sentence. That kill-on-sight strategy gave the Mazikin a way to escape, because we—and Malachi especially—were more eager to save the lost than to punish the monsters. When we discovered the lie, we found out that those human souls were actually trapped in the Mazikin realm forever.

"I looked for Takeshi for a while, and then I realized . . . he wasn't in the Countryside," said Ana. "And the moment I understood that, the Wasteland appeared before me."

"What?" I rose up on one elbow, trying to marshal enough strength to get out of bed. I remembered what Henry had said about the Wasteland. Full of killers. The worst of the worst. Definitely not where I expected Takeshi to be.

Ana looked haunted as she recalled the place. "It's like this wide canyon, full of crazy barbarians. Hunchbacks and traders who take advantage of the vulnerable. Wolves and vultures who pick off the weak and scavenge the dead. I think people stay there forever, dying over and over in horrible ways, becoming less and less human every time." She paused, looking regretful. "Well, most of them, at least. Anyway, the Mazikin city is there, way out in a desert. Under a dome."

Just like the Judge had shown me.

"Somehow, I knew he was there," Ana continued. "I mean, why else would that place appear right in front of me when no one else seemed able to see it? So I went." She laughed and shook her head. "I was convinced I was just going to go in there and get him out."

"And it didn't go as planned . . ."

"I couldn't get through the dome. But I could see through it, to the other side." Her eyes met mine. "And what I saw was Malachi." Her tone had regained its edge.

I sat up all the way. "Was he okay?"

Her knife suddenly stopped twirling, with the tip pointed right at my face. "What did you do, Lela? I was standing right there when he fell out of a black hole at the edge of the sky. He hit the ground hard, right in front of the Mazikin city gates. He was naked. Dazed. Totally defenseless. And they were waiting. A whole crowd of them." Her voice shook—but she held the knife steady.

I pressed the heels of my palms against my eyes to keep the tears from falling. "Of course they were," I said hoarsely. "They had it all planned."

"But in seventy years, Malachi never even got close to being taken." Ana's voice dripped with accusation. "So what I want to know is how it happened—and what *you* had to do with it."

At least now I knew why she'd hurled the knife. "You think it's my fault."

Her gaze slid along the edge of her blade, and I wondered if she was considering stabbing me again. "If it's not, you tell me how one of the best Guards who ever served is now at the mercy of the creatures he dominated for decades."

I swung my legs over the side of the bed. "If you want to blame me, go ahead. He was trying to free prisoners who he thought were human, not realizing the whole thing had been set up to capture him. He thought the Mazikin wanted *me*, but they didn't. He was too busy protecting me to realize it."

We stared at each other for a moment. "I could have predicted that," she said quietly. "I think I knew he was in love with you before he did."

I impatiently wiped a tear from my cheek. "I love him, too, Ana." I cleared my throat. "And I'm going to get him. I've already met with the Judge, and she gave me my mission."

Ana threw her arms up and groaned. "I should have known she would do something like this."

"What are you talking about?"

"She told me I could go on an official mission into the Mazikin city. She said I'd have a chance to get Takeshi out. And then she told me I'd have a new Lieutenant. I assumed it would be an actual Guard."

"Ana, I *am* a Guard."

Her eyebrows rose. "What?"

"She didn't tell you? Malachi and I were back in the land of the living for the last few months." I gave her the two-minute rundown, leaving out all the angsty drama between Malachi and me. We'd gotten through it, and that was what mattered.

"Huh," she said, eyeing me up and down once I'd finished. "I could not have predicted *that*."

"Me neither. And I'm sorry about Takeshi. I really hoped you guys would get to be together after all those years apart."

"Me too," she murmured. "But it's going to happen. That's why I'm here."

Looking at her, so fierce and strong, it suddenly felt possible. She and I would face the Mazikin together, and there was no one else I would have rather had as my Captain as I tried to rescue Malachi. "Did she tell you the other stuff we have to do?"

Ana nodded, then seemed to realize something. "Hey, I was thinking you came from the dark city, but you said you were back in the land of the living. As in, alive. How did you get here?"

"I . . . I kind of lost it when Malachi got taken. I jumped off a cliff."

"You committed suicide?"

"Kind of? I had a feeling Raphael would stop me. It seemed like the quickest way to get to the Judge. I couldn't let the Mazikin take me. I mean, it would have gotten me to the Mazikin city, but then there would have been a possessed Lela running around in Rhode Island, and she would have hurt people I care about."

Ana finally sheathed her knife and gave me a hard assessing look. "But you would have let them take you? If it was the only way?"

I stood up. "I would have done anything. I *will* do anything."

She sighed. "All right. I'm sorry for throwing a knife at you. It was just . . . seeing Malachi like that sent me over the edge."

My throat tightened up. "Do I want to know what they did to him?"

"It wasn't what they did. They just picked him up and carried him into the city as he tried to fight them. It was how he looked." She winced and scrubbed her hand over her face.

"Tell me," I said, the tension knotting along my spine until I felt like it was about to snap.

She shifted restlessly, looking down at the floor. "He looked scared, Lela. He looked really scared."

I walked toward the door, unable to stand still any longer. "Can we go, *Captain*?"

Ana got to her feet. "Are you ready for this?"

"Absolutely." I sounded more confident than I felt.

"You better keep up with me." She crossed her arms over her chest. "If we're going to succeed, I can't take care of you."

Which was what she'd done in the dark city. "You won't have to." I swallowed my tears. "Malachi taught me a lot. I can hold my own now."

"You'd better. We're going to a place that makes hell look like a picnic." She stalked past me and out into the hall. "So we're going to go in armed. Let's go see Michael."

I followed Ana down a hallway covered with brightly flowered wallpaper. "Where are we going?" I asked. "I thought Michael's workshop was at the Guard Station in the dark city."

She shrugged. "He's wherever we need him to be."

Considering he'd appeared in the basement of the Guard house in Warwick back home, I supposed she was right. As we neared the end of the ridiculously long corridor, the wall-paper changed to a dark burgundy, our path lit by elaborate lanterns dangling from silver chains. At the end of the hall was an intricately carved wooden door, in front of which one of the enormous Guards stood at attention. When we reached him, he saluted us, then pulled the door wide, allowing a wave of sound to flow out, all sharp clangs and roared curses.

We entered the workshop and walked down aisles with shelves of blades, bows, staffs, and other weaponry rising nearly two stories above us. As we turned a corner, Michael looked up from his forge, holding his heavy iron hammer high. Thick folds of fat wobbled beneath his arms.

"You're late!" he shouted, his jowls trembling as he slammed his hammer down. His cheeks were bright red, but the rest of his complexion was gray.

I gave Ana a sidelong glance. "Sorry. We got held up."

He pursed his lips as his gaze settled on Ana. "Ah. Yes. Raphael told me you got temperamental. I've half a mind to leave you unarmed."

Ana lifted her chin defiantly but didn't make any excuses. Michael gestured impatiently at us, throwing off shimmering drops of sweat that hit the forge with a sizzle. "Get over here. No time to waste."

I stared at him. Usually, he was telling us to keep our hair on, to let him work. But today . . . no insults, no flirting, no cursing in his chosen language of the month. Just action. He already had a fresh set of knives waiting for me, their narrow forward-curving blades reflecting the fire of his forge. Unlike Ana, I rarely threw my knives, preferring to use them in direct hand-to-hand combat to slash and stab. As I picked them up, I found them to be nicely balanced and deceptively heavy. Michael also supplied me with a belt and sheaths for my thighs and ankles.

"How did those gloves work out for you?" he asked. "The ones for the dance?"

Ana's brow furrowed. "You got to go to a dance?"

I looked over at Michael, expecting him to say something about my dress or my breasts or . . . something. But he was simply looking at me expectantly, waiting for an answer. "They were awesome," I said. "I punched through a thick plastic barrier without a problem."

He nodded briskly. "Made you a pair for this mission." He held up a set of long gloves, but instead of silvery satin, these seemed made out of leather. They were the same shade as my own skin.

While I slid them on and tried them out, swinging my fists to adjust to the weight of the steel shot sewn into small pockets over each of my knuckles, Michael provided Ana with a set of double-edged throwing knives. "I'd give you batons, but they'd be easier to detect than the blades and instantly recognizable as Guard weapons," he said. "I'll give you something else, though." He reached under his worktable and brought out a box filled with small black spheres. They were the size of golf balls, but they were smooth, except for a single concave button on each of their round faces. He nodded down at them. "Just hold that button down, and you have ten seconds," he said. "Boom."

Ana blinked. "Boom," she echoed softly, probably remembering her last encounter with one of these grenades. She hadn't lived through it.

"Who gets these?" he asked.

"I do," said Ana, somewhat hoarsely. "I have more experience with them."

"Thanks," I said, watching Michael slide eight of the grenades into a thickly padded strip of leather.

He held it out to her. "You'll be able to fight without triggering them. The buttons are recessed, and you really have to push with some strength. They won't go off until you want them to. But remember—you only have ten seconds after you press that button. Get clear as fast as you can."

Ana positioned the thick strip of deadly grenades diagonally over her chest, looking like she'd rather wear a poisonous snake. She adjusted it and straightened her shoulders. "Can you tell us more about the city?"

He shook his head, sending more drops of sweat onto the forge. "No. I can only tell you what they started with, not what they have now."

"What do you mean?"

"Everything has a beginning, even Mazikin. And theirs wasn't in that city, under that dome."

"Well, tell us what you do know," said Ana. "Anything might help."

Michael nodded. "They weren't always imprisoned. It wasn't until they tried to take over the Sanctum. They wanted to rule. And the Judge, he let 'em." The Judge could take on any appearance, and apparently, to Michael, the Judge was male.

I held up my hand. "Wait, what? The Judge *let* them take over?"

Michael snorted. "Not here. He gave them their own place, and enough resources to be self-sufficient."

I gaped at him. "Why would the Judge do that?"

Michael gave me a strange look. "Because he loved them, Lela. He was the one who created them in the first place."

THREE

"SHE FORGOT TO MENTION that," Ana and I said at the same time. My hands became fists. We were being sent in to clean up a mess the all-knowing Judge had made.

"It wasn't necessary for your mission," said a voice coming from behind us. I looked over my shoulder to see Raphael standing next to a neatly stacked set of crossbows.

Michael picked up his hammer. "I don't come into your quarters and interrupt your conversations."

"Don't be peevish, Michael. Are they ready?" Raphael walked forward. He was carrying several garments, which appeared to be made of different shades of brown leather, stitched together haphazardly.

"Nearly," Michael grumbled.

While he finished arming Ana, I walked over to Raphael. "Knowing the Judge created the Mazikin may not fall under 'need to know,' but the more we understand about them now, the better equipped we'll be," I said to him. "What's their city like? How did they get ahold of the portal she's sending us in to destroy?"

"The Judge only gave them what they needed to survive. She never intended them to escape. They have access to water and other natural resources. She gave them a herd of prey animals as a food source. Goats, actually. As for the portal . . ." He and Michael looked at each other for a moment, then Raphael gave him a brief nod and continued. "The Mazikin were the animal companions of the Judge."

"The Judge's idea of the perfect pet is a horde of crazy hyenas?"

"In the beginning there were only two." Raphael gave me a beautifully enigmatic smile. "She has a soft spot for animals."

"Apparently. But these can't be ordinary animals."

He shook his head. "Far from it. They are nearly as intelligent as humans, or the first two were, anyway. And the pair of them had the run of the Sanctum." He made a mildly disapproving face, and I suddenly pictured him following after a large dog, carrying a baggy full of poop. "Unfortunately, by the time they rebelled, they had learned some of its secrets, and when they were banished, they stole the material needed to make a portal. Then they used their knowledge of the boundaries between the realms to make one for themselves. We found this out later, when it was discovered the Mazikin were possessing human bodies within the dark city."

"Why the dark city?" Ana asked, coming over to join us. "Taking over the bodies and minds of people who chose to end their lives cannot be a fun experience. Seems like they'd have done better almost anywhere else."

"But the people in the dark city are far more passive," said Raphael. "And, as you discovered in the land of the living, Lela, Mazikin like the dark."

"How long ago did they escape their city?"

"It has been a very long time since the Mazikin were contained under the dome. We think they found a way out only about eight hundred years ago."

"Only." I suddenly wondered how old Raphael himself was. Even though he looked about thirty, for all I knew, he might have existed since the beginning of time. So few people I'd met in the afterlife looked their age. Malachi looked about eighteen, but . . .

Thinking of him was like being stabbed in the chest, and I crossed my arms in front of me and looked away. It was too late, though. His face loomed large in my mind, the heat of him, the sensual, earthy scent of his skin, the sound of his voice as he whispered fiercely in my ear: *You will kill whoever comes at you. You will do whatever it takes . . .*

I drew in a shuddering breath. That was exactly what I would do. Whatever it took to get him back. "When can we leave?"

"As soon as you change," said Raphael.

I raised my eyebrows.

"We're going into a self-contained city, Lieutenant," Ana said.

Raphael nodded. "If you go clothed in materials that cannot be found in the city, they will spot you immediately." He eyed my hair. "Which is already a possibility, mind you. But it would be best not to make it too easy for them." He held up the garments folded over his arms. "Goatskin."

He handed me a pair of pants, a smock with a thin strip of leather lacing up the front, and a cloak. "I have boots for you as well. The material is durable and will help you withstand conditions under the dome, which are likely to be extreme."

I walked into one of the aisles to get a little privacy. A second later Ana joined me. Apparently, she wasn't too keen on getting naked in front of Raphael and Michael, either. Barely looking at each other, lost in our own mental preparations, we stripped off our clothes and put on the surprisingly supple goatskin.

"It will double as armor," Raphael called. "I created it so that Mazikin teeth and claws won't penetrate it, unlike the garments you would find within the city. Metal blades are a different matter, though. Be careful."

I strapped the sheaths for my knives over my thighs and pulled the cloak around me, then glanced at Ana, who was adjusting the row of grenades beneath her smock. "What happens if they find us with those?"

"My guess is we'll be strung up next to Malachi," she said in a low voice. "But we won't go down without taking a few of them with us."

I nodded. "How about a lot of them?"

She gave me a grim smile. "I'll do my part if you do yours."

"You got it, Captain." I pulled up the hood of my cloak. It smelled sharp and sour, and I wrinkled my nose.

"What in the hell is taking so long?" Michael roared.

My cloak fluttering around my ankles, I emerged from the aisle to see Michael staring at us with red-faced fury. Raphael held out a pair of leather boots to me as he said calmly to Michael, "Stop rushing them."

Michael exhaled through his flared nostrils, like a bull about to charge. His skin began to give off the same glow as Raphael's did when he was really pissed. And that's when it occurred to me: Michael was upset about Malachi, too. Whenever they were together, Michael had always given Malachi a really hard time, calling him names and hollering at him to stop mistreating his weapons. But looking at Michael now, it seemed like he was ready to go into the Mazikin city himself. And the Mazikin probably wouldn't stand a chance if he did.

"Are you sure you can't come with us?" I asked.

Michael opened his mouth to answer, but Raphael interrupted. "He can't. Neither of us can. The Judge's promises are never broken."

"Doesn't mean we wouldn't like to," Michael growled, gripping the handle of his hammer with his meaty fingers. He glared at me with red-rimmed eyes. "You get him out, you understand me? He doesn't deserve this."

"This isn't about deserving," Raphael said. His voice was gentle, though. "You know that."

Ana emerged from the aisle, her hood pulled back from her face. "If it was, Takeshi wouldn't have been there in the first place."

"Too right," Michael said, shaking his head.

Raphael held out a pair of boots to her and watched as both of us pulled our footgear on. "You will not need to eat while you are inside. You don't belong there, and nothing in the city will nourish you."

"But does that mean—?"

He nodded as he met my eyes. "Like your time in the dark city, you will grow weaker the longer you are inside. You won't die, but you won't be as strong as you are now. And if they kill you, you will become part of the city, and it will be easier for them to control you. Do not allow this to happen."

"Work fast and don't die," Ana summed up. "Generally good advice."

"Are you ready?" Raphael asked.

I looked over at Ana, my new Captain. Her determination was written on her face, blazing and fierce. She had the same reason I did for walking into that hell, and that love would drive her as far as she needed to go. "We're ready," she said.

Raphael placed his burning hands on the backs of our necks. Right before we disappeared, I saw Michael's fury fall away like a mask, and in that moment I knew the truth, and it sliced through my body with icy dread.

He didn't think we were coming back.

My boots hit the ground, and I stumbled, crashing into a hard surface and bouncing off. Crouching, I ripped my hood away from my face, my hair flying out around me in crazy, flyaway curls. Dull orange light reflected off the wall in front of me, and I blinked as my eyes adjusted to the dim twilight. In front of me was a smooth surface, like a bubble with thick, hard skin that swirled lazily with an oily prism of colors. In it, my own face was reflected, my amber-brown eyes wide and haunted, my dark hair bouncing around my face. The cloak flapped around me as I pressed my hands to the dome, which emerged from the sand and rose so high I could barely make out the curve as it arced over the city. Even through my gloves, I could feel it pulsing with the misery inside, and I closed my eyes for a moment and absorbed it. Malachi was in there. I was closer to him now, and that thought was enough to raise the tiny hairs on the back of my neck. Somewhere in this walled city, the Mazikin had him. Naked, Ana had said, and scared. Furious, I slammed both my fists against the dome with all my strength. The impact shuddered up my arms and knocked the breath out of me. The steel shot in my gloves protected my knuckles from splitting, but the barrier hadn't dented or cracked.

"It's to keep them inside," Raphael said. He stood behind us, looking small and insignificant, one man surrounded by a sea of sand bounded by two mountain ranges, with the orange glow of the morning horizon behind him. "I will create an opening when you're ready to go inside, and I'll be waiting to let you out."

"*If* we complete the mission, you mean," Ana said. She had her face mashed against the dome, peering inside.

"That's correct," Raphael answered. "If you succeed. You have to make it back to the gates and out of the city. I can't come in to get you."

I watched him for a moment, looking for some flicker of feeling in his light-gray eyes, some hint as to whether he thought we'd actually make it out. But as emotional as Michael had been, Raphael was the opposite. He stared steadily back at me with what appeared to be only mild curiosity. I turned from him and squinted, trying to sce through the dome. Beyond its thick barrier were dark, pitted bricks, black mortar binding them together.

"Like many of the realms within the Shadowlands, it's a walled city," Raphael said.

"Why the wall, if they have an impenetrable dome?"

"So they can control the entrance to the city." Ana tugged at my sleeve and began to walk along the edge of the dome like she knew where she was going. Cold sweat prickled over my scalp as I followed, my soft-soled boots sinking in the loose sand. A stiff gust of wind sent the diamond-hard grains pelting against my cloak and the side of my face.

Raphael pointed to the dome. "We're next to the gates."

"There they are," Ana whispered as she pushed her face close to the dome's reflective surface again.

I cupped my hands around my eyes and leaned in. In front of us were high, heavy gates, twisted metal with jagged spikes jutting out at odd angles.

They were open. Two creatures stood on either side of them, upright but definitely not human. They were clothed in what looked like the same leather we were wearing, including cloaks with hoods. The tan material hung over their powerful bodies, broad barrel chests, and thick necks. They had humanlike hands and booted feet instead of paws, but in place of fingernails, curled black claws sprouted from each fingertip. Their faces were covered in short, dusky brown fur, and their eyes were solid black marbles, round and shining with an eager, cruel sort of mischief. They had rounded ears on the tops of their heads, and blunt black snouts. Their mouths were ridged with gleaming fangs, and threads of saliva stretched thin as they grinned.

The two of them paced back and forth on all fours, then rose to their hind legs, their ears twitching as they looked at the surface of the dome and conversed. It was all wrong—they were too human to be animals and too animal to be people. They looked like hyena-human hybrids.

"The Mazikin," I whispered. These were the things that forced themselves inside human bodies, that took them over. This was what Juri, Malachi's sworn enemy and the being who had haunted me for the longest time, looked like in his true form. I'd always pictured him as human, despite the fact that he behaved like a depraved animal, but now it was clear that was exactly what he was.

"That's them," Ana said, impatience creeping into her voice. "But look." She jabbed her finger into the unyielding surface of the dome.

In front of the gates, people kept appearing out of nowhere, sprawled in the sand on hands and knees, naked and trembling. One woman was curled into a ball, her head tucked against her knees, like she was trying to avoid acknowledging where she was before the inevitable caught up with her. A Mazikin guard grabbed a leather garment from a large pile by the gates and tossed it at her. When it hit her, she frantically pulled it on, but as soon as she did, the Mazikin grasped a handful of her hair and yanked her head up. Then it leaned into her face and said something. The woman, her eyes open and helpless, her face slack, nodded in this pathetic, defeated way, then got to her feet and trudged toward the gates. Two other naked humans appeared out of thin air a second later, shaking and blinking.

I turned to Ana. "These people are materializing, like new arrivals at the Suicide Gates. You said Malachi fell out of a hole in the sky."

"He did."

"Those people died inside the Mazikin city," Raphael said. "They aren't recently possessed."

"So if you die, you end up back at their gates. Just like in the dark city. Except you're naked." The anger twisted inside of me. It was like this place had been designed to humiliate. To oppress. I hated the looks on those people's faces and had to turn away to keep myself from punching the dome again.

Raphael's eyes were also on the hunched bare backs of the humans inside the dome. "Yes."

So there was no escape. Ever. My chest aching, I watched as a few more people appeared in front of the gates and were herded back inside. The Mazikin cheerfully shoved the humans over the threshold of the city, some of them to the left, some to the right, like they knew exactly which way each person should go.

"How are we going to get in?" I asked, my voice trembling. This was it. Was I ready? Was I strong enough?

I had to be. Ana and I were the only rescue squad available.

"They'll see us come in," Ana said. "The crowd isn't big enough for them not to notice us crawling through the opening you make."

"Have a little faith," said Raphael. "I'll get you in without incident. Once I do that, though, you're on your own." My heart stopped as his voice hitched, catching on those final words. Somehow, that tiny emotional breach was worse than Michael's red-rimmed eyes and roared curses.

I stepped back from the dome. "Be honest with us. Is this possible? Or is this a suicide mission?"

I expected him to smile calmly and repeat his standard reply, that I didn't need to know. But his freckled face was arranged in a very strange expression: part pity, part sadness, part uncertainty. And then he looked up at the sky, closed his eyes, and drew in a breath. It was the most human thing I'd ever seen him do.

"If anyone can complete this mission successfully, the two of you can," he said as he opened his eyes and turned to the orange glow at the horizon. He stared without blinking at the thin strip of flame forming as the sun began to rise from the sand. "You have everything you need. It is only a question of will and gut, and of the choices you make."

I turned to Ana. "Say the word, Captain."

Her dark eyes met mine. "Fast and focused, Lieutenant. We go in, get our men, destroy the portal and the Queen, and get out."

I nodded and put my hands on my thighs, feeling for the blades through the thick material of my cloak. Malachi had trained me well. I knew how to survive. How to kill. How to endure. And I knew what I wanted. Him. Only him. "Let's go."

Faint lines creased the corners of Raphael's mouth as he turned away from the rising sun, his gray eyes now blazing with an oddly orange tint. "Very well. When I give the signal, dive for the sand. And good luck."

He spread his arms, and twin balls of bright-yellow fire formed on his palms, like two tiny suns. I spun around, facing the dome. I watched his reflection as he lifted his head, his eyes still glowing, and hurled the balls of flame into the air. They hit the dome with a deafening explosion, right over the Mazikin guards. Their heads jerked up, their mouths wide and snarling; at the same time Raphael's hand reached between Ana and me. He drew his finger across the dome, then grabbed at its surface. It crumpled and tore like paper, letting the cool, fetid air of the Mazikin city rush out.

I dove through the window he created, landing in a heap a few feet away from the edge of the dome. I scooted toward the center of the sand as the Mazikin hooted and growled, their attention riveted on the dome above them. A muffled crack and a blinding light made me duck my head. Probably more balls of flame to keep them distracted. Ana grunted as she hit the sand next to me, spraying the yellow-gray granules across the tops of my gloved hands.

I turned my head in time to see Raphael's face through the opening of the dome, the night-blue sky behind him, wide and endless, the sun a half circle on the horizon. He nodded at me, then swiped his hand across the dome once more. Shutting us in.

He disappeared, and all I could see was my own ashen face reflected in the wall of my new prison. My fingers dug into the sand.

The Mazikin were still growling at each other, their shoulders drawn up and their claws twitching.

"They're nervous. Never seen anything like that," Ana whispered as we scrambled to join the small crowd of clothed humans huddled next to the Mazikin guards. She cursed. "They're saying they should report it."

"You can understand them?" I muttered softly as we pressed ourselves in among the others. Then I realized that made sense, because Malachi could understand them, too, after decades of eavesdropping on them in the dark city.

If she answered, I didn't hear. Because that was the moment when the Mazikin grabbed my hair and wrenched my head up. His black-marble eyes gazed deep into mine. His rotten-meat breath fanned across my face. I gagged and tried to turn my head away, but he only leaned closer, nuzzling his warm, wet snout along my cheek. "Ah," he sighed. "English?"

His black-lipped smile glistened when he saw the recognition on my face. An involuntary sound of disgust squeaked from my throat as he drew his tongue across my forehead. "These two must be straight from the Queen's dinner hall," the other Mazikin said. "They smell delicious."

Somehow I knew he was speaking English because he wanted us to be scared. The Mazikin stationed at the gates probably knew several languages, to help them terrorize efficiently. And it was working. The Mazikin holding me nodded, still looking in my eyes. He grunted at his friend, who was holding Ana in a similar grip. Then they shoved us toward the open gates. My elbows hit the sand as I fell, but all I felt was relief. They were herding us into the city, as we'd hoped.

Ana didn't appear to agree with my rosy assessment of our situation. Crawling forward on her hands and knees, she grumbled under her breath as we drew even with the city gates.

"What is it?" I whispered as we inched toward a huge cart crammed with a few dozen cloaked women, all wearing completely defeated expressions. The Mazikin standing next to the vehicle were watching us, clearly expecting us to climb aboard.

"The Mazikin guards have pronounced us edible," she said quietly. "We're being taken straight to the meat factory."

FOUR

"I THOUGHT THEY ATE goats!" My heart thrummed as I stared up at the waiting Mazikin. They were using canes tipped with metal hooks to poke at the whimpering women inside the cart. Their yellow-white fangs flashed as they snarled at their victims.

"Either there weren't enough or their tastes have expanded," said Ana.

We were only a few yards from the cart now, still on our hands and knees in the middle of a small square. Three crumbling roads led away from the city gates. A similar cart, this one holding several gray-faced men, was sitting on the other side of the square, near a road that ran right along the wall. In the distance, high smokestacks belched black plumes that curled in wisps as they hit the top of the dome. The faint clamor of industrial machinery reached my ears over the sounds of human suffering in the square. There was some type of factory up there, and my guess was that the men were the labor force.

On Earth, the Mazikin had been most fond of the night, and now day was breaking. Here, all the Mazikin in the square were growling impatiently at their human charges and glancing over their shoulders as the sun, the only thing visible through the dome, peeked over the bricks of the wall behind us.

I sucked in a breath of cool, moist air that left a sour taste on my tongue. The smell of this place was incredibly bad: rotten eggs, acrid smoke, and raw sewage. "Orders?" I asked, hoping Ana had a brilliant plan that did not involve becoming a nice flank steak.

"We get in that cart," she said, leaning close and speaking directly in my ear as we inched forward. "I think we're going to have a chance to get away when the sun gets higher, but if we try it now, the entire city will know we're here. They're already on guard because of Raphael's fireball-juggling act. Don't do anything to draw attention to yourself."

I tugged my hood low over my face as I reached the boots of the Mazikin waiting at the cart. Mazikin feet were broader than human feet, and their knees seemed to bend backward—much like a dog's. Still, they alternated between standing on their hind legs and running around on all fours. They also had no trouble kicking—my captor's boot made a firm connection with my ribs. "Up," he snarled.

I let out a pathetic whimper and obeyed, despite my desire to whip out one of my knives and get to work. Ana was right—this seemed like the quickest way to get deeper into the city. Closer to Malachi, wherever he was. As convenient as it would have been, I'd known he probably wasn't hanging out right next to the exit to the city.

The cart rattled as Ana and I climbed aboard. It was powered by a huge clunky exposed engine at the front with crazy coils of pipe and gauges sticking out at seemingly random places. It sputtered as the Mazikin driver twisted a key in the ignition, making the vehicle shudder and creak. The woman squatting next to me wrapped her skinny fingers over the metal edge of the cart, as did the woman on her other side. They bowed their heads, waiting. I bowed my head in imitation, then jerked it up when I felt a sharp jab in my shoulder.

A Mazikin was standing right in front of me. "Hands out!" he barked, then repeated the command in a few other languages. Like all the others, I wrapped my fingers over the metal wall of the cart, waiting for him to notice I was wearing gloves and preparing to punch my fist right through his face if he made a move. But he barely looked at me. All he seemed to care about was getting the job done. He flicked an irritated glance at the rising sun, and with quick, practiced movements, snapped a metal cuff onto my wrist. I flinched back out of sheer reflex, but not fast enough to keep my other wrist from being captured. Without looking at my face, the Mazikin fastened the cuffs, connected by a rusting chain, to a metal ring on the floor of the cart. Two other Mazikin were doing the same thing to the other captives, none of whom resisted. I met Ana's eyes and saw a flicker of uneasiness.

Chained inside the mechanized cart, squatting on the floor, shoulder to shoulder with Ana and a bunch of other women, I tensed as we lurched into motion. The woman next to me, her hood covering her face, sniffled and sobbed. "Oh God," she whispered over and over again, and I couldn't help but picture her prayer rising high in the air . . . and then hitting the dome and falling, unheard, to the dirty streets below.

We rumbled along the rough road as the sun finally broke free of the city wall and turned into a circle of fire. As the heat struck me, I lifted my head and let the hood fall away. The air had turned from cool to warm in a matter of a minute, and the temperature just kept rising, drawing tiny beads of sweat along Ana's temples as she scanned her environment with a predator's calm. The Mazikin driver shook his big hairy head back and forth, his ears twitching as if trying to toss off the heat. The engine belched, and the cart accelerated sharply, throwing me off balance. Not that it mattered—we were packed in so tightly that I couldn't have fallen over if I tried.

I sucked in a breath of scorching air and tugged at the shackles on my wrists. The rusty cuffs were crusted with dried blood, and maroon flecks scraped off with my movements, remnants of someone else's pain and desperation. On either side of the road were gray concrete buildings, all of the same design. Three stories high, square openings every ten feet or so, windows without panes, dark inside. The only thing that distinguished them were the paintings all over their exteriors. Some of the markings looked like graffiti, black and jagged, and some of them looked more like murals. But all of them were chipped and pockmarked, cracked and faded. Nothing thrived here.

That thought stamped itself on my brain as we passed by a Mazikin trotting down the street on all fours—walking a woman on a leash. The human was young, but the look on her face reflected a century's worth of suffering as her captor yanked the leash tight, making her gulp for air. The Mazikin dragged her through the entrance to one of the buildings. All around us, the creatures were fleeing indoors as the temperature rose and the sun's light was magnified through the dome, pouring over the city with brutal thoroughness.

"Get your hood up or you'll burn," muttered Ana. "God, this is awful."

I gave her a sidelong glance. She was twisted into a weird position, with her hips pressed downward and her back bowed. Her fingers stretched and scrabbled . . . She was trying to reach her knives. "I can help," I whispered. "Stop tugging on those or you'll hurt yourself." Unlike me, Ana wasn't wearing gloves.

"I'm pretty sure I can pick the lock," she told me as I leaned down. My hood flopped over my head as I fastened my teeth onto the hilt of one of her double-edged throwing knives. I began to draw it back just as we went over a bump. My forehead smacked the metal edge of the cart, and for a second I saw stars, but then I returned to my task of unsheathing the knife. After a few seconds, I pulled it free, and then bent sharply so she could snatch it from my mouth.

As I straightened up to give Ana room, I turned to see the woman wedged in next to me watching us carefully. "Are you part of the Resistance?" she asked me, her eyes darting back and forth like she was afraid we'd be overheard despite the roar and cough of the engine, the rumble of the cart along the potholed road, and the sobbing women around us, who were babbling in a dozen different languages.

My heart skipped. "Resistance?"

She paled when she saw the clueless look on my face. "No, no," she stammered. "That's not what I said." She ducked her head and pressed her forehead between her hands, her shoulders trembling.

Next to me, Ana was working on her shackles, her cloak concealing her movements. I shifted onto the balls of my feet and pulled myself forward to get a good look at where we were going. Dozens of blocks ahead was a massive building, partially obscured by greenish-brown smog, through which I could make out the tips of a few smokestacks.

I could already smell the oily scent of roasting meat.

I blinked away the image of what awaited us at the meat factory in time to notice a black-cloaked figure disappearing between two buildings a block away. From the shape of the silhouette, I could tell it was a human and not a Mazikin, but he moved with sure-footed confidence rather than the broken, raw fear that bent the backs of the humans I had seen so far. I tingled in anticipation as we drew closer—I wanted to see where he was going, what he was doing. But we ground to a halt behind another mechanized cart, this one carrying a load of concrete blocks. It had hit a huge pothole and canted to one side, spilling several bricks onto the street and sidewalk. The driver was galloping around, prodding at two humans who were trying to push the vehicle's tire out of the hole.

Our driver stood up and began to grunt at the other Mazikin, who raised his ugly head and spat at our cart. He rose to his hind legs and brandished a club that looked strikingly like a human femur. Our driver sat back down, growling to himself and pulling his hood up against the sun. My own skin felt like it was slowly cooking, especially now that we didn't even have the heated air rushing over us as we flew down the road. "How are you doing?" I asked Ana, who had yet to raise her head from her work.

"Almost there," she mumbled from beneath her hood. "Why are we stopped?"

"Broken-down vehicle. They're clearing the road." I watched the straining forms of the men struggling with the loaded cart. They were naked from the waist up, and the skin on their backs was blistered, scarred, and oozing with sores. The driver of the concrete cart smacked one of them in the legs with his bone club, but the man didn't cry out. He merely nodded as his Mazikin master hooted at him.

"He's telling them to hurry before the 'fire hour' arrives," Ana said. "No idea what that is, but I think I'd like to be inside when it happens."

"Me too."

The men, perhaps motivated by the reminder about fire hour, finally shoved the wheel of the cart out of the hole. With near-frantic movements, they tossed the fallen bricks back in the cart and leaped on top of the load, hanging on as the vehicle rolled forward. Our own driver cackled, then gunned the engine of our cart.

"Got it," whispered Ana, and by her movements I could tell she was completely free. "Your turn. Hold still or I'll end up cutting your fingers off."

I clutched the edges of the cart and leaned back as she went to work on my shackles. As we bumped down the road, I squinted up the block where I'd seen the black-cloaked figure run, but there was no one in the streets now. At least, not that I could see.

Some of the women in the cart had noticed our efforts and were watching us with a mixture of curiosity and fear. From behind me, I once again heard the word "resistance," followed by the soft hiss of whispering in a language I didn't understand. I tilted my head toward the woman who'd spoken to me initially. Her forehead was still pressed between her hands.

"What's the Resistance?" I asked. "If you're afraid of getting in trouble, don't worry. I won't tell anyone."

Her knuckles turned white, which stood out in stark contrast to the red skin on the backs of her hands. "I don't know what you're talking about," she said, her voice muted by the leather folds of her clothing. "But don't let them hear you mention it." She jerked her head toward the front, where the driver had his shoulders hiked nearly to his ears as we raced toward the meat factory. It still loomed far in the distance but was growing closer by the second.

The cuff around my right wrist clicked and fell away, and Ana pressed the knife into my free hand. "Do the other one yourself. I'd practically have to lie on top of you to do it, and we're already drawing too much attention."

She was right. The low whispers around us were nonstop now. It was only a matter of time before the driver heard them. I grabbed the knife with my right hand and jammed the tip into the keyhole on the underside of the cuff on my left hand, knowing one pothole could cause me to slit my own wrist. My heart pounded as the cart slowed to keep from hitting a massive truck rumbling along in front of us. I didn't know what was in it, but a thick reddish-brown substance was leaking from beneath its rear door. We almost came to a standstill as it negotiated the deep divots in the road. The gouges were regular, set across the road in a way that made them nearly unavoidable, like speed bumps. It almost looked like someone had created the holes with a pickax or something. Next to me, Ana was chanting—*hurry, hurry, hurry*—like she was about to explode. I couldn't blame her. The only thing keeping us in this cart was the fact that I wasn't very good at picking locks.

I rotated my wrist, trying to slip the blade deeper into the keyhole, then hissed as we hit one of the divots and the knife poked into the fabric of my glove, just missing the skin. I yanked it out and got back to work, raising my head in time to see another dark-cloaked figure standing in the alley between two buildings. The person pressed further into the shadows as we passed. The face was hooded—I couldn't tell if it was a man or a woman. But it was definitely human; I caught a glimpse of bare skin peeking from beneath the cloak.

Ana nudged me with her shoulder. "We need to get out before we speed back up. This is our chance."

"Doing my best, Captain," I said from between clenched teeth.

In front of us, the massive truck, now leaking the reddish-brown fluid in a steady stream, slowed further and began to pull over to the side of the road. Up ahead, the smokestacks of the meat factory were easily visible, and the odor of cooking flesh hung heavy in the air, a stench that made me very glad my stomach was empty. "Jump," I said. "I'll catch up with you."

"Shut up and work. That's an order," Ana snapped.

I'd never stopped trying the lock, but it wasn't getting me anywhere. Still wriggling the tip of the knife in the keyhole, I turned to her. "Go, Ana. Before it's too late."

She shook her head. "Not without you."

"You said you wouldn't take care of me. So don't," I whispered, glaring at her. Sweat tickled the back of my neck as I bent over my shackled wrist again, wanting to scream in frustration.

Our driver yanked the steering wheel sharply as he started to pull around the now-stopped vehicle. Right before we passed the cab of the truck, I felt a breeze and heard the lightest of footfalls on the road behind us, and I knew Ana had jumped. The women around us grew silent; I was sure they were watching her. I closed my eyes and hoped against hope they wouldn't alert our driver to her escape. But as the seconds ticked by and they stayed quiet, I realized they weren't going to betray us.

It was in that moment I understood how many people must be trapped in this city. How many good people who didn't deserve this hellish fate. I'd known it before, but only at a brain kind of level. Now I felt it in my gut—the agony, the suffering, the sweat and blood in the air. The horror rolled over me, sending a chill up my spine despite the sweltering heat. I'd come to rescue Malachi. Ana had come for Takeshi. No one would ever come for the others.

Our vehicle picked up speed as we passed the enormous truck, and I made one last frantic twist of the knife—*click*. The shackle at my wrist fell open. Feeling victorious, I pulled my left hand free.

And saw that we were now going at least twenty miles an hour.

Well, shit.

Staying low, I held on to the edge of the cart and threw my leg over the back, then clung to the closed tailgate as the buildings zipped by. The hot wind blew my hair around my face, leaving strands of it sticking in the sweat on my forehead and neck. *Let go,* I coached myself. *You have to let go.*

Then I made the mistake of looking down. When I saw the road passing under me in a blur of rocky asphalt, my fingers wouldn't obey me. The woman I'd been chained next to turned her head. Her startling blue eyes met mine, full of pleading—and hope. She knew I was different. She wondered if I would help her. She nodded at me, urging me to go on.

My fingers straightened, and I let go.

My boots hit the blacktop, and I pitched forward into a roll as the air was driven out of my lungs. My shoulders and hips cracked against the uneven pavement. Sick-hot agony zapped along my bones as I came to a stop along the side of the road. The vehicle was disappearing into the distance, but that woman's eyes were still clear in my mind. Hands closed around my arms and tugged at me. "Get up," Ana said. "We have to get off the street."

With her help, I staggered to my feet. Though every part of me hurt, no part of me seemed broken, miraculously. I pulled my hood over my head and followed Ana into the nearest alley. She whirled around to face me, her eyes bright and intense.

"Hey, I'm okay," I said to her, eager to show her that I could hold my own, that she could be my Captain and not my babysitter.

She shook her head dismissively. My welfare wasn't what was on her mind. "You have to see this," she said, grabbing my sleeve and pulling me back along the alley that ran parallel to the main road. The buildings sheltered us from the brutal sunlight as our boots squelched through sludgy garbage.

"I can't believe it," Ana muttered as she finally came to a halt at the mouth of an alley. "You won't believe it." She threw her arm in front of me to keep me from blundering onto another road that ran off at an angle to the city wall. "Look." She pointed across the street.

In front of us, riveted to the side of a concrete building, was a metal billboard. Painted across its surface was the face of a man. Below it were words, in all different languages. My eyes searched for ones I could understand and found them in the bottom row. Wanted, it said, for crimes against the true citizens.

My eyes traveled back up to the man's face. It was crudely rendered, but I was almost sure I knew who it was, because I'd seen a painting of him before. One glance at Ana told me I was right. She stared at that picture like it was her salvation.

Takeshi.

FIVE

"I GUESS THAT'S OUR confirmation that he's here," I said.

Ana smiled, blinking away tears. "Yeah." She swiped her sleeve over her cheeks and cleared her throat. "Sorry. It's been awhile since I've seen his face."

"It's all right. It looks pretty recent, doesn't it?" The paint was shiny, not chipped or cracked. Compared with the other signs I'd seen so far in the city, this one was much newer. "What do you think it means?"

Her look was all grim satisfaction. "I think it means he's on the loose, and they're not happy about it."

"When we were on that cart, I heard the others talking about some sort of resistance movement. Do you think—?"

"I think, if there actually is one, he'd be at the heart of it." Ana was still staring hungrily at his face, at the rough sweeps of paint forming high cheekbones, a wide forehead, sharp brown eyes, and a shock of black hair. "He would never be satisfied with hiding out. He'd want to destroy the Mazikin." The pride in her voice was evident—as was the hope.

And it was contagious. "Do you think . . . do you think maybe Malachi could get away from them too?"

She gave me a smile that was meant to be reassuring but didn't reach her eyes. "Maybe. Takeshi taught him well."

Wishing hard, I imagined Malachi's face on a billboard like this, his defiant, angular features rendered in shades of brown and tan, his dark eyes almost as black as his hair. If anyone could get away, it would be him. And we would find each other, and find a way out of here. I couldn't contemplate any other alternative.

I peered up the street. The glare of the sun was blinding, warping the air with heat. "I don't blame the Mazikin for hating the sun. I'm starting to hate it, too. But it gives us a chance to get deeper into the city."

The quiet, garbage-strewn streets were bounded by dark-gray buildings, stolid cubes of thick concrete squatting beneath the dome, sheltering the monsters. The only sound was the distant crash of machinery. Factory noises. Not everyone was sleeping.

"Which direction should we go?" I asked.

Ana reluctantly tore her eyes from the Takeshi billboard and pointed up the road that would lead us away from the wall and straight to the center of the Mazikin realm. "We have to find the Queen. If we find her, we find the portal."

"How are we going to find Malachi and Takeshi, though?"

"It won't matter if we can't complete our mission." She glanced back at the rendering of Takeshi's face. "Come on."

We pulled our hoods over our heads and walked up the road, looking for danger. Thick poles were sunk into the roadside every twenty feet or so, a few feet from every building, holding up bare wires that glinted in the sunlight.

"There's more technology here than I thought there would be."

"That's for sure," said Ana. "I don't know exactly what I was expecting, but it wasn't trucks and roads. I mean, I saw the smokestacks . . ."

"They have oil. Gas. Metal. Electricity. Raphael said they were only given what they needed to survive."

"Yeah, but think about how many bodies they've possessed, and how much knowledge they've stolen. The people who knew all that stuff are also here in the city. Somewhere along the way, the Mazikin must have learned how to mine for what they need. And the more people they possessed, the more free labor they had."

We reached an intersection where a mechanized cart had crashed into the side of a building, leaving a pile of twisted metal. Wisps of black smoke still rose from the engine, like the wreck had happened pretty recently. A smear of red against the concrete wall told me the driver probably hadn't walked away, but there were no bodies in sight. Ana and I peeked into the building it had collided with, which looked the same as every other we'd seen so far. Even though there was electricity in the city, the insides of the buildings were dark, like maybe it was turned off during the day. There were no doors on the buildings, only wide openings, letting us see the empty spaces inside. No furniture, no people, no Mazikin. The living creatures were all tucked below or above, leaving the street level deserted as the sun beat down.

After a few blocks, we passed another Takeshi sign, this one older and faded. Ana smiled. "He's been free for a while."

I smiled, too, and rubbed at the ache in my chest. Where was Malachi—was he free as well? Could he have escaped the Mazikin's control? "If there's a resistance movement within this city, we're going to want to find those people. Maybe they can help us destroy the portal and take care of the Queen."

"Maybe." Ana nodded toward the flutter of a dark cloak disappearing around a corner up ahead. "And they may have already found us."

We picked up our pace, our leather soles nearly silent on the concrete. Everything in the city was fashioned from cement and metal. Like the dark city, nothing green seemed able to survive in this dome, but ugliness flourished. Only here, it was sharper. Harsher. Cruel.

We reached the corner we'd seen the dark figure disappear around, but as we looked the streets up and down, they appeared deserted. "You think they're watching us?" I asked quietly, wiping my hand over my sweaty face and tucking my hair behind my ear. It lay like a thick, wet blanket over the back of my neck.

"I don't know," said Ana. "The only thing we can do is keep going. It's damn tempting to hide out in one of these buildings until the sun calls it quits, but we have to take advantage of the empty streets."

I was melting inside my cloak, but I had a feeling that I'd be blistered and charred without it. The heat was nearly unbearable, but—"You got it, Captain."

Our heads snapped up at the sound of a low moan. A man lay crumpled in the road about a block ahead. Blood oozed from a gash across his forehead. Ana and I locked eyes, then crept toward the man, sticking close to the shelter of the nearest building. Ana reached him first and knelt at his side. The back of his neck was blistered and raw from lying in the sun, as were the backs of his hands. He wore a stained and torn leather smock, similar to the ones Raphael had given us. His lips were a startling color, redder than the most chapped lips I'd ever seen. He groaned as Ana touched his shoulder. "Hey," she said to him. "You need some help?"

The man said something in a language I didn't understand. I turned to Ana, who spoke several languages, but she looked as lost as I felt. "Let's at least get him off the street," she said. "He's roasting alive."

We grasped the guy under his arms and lifted him off the road. His blistered fingers clutched at our cloaks, and he licked at his crimson lips with his tongue, which was an equally violent shade of red. Though I wanted to help him, revulsion made my throat tighten.

"It's all right," Ana soothed as we dragged him toward the nearest building. Both of us sighed with relief as we entered the shaded, dank space. It was at least twenty degrees cooler than the street and felt downright awesome. We set him on the floor and began to rise, but our wounded companion grabbed our cloaks, speaking urgent words we couldn't decipher.

I squatted next to him, trying to get him to look at me, to see we didn't mean him any harm. Next to me, Ana stood up abruptly.

"What should we do for him?" I asked her.

"Nothing," she whispered. "I think he's served his purpose."

Then I heard the growl, deep and vicious. It rolled like a wave up my spine, raising goose bumps. The bleeding man let go of my cloak, shot to his feet, and scrambled across the space to press himself against the wall. I looked over my shoulder. Ana stood between me and the threat. She'd already drawn her knives. "He was a decoy," she muttered.

I looked over at the man, whose eyes were fixed on something just beyond Ana. My hand traveled to my thigh, drawing a knife of my own as I rose.

The Mazikin, standing on his hind legs, his claws flexing by his sides, grunted at us, rhythmic and guttural.

"They want to know who our master is," Ana said.

"They?" I stepped to the side—we were completely surrounded. Four Mazikin had emerged from the shadows. All on two legs, their black eyes shining like oil slicks, their mouths snarling.

I let out my breath slowly, focusing. "Orders?"

"Hold your own and let me do the heavy lifting."

As soon as she said it, the knives flew from her hands, and the room erupted in chaos. Two of the Mazikin let out choked shrieks as the knives hit home with muffled thumps, but the other pair moved before Ana could draw again. They leaped at us, and we only had time to get our arms up to shield our faces from their claws. My shoulders hit the wall behind me, but I kept a grip on my knives, even as a Mazikin closed its jaws around my forearm. It felt like my bones were being crushed in a vise, but its teeth didn't penetrate the sleeve of my leather smock, and its claws scraped down the side of my cloak without tearing it.

Ana cried out and rolled to the side, entangled with her opponent. I threw my weight forward and twisted as my own attacker held on tight, its eyes squeezed shut as it shook its head side to side, trying to rip my arm off. I rammed my steel-shot-coated fist into its body over and over again as it clawed at me, searching for vulnerable flesh within the folds of my cloak. Finally, it let out a whine as I drove my fist into its ribs, and its mouth opened wide enough to allow me to tug my arm from its jaws. With a fierce growl of my own, I grabbed the Mazikin by the ear with my newly freed hand and slammed my knife straight down, burying it in the Mazikin's eye socket. It let out a soft whimper and fell limp to the ground.

I stumbled away from it to see Ana wrestling on the floor with the other Mazikin; it had both of her arms pinned and was going for her throat. I dove forward, planning to bury my blade in its side, but before I reached it, it jumped to its feet with a snarl. It grabbed my raised arm and twisted, filling the echoing space with a sick popping sound. Lightning strikes of agony jolted through my shoulder, and my knife clattered to the floor. With a strangled scream, I landed on my back, waves of nausea crashing over me. My tunic had flown up to expose my belly, but I managed to get my feet up to shove the Mazikin away from me before it could tear my stomach open with its outstretched claws. It disappeared from my line of sight, but the shuffling feet and growls told me Ana was up and had taken it on.

I rolled to my side, cradling my limp right arm. I tried to rise to help Ana, but then I heard a gurgling whine, followed by the splatter of blood hitting cement, and I knew that she could take care of herself. She appeared by my side a second later, breathing hard. "Thanks for having my back," she said, looking at my limp arm. "Can you move it?"

I tried and then doubled over, retching with the pain. I closed my eyes and pressed my forehead to the cool concrete, trying not to faint. "Is it broken?" I gasped out. My whole arm was limp, and there was an odd bump on the front of my shoulder.

"Dislocated." Ana hunched over me. "We're going to have to—"

She froze. And over the uneven sound of our breaths, I heard it. Claws, clacking together.

Yet another Mazikin stepped from the shadows. It had a cloak pulled low over its head, so all I could see was its ugly snout and half-open mouth. And its clawed hands, slapping together in a muffled slow clap that reeked of amusement. Ana cursed. A second later, her knives were flying.

They clattered against the concrete walls as the Mazikin moved with a speed I couldn't even track. The dark blur ducked and dodged, able to anticipate Ana's every movement. A deep, guttural laughter rumbled from the shadows far across the room.

"I think this is the last one," said Ana in a low voice, her attention on the black corner where the Mazikin lurked. "But it's faster than the others. Can you get up?"

I shoved myself up with my good hand but couldn't stop the gasp of agony at the dead weight of my right arm pulling on the socket. I wrenched myself to my feet, then grabbed my dangling limb and pressed it against my stomach, my breath whistling from my throat.

"Get against the wall. You're useless," she said, but her voice was gentle, protective.

I took a few steps back at the same time the cloaked Mazikin emerged from the shadows. I couldn't see its eyes, but somehow I knew it was focused on Ana—the only other dangerous predator in the room. It grunted at her as it stalked forward, more like a tiger than a hyena. She stepped to the side, drawing its attention away from me as I withdrew into a corner and noticed the wounded man was gone. Had he been a victim forced to be bait, or a willing collaborator in this trap set for anyone strong enough to show mercy?

As Ana and the last Mazikin circled each other, my gaze darted to the bodies of the ones we'd killed. All of them wore dark leather cloaks with a black triangle sewn onto the back. I wondered if they were part of the Mazikin guard, some kind of enforcement squad. I looked at the Mazikin squaring off with Ana. His cloak, too, had a black triangle. I suddenly wished I was better at throwing; I would have loved to bury my blade in that thing's back. But as I shifted my weight and considered trying, my knees buckled with another shock of pain.

I sank to the floor and watched helplessly as the Mazikin leaped at Ana. She lunged with her knife, but it caught her wrist in its clawed hand and spun her around. She jabbed her knee into its belly, but it arched back and received only a glancing blow. Ana's face was alight with frustration as she pressed her attack and the Mazikin knocked away her punches and knife jabs with relative ease. It was playing with her.

Her eyes glinted with the same realization. She glared at the beast, searching for its vulnerability. Without letting her gaze waver from her enemy, she shed her cloak to give her more freedom of movement. Her black hair was so long that it fell over her shoulders from the ponytail high on her head.

The Mazikin made the oddest sound, this faint, hungry sigh, and its arms dropped to its sides. I watched Ana, expecting her to take advantage of the Mazikin's loss of concentration, but instead, her eyes went round and filled with tears. “It’s you, isn’t it?” she whispered.

The Mazikin let its hood fall away from its face. Ugly stitches tracked along its skin and neck. “Only if it’s you,” it said softly.

SIX

THE MAZIKIN TUGGED AT its own ears, lifting its head away—and dropping it to the floor. A mask. It had been hiding a man who stared at Ana like she was the only person in the universe. His honey-colored skin was flushed with exertion, and his breaths sawed from his lungs as he pulled furry, clawed gloves away from his very human hands.

"Ana?" His shaky voice drove the breath from my lungs, because it was pure, raw *want.*

Takeshi had found us.

Ana's face crumpled as she dove into his open arms. Muffled Spanish flowed from her lips as she clung to him. He bowed his head into her shoulder, his arms trembling as he threw them around her. Something about their embrace made my chest feel like it was ripping right down the middle. I closed my eyes, unable to bear it.

A few minutes later, a hand touched my good shoulder, and I looked up to see Takeshi crouching in front of me. Ana stood behind him, tears dripping down her face. "Lela, this is Takeshi," she said like she couldn't quite believe it.

"Hi." I couldn't summon more than that.

"She said your shoulder is dislocated," he said in faintly accented English, lifting a fold of my cloak to peek at my right shoulder. "*Aaand* she was right. Can you stand up?"

He offered me his arm, but I couldn't reach for it. I needed my left arm to hold my right against my body. It was the only way to keep the pain at a level that allowed me to stay conscious. I braced my feet and used the wall to push myself up.

Takeshi rose as well, giving me an assessing look. His gaze lingered on my face for a few seconds before he said, "Neither of you were possessed, were you?" He lifted my cloak again to eye the knives strapped to my legs and waist. Quick as a cat, he snatched one of my blades from its sheath. He held it up to the faint light flowing in from the street. "I know exactly who made these, and it wasn't anyone in the city. How the hell did you two get here?"

"Raphael made an opening in the dome," Ana said.

"This is an official mission?" His eyes were wide. "The Judge sent you here? Or"—his jaw clenched—"did she sentence you here?"

Ana put her hand on his shoulder, and he turned to her. "She didn't sentence us, but she did send us."

"The lights and the explosions against the dome this morning—was that when you came in? It's got the guards on the lookout. But I never thought, I never even considered—"

"Malachi was taken," I blurted out.

"What?" The shock and disbelief on Takeshi's face sliced right through me. "When?"

"A day or so ago," I said, my voice breaking. "I don't know how time passes here, but it hasn't been that long." Though it felt like forever.

"*He's* the one," he muttered, still looking stunned. "The rumors that they've captured a Guard are spreading through the city. I was heading to the square to find out for myself. But I didn't for one moment think it would be Malachi."

"Things have changed for him," said Ana, her gaze drifting over his shoulder to land on me.

Takeshi twisted around to look at me again, almost like he was seeing me for the first time. "Who are you exactly?"

"She sneaked into the dark city from the Countryside to try to rescue a friend of hers," said Ana. "Malachi . . . well, I think he was done from the moment he saw her. And I guess Lela here got herself sentenced to be a Guard right alongside him."

Takeshi gave me the faintest of smiles. "Poor Malachi."

I couldn't return his smile, but I had to agree with his words. If Malachi hadn't met me, he wouldn't be here. "The Judge agreed to allow us to try to get him out, as long as we destroy their portal and kill the Queen."

Takeshi laughed, then stifled it with his sleeve. "So sorry," he mumbled. "That's quite a mission."

"We've heard there's some sort of resistance movement here in the city. Are you part of that? Could they help us?" Ana asked.

The laughter died immediately, and he frowned. "The Resistance is a myth, bred by people who haven't yet given up hope."

Ana's brow furrowed. "You haven't given up hope."

"I will *never* give up," he said, so softly I knew his words were meant only for her. Especially when his voice hardened as he added, "But here I take care of myself, and I cause as much trouble as I can, and that is all there is. All there has been for a very long time."

Ana glanced at me and looked away. When she'd told me she thought he'd be part of the Resistance, she'd said it with such pride, but this was a reminder she hadn't seen this man in a decade or so. It was certainly a reminder to me—he'd been a Guard, but did that mean we could trust him? What had so many years in this hellish place done to him and his allegiances?

A soft crackling sound from the street drew our attention. Takeshi cursed. "I lost track of time. The fire hour is coming. We need to get below, and then we're going to put your arm back in its socket."

He said it like he did that kind of thing every day. I shoved off the wall as he strode to the center of the room and picked up his Mazikin disguise. "I have a place close by. We won't be on the streets for long. Still"—he pulled the Mazikin face on over his own—"best to be cautious."

While Takeshi collected Ana's knives from the bodies of her victims, Ana tugged on her own cloak, then came over to me. She pulled my hood over my head as I clutched my right arm and swayed unsteadily. Even distracted by my pain, I could see the glow on her face. She didn't care whether Takeshi had changed. She had been waiting for this reunion for years, and now she had it. I couldn't begrudge her—I was hoping to have a reunion of my own very soon.

With our hoods low and our cloaks pulled around our bodies, we exited the building. The heat nearly flattened me as I drew the searing air into my lungs. Ahead of me, Ana cringed under the blazing sunlight. The enormous ball of flame, magnified through the dome, was directly overhead. Takeshi glanced up and growled something incomprehensible, and both he and Ana began to jog. I stumbled along as quickly as I could, but each step jarred my shoulder joint. It was all I could do to keep from screaming with every footfall.

A sudden explosion close behind me sent me careening off a wall. Takeshi pivoted on his heel toward me, his cloak swinging, his half-open Mazikin snout leading the way. It bounced off the side of my face as he slid a steely arm around my back and wrenched me away from the wall. He hustled me down the street, muttering urgently in Japanese. A flash of flame erupted not a block away, and I started to turn my head toward the threat, but Takeshi lugged me forward with a sharp, merciless strength.

"Up ahead," he said to Ana, who was right in front of us, her steps halting as she tried to figure out where to go. She froze in place as another nearby explosion sent a wave of heat at us. Black smoke billowed into the air from the flaming carcass of a mechanized cart up the block.

"Are those car bombs?" I asked as we drew parallel with Ana, Takeshi practically carrying me as I tried to hold my arm still.

"No. It's the rays of the sun magnified under the dome. We're going to combust if we don't get inside," he said, his voice muffled by his mask.

Ana's eyes flew wide. Takeshi's arm was so tight around my waist that I could hardly draw breath. His gloved, clawed hands were digging into my side. "Here, right here," he said as he propelled me into a generic concrete building, right as a power line crackled above us.

Ana burst through the doorway in a shower of sparks. She threw her hood back and smiled, and I felt Takeshi's rigid body relax.

"Let me guess," she said to him. "The fire hour." Her statement was punctuated by another explosion outside.

"As the sun moves directly overhead, it gets focused through certain weak spots in the dome," Takeshi replied as he led me across the space, toward a back room filled with a pile of rubble. "The Mazikin have their private dens above and below. The first floors of every building in the city are meant to allow shelter if anyone gets caught out. They are public ground."

He led us around a few piles of crumbled cement and metal scraps, toward a thick wall at the center of the building. He moved aside a thin sheet of concrete to reveal a large jagged crack. Murmuring to Ana, he guided her inside—and down a hole. My heart beat a little faster as she disappeared. He turned to me. "This is going to hurt."

I leaned over. Ana was standing in a dimly lit space right below me. "I'll catch you," she said softly.

"This is *really* going to hurt," I muttered, and Takeshi chuckled. Steeling myself, I clumsily edged to the opening in the floor. The hole was about six feet deep, judging by the fact that Ana's head was right next to my boots as they dangled below me. I could do this. I could take it. I could—

"No more thinking," Takeshi said. Then he shoved me. With a yelp, I plunged down, landing hard, but Ana managed to catch me before I collided with the floor. Agony exploded in my shoulder, and I clamped my teeth together to keep from screaming.

Takeshi landed lightly next to us, leaving the hole above us completely dark—he'd replaced the sheet of concrete. He pulled his mask off and didn't look the slightest bit apologetic as he glanced over at me sweating cold drops of distilled pain. "All around you are Mazikin," he said. "They mostly hide from the elements and sleep during the day, but you never know when one will happen by."

He gestured at a narrow, rocky tunnel leading downward. Bare, crudely fashioned lightbulbs had been strung every twenty feet or so, allowing me to see that we had a walk ahead of us. Ana went first, and I was behind her. I tried not to be nervous about having Takeshi behind me, but it was hard to relax around him. Finally, after hiking a shallow downward path for a few minutes, we reached a metal door closed with a heavy padlock. Takeshi fished a skeleton key from his pocket and jammed it into the lock, then pulled the door open. His razor-tipped fingers were firm under my elbow as he guided me down another set of stairs, past dripping rock walls toward a glowing light at the bottom. We were deep within the earth, the temperature much cooler than it had been above. My boots slipped on the moist stairs, and I nearly fell, but Takeshi caught me. His build was slim, and he was only a few inches taller than me, but he was clearly stronger than he looked.

At the bottom of the steps lay an open cave-like chamber, complete with a thick pile of goatskin blankets and a satchel leaning against the wall. Takeshi led me to the mound of blankets and gestured for me to sit down.

"You live here?" Ana asked as she reached the bottom of the steps.

"I live nowhere and everywhere," said Takeshi as he tugged on my cloak, carefully pulling it off me. "There are salt caverns like this all over the city, and I've made a few of them into safe chambers. None of them last forever—they eventually cave in or are discovered, and I move on." He tucked the skeleton key away in his pocket and bent to remove a few of the goatskin blankets from the pile I was sitting on. I leaned to help him and moaned as it jostled my arm.

Takeshi carried the blankets across the room and set them in a corner. He met Ana's eyes. "We have to get her shoulder back in the socket, then we should all rest. We can't be on the streets for the next few hours, unless you feel like being cooked alive. You two were taking an incredible risk by being out there at this time of day."

"Tourist mistake." Ana stepped around him to squat in front of me. "You okay, girl? You're really pale."

"I'm great." I leaned back against the cool, damp wall and closed my eyes, fighting the urge to puke.

"You don't have to be tough, Lela," Ana said gently. "You don't have anything to prove. That Mazikin would have torn my throat out if you hadn't been there."

"Just help me get my arm working again. I won't be able to fight with my shoulder like this." The idea of being unable to defend myself in this hellish place was terrifying.

"You'll be ready to throw punches before the next fire hour." She inclined her head toward Takeshi. "He's done this for me before. He's a pro."

"But it's going to be painful," Takeshi warned.

I didn't see how it could be more painful than it had been when I was shoved without warning into a hole, but whatever.

He got on his knees in front of me and secured my gaze. His eyes were a cinnamon brown, and I let myself stare, taking in the finely sculpted lines of his face. Silver-pink scarring tracked down the left side of his cheek and neck, but it didn't ruin him, only made him look more intimidating.

"Try to relax," he said as Ana scooted over next to me and took my left hand. Takeshi had removed his Mazikin gloves and now cradled my limp right arm in his warm hands. "You have to release the tension in your muscles, Lela, or this isn't going to work. They're all seized up around the injury."

Ana pulled the heavy glove off my arm and stroked the back of my hand. "You're safe. Just take a deep breath and think of being far away from here." She paused. "Think about that dance you got to go to."

"Um, it wasn't that relaxing, but I'll try." And I did. As Takeshi slowly moved my arm, pressing the elbow against my side, I thought back, not to the dance, but right after, to the last time I'd been in terrible pain. Malachi's voice, soft against my skin, whispered, *I've got you. Just hold on to me . . .*

I didn't close my eyes quickly enough to contain the tear that streaked down my face at the memory of how, in that moment, with his cheek pressed to mine and his voice in my ear, I'd given myself over completely, letting him hold me together when I couldn't do it myself. It had been the best and worst feeling in the world. And now all I had was the shape of it carved onto my heart, the hole he left behind.

Ana's fingers brushed against my face. "You're doing great, Lela. Doing great."

Stars exploded behind my closed eyelids as Takeshi held my elbow still and abruptly levered my lower arm away from my body. As the pressure and pain ratcheted up, I let out a slow breath and imagined Malachi holding me down, keeping me from shattering.

I cried out as my shoulder popped back into place, then sagged as the burst of pain gave way to instant relief, leaving me aching but able to move my arm without agony. When I opened my eyes, Takeshi was smiling. "Well done," he said. "Now lie down."

I sank into the surprisingly soft goatskin pallet. My shoulder was okay, but the rest of me still felt pulled out of joint. "Just for a little while."

"Only a few hours," he agreed. "I need to rest, too, and then we'll move toward the center of the city. The Mazikin would keep Malachi in the square. That's where we'll go."

"Why do you think he's there?" I asked.

His eyes were steady on me. "To be an example."

My stomach dropped.

"Do you think he might have escaped?" Ana asked, joining Takeshi in the center of the room. His fingers drifted across her cheek, but he was frowning.

Then he caught me watching him and flashed me a reassuring grin. "If anyone could, it would be Malachi."

He turned away, but not before I saw his smile fade. He whispered something in Ana's ear, and her eyes flicked over to me. "Try to sleep, okay? We'll be on our way again before long."

I knew they weren't telling me everything, but I was too thrashed to demand that information right then. I turned to the wall and wrapped my sore arms around me, drawing my knees to my chest as the lightbulb clicked off. My thoughts swarming with a million plans and unknowns, my mind racing with countless what-ifs, I lay in the dark and counted the seconds and minutes, forcing my breathing into a long, slow rhythm, hoping my body would rest even though my brain couldn't.

And then, deep within the dark, I heard sounds that burned me in a million different ways.

The soft sighs, the sharp intake of breath, the swish of fabric as it fell to the floor, the quiet shudder of surrender. Ana and Takeshi. Together, finally, after so many years apart. I let the tears roll down, wishing I was anywhere but right there, having to bear witness to something so private and intimate. My chest felt like it was caving in with every uneven breath, every whispered word in languages I couldn't understand but had no trouble translating. *I love you. I never stopped loving you. You are the home for my soul.* I flattened my hands over my ears and sank deep into my own head, the only way to escape.

Malachi was waiting for me there. The way he pressed my hand to his chest and told me his heart beat for me. The burning look in his eyes as he watched me, how he kissed me like he could never get enough, how his hands shook as they slid over my body. All those images of him, all those sensations, washed over me, leaving me hungry and aching and grieving. Inside of them I drifted, reaching for him, never quite able to catch hold of his sleeve, never quite able to touch his face or make him hear me.

Someday, I promised. *Someday it will be you and me, face-to-face, and I will tell you how I feel.*

I lay there, hurting inside and out, thinking *someday* couldn't possibly arrive soon enough.

SEVEN

SOMEONE PRODDED MY ACHING shoulder, and I lurched awake from a dream of slow dancing with Malachi in an abandoned warehouse as it collapsed around us.

"Takeshi went up to scout. It'll be sundown soon. We're packing up to head out," Ana said softly. Her hair was freshly braided, and she looked happier than I'd ever seen her. The sling for the grenades was on the floor next to her thigh sheaths, laid out so she could arm herself.

I directed my gaze at the wall. "All right. Hey, did he tell you how he found us so quickly? This city seems pretty huge."

"The explosions against the dome got everyone's attention," she said, sliding a knife into a sheath. "He was following the enforcement squad to try to find out why. Apparently, Ibram commands them, and he's close to the Queen. And Tak loves to make their lives more difficult."

"Does Takeshi seem the same to you, Ana? Is he the person he was before he was taken?"

She raised her head and stared at me. "Are you implying something?"

I shook my head. "It just seems like this place would change a person." Into what, I didn't know.

Her fingers curled around the hilt of the knife. "He is still Takeshi."

I looked away from her predatory glare, hearing footsteps on the stairs. I sat up as Takeshi descended into the safe chamber. A single lightbulb hung from a twisted wire that threaded its way along the ceiling, nearly brushing the top of his head as he joined us. "How's the shoulder?"

I moved it gingerly. "Achy. But all things considered, pretty good." It hurt like a bitch, but there was no way I was going to complain.

"You're lucky," he said, watching me swing it in a slow arc, testing my range of motion. "People in the city heal quickly but badly. It's hard to die here, but it's also hard to stay whole. Like everything works to increase the suffering."

He turned to Ana. "What's that?" he asked, pointing to the sling.

Ana let out a dry laugh. "Grenades. Michael came up with them after you were gone. They explode ten seconds after you push the button."

Takeshi knelt next to her and picked up the belt. Carefully, he lifted a flap on one of the little pouches and peeked inside. "Amazing. They're so tiny. How powerful?"

"Really powerful," Ana said in a choked voice, and I had no doubt she was remembering the blast that had taken her out.

Takeshi brushed a few tendrils of hair away from her cheek, but then returned to examining the grenades. "These are very valuable. There is no one in the city who wouldn't want them."

"What are you talking about?" I suddenly wanted to take the sling out of his hands.

He seemed to sense that, because he set it down next to Ana. "There is no currency here. It's a barter system. And with those, even one of those, you could have nearly anything you wanted."

"All we want is to find Malachi and get out of here." I didn't like the bright look in his eyes as he stared at our most powerful weapon against the Mazikin, and I couldn't help but remember what he'd said about looking out for himself and no one else. He'd been nothing but kind to me, and he obviously loved Ana, but I guess I'd expected someone more . . . noble?

I pushed myself to my feet and scooped my cloak from the rocky floor of the chamber. "Have you been free all these years?"

Even if he really had safe chambers all over the place, I didn't see how it was possible for him to get around so easily without allies or friends. His face was painted on walls all over the city.

Takeshi leaned back from Ana and looked at me. "I got away from them very quickly after they brought me into the city. After that it was a matter of survival."

"And who helped you with that?"

His eyes narrowed. "I've bartered or stolen what I needed. I don't take human lives unless they threaten mine. If some have helped, the alliances are fleeting and motivated by a mutual need to survive, nothing more. There isn't room for more, not here," he said bitterly.

Ana frowned but remained silent.

"But you don't think Malachi got away? You don't think anyone would have helped him?" I watched him closely, looking for the truth. As soon as I saw the corners of his lips hitch upward in another show of fake optimism, I shook my head. "Don't bullshit me."

He stood up. Without his cloak, I could see that the scars on his face weren't the only ones he'd collected. Silvery gashes laced along his honey-colored skin, descending into the neck of his shirt. "I don't know what the truth is. But if you want my opinion, I'll give it to you. When the Mazikin captured me in the dark city, it was luck. I was weak, and they pounced on the opportunity. When they brought me into the city, they underestimated me. They treated me like anyone else. They thought it wouldn't take much to keep me contained, and they were wrong." His eyes met mine, cold despite the natural warmth of their color. "But Ana told me they were waiting for Malachi, that they had planned to take him."

I swallowed back nausea. "They set a pretty elaborate trap, made just for him. Juri was waiting to take over his body."

Takeshi tilted his head. "They will take no chances with such a valuable prize."

"So you think they have him," I said, ashamed at how small and broken I sounded. From the moment I'd found out Takeshi was free, some tiny part of me had hoped Malachi had gotten away, too, that he would find me the way Takeshi had found Ana.

Takeshi nodded, slow and deliberate. "I not only think they have Malachi—I think they will guard him with every bit of cunning they possess. And I think they will show him absolutely no mercy. I think they will destroy him, over and over again."

"Takeshi—" Ana began, but he held up his hand to silence her, never taking his eyes off me.

His voice was deadly but gentle, which made it all the more brutal. "No, Ana. She wanted to know. Didn't you, Lela?"

"Yes," I whispered, aching to slit the throat of any Mazikin that laid a clawed hand on Malachi. "And that's why I'm here. Can we leave now, Captain?"

"If you're ready," Ana said, a shade paler after Takeshi's blunt words.

Takeshi released her and moved across the room with a barely contained sort of energy, controlled but crackling with life. It might be difficult to stay whole in this city, but it seemed like Takeshi was in his element. He swung the satchel onto his back and took Ana's hand. "When we go topside, I'm going to wear the mask," he said to her. "And I want you two to wear disguises, too. Few humans walk these streets independently, and as you saw, there are traps to capture those who do. Nearly every person in this city is a slave, every creature a master."

Ana wrinkled her nose. "Ugh. That Mazikin skin stinks. I don't want to wear one of tho—"

"You don't have to," Takeshi said, arching an eyebrow. He reached into his satchel and pulled out a studded collar, connected to a long black leather leash. "You can wear this."

The sun hung low and menacing at the rooftops when we left our underground haven. It was still hot, but no longer unbearable. "The Mazikin will be emerging from their dens soon," Takeshi told us. "Fortunately, the crowds and the darkness will help us more than they hurt. Unless we're caught. Keep your heads covered and follow my lead."

He smiled and yanked playfully on Ana's leash. Anyone else would have had one of Ana's knives rammed into his soft spots, but Ana rewarded Takeshi with a look hot enough to make me blush.

I pulled my cloak around me and tucked the end of my now-braided hair under my tunic, fighting the urge to tug at the stiff collar around my neck. "Where are we going?"

Takeshi led us over to one of the doorways. "The square, the central meeting place. It's just south of the Bone Palace, and it's where they hold the lotteries and . . . other events they want the public to witness."

"The lotteries?" Ana asked, making sure her own hair was fully concealed beneath the hood of her cloak.

"It's how they decide which of them gets to go through the portal. The favorites of the Queen may go at her command, but the rest go by lottery. They enter their names and vie for the chance to possess a human body—to escape. The drawings take place every night. Even Mazikin need hope." His jaw flexed with tension. "It will take us a few hours to walk."

With my head bowed, I followed him onto the road, Ana trudging next to me, her powerful stride reined in. I flinched as a growling, distorted voice rang out over some kind of public announcement system, echoing above the din of the street. Takeshi stopped dead, listening, and then continued on. Ana cursed under her breath.

"What is it?"

"They're calling all citizens to the square at the black hour," she translated.

"It's the coldest hour of the darkness," Takeshi said. "Think of it as midnight."

"For the lottery?" I asked.

"No." Ana reached for my hand, and I let her take it in hers. It seemed less like an affectionate gesture and more like an attempt to hold me in place. "The Queen is playing host to the newest resident of the city," she said in a hollow voice.

I focused on the pressure of her fingers to keep from screaming, from flying apart. As the growling speech went on, Ana's grip steadily tightened until she was nearly crushing my hand, but she didn't translate any more for me. I was about to ask her when the voice cut off with a blast of screeching feedback, allowing me to hear the noises of the street, the sounds coming from the buildings around us. Since we'd arrived in the city, it had been mostly quiet, save for the distant industrial noise coming from the factories. But now, all around me, the Mazikin hooted and snarled. Engines roared. Metal rattled and clanged.

Humans screamed and moaned.

In the gray twilight, the electric lights began to wink on, just enough to show the way. Shadows danced on the black pavement, silhouettes of snouts and rounded ears, of barrel chests and clawed hands. And more human shapes, too, hunched backs, trembling shoulders. The Mazikin and their slaves.

"There are more humans in the city than Mazikin." Takeshi patted my head as he spoke, as if I were his mute and devoted dog. "About twice as many."

"If they outnumber the Mazikin, why are they slaves?"

"I'd start with the fact that nearly all of them came from the dark city," said Ana. "It's not as if they were in fighting form when they got here. They were already hopeless enough to have taken their own lives."

"And those who fight are punished in terrible ways," added Takeshi. "In a place where there can be no escape, where you go on and on, and so does your suffering, that's a terrifying prospect."

"But not all of them have given up," I said, thinking of that woman in the cart, chained and on the way to the meat factory, looking at me like I might save her. I hadn't come here for that woman, and she wasn't part of my mission, but I couldn't help wanting to be worthy of that hope in her eyes.

Takeshi assessed me coolly and tugged my leash as we crossed the street. I shivered as chilled air crept under my cloak; now that the sun had fallen below the skyline, the temperature was dropping as rapidly as it had risen. I pulled my gloves from my waistband and slipped them on.

From behind us came a grunt, and Takeshi responded with a fierce growl and a wave of his clawed hand. The streets were growing crowded as the Mazikin came out to play. The pungent musk of their fur and the deeper scent of human misery—sweat and blood—wafted over me as I bumped shoulders with other leashed slaves and shied meekly away from the cloaked Mazikin who strode down the middle of the sidewalk. I could almost tell which ones had occupied human bodies. Some of them bounded up the street on all fours while others walked upright. Some wore jewelry and had styled the tufts of hair on their furry heads, and others wore no adornment at all—but all of them wore some kind of clothing. And with their humanlike hands and ability to speak, with the eerily intelligent gleam in their eyes, there was no mistaking them for ordinary animals.

"Aren't there Mazikin cubs somewhere?" Ana asked. We hadn't seen a single one since we'd entered the city. "Do they keep them underground or something?"

Takeshi made a disgusted noise. "No, the cubs are kept in a single nursery until they're released into the city." He barked and lunged at a Mazikin who came up to sniff at Ana, and the creature yelped and scurried away. "Now's the time to be quiet," he muttered. "Too crowded here."

As we hiked north, Takeshi played his part with authority, stepping aside for no one. His cloak concealed most of his face, but his mask was arranged in a vicious snarl that made him seem like a bad choice if someone was looking for a fight. Which was good—because others weren't so lucky. Scuffles broke out every few blocks. We passed by one Mazikin lying in a heap against the wall, holding a torn leash and bleeding from a gash across its chest. Its rapid, shallow breaths puffed in red-tinged clouds. Someone had wanted its slave and had taken the human by force, leaving the loser to drown in its own blood. Takeshi shortened the lead on our leashes, and through the collar I felt his tension vibrating.

Mechanized carts, trucks, and cars, their enormous clunky engines exposed and sputtering, their exhaust pipes belching oily black fumes, rumbled up and down the potholed roads, occasionally scraping against each other as they tried to pass on the rocky, crumbling terrain. The technology in the city looked to be about a hundred years behind Rhode Island, nothing sleek, nothing quiet. It was all clamor and stink, loud and brutal. Exactly like the

Mazikin themselves. There didn't seem to be any separation between public and private. More than once, we passed by pairs or groups of Mazikin, up against cars or walls or lying on the sidewalk, engaging in acts that turned my stomach. Sex. Death. Pain. Pleasure. All right there, all hideous.

These were the creatures holding Malachi prisoner.

And somewhere, in all of this, they had a few of my classmates, too, the ones unlucky enough to cross the paths of the Mazikin who had invaded my hometown. Somewhere out there, Aden the baseball star and Evan the drug dealer were enslaved and suffering. Some of the people I had met in the homeless camp in Providence were here, too. And, somewhere in this seething hell, my mother was lost and in pain. Even if I freed Malachi and completed this mission, what would it be like to escape the city knowing they were still trapped?

"Only a few more blocks," Takeshi said in a low voice, steering us through the massing crowd. It was slowgoing now, because the streets were packed with creatures and humans. Most of them, though, were headed in the same direction we were. Toward the square.

Takeshi halted abruptly, and I bonked my head on his back. "This way," he hissed, yanking my leash to the side, hard enough to make me stumble. Then he growled and barked at something beside me. I raised my head to see a big black-spotted Mazikin with a torn ear standing a few feet away. It had a fistful of Ana's hood and was eyeing her with greedy eagerness. Ana was standing very still, her mouth set in a thin gray line. Her hands weren't visible—they were hidden beneath her cloak—she probably had already grabbed knives, ready to defend herself.

With an earsplitting burst of feedback, the PA system flared to life again, and the deep grunts of the Mazikin announcer echoed off the cement buildings. As Takeshi continued to argue with the torn-eared Mazikin, the crowd drifted toward an open square up ahead illuminated by high stadium lights. The entrance to the square was only a few car-lengths away, and bodies were flowing into it, their heads upturned, their gazes focused on something above street level. Mazikin stood atop the buildings, too, looking down on the square, while those in the streets pressed forward, trying to get a view. I took a few steps and realized Takeshi was so absorbed in the discussion with the other Mazikin that he'd let go of my leash. I toppled forward as three leashed women with sunken faces tried to press by, and I had to stutter-step to avoid getting trampled.

Then I heard it, amidst the growling over the public announcement system, one word in English, wedged between hoots and whines. One word that made my heart seize up.

Captain.

Barely breathing, I let the crowd carry me, oblivious to everyone else, human and Mazikin alike.

A few dozen steps were all it took to make it to the square.

A few seconds was all it took to shatter me.

At the opposite end of the plaza, on a tiered platform, his arms outstretched, shackles around his ankles, wrists, and throat, the cement wall behind him splotched with reddish-brown stains, clothed only in his own blood, was Malachi.

I lunged forward, a desperate, soul-wrenching cry exploding up from the center of me. But then a clawed hand closed over my shoulder, and a furry limb snaked around my neck, cutting off my scream before it escaped my throat.

EIGHT

I LIFTED MY FEET off the ground and tucked my neck against my body, trying to wriggle away, but the Mazikin wrapped its arm around my waist and lurched backward until I could no longer see Malachi. Not that it mattered. The image was stamped on my brain. His eyes had been closed, but his face . . .

My heels scraped against the sidewalk as the Mazikin dragged me back the way I had come. No one in the crowd seemed interested in us; their eyes were all riveted on the spectacle in the square. And if no one cared, maybe they wouldn't notice if I slit this Mazikin's throat. I was reaching for my knives when the thing hurled me to the pavement. I hit hard, knees and elbows first. Above me, my Mazikin captor stood astride me and jabbed its clawed finger into Takeshi's chest. With a knee-high leather boot, it kicked me lightly in the side and stepped over me, wedging itself between Takeshi, whose hood was pulled low over his Mazikin mask, and the torn-eared Mazikin he'd been arguing with. The Mazikin who'd grabbed me was shorter than Takeshi, but its claws were long, curved, and gleaming—and painted hot pink. Snarls came from deep within its barrel chest as it swiped those claws in front of the torn-eared creature's face, and though bigger, Torn-Ear actually stepped back. A second later, Ana thumped to the pavement next to me.

"Are you okay?" she asked as soon as she saw my face. "You look like you've seen . . ." She grimaced. "We'll get him, Lela. But first Takeshi has to convince Ugly up there that I shouldn't be his new slave." She jerked her chin at Torn-Ear, who had taken another wary step back from Takeshi and the small pink-clawed Mazikin that had hauled me away from the square.

I should have been trying to figure out how to help, but I was numb to anything except the memory of Malachi, the livid ruby scars that streaked his legs and ribs, the bite marks on his calves and hips and arms. And his face . . . "Malachi," I breathed, trying not to pass out.

"Stay with me, Lela." Ana edged up close, speaking right in my ear, somehow penetrating the swirl of panic. "I don't know why, but that small Mazikin who grabbed you is claiming Takeshi is her mate. She's insisting we all go with her, because she's exercising her blood right."

"Her *what*?"

"I think she means we're all her property," Ana said quickly, right as Takeshi grabbed her by the shoulders and wrenched her up. The small pink-clawed Mazikin did the same to me, and before I could draw my knives, I caught the barest shake of the head from Ana. So I let the creature practically carry me back along the block, down an alley that stank of raw sewage, and then through a narrow space between two buildings. I glanced up at the creature who had taken control of us. She had a crescent-moon-shaped scar next to her eye, which gave the sense that she had fought and survived on more than one occasion. Her grunts vibrated against my back as she wrestled me through a doorway and then through a maze of rooms that reeked of wet fur.

I stumbled up a few flights of concrete steps, the toes of my boots catching as I tried to keep up, my thoughts painted red with visions of Malachi. The Mazikin reached a metal door and wrenched it open, revealing a shallow room with three windows opening onto the street below. The pink-clawed Mazikin slammed the metal door, threw the dead bolt, and looked down at me, her fangs only a few inches from my face. "Lela," she growled. "Lela . . . girl."

My breath caught in my throat as I stared into her black eyes.

Takeshi ripped his mask from his face and let it fall to the floor, then stepped up next to us. "Lela, this is Zip."

"What . . . what . . ." I stuttered, trying to figure out why Takeshi had been talking to this creature, and why she knew my name.

Zip turned to Takeshi and spoke in her snarl-hoot-grunt staccato, and Takeshi nodded before giving me a careful look. "She says she knew you. In the land of the living. When she . . ."

He glanced at Ana with a worried expression, and Ana walked over to me and leaned so all I could see was her face. "She says she's the Mazikin who possessed your mother."

The Mazikin released me, and my knees gave out. I hit the floor in a boneless sprawl of limbs, unable to decode all the images and words and thoughts in my head. I looked up at Zip, the Mazikin who had taken my mother. "You—"

"Tu mamá te ama a tí, Lela," she said softly.

"Have you seen her?" I asked, peering into the dark corners of the room as if I'd find her there.

Zip and Takeshi exchanged words, then he knelt by my side. "She's in a safe place. Not here. You'll see her soon."

"Safe place?" My laughter was hoarse and broken, my voice cracking on each word as I rolled to my hands and knees. There was no such thing as a safe place in this city. I fixed Takeshi with a hard stare. "Why is she here? Why are *we* here? Malachi's out there. I just saw him."

"And there's nothing you can do about it right now," Takeshi said. "That square is teeming with Mazikin, and unless you want to be chained next to him, we have to wait for a better time."

I drew a deep breath. The damp concrete floor cooled my blood and slowed my heart, uncramping my muscles and allowing me to stand. "I still don't get why this Mazikin's acting like she's our friend. She's the reason my mom is here in the first place. Why would she care about her safety? Or ours, for that matter?"

"I'm not entirely sure." Takeshi's gaze wandered over to Zip, who was staring at me with total focus. "Is there something unusual about your mother, Lela? Something—"

"Nothing apart from the fact that she's completely insane," I said bitterly.

He nodded. "Ah. Well, Zip here is a young Mazikin, and your mother was probably the first and only human body she possessed. I think she probably got a bit lost in your mother's head."

"That's what Sil told me," I murmured, remembering the moments right before he cut my mother's throat.

A rumbling growl rolled from Zip's throat. "Sil." She bared her teeth. Her curved claws clicked together.

"She still seems a little confused," said Ana, eyeing Zip. "She has strong feelings for you and your mother, as if she's part of your family." Ana's hands had disappeared beneath her cloak again, and I had no doubt she was ready and willing to put Zip down if she needed to.

"My mother's not really my family," I said, hugging myself. I wanted to be numb, truly numb, so nothing else would hurt. But as much as I'd tried to forget her, Rita Santos was an open wound, hurting me from the inside out. My mother had deserted me when I was only four years old. She'd let the system take me, chew me up, and spit me out. I edged away from Zip as a shout went up from the crowd. Zip whined quietly, then turned to Takeshi and began to speak again.

"She's taking care of your mother," Takeshi said when she was finished. "When Zip was returned to the city, she was determined to find her. She saved your mother from a meat cart and took her as a slave. I get the sense she treats her more like a pet, though. It's a better fate than many here have."

"Well, thanks," I whispered, not wanting to think of how many times my mother had taken a ride on the meat cart before Zip rescued her. I got up and walked to the window.

Like a punch to the gut, the sight hit me hard—we were right over the square, near the top floor of one of the surrounding buildings. Maybe a story below, and only yards to my right, Malachi was chained to the bloody platform.

My hands clutched at the rough cement of the windowsill as I took in the blood, the gruesome, barely healed wound just beneath his rib cage, the heavy manacles pinning him against the concrete wall behind him. My fingers curled into shaking fists as I gazed at his harshly beautiful face. They'd tried to ruin it. Or half of it, at least. His right cheek was a maze of claw marks, but the left appeared untouched. What hurt the most, though, was seeing his eyes. They were open, and the agony in their black-brown depths was miles deep. He gazed up at the black haze hanging above the stadium lights, like I'd seen him do in the dark city, when he'd stared at the wild forest beyond the city wall. He was escaping in the only way he could.

A shrieking blat of music split the frigid night air, and the crowd roared, the Mazikin's black-clawed hands waving. The humans in the square cheered, too, like they were just as bloodthirsty. What the hell? Malachi had spent years protecting the inhabitants of the dark city . . . but of course, these were the people he'd failed, and he didn't have any power here. The Mazikin were the masters. Takeshi's claim that the Resistance was a myth made perfect sense as human shouts mingled with the snarls and hoots of the Mazikin. But then a flurry of movement to my left caught my attention, and I leaned from the window and looked down at the alley beside our building. I glimpsed pale-blond hair blown by a chill wind, a flash of milk-white skin as a hand pulled a hood forward, a dark-cloaked human sinking back into the shadows. Then the figure was gone, and the crowd near the alley reshaped around the person who had been there.

All eyes in the square were now focused on an archway of enormous cement blocks, which had been stamped with the image of a Mazikin, a grinning, fanged face keeping watch over the square. The archway was to the side of the platform where Malachi was chained, and through it loomed a dark, vast building, partially obscured by the haze. As the music screeched, discordant and earsplitting, it was joined by the rumble of a powerful engine. The mob parted as a mechanized cart rolled beneath the archway, the exposed coils of its engine gleaming under the stadium lights. Its driver wore a black leather cap with holes cut out for his ears, which twitched as he steered the vehicle into the center of the square. The rear of it became visible; the cart had a long, open back, like a stretch limousine without a hardtop.

And lying in the back of the shining silver cart, on a broad, intricately welded wrought iron throne, was a coppery-furred Mazikin. It was propped on its elbows with its head up, like a dog on a bed, wearing a flowing black leather gown and a crown of creamy ivory . . . No, there were no elephants in the city . . . It was bone. Had to be. The creature was wearing a crown of bone.

The Mazikin Queen.

Her black eyes swept over the square as she pushed herself up to sit. She raised her hand into the air, revealing long, straight claws that looked like they had been dipped in silver. They gave off a steely glint as she waved to the crowd, who cheered, mouths gaping, tongues lolling, teeth flashing. Behind the Queen stood two large black-spotted Mazikin with curving ebony claws. Slick leathery cloaks marked with black triangles hung from their broad shoulders, and their blunt snouts peeked out from under wide hoods.

As the cart rumbled and bumped over the rough pavement, their cloaks flapped and swayed, revealing the daggers tucked into their belts. "Sil and Ibram," Takeshi said from behind me. "When he inhabits his own body, Juri has a place in the Queen's entourage as well. He's one of her favorite companions."

I stared at the two Mazikin. The one on the right eyed the crowd with a cold, haughty indifference, but the one on the left, with a deep scar denting the top of his snout, had darting, cautious eyes that never stopped flitting over the crowd. The tip of his nose twitched and trembled, like it was picking up scents in the air. As the cart approached the raised platform, he inhaled deeply, and a wide, malevolent grin split his ugly, spotted face. His gaze swung smoothly up the cement steps and landed on Malachi. I was willing to bet almost anything that the Mazikin with the scarred snout was Sil. His expression was so similar to looks he'd given me when in his human body—when he knew he was winning, even when I hadn't figured it out yet.

The driver of the cart pulled to a stop in front of the steps. Slowly, the Queen edged herself off her throne and rose on her hind legs. She pointed a razor-tipped finger at the sky, and the crowd abruptly fell silent.

Halfway up the wide cement steps leading to Malachi's platform stood a Mazikin at a podium—the announcer. Heavy silver loops hung in a row from each of its ears. Its teeth were stained a vibrant red, as were its claws. Its furry arms were brown, but its face was a bleached white. It grunted into the microphone, then let out a hooting growl and gestured at the Queen.

The crowd—including the human slaves—clapped and cheered as the Queen stepped ponderously from the cart, assisted by Sil and Ibram. The folds of her dress stretched tight against her oddly swollen belly. She put a hand to it as she stepped onto the stairs leading up to the platform. With Sil and Ibram close by her sides, she approached the announcer, who bowed low and moved aside to allow her to take its place. The announcer dropped onto all fours to straighten the Queen's skirts, spreading the black leather material in a neat circle around her feet. For a moment, the Queen's gaze slid up the front of our building, and I quickly shrank back into the shadows as an iron-edged chill rippled through my body.

Sil, Ibram, and the announcer descended the steps, leaving the Queen alone at the podium. A few steps above her, Malachi stood chained on the platform. His dark eyes were still directed at the sky, like he was unaware of his surroundings. His expression hadn't changed at all. I wanted to scream for him. I wanted to leap from the window and free him. The dread was nearly strangling me.

The Queen began to speak into the microphone, her deep, rumbling voice rolling over the crowd. Takeshi leaned close and spoke in my ear, translating. "Citizens, you know of my devotion to you. I am your provider, the one who paves the way. I am your lover, the one who gives you young."

I shuddered at the sound of her voice and his, the growl and the whisper, and the way she patted her belly as she continued to speak while Takeshi translated. "I am your mother, and a mother protects her cubs. I am your Queen, and a Queen destroys her enemies."

She bared her teeth, and my stomach clenched. She pointed a silver claw at Malachi and snarled something that made the crowd erupt. Takeshi's hand closed over my upper arm, and he began to tug me backward. "Lela—"

I jerked my arm away and pressed closer to the window as she mounted the steps on her hind legs, slowly closing the distance between her and Malachi. My heart choking me, I saw the *exact* moment he came back to himself, the moment escape was no longer possible. His eyes darted to the Queen as she reached the top step, and then he closed them tightly. With the heavy manacle around his neck, he couldn't even turn his head, but every muscle in his body flexed. I bit the inside of my lips to keep from screaming. Next to me, Takeshi was talking as he pulled on my arm, but his voice was merely a buzz in my ear. As the Queen stood in front of Malachi, her gown billowing behind her, I could only hear the voice of Clarence, a Mazikin I'd interrogated in the land of the living, saying eight words about what his Queen would do to him if he betrayed her.

Eight horrible words.

The Queen laid one of her hands against the side of Malachi's face, and suddenly I knew why he had scars there, why they were only on that side. She leaned forward and whispered something in his ear, as tenderly as a lover, and licked the undamaged side of his face with her black tongue. Even from my spot across the square, I could feel his shudder. And then her claws scored down his cheek as her other hand—claws sheathed in those silver blades—jerked forward suddenly, right at the center of Malachi's body, just below his rib cage.

His eyes flew open. The veins at his temples stood out blue against his reddening skin. Blood welled and trickled from the corners of his mouth, which opened in a silent cry. I jumped onto the windowsill, Clarence's words deafening me, destroying me.

She will eat my heart in the square.

I was halfway out the window when I was jerked back, hitting the floor hard enough to knock the wind out of me. A calloused palm slapped itself over my mouth. Steely arms held me down. I fought and bit and kicked, every part of me screaming: *Malachi Malachi Malachi.* Nothing but his name in a never-ending loop, the soundtrack to the horror in my head, the sight of my love being torn apart, the knowledge that the heart that beat for me was being ripped away by steel-tipped claws.

I grabbed for my knives. Nothing would stop me from getting to him. My fingers closed around their hilts, and I drew my only allies from their sheaths, ready to lay waste to anything that stood in my way.

But then the inside of my skull exploded in a million pin-pricks of light, and darkness took me.

NINE

MY EYES FLICKED OPEN, then closed against the bright light overhead. A bare lightbulb hung above the spot where I lay. The rocky floor beneath me was thinly padded by a goatskin blanket, judging by the sharp, tangy smell of it. Next to me, I heard Ana whisper, "She's waking up."

I slowly moved my arm up to cover my eyes. My muscles ached like I'd had a brutal workout. My stomach burbled uneasily. Somewhere in the room, a voice muttered in Spanish, but it wasn't Ana's. I rolled to my side and drew my knees to my chest, curling into a ball to protect myself from the memories that flooded me, of lying in the dark with hot tears hitting my face like rain, of the scratchy blanket under my chin and the ratty teddy bear in my arms, of the shaking fingers that smoothed my hair.

"Mi bebé, mi bebé," the voice repeated.

It was my mother.

A hand stroked down my arm, and I jerked away, then retched as the motion split my brain right down the middle.

"Lela, it's Ana. You're safe."

"Where are we?" I winced as the sound rushed from my raw throat.

"Zip brought us to the bottom level of her den. We're below the square."

The square . . . I dug around in my brain for the sequence that had landed me here. I remembered being in the square, seeing Malachi—

I sat up suddenly, my heart jabbing against my ribs. I was in a cement-walled, windowless room with a steel door. Goatskins were piled in one corner and spread over wide concrete-block chairs. There was a concrete table in another corner and a row of buckets in a third corner. The place reeked of wet fur and goat.

Zip was in the corner, hunched over a rocking, mumbling human, stroking the woman's wild, curly hair. My mother.

I'd gotten halfway off the floor before Takeshi appeared in front of me. He grasped my shoulders, his expression grim. "Stay down. Or you'll probably fall down."

Dizziness making the cinder-block walls undulate like snakes, I allowed him to guide me back to the floor. "Malachi," I said in a scratchy whisper. "She killed him."

"No, she didn't." Ana scooted toward the goatskin pallet I'd been lying on. "Apparently it takes more than that to kill someone here."

I rubbed my hand over my chest. "She tore his heart out, didn't she?"

Ana's eyes were full of sorrow as she nodded. "But according to Zip, she's done that to him every night since he arrived."

My face crumpled as I tried to keep from crying. That was why he had that barely healed wound in the center of his chest. That was where her silver claws had torn him open and claimed their prize. "How could that not kill him?"

"I told you it was hard to die here if you're a human," Takeshi said quietly. "You have to be decapitated, or your body has to be completely destroyed. But if you're wounded, even something that would be fatal anywhere else, you'll heal. Badly, though. You're never quite the same. I've seen it many times. I've lived it."

Ana took his hand, and seeing that connection between them made me feel like my own heart was being ripped out. "What will happen to him?" I choked out.

"His heart will grow back. It grows back every day. And every night, the Queen—"

I held up my hand, and his mouth snapped shut. "How long have we been here?"

He sank to the pallet next to Ana, all slender animal grace. He'd claimed to have lived through that awful kind of wound, but he looked pretty whole to me, pretty healthy. "We haven't been here long. We brought you here when you—"

"When I lost it. You hit me, didn't you?"

He nodded. "It was the only way to stop you from killing yourself."

"I wasn't trying to kill myself."

"That's for sure. You were trying to kill *us*, Lieutenant," Ana said in a hard voice as she rubbed her temple. "But you were also trying to hurl yourself from the fourth story of a building, straight into a hostile crowd that would probably enjoy seeing you disemboweled by their Queen."

She was right. I wasn't about to thank her, though. A bump on the side of my head throbbed with the hot, sick beats of my heart, sending another wave of dizziness rolling over me. From the corner, I heard more Spanish mumbling, then a shuffling of feet and hands. My mother was crawling toward me, her amber eyes riveted to my face. She paused a few feet away, her head tilted. Her hair was combed and pulled into a bushy ponytail. Her cheeks were sunken. Her fingers twitched like she wanted to touch me.

That was when I realized—this woman, my actual mother, hadn't laid eyes on me since I was four years old. I'd seen *her* much more recently, but only while her body was occupied by Zip. The real Rita Santos had already been here, trapped in the Mazikin city, apparently serving as a renewable food source for these creatures. I watched mutely as she edged closer. A few tears fell to the bare concrete floor. Hers, not mine. I was too emptied out to cry, even when she tucked herself against my arm and leaned her head on my shoulder, whimpering softly.

"Hi," I said, hating the way all eyes in the room were fixed on me. "How are you?"

I had no idea what to say to her. Once upon a time, we had shared a language and she had loved me. I had loved her, too. She had been the ground beneath me until she crumbled and fell apart, leaving me with nowhere to plant my feet. Now she was a stranger with familiar eyes. We needed a translator to understand each other. And in looking at her, I wasn't even sure that would be enough. She was rocking again, humming vacantly to music only she could hear. Finally, she started to whisper to no one in particular, a rapid-fire mumble of Spanish.

Ana tried to translate in hushed tones, but after a few seconds she shook her head. "I can't . . . Lela, she's not making sense. I'm not sure how to . . ."

"Don't bother." I closed my eyes and bowed my head against my knees. My mother stroked a tentative hand down my arm while I fought the urge to pull away. "My mom's mentally ill. Schizophrenia. Heard of it?"

From the corner, Zip let out an anxious whine. Ana and Takeshi were silent. They were from different times and places, and I didn't expect the term to make sense to them. It barely made sense to me. All I knew was that my mom had lost her grip on reality, that her world was flimsy and drifting. She couldn't take care of herself, let alone her daughter. Sil had told me that when the Mazikin took over her body, my mother's soul slipped free without a struggle, because it had been hanging on by a thread. And now she was here—one more thing I had to worry about.

I raised my head and looked at her, feeling the trail of bitter regret for what should have been. In that moment, I missed Diane so badly that it was a physical pain. If she were here, she wouldn't be huddling against my arm, singing to herself. She'd be fussing over me in a way I used to hate but had grown to count on.

Rita, on the other hand, seemed like she was the one who needed to be fussed over. She sounded forlorn and lost as her bony fingers touched the back of my hand. She squinted, leaning forward and placing her palm against mine, lining up our hands. Ana looked worried, probably because she'd witnessed me flinch away from touch on more than one occasion. I was more able to tolerate it now, but not without some effort. The only person in the world whose touch I craved was . . . I pulled my hand away from my mother's and rubbed my palm along my pants. "I'm sorry," I said as her eyes met mine for the first time.

"Lela?" she whispered.

"Yeah." And—I couldn't help it—hearing her say my name did funny things to my heart.

She mumbled something else and curled against my side, sinking into herself again.

I drew a slow, determined breath. "Can somebody tell me how we're going to get Malachi out of that square?" I couldn't bear the thought of him suffering a moment more than was necessary. "And then how we're going to get to the portal?"

Takeshi gave Ana a sidelong glance and looked away.

"What is it?" Ana asked.

"I want to free Malachi as badly as you do. If you'd never shown up, I would have done it by myself. But destroying the portal and killing the Queen? That is an impossible mission," he said. "It was cruel for the Judge to send you here, but it doesn't surprise me in the least."

"She didn't force us," I said. "We pretty much demanded a chance to come."

"That doesn't mean you owe the Judge anything."

"Are you saying you want to let the Mazikin keep possessing people?" I stared at him.

"I'm saying I'm not particularly interested in what the Judge wants."

"What about us?" Ana whispered. "If we do this, we could get out, Tak. We could be free."

He laughed. "What makes you think the Judge will ever set you free, love?"

Ana's jaw clenched, and Takeshi pulled her into his arms and kissed her forehead. "I'm sorry," he murmured to her. "I'll help you." He framed her face with his hands and stared into her eyes. "I'll help *you*."

I looked away from them. Once we had Malachi back, he would help. I knew that for sure. Not because of his feelings for me, and not because the Judge ordered it. Because of *his* sense of justice. Malachi cared about so much more than himself. That was simply who he was.

"Since you hate the Judge and don't seem to care about our mission," I said to Takeshi, "tell me what Malachi is to you. I need to hear it."

He sighed, squeezing and releasing Ana's hand before moving to squat in front of me. He tipped my chin up with his fingers, and I was so caught by his solemn expression that I didn't pull away as he started to speak. "The only thing that kept me sane when I first arrived here was knowing Malachi would take care of Ana, that he would protect her when the Mazikin who'd possessed me went after her. If I were in that square and he were here, he would be plotting my rescue, as surely as I'm planning his. He is one of the strongest, best men I've ever met, and the one I'd want at my side if I went into battle. I love him like my own brother, and I will use whatever skill and knowledge I have to help you free him—and to keep you whole while we do that. Because, if what Ana says is true, Malachi feels for you what I feel for her. So if I happen to hit you over the head in the process, I'm sorry, but I'd do it again if that meant saving him from losing you forever."

"He could never lose me forever," I said hoarsely. "But I appreciate your help."

Ana put her hand on Takeshi's shoulder, and he rose to his feet as she said, "We should try to get to Malachi at dawn, when the Mazikin have fled to their lairs. He might still be guarded then, but the crowds will be gone."

Takeshi gave her an uneasy look. "That's only a few hours away."

Zip crept over and laid her clawed hand on my mother's shoulder. *"Le ayudaremos,"* she said as my mother crawled back into the protective circle of Zip's furry arms. The Mazikin spoke in Spanish to Ana, who translated: "You get the Captain and bring him here. We will take care of him."

"Something tells me it won't be that easy," I said.

Takeshi pointed to a darkened hallway at the far end of the room, opposite the steel door. "Zip's got a few ways out. She's pretty resourceful, and she has some means. She said she works at the Bone Palace, in the kitchens, so once we get Malachi, perhaps she'll help us get in." He gestured at the door. "That passageway connects to an underground tunnel beneath the square, but there are several other passages that lead to other dens and tunnels. We're in a warren of sorts, and as far as I know, none of it is mapped. That's the way the Mazikin live. Little planning and no control. The Queen rules with fear and promises, and the enforcement squads are brutal but disorganized. It's one of the reasons I've remained free for all these years."

I eyed Zip, and she hooted softly at me. "How can we trust her?"

Ana shrugged. "We can't, not completely. But she's already risked herself a few times to help us. That torn-eared Mazikin was about to fight Takeshi just so he could claim me as a slave, and Zip saved us. And she got us down here after you freaked out. I'm willing to give her the benefit of the doubt. If that doesn't work out . . ." From beneath her cloak, I caught the dull glint of one of her blades.

"Would this be a safe place to bring Malachi?"

"It's a good first stop," said Takeshi quietly. "From here, we can plan the assault on the palace."

I pushed myself up to a kneeling position, already reaching for my weapons. "Then let's go now."

Ana shook her head. "We can't just walk into the square unprepared. It's not only a matter of fighting the guards. He's in chains."

I looked down at my blunt, broken nails, my plain, weak, human hands. If the strength of my feelings was all that mattered, I would have been able to tear through those manacles like paper. But since my feelings barely mattered at all, we needed something better. I looked up at Takeshi. "When you unlocked that safe chamber right after you found us, you used a skeleton key. Where did you get it?"

Takeshi gave me a wry grin. "Stole it from the Smith." He pulled the thing from his pocket and held it up. "He runs the metalworks on the east side of the city."

"Is he Mazikin or human?" Ana asked, taking the key from him and examining it.

"Human. But he's been here for a very long time. He and his human slaves make all the weapons for the Mazikin guards." He gave me a cautious look. "He's the one who made the Queen's steel claws. And if we want to unlock Malachi's chains, we'll need to get the key from him."

I got to my feet. "Sounds good," I said, entertaining thoughts of dipping this Smith person face-first into a vat of molten metal.

"He sells his wares in a market west of the factory. We'll need to steal his master key, and he's very well protected. Our best chance is to do some reconnaissance and see if we can slip in to his inner sanctum."

"He can't be bargained with?" I asked.

Takeshi shook his head. "He is *not* our friend."

"Wait," said Ana. "You said all humans were slaves. But this guy runs a factory and sells stuff?"

Something cold flashed in Takeshi's eyes. "He's their ally, so he has special privileges as long as he obeys them. It's the same for the Tanner on the west side of town, who is responsible for clothing the entire city. The Tanner and the Smith have expertise that has been useful to the Mazikin, and they've been highly cooperative with the creatures." He rose from the floor in a single smooth movement. "They are as much the enemy as the Mazikin."

"You've never tried to stop them, though?" I asked. When he shook his head again, I continued. "But you said you've caused trouble."

"Habit. Nothing more."

"So you're just pissing them off," I snapped. "And what do you bet they're taking some of that out on Malachi?"

"Malachi has caused them enough trouble all on his own, Lela. He was very good at it, as I recall."

"But the trouble he caused was always intended to help the people he was supposed to protect."

"Am I a Guard here, Lela? Who am I supposed to serve?"

"I—"

Takeshi's dark eyes went bright with sudden fury. "That's what they call me here. *The Guard.* I hadn't been called by my name in years, not since I heard it fall from Ana's lips yesterday." He leaned closer to me, tension emanating from him. "I was forsaken by the Judge after a hundred forty years in her service, right when I should have been released into the Countryside. Unlike she has apparently done for Malachi, our all-powerful Judge didn't send *anyone* here to rescue me. For a decade, I have been one man among a million slaves and a million carnivorous enemies, with absolutely no means to escape this hell, including death."

"Tak—" Ana began.

"No." He lifted his hand to stop her and got right in my face. "Forgive me if I haven't tried to play the hero," he said in a quiet voice. "And I'll forgive you for making judgments without knowing anything about me or what I've been through over the last century and a half."

"Then tell me what I should know," I said, ignoring Ana's warning glare.

Takeshi leaned back and wrenched his shirt up, revealing a thick diagonal scar across his stomach. "The Judge is not the first of my masters to betray me."

I stared at the horrible scar. "Your master did that to you?"

He let out a bark of laughter. "No, Lela, *I* did that to me. Where I came from, suicide was sometimes the only honorable death—much less shameful than accepting defeat. But that was not how it happened for me." He let his shirt fall over the scar. "I was a warrior, and I served my master well. With all I had, from the time I was a boy. When he told me to kill, I killed, and I was very good at it. Perhaps too good. When he sent me to help another lord secure his lands from raiders,

I did. But instead of being grateful, that lord turned on my master."

"I take it your master wasn't forgiving."

Takeshi ran his hand over his stomach. "It was worse than that. When I saw that this rival lord was trying to undermine my master, I sent a message, and received the assassination order in reply. I killed that rogue lord, which enabled my own master to take his lands." He bowed his head. "I thought he would be honored. But the dead lord was well loved by his people, and they rebelled against their new lord. They wanted blood."

He looked at me. "I was summoned before my master. In front of all his men and the subjects of his dead rival, he asked me why I had so hastily and unjustly executed the lord. I had a choice—to betray my master by revealing that he had ordered the assassination, or to take the blame." His fists clenched. "I did what my honor dictated, and I hoped for clemency."

"But you didn't get it," I said softly.

His palm spread over his belly. "*Seppuku* is a ritual. Once you make the cut, your *kaishakunin*—your assistant—ends your suffering by cutting off your head. It is quick." His voice was hushed and his eyes glazed. "My master told me he would be my *kaishakunin*. And I remember thinking, 'I am willing to die for this man. To be the sacrifice that pacifies his new people.' I thought he was honoring me by performing this service, that this was his final acknowledgment that I had served him well. So I knelt before him, and I plunged that knife into my belly, and I sliced my insides like this." He slashed his finger across the path of the scar, from the lower left side of his stomach up across his belly to the right.

Ana winced and pulled his hand away from his body. He watched their fingers tangle. “Do you think he was honoring me, Lela?” Takeshi whispered. “Do you think he repaid my loyalty by ending my pain?”

I folded my arms across my chest and shook my head.

“He stood over me, sword in hand. But he didn’t carry through. Instead of ending my pain, he watched me suffer. And it hurt as much as the wound, the knowledge that he was throwing me away, that I was merely a tool to be discarded when I had served my purpose. He let me die that way, at his feet. He even said, ‘Mercy is too good for you,’ loudly, so all could hear. To cement their allegiance, he heaped shame upon my head. I died knowing that I was worth *nothing* to him.”

Takeshi gestured at the scars on his face, made by claws instead of blades. “When I arrived in this city, I was stupid enough to hope. But as time passed and no one came for me, I understood. It had happened again. Years of service. Years of suffering. And still, I was worth nothing to the master I had served so faithfully.”

Ana’s arms coiled around Takeshi’s waist, and she laid her forehead on his shoulder. Her eyes were tightly shut; it looked like she was trying not to cry. My own eyes stung as I watched their pain. “I’m sorry, Takeshi.” I had no idea what else to say.

“Thank you,” he murmured, then turned away abruptly and approached his Mazikin disguise, which was propped up against the wall, the face snarling and scarred. For the first time, I thought about what he must have done to make it. His graceful, elegant appearance was simply another disguise, one that made him all the more dangerous, because it was easy to forget that this was the man who had trained Malachi and Ana to kill, and who had done a really good job of it. But when the time came, would he really help us complete the mission? Did he even have it inside of him, after everything that had happened?

He stuffed his disguise into his satchel. "We should get going if we want to do this today. The Smith's domain isn't far. Maybe ten blocks down, in the factory district. And everyone's still in the square. They're having a lottery."

"To see who gets to go to the land of the living." And possess the body of a homeless person. Or one of my classmates. "If we kill the Mazikin bodies here while their spirits are inside humans there, will that end them for good?"

"Maybe," said Takeshi, casting a wary glance at Zip, who had pulled out a comb that appeared to be made of polished bone and was brushing my mother's hair while cooing softly to her. They seemed to be in their own bizarre little world, and I was happy that neither of them understood a word we were saying. "Mazikin don't have eternal souls. Not like humans. Once their bodies are dead, they're gone, as far as I know. They don't appear at the gates and come in again. They're tough creatures and hard to kill, but unlike us, they stay dead. If their physical bodies die, their spirits, the aspects of them that possess humans, die as well. I'm sure the bodies of the Mazikin that are currently possessing humans are kept in a protected place, though. Probably near the portal, which is likely to be located in the Bone Palace."

"So . . . the *Bone* Palace . . . ?" Ana made a face.

"It's exactly what it sounds like," said Takeshi in a flat voice. "I haven't ever been inside, but there's no other place the portal could be."

"Then we'll check it out after we get Malachi to a safe place so he can recover," Ana said.

I reached for my cloak and gloves, which had been folded and left on a patch of bare rock next to the goatskin pallet I'd been lying on. If I gave myself time to think about Malachi and how he was feeling right now, I thought I might start screaming and never stop. So I pulled the gloves on my hands, tied the cloak at my neck, and strapped my knives around my thighs.

Ana gave Zip and Rita a vague explanation of where we were going but didn't tell them our specific plan, just in case. Zip promised to stay in the lair and to be ready when we arrived later, and then she comforted my mother, who burst into tears when she was told I was leaving. Although she'd seemed barely aware of me for the last several minutes, she came toward me and took my face in her hands, looking at me with amber-brown eyes full of concern—and startling clarity. *"Cuidado con los monstruos. No deja que te roban los dientes,"* she whispered, leaning forward to kiss my cheeks.

I pulled away from her grasping fingers gently, even though part of me wanted to scream at her—*Too little, too late, too little, too late.* I didn't know how to be her daughter. I didn't know how to accept the loving words or the worried looks, especially when they came so suddenly, rising out of the haze of her illness and sinking back in just as quickly. So I waved to her, pulled my hood over my face, and followed Takeshi as he led us along a rocky, deserted passage and up to the street.

He didn't make us wear the leashes or collars this time. Those were safely tucked away in his satchel. Takeshi told us to stay close to him and keep our heads down, then he guided us into the predawn chill, which bit at my cheeks and made my breath puff out in white clouds in front of my face. In the distance, the crowd in the square cheered raucously. "Are they hurting him?" I asked, rubbing away the pain in my throat.

"I don't know," answered Takeshi. "He's probably not feeling much at the moment. It would take awhile for him to regain consciousness, for his regrown heart to get enough oxygen to his brain to allow him to feel pain."

I wanted to vomit all over the crumbling concrete at my feet. Ana's shoulder bumped mine, letting me know she was next to me. It was as much a reassurance as a warning to keep it together, a reminder that I didn't have the luxury of acting pathetic.

"Is there anything here that isn't made of concrete or steel?" Ana asked, probably trying to distract me from thinking about Malachi—wondering whether his heart would beat the same way after it had been torn from him repeatedly, whether his mind would survive intact after his body had been abused so terribly.

"It's really all the building material they have," Takeshi replied. "Unless you count bone."

Ana grimaced. *"Ugh."*

We crossed a deserted intersection. Down the block, I heard moaning and screeching, but I didn't turn my head. Ahead of us, the factories loomed, bright lights fogged by black smoke. The air here was slightly warmer but filled with an acrid, metallic scent that burned my eyes. "No wood?" she asked.

Takeshi laughed. "No trees. But there is *plenty* of sand. Between these factories and the city gates is the mining zone. Salt and sand and limestone and iron. Oil, too. These are the materials available to them, and so they make concrete and steel, and they refine oil for fuel. There is a river that flows beneath the city, and it's the only water source. This is a hard place." His gaze traveled from the street to the massive smokestacks looming in front of us. "Can you blame them for wanting to escape it?"

"Yes," Ana and I said at the same time.

I bumped into Takeshi's back as he stopped abruptly. "What is it?" I asked.

"In the alley," he said in a low voice. He sniffed at the air.

I looked in the direction he was peering, down a side street to our left. Was that a flash of white skin and dark cloak? "I could go—"

"No. Wait here," Takeshi said, then plunged into the alley. He disappeared from sight almost immediately.

"I've seen that cloaked figure twice now," I said to Ana as I stared at the mouth of the alley.

"Least of our problems." Ana's voice was tight with anxiety.

I spun around to see her standing alone in the intersection, her eyes wide. "What?"

"It is against the law to roam the streets without a master," said a voice from the shadows. My blood went cold as no fewer than ten men stepped from buildings and alleys all around us, knives drawn. Instantly, I felt a blade against my throat and heard a sharp cry that told me Ana was in the same situation. My captor pulled me against him. He stank of sweat and goat. I fought to hold back my panic.

"Do you have a permit to walk free?" the man demanded.

"Yeah," I said. "I've got a permit right here." But before I could reach for the knives at my thighs, a sharp slice of pain in my throat made me gasp. My assailant's gravelly voice rumbled in my ear. "Try it, and I'll remove your pretty head." The warm trickle of blood into the neckline of my tunic told me he was serious.

As much as I could with the knife at my throat, I glanced over at Ana next to me. Her hands were out to the side, and her throat was sticky red, but her face was a blank mask. I couldn't tell if she knew what was going on any more than I did. Where was Takeshi? Had he known we were being watched?

I felt the blade withdraw a bit. Instead, thick fingers wrapped around my neck and wrenched my head up. A dark-skinned, bearded man who looked to be in his thirties stepped in front of me while the person behind me kept the knife close to my skin. While my attention was focused on the bearded guy, one of his friends ripped a blade from one of my thigh sheaths and held it up to his lantern. "That wasn't made by the Smith," my bearded assailant growled.

"Who could have made it then, Nazir?" the other man asked, peering at the edge of the blade with sharp curiosity.

"Someone on the outside," hissed Nazir.

The other man's mouth fell open as his eyes lit on me. "Outside?"

The man behind me released his grip on my neck as Nazir said, "Strip their weapons."

My thigh sheaths were ripped from my legs, and the blade moved away from my throat, allowing me the chance to look around. What I saw made my heart sink. Ana's hands were being tied behind her back. The only weapons we still possessed were the grenades strapped to her chest, but seeing as our hands were now being roughly bound, they wouldn't do us much good at the moment. "Four of you stay to monitor the market," ordered Nazir, grabbing my arm and tugging me forward. "The rest of you, come with me. The Smith will be eager to meet these two."

TEN

THE HUMAN POSSE LED us down the street. Six men, relatively straight-backed and fit, though many bore ghastly scars, mostly claw or bite marks and signs of blistering. From the way they held their weapons, I could tell they were competent with them, but they weren't warriors. Their eyes darted from street corner to street corner, as if they were afraid something might leap out and attack at any moment. Though most of the buildings in the area were illuminated, their first floors were largely empty, and the roads were quiet except for the shouting and cheering that could be heard blocks away in the main square. Every wave of noise felt like a celebration of Malachi's pain, cranking my rage and frustration a notch higher. We were wasting time. Every moment we spent in captivity was another delay in our rescue plan.

And where had Takeshi gone? Had that cloaked figure gotten him? Had it been a trap to draw him away? It seemed like one person couldn't possibly stop him. But if that was true—why hadn't he stayed to fight? Between the three of us, we might have been able to beat these guys. Was he trailing us? Planning to rescue us? Or had he slipped away? Was he going to find a way to sneak into the Smith's lair, as planned? All of these questions and speculations flew through my brain so quickly that it almost made me dizzy.

Ana and I were shoulder to shoulder, but it wasn't a safe time to chat. Now that we were down to six human guards, it seemed even more likely that Takeshi could use this as a rescue opportunity. Though with every step we took toward the three-story-high steel archway that marked the entrance to the metalworks, my hope for a Takeshi ambush faded.

We reached the final block before the archway, a series of buildings where the open first floors hummed with activity. As Takeshi had described, it was a marketplace, full of glittering metal. Furniture in one building, mechanized carts in another, tools of various types in the next, weapons in the one closest to the factory, which loomed in front of us, belching black smoke into the night. The market was staffed by humans wearing collars, which marked their status as slaves. They hovered near the goods, conversing with the Mazikin who were looking over the wares in each stall.

As we passed the space where the tools were displayed, one of the Mazikin customers growled and swiped its long claws across a frail human's throat. The poor man cried out and fell to the ground, clutching at his neck as his blood spilled on the concrete floor. Two other men ran to him, but instead of helping him, they matter-of-factly dragged him behind the display of tools and dumped him there before scurrying back to their stations.

One of our captors, a man with horrific burn scars all over his face, cleared his throat. "That's Carlo."

"Should I take care of him?" asked another, a dude with a giant blistered bald spot and a knotty scar of his own winding down the side of his face. His dark eyes were riveted to Carlo as we walked past the display that concealed him from the customers' sight. The victim's claw wounds still wept blood. Anywhere else, he would have bled to death. But here . . . Takeshi had said injuries would heal badly but wouldn't kill.

"You'd have to wait until one of our agents is back at the gates, Phil," snapped Nazir, giving me a little shove. "Otherwise, he might get sent to the meat factory."

"Might as well let it heal up on its own then," rumbled the guy who was holding on to the back of Ana's neck, the tip of his blade pressed lightly between her shoulder blades.

Phil, the guy who wanted to "take care" of Carlo, merely grunted. I couldn't tell if he had wanted to offer Carlo mercy or had been trying to figure out how to keep him functional enough to work.

Finally, we were escorted under the massive metal archway and along the front of the factory building, then down a long passage. The scarred posse marched us through a long, narrow room dominated by a concrete conference table and high-backed steel chairs, then along another corridor that opened onto what appeared to be some sort of showroom for weapons. Hanging on the walls were heavy battle axes, long pikes and spears, and curved blades with barbs that looked like they could rip a man's guts out with a simple twist of the wrist—weapons made for the Mazikin by the traitorous Smith to hurt people like us. My own knives suddenly seemed useless, their effect like the sting of a mosquito compared to the bite of a great white shark.

By the time we reached an alcove furnished with goatskin-upholstered chairs and curved punched-steel tables, I realized our plan to sneak in had been pretty unrealistic. The place was a heavily guarded maze, and every person here was cautious and alert—and they all seemed to know each other. Nazir and his men pushed us farther into the little chamber. Sitting at one of the chairs at the back was a very short man. Even though he was seated, I could tell he'd be lucky to crack five feet with lifts in his shoes. His thick legs were crossed, and his boots, which had pointed toes, were a rich brown, though they seemed a little worn. He peered at us from beneath some of the bushiest eyebrows I'd ever seen, but they couldn't hide the calculating glimmer in his eyes. He looked about forty, solidly built with square shoulders. His black hair was smoothly combed and greased, his skin a dark-olive tone.

"What have you brought me?" he asked with a low, melodious accent. Italian, maybe? Greek? Those eyebrows twitched as his eyes darted over our scar-free faces and bodies. "Did you bring them straight from the gates? Is this their first go-round?"

Nazir tossed one of my thigh sheaths at the Smith, who caught it in his meaty hand. "Nabbed 'em only a few blocks from the market, headed in this direction. They were carrying these."

The Smith plucked one of my knives from its sheath and held it to the light. His eyes went wide. "Where did you get this?" he whispered as his gaze returned to me.

"Found it on the street," Ana said.

The Smith's plump lips quirked into a smile. "Liar."

"These are hers," said Phil, tossing Ana's throwing knives onto the low steel table in front of the Smith. Metal hit metal with a terrible clatter, but it didn't seem to bother the Smith. He muttered in some foreign language as he gave Ana an intrigued once-over.

"Throwing knives? Can you wield these, my dear?"

"If you untie my hands, I could give it a try," said Ana sweetly.

The Smith snorted. "Perhaps later."

"They came from the outside," Nazir told him. "I'm sure of it."

"So am I." The Smith looked out at his scarred posse. "We have been here for so long," he said, a hint of sadness in his voice. "But none of us has forgotten that there are worlds outside of this dome. Which means we have not forgotten that we've been forgotten—and all the while we suffer"—he tossed Ana's knife onto the table—"we blister"—he pointed to the man whose entire face was badly burned—"we scrape and toil to avoid the slashing claws"—he gestured at the man with the knotted scar down the side of his face—"and we die."

His pitted nostrils flared. "Do you know who our Mazikin masters are entertaining in the square at this very moment, Nazir?"

"Someone they call 'the Captain,'" said Nazir. "All I know."

I gritted my teeth as the Smith chuckled. "Well, let me enlighten you. The Captain in the square is not the first of his kind to come to our city. There is another. He has caused more destruction than any other human under this dome."

Nazir's eyes went wide. "The Guard?"

The Smith nodded. "They are mortal enemies of our Mazikin rulers. Ibram told me so himself, how much pain and fear these Guards have caused. And we all know the Guard is no friend of ours. He hides in the city while we pay for his crimes. So no, this 'Captain' was not the first to come here." His eyes glittered nastily as he turned to Ana and me. "Nor, it seems, is he the last."

The men behind us began to mumble to each other, but the Smith silenced them with a glare before returning his attention to us. "How did you get here, darlings? You weren't possessed, were you?"

Both of us stared at him mutely.

He smirked. "And why are you here?"

Again, neither of us responded. I honestly had no idea what the right answer was. If we said we were here to save Malachi and kill the Queen, it seemed like the quickest way to get chained up alongside Malachi, and possibly another reason for them to hurt him. But there was no lie that seemed reasonable. The Smith knew who we were, sort of, and he knew we'd come from the outside.

"Are you here to save your comrades?" he asked, his voice quiet.

Ana glanced at me. "Nah, we're just tourists."

I knew she expected me to go along, but I couldn't help but feel that her joking lies would only get us in trouble. "We're here to save everyone," I blurted out as Ana's eyes narrowed in anger. She was my Captain, and this was on the bleeding edge of insubordination. But the certainty rose up inside me—this was what we should do. I had to hope Ana would see it that way . . . sooner rather than later. “We could get you out, too, if you help us.”

Whatever he’d expected me to say, it wasn’t that. He blinked, his face reddening, and then he began to laugh again. The sound bounced off the walls, the tables, echoing mercilessly. He slapped his hand across his thigh, tears streaking from the corners of his eyes. Snot began to leak from his nostrils, and he swiped his sleeve under his nose. The men around us were silent, either too afraid or too stunned to laugh. Or maybe they had no clue why he was laughing in the first place. “Ah, that is impossible,” he said. “The Judge has sent you on a suicide mission.”

Next to me, I felt Ana freeze. The Smith noticed it, too. “You didn’t think I knew about the Judge? I wasn’t *born* here, Guard. None of us were. And nearly all of us had some experience with death before we came.” His voice grew louder, angrier. “I’ve been here for hundreds of years, though I have no idea how long I was in the dark city before I was taken by the Mazikin. But I saw Guards on the streets. I’ve seen the Sanctum. And I’ve heard about the Judge who presides there. For the first many years I was here, I held out hope that justice would prevail. Isn’t that what a Judge is supposed to ensure? But *never* has your precious Judge sent anyone to save me, let alone all the other helpless wretches in this city.”

He and Takeshi had more in common than either of them knew.

Suddenly, he rose to his feet and kicked the metal table out of the way, sending Ana’s knives flying and his own men scattering as the blades whipped through the air. He stumped toward me until his belly nearly touched mine. “I don’t believe, even for a moment, that you came here to do anything except to take care of your own," he growled.

"Fine," Ana snapped. "So what if that's true? We didn't come here to hurt you, so how about you let us go?"

The Smith shook his head. "You should have stayed far away from here. If I were to capture two Guards and then set them free, me and mine would be in the square right next to your Captain."

"So what are you going to do with us?" I asked, trying to keep my voice from trembling.

The Smith grinned. "I will use you to draw out the Guard. The one who has been terrorizing our city for a decade. And once I have all of you, I will present you as gifts to my Queen."

"He won't come," blurted Ana. "He won't let himself be taken."

I'd never wanted to kick anyone more than I wanted to kick Ana in that moment. The Smith, of course, looked absolutely delighted at her response. "Well then. I'll enjoy *trying* to draw him out." He turned to Nazir. "Take them to a cell while we prepare the yard."

I crouched in the corner of the cell, my back to the wall, my eyes on the guard pacing the corridor in front of us. Ana sat in the cell next to mine, doing the same thing. I had no idea how long we'd been here, but the dude, his pointed, blistered nose leading the way, had walked by ninety-seven times. He was starting to look bored.

We'd been shoved in here with the ominous promise that the Smith would come for us when he was ready. I could hear distant sounds of construction, the clang of metal on metal, the roar of engines. The vibrations of heavy objects being shifted and dropped jittered through the floor. I imagined what they might be building—probably a platform like the one where Malachi had been chained. Would the Smith call his Mazikin friends? What would they do to us if he did?

The guard was taking his time now. We hadn't moved since being stowed in these barred cells with concrete floors, and he was probably thinking we weren't a threat. Finally, I heard him settle himself heavily down the hall, near an open window where he could see the construction. From what I understood of this city, the fire hour was coming soon, so I was betting they'd have to take a break and hide from the heat. And maybe we'd be able to escape while they did. I was willing to brave the fire if it meant getting back on track with the rescue mission.

"Ana," I whispered, scooting a little closer to the bars that separated my cell from hers. When she looked over, I drew my finger along my chest in a diagonal motion. "Grenades?" I mouthed. One toss down the hall and we'd have chaos on a grand scale. And hopefully, a hole in the side of the building big enough for us to climb through to the outside.

Ana looked away. "I don't have them."

My stomach dropped. "What?"

Her fingers tightened over the bars. "When we were repacking to come here, Takeshi offered to carry them in his satchel."

I grasped the bars between us. "You said you would carry them."

"I changed my mind, *Lieutenant*."

My knuckles were turning white. "So now Takeshi's disappeared with our grenades," I hissed. "He looked pretty damn interested in them, didn't he?"

She slowly turned her head. "What are you saying?"

"I don't know the guy, but let's add it up. He said they'd get a great price on the black market, and he straight-up said he didn't consider himself a Guard anymore. He never sounded all that interested in helping us destroy the portal—he said it would be suicide. And you gave him our only means of escape!" I shut up when I heard the guard shift and stand again. I pressed my face close, and Ana's jaw tightened. "How do you know he hasn't gone on his merry way to use them for trade? Or to cause more destruction that will only make the Mazikin more determined to hurt Malachi?"

She leaned toward me. "You're right," she said. "You *don't* know Takeshi."

"Are you sure you do? Takeshi has been gone for ten years. People change. You thought he'd be some noble leader of a resistance movement, and instead he's been out for himself the whole time."

"What would you have done if you were in his position, Lela? Tell me, since you're apparently better than the rest of us."

I sagged, defeated, and rested my forehead against the warm metal bars. "No idea. I just don't get why he disappeared. And why he hasn't tried to rescue us."

"I don't know," she whispered. "But I do know he loves me. He never stopped. And he loves Malachi. He won't let him continue to suffer."

"By leaving us in here, that's exactly what he's doing." I wanted to rip the bars from the wall. I wanted to knock the building down with my bare hands. Somewhere out there, Malachi was about to endure the fire hour. Chained in the middle of that square, with nothing but a flimsy metal roof over his head. His shackles would get so hot they would burn his skin. The mere idea of it made me want to shriek.

"You should be more worried about what they're going to do to us," she said softly. "We're going to have to try to make a break for it before they chain us up. We need to come up with a plan."

I sank to the concrete, my hands falling away from the bars. "I was trying to." I bowed my head on my knees, suddenly so weary that I could no longer hold it up. No grenades. No allies. No way out. A few hours until we became a public spectacle. "Any ideas, Captain?"

Ana sighed. "None at the moment."

"Let me know when you come up with something."

She didn't answer. If we were lucky, they'd decapitate us. Maybe if we appeared at the gates of the city, we'd have another chance to escape. I chuckled grimly to myself. "Lucky" took on a whole new meaning in the Mazikin realm.

As the banging and roars outside fell silent, I drifted into dreams of Malachi, hoping that somewhere in their shifting sands, I would find our path to escape.

ELEVEN

I AWOKE TO THE sound of clanking chains. Next to me, Ana was getting to her feet. “Lela,” she whispered. “Here they come.”

I slid up the cement wall, my heart starting to pound. Memories of Malachi, covered in his own blood, his face a mask of pain, flooded back. Was that what lay ahead for us?

“Orders?” I asked as heavy footsteps clonked down the corridor.

“We’ll have to see what they’ve set up,” she answered in a low voice, talking fast. “If you can grab a weapon, go for it. I’ll do the same.”

“Sounds good,” I whispered as two men reached our cells. I might have considered taking them on once they opened our doors, but from the scuffling sound of boots I could tell that they’d brought a squad of helpers. There was only one exit from this corridor apart from the barred window, and without weapons, Ana and I were unlikely to be able to plow through all of them.

A bear of a man with pale-gray eyes lifted a set of shackles. "Some pretty jewelry for you," he said, grinning.

Standing next to him, Nazir did not look amused. "Get them out and chained, Holloran. Don't talk to them."

"What are you going to do to us?" I asked.

Nazir's eyes met mine, and in them all I saw was regret and pain, no softness. It was like everything kind or compassionate inside him had fossilized ages ago, leaving only stone. "He'll make an example of you. He'll put on a show for the Mazikin. And he won't be satisfied until he has what he wants."

Which was Takeshi, who had abandoned us. Me, I could understand. I didn't mean a thing to him, really, and I'd never fully trusted him, as much as I'd wanted to. But I had trouble comprehending how he could have left Ana to this fate. I'd seen the way he looked at her, his eyes reflecting secret shared moments and years of want.

Nazir pulled one of those elaborate skeleton keys from a ring latched on to his belt and unlocked my cell. I held still while Holloran chained my hands in front of me and shackled my ankles. Once I was fettered, he and Nazir did the same to Ana, who stared at them with such intense hatred that it was a wonder their faces didn't melt off.

Nazir took me by the arm and led me into the corridor. His grip was firm but not painful. Armed men and women, scarred and blistered and wearing pale leather cloaks, stood on either side of the hall. Every one of them held a weapon, knives of various shapes and sizes—some hooked and barbed, some long and broad, some curved and narrow. All deadly. They weren't taking chances on us. Holloran walked behind Ana, his meaty fingers closed around the back of her neck. Her posture was taut as a bowstring despite the fact that her steps were hampered by the chains. The group turned toward the wide door in unison and one of them held it open for us.

As we filed out of the hallway and through a massive set of metal doors, I waited for my chance. Nazir let go of my arm when we reached a huge fenced-in space filled with humans and a few Mazikin wearing the cloaks with black triangles that I now assumed marked them as members of the enforcement squad. They stared at us with leering eagerness. Probably none of them recognized us, but the Smith had invited them in the hopes of drawing out the man who had been the scourge of the city for a decade, and they were here to make sure he didn't leave a free man. There were at least twenty of them in the crowd, weapons sheathed at their belts, teeth bared. The humans gave them a wide berth, as if scared to draw their attention. Only Nazir and Holloran kept their heads high as we passed.

The crew led us through an opening in the crowd, and as Holloran moved to the side and shoved Ana next to me, our destination came into view. We were at the southern side of the factory, by the looks of it. To our right was the wall of the city and the filmy dome above us, smog curling against its surface, lit by lights below. Night had fallen while we were imprisoned, which probably meant, somewhere out in the city, my love was about to have his heart ripped out once again. I had wanted to save him from that, and I had failed. But I wouldn't give up. I would endure whatever they did to us and take any opportunity to escape. I supposed one advantage of not being able to die was that I had endless chances to try. That also meant endless chances to be hurt, but I'd survived pain before. And I'd never had a better reason to go on.

The "yard," as the Smith had called it, was surrounded by a high sturdy metal fence, barbed wire coiled at its top edge, large stadium lights blazing down on us. The space was about the size of a football field, and there was scaffolding ahead with a platform near the top and metal steps leading to it. As I had feared, the setup reminded me of Malachi's platform in the square, and I was betting the Smith had very similar plans for Ana and me.

He stood on the platform, all four and a half feet of him, sporting a black cloak. He watched us approaching, his face grim, and then glanced at a low table next to him, his fingers grazing an object that lay atop it. He had a makeshift bullhorn in his other hand, attached to a wire that connected to enormous speakers on the metal roof over his head. He lifted the device to his lips as we reached the bottom of the steps. "Unfasten their ankle shackles. Let them approach their fate on their own two feet." His voice blasted from speakers positioned against the factory building and at the top of metal columns between stretches of fencing.

Nazir unlocked my shackles and then knelt at Ana's feet. As soon as he got Ana's chains open, Holloran shoved us up the stairs.

The Smith's huge round head came into view again as we climbed, our boots clanging softly against the metal steps. The top of the platform had no railing. One wrong move and someone could go plunging twenty feet or so to the ground below. An interesting prospect, though it looked like it would take a Mack truck to knock the Smith more than a few inches;

he was built like a tank and had a low center of gravity, being so short. I looked around, trying to map a possible escape route. We were about ten yards from the high barbed fence that marked the boundary between the factory grounds and the city on the other side. Blocks of three-story cement buildings were all that lay beyond. About a mile away, I knew Malachi was on his platform. I wondered if I was imagining the distant cheers.

"Welcome," murmured the Smith, his eyes skating over me and Ana. His thick fingers toyed with a ring of keys at his belt. That key ring probably held the one that could unlock Malachi's chains, but though it was only arm's length away, it was far out of reach. The Smith turned to Nazir and Holloran. "Put them in position."

Nazir abruptly grabbed my arms and wrenched my bound hands over my head. Something in the movement drenched me in terrible black memories, and before I could stop myself, my knee jerked up and slammed him in the groin. He groaned and dropped to his knees.

"Men!" shouted the Smith, and the thunder of footsteps told me we wouldn't be alone up here for long. To my left, I heard a wheezing grunt, and I glanced over to see Holloran tumble over the side of the platform, the victim of a sharp side kick from Ana. Yowls from below told me he had landed on startled members of the crowd.

I spun around, preparing to knock as many men off the platform as I could, but pain blasted through my back. I looked down to see the tip of a metal blade poking through the middle of my leather tunic. Someone had stabbed me straight through. As sticky drops of blood fell heavy on my boots, I sank to my knees. Ana called my name, but I couldn't answer. And then the Smith's breath was hot on the side of my face. "I take no pleasure in this. You gave me no choice, Guard." He yanked the blade out of me, ripping a wet scream from my lungs.

I began to tip forward but was caught by a woman at the top of the steps. "Get her in position," yelled the Smith.

The woman grunted as she lifted me. "Don't fight him," she whispered.

Senseless with pain, I was pressed up against a cold metal surface, my arms forced above my head. Two men held me there, their sweat-scented bodies keeping me upright as a third man fastened my wrists to the wall. And then I was left to hang, my toes brushing the platform's surface. Ana, still struggling, was chained next to me a moment later.

"Are you okay?" I asked, barely able to get any volume. Below us, the crowd cheered our display.

"Better than you," she said.

I looked above me—I wasn't locked to the platform. My shackles had merely been looped over a hook in the wall. If I had the strength, I could get free. But I didn't. And I couldn't move my legs. Was I paralyzed? I hadn't considered this, being alive but unable to run. "Ana," I whispered, my voice breaking. I was useless once again, and the knowledge amped my pain to an unbearable level.

"See what happens to the enemies of our masters!" shouted the Smith. "See what happens to those who cause trouble in our city!"

His bullhorn PA system carried his booming voice over the crowd's waving arms, overpowering their screams and cheers. He looked over his shoulder at me, focusing on the bloody mess of my torso. I swear I saw a flash of regret, but it didn't last long—he was grinning as he turned back to his people. "How should I punish them?"

He looked at the Mazikin, who were the only ones not cheering. They looked wary, their round ears twitching, their black noses trembling. The Smith's smile wavered, then turned into a line of determination. His thick fingers closed over a curved knife on his table, which was laden with instruments of torture—pliers, blades, tools I couldn't even identify—all of which seemed designed solely to cause pain. I closed my eyes. If we had any chance at all, it was Ana. If I could draw the abuse and hold his attention, she could stay strong and maybe escape. I pushed a laugh from my tight throat, and the Smith turned back to me with surprise. "This amuses you?"

I swallowed back the metallic taste of blood on my tongue. "It's funny, that's all. How pathetic you are."

"Shut up, Lieutenant," Ana snapped.

The Smith's attention remained focused on me. "You have an odd sense of humor."

"No, I just realized that old cliché is true." When he gave me a questioning look, I continued, forcing my voice into steadiness. "You're just a little man who drew a short straw." I let my gaze flick to his pants. "And you're working hard to compensate." I chuckled again, though it caused waves of agony. "Don't let me stop you, dude."

"You couldn't if you tried," he growled. He raised his curved blade and came toward me, and I closed my eyes again, willing myself to be elsewhere.

"But maybe *I* could," said a voice distorted by the screeching feedback of the audio system.

The Smith flinched, and the crowd hushed. "Who is that?"

"You invited me here," said the voice.

"Show yourself," the Smith roared. He stepped up to me quickly and pressed his blade to the side of my face. My eye twitched as the knife's edge cut into my skin, but I stayed quiet.

"Let them go, and I won't hurt any of you."

The disembodied voice had a remarkable effect on the crowd. Many of the people crouched low, their eyes darting from speaker to speaker as if the challenger were actually hiding inside one of them. The Mazikin had dropped to all fours and moved to the edge of the courtyard, by the fence, frantically scanning the crowd, their fangs glistening, their claws curled.

The Smith laughed. "If you are who I think you are, you're alone. And one man. Your threats are empty."

The voice *tsk*ed. "I am one man." A chuckle. "But I've always considered myself special. Let them go."

The Smith's blade carved a hard line of pain down the side of my face, and I screamed. "Show yourself, and then we can talk," the Smith said, sounding bored. But his hand shook as he wiped his bloody knife on my tunic.

"Very well, Smith. Here I am."

This time, the voice hadn't come from the PA system.

It had come from only a few feet above us. A man swung down from the metal roof of our platform, sending a few other men plummeting to the ground as he cleared a path to the Smith using his fists and feet. He lowered his hood and grinned as the Smith backed against the table of torture implements.

Takeshi's black hair stuck up in every direction as he leaned over the Smith and raised his eyebrows. "It's nice to finally meet you."

TWELVE

TWO OF THE SMITH'S men grabbed Takeshi's arms and dragged him back from their boss, but it only took a moment for him to dispatch them. His eyes flashed dark and fierce as he vaulted over the Smith and onto the table. He raised his hand above his head.

He was holding a grenade. "I brought you a present," he said quietly to the Smith, who pressed himself next to Ana, against the metal back of the platform. "Watch this."

Takeshi threw the grenade over the heads of the crowd. It landed near the group of Mazikin who had been hovering by the fence. They flinched away but then padded closer to the small black sphere. Their noses twitched as they sniffed at it.

I turned my head as the deafening explosion flattened me against the metal wall and rattled my chains. When I opened my eyes, Takeshi was standing in front of me and Ana, single-handedly battling three men. The Smith was nowhere to be seen. Screams and shouts melded together in a tidal wave of noise.

A skinny man with knobby fingers slipped behind Takeshi and began to reach for him, but Ana wrenched her legs up and around his neck before the guy could do much else. With a sickening crack, he fell to the floor of the platform.

"Thanks," Takeshi called out without turning around.

"Back up a few," said Ana.

He obeyed her immediately. She wrapped her legs around his waist as he continued to fight, and in an instant, she'd pulled her shackled wrists from the hook above her head. She dropped to the platform. Her dark eyes slid over me. "Hang tight."

"Very funny," I muttered.

In an instant, she'd commandeered the torture table. Even with her hands shackled, sharpened implements were flying in all directions, felling opponents who went plunging off our raised stage with screams and surprised yelps. "We have to get to that opening in the fence," she said in a breathless voice.

"Or I could make us another one," said Takeshi as he finished off another opponent. He reached into the pocket of his pants and pulled out another precious grenade. He hurled it toward the section of fence closest to us, knocked yet another man off the platform, and whirled to face me. "Time to go, Lela," he said softly, then grasped my waist and lifted me. My hands pulled free of the hook, and my arms fell limp in front of me. Searing pain radiated from the hole in my stomach, causing me to stumble.

"Sorry I couldn't stop him before he did that," Takeshi said. "I didn't expect you to fight them."

"Instinct," I gasped as he dragged me to the steps of the platform.

"Ana," Takeshi called.

"Behind you. I'll cover your exit," she replied.

Boom. We were knocked backward as the fence in front of us was blasted open in a blinding flash that shook the steps beneath our feet. People squealed and scattered, so that the square was now dotted only with a few Mazikin and a handful of the Smith's guards. I had no idea where their leader had fled to, though I wished he'd stayed to fight. I would have enjoyed seeing Takeshi give him a taste of what it felt like to have a blade thrust through his stomach.

We heard Mazikin growls and snarls behind us. They were closing in fast. Takeshi carried me toward the wide section that had been blown open in the fence, but from the corner of my eye I saw a member of the enforcement squad galloping toward us on all fours. "Tak—" I began, but then the Mazikin was felled by Ana—with a knife to the skull.

Halfway down the steps, she waved us toward the street as she turned to face another charging creature.

Downed Mazikin were scattered around the yard, torture implements embedded in their throats and chests. Takeshi dragged me onto the road beyond the fence and dropped me there. "Ana," was all he said by way of explanation.

I lay on the rough concrete, staring at its crumbling surface and listening to the animal cries of pain coming from the yard. Then Ana and Takeshi appeared. They each grabbed one of my arms, and we were off, my toes skimming the ground as we fled along near-empty streets. We took a series of turns down dark alleys before diverting into a sort of alcove that smelled of garbage and pee. As we paused, I heard distant cheering once again. Ana cursed and said something in Spanish to Takeshi. He replied, and she fell silent.

Takeshi leaned close and examined my face in the dim glow of lights from windows above us. "I took the first chance I had to get you out."

I wanted to ask him where he had disappeared to, but I didn't have the breath or strength.

"It's all right," said Ana. "Except . . ." She pressed in next to him and gazed at my face. "You are so stupid," she said to me, giving me a little shake. But her voice was gentle.

"She'll heal," said Takeshi. "Though not completely and not well."

Ana's expression twisted. "Is there anything that would help?"

Takeshi pursed his lips. "I can think of one thing, but Lela might not like it. We have a choice now, go to my safe chamber or—"

"Anything," I said in a weak voice. "I need to be able to fight."

"In all my years in the city," said Takeshi, "I have seen many strange things. But the strangest of all might be the key to Lela's recovery. It's rare, but I've seen it work. Lela's one of the few people in the city who might have access to it."

"And what's that?" asked Ana.

"Come on," he said, picking me up again. "I'll tell you when we get there."

"Where are we going?"

"Back to Zip. Lela needs to be with her mother."

Takeshi and Ana supported me as we crept along alleyways and scrambled across streets, making our way closer to the square.

"What about the Smith?" Ana asked as we walked. "Won't he alert the Mazikin to our presence? He knew we were here for Malachi, even if he doesn't understand the entire plan."

"Oh, he'll warn them. But we made sure none of the Mazikin in the yard lived to tell about it, and most of the people and creatures out tonight were already near the square where the Queen is putting on her show. Only those loyal to the Smith and his Mazikin cronies went to see who he'd captured. He has a history of torturing troublemakers in his courtyard, and I suspect no one thought you were much different."

"But he knew we were like you," said Ana. "And he was furious. He wanted to catch you."

"He wanted to please his masters," answered Takeshi in a tense voice.

"He said you'd caused a lot of trouble," I mumbled. I hated the Smith, and hated what he'd done, but in a way, it made sense. Takeshi had been hell-bent on provoking the Mazikin, but I wondered if he'd considered the repercussions for the ordinary humans in the city. The Smith said they'd been punished for the crimes Takeshi committed. No wonder they hated him.

"We have a little time before they're alerted." Takeshi pulled me into yet another alley barely in time to avoid being hit by a passing cart that was spewing black fumes into the lamplit road. "We left a real mess for the Smith to clean up, and by dawn, no one will be on the streets. But as soon as the sun goes away, he'll send someone to warn the Queen."

"Which means we have to rescue Malachi before then," Ana said quietly. "If the Mazikin know we're here to rescue him, they'll try to make it impossible. Tonight might be our only chance to get him out of there."

"Agreed," I said in a choked voice.

"Agreed," echoed Takeshi. "Here we are."

They guided me down a set of cramped stairs and into a rocky tunnel. My pants were stiff with blood and God knows what else seeping from the gaping hole in my stomach, and it felt like half of my face had been torn away. We reached a closed metal door. Takeshi scratched at it and whined and coughed, no doubt saying something in the Mazikin language.

The door opened quickly, and Zip appeared, wearing a goatskin dress. Her claws were now painted white. As they carried me into her den, I heard a tangle of languages I couldn't understand. Takeshi spoke in Mazikin to Zip. Ana spoke in Spanish to both of them. Takeshi and Ana spoke Japanese to each other. I let them lower me to a goatskin pallet, staining it red. The hurt was fathomless. I was drowning in it.

Someone poked at my forehead. *"Qué se robaron los dientes?"* whispered a voice I knew to be my mother's.

Ana answered her in Spanish, and whatever she said made my mother cry out. She turned me over and pulled me against her, amber eyes gazing into mine. They were lucid once again, full of concern. She squinted at my mouth, ignoring my attempts to shrink away. *"Me alegro que todavía tienes los dientes. Pero si te los hubieran robado, te daría los míos."*

"Why does she keep asking about Lela's teeth?" Ana asked.

Takeshi shrugged absently, completely focused on me and my mother. "I don't know if this will work."

My mother began to stroke my hair.

"Stop," I said hoarsely. It was too much. Too weird. Too painful. But I was too weak to move, so all I could do was beg her in words she didn't even understand. Tears burned my eyes as my gaze found Ana's. "Make her stop. Make her leave me alone." I feebly swiped at her hands as they smoothed curls off my forehead.

Takeshi's face appeared over mine. "We can't, Lela. Not if you want to heal."

"Can't I heal without her squeezing me like this?" I could barely breathe.

He shook his head. "Sorry. She has to be touching you." He gave me a faint smile and explained. "Many years ago, I was hiding in an abandoned den when I heard a commotion outside. I peeked out to see a man carrying a woman who had been badly mauled by a Mazikin. He set her down, both of them too tired and injured to go on. And there, right in that quiet tunnel, I saw the only miracle I have ever seen in this terrible place. He kissed her face and held her close. He was crying. Though I've seen many tears here, most people are in too much pain to cry for anyone but themselves. But he was crying for her."

"So the fact that he cared for this woman was a miracle?" Ana asked, sounding unimpressed.

My mother began to rock me. She was singing some song that echoed in my head uncomfortably, scraping the walls of my skull, making it impossible for me to pull away from myself. Her heart beat loudly in my ears.

"If you understood what it was like here, you'd know that it was a true miracle," he said softly, turning to Ana and running his fingers along the side of her face and her throat, then down her arm. "But also, it was more than caring, and more than simple kindness. It's the only reason I can think of for what happened next. The woman healed. So quickly that I couldn't believe it, so well that within an hour, she was rising to her feet, despite the fact that she'd almost been gutted. Her skin knitted together and—"

Takeshi leaned down and pulled up my tunic. I grabbed his wrist automatically, and he grinned. "You've got some strength back in your grip." He looked over at Ana. "It's definitely working."

I released his arm, meeting his eyes as he added, "And your wound is closing."

Stunned, I glanced at my belly, blood-smeared but no longer bleeding. My mother hadn't loosened her grasp, and she was still singing, smiling to herself dreamily, her cheek pressed to mine, like it were seventeen years ago, when I was still her baby and she was still herself.

"Love," he whispered. "You are one of the few humans in this city who is *loved*, Lela."

I blinked up at him, noticing how the pain was fading, how my belly tingled and my whole body felt warm. This was so much better than the healing I'd experienced at the hands of Raphael, whose technique felt more like being burned alive. This was . . . nice. It was comforting. And as I lay there, my mother's unfamiliar arms wrapped around me, a truth bled into me and spiraled its way along my limbs. Rita Santos—my mom—loved me. She might have left me. She might have failed me. But despite that, her love was real. Imperfect, yeah, but deep and enduring. It was a big feeling, pushing at the fortress around my heart. I squeezed my eyes shut.

Takeshi and Ana settled in against a wall next to us, seeking rest and haven in each other. "We'll go at sunup," said Takeshi. "Before the fire hour. We'll rest until then."

"Malachi," I whispered. "We never got what we needed to unlock his chains."

Takeshi chuckled. "You think I'd let your sacrifice go unrewarded?" He reached into his pocket and held up a beautiful, intricate metal treasure. "It's why I had to wait for the right moment to rescue you. I needed to snatch the Smith's master key."

A few more hours and we'd save Malachi. With that knowledge, I sank into my mom's arms, letting her improbable, flawed love make me new again.

THIRTEEN

I CROUCHED IN AN alley a block from the square, sweat dripping down the side of my face.

Ana squatted next to me, peering at the sunbaked concrete. "It must be like an oven in that square. Takeshi said it's almost the fire hour."

"So I guess we'd better hurry." I stared into her dark eyes.

"Hey, who's the Captain here?" she said, but it lacked bite. I knew she wanted to get Malachi out of there. She just didn't want to be incinerated in the process, and I couldn't blame her.

Takeshi appeared silently behind us. "There are only two guards in the square, at least that we can see. There are probably a few others in the buildings around the perimeter. Very soon, they'll all be inside when the fire hour arrives, but that will also be the most dangerous time to enter the square.

Malachi is under a shelter because they won't allow his body to be entirely destroyed."

Unwilling to offer him even a few hours' worth of wholeness, they didn't want him to die and reappear at the city gates. Instead, they kept him barely alive and suffering constantly. My rage flowed through me, powerful and hotter than any flame.

"We can't let any of them escape and raise the alarm," said Ana.

"Then we should go now." Takeshi raised his hood and then reached into his cloak and pulled out the Smith's master key.

"You want me to do it?" I asked.

Ana nudged my elbow, urging me to take it. "I think you're the best person for that job."

I accepted the key. "You two can handle the guards?"

Ana nodded, eyeing the grenade belt slung over Takeshi's chest. We didn't want to use them if we didn't have to—we had only six left thanks to Takeshi's efforts in the Smith's yard. But if we needed them, the fire hour would be the perfect cover, since explosions were common at that time of day and therefore wouldn't bring Mazikin running to investigate. "We'll take care of them." She turned to me. "Malachi will need to hear your voice, Lela. Make sure you talk to him. He'll need any motivation you can give him to climb down off that platform." She gave me a sad, solemn look. "He's in bad shape, and—"

"I know, Ana. Let's just go get him, okay? Is Zip waiting?"

"She is," said Takeshi. "She has a view of the square from one of the passages above her den. She's watching and ready."

"Then that's it. Thank you both," I said quietly, gripping the key in my fist.

I followed Takeshi along the alleyway. The heat intensified the stench of the city: roasting meat, gasoline, blood and shit and sweat. *This,* I thought, *is what hell smells like.* I pulled my hood over my hair as the sunlight hit me, searing my skin. Amazingly, though, I felt strong, ready to roll through my enemies. Love had healed me, and now my love would save Malachi. It had to.

We stood in a corner of the square looking out across the expanse. I'd have to run straight across it and climb the steps to get to Malachi, who stood beneath a broad piece of corrugated metal. His sweat ran in trickles, working thin rivulets through the blood that coated his skin. His eyes were closed. The wound stood out, ghastly and huge, below his rib cage. Tears pricked my eyes as I watched him. Once again, I considered what all of this trauma might have done to him. Was he still in there?

I pushed the fear away. He would be whatever he was, and the only thing that mattered was saving him from more suffering. "The guards look pretty miserable over there," I whispered, pointing at the bedraggled-looking creatures that crouched on either side of the steps with their hoods pulled low over their heads, not even their snouts peeking out.

Takeshi, who was standing beside me, inclined his head toward a wide building that took up most of the block next to the huge cement archway that marked the road to the Bone Palace. "The other guards are probably there. The only threat they expect is from Malachi himself, but they can see as well as we can that he can't go anywhere now."

"Okay," I said hoarsely, tucking the key into the pocket of my pants. "I can take out one of those guards by the platform, but not both." I pulled a knife and held it in my right hand, the solid, welcome weight an extension of my body.

"I'll take the one on the left, closest to the archway," said Ana.

"And I'll take the ones in the building," said Takeshi. "They'll be sleeping. Ana will help me when she's finished with hers. Lela, when you get him loose, the entrance to Zip's den is there." He pointed to an alley at the opposite end of the block from us. "She'll be waiting to get him below before anyone knows what's happening."

"Got it." A few blocks away, a percussive boom shook the ground at our feet. The fire hour was starting.

"Now!" Ana cried.

We sprinted into the square. My cloak billowed behind me as my feet pounded the concrete. My soft-soled boots were so silent the Mazikin guard wasn't aware I was coming until I was less than twenty feet away. It yipped loudly and reared onto its hind legs, but I was on it before it could draw the dagger from its belt. I used its upward motion against it, ducking low and driving up knife-first, burying my blade in the guard's stomach and twisting. Blood flowed over my hands as it jerked. I yanked the knife out quickly and wrapped my arms around its flailing, snapping body, then hurled it to the ground. Across the square, the screech of the other Mazikin guard stopped abruptly as Ana did her thing. My opponent was still kicking and gasping. Its claws caught in my cloak but didn't tear it, and I let it struggle as I straightened up and stabbed down with all my strength, right into the Mazikin's throat. It gurgled and went limp.

I jumped for the steps, still hearing the sounds of frantic fighting coming from inside the building where Takeshi was taking on the remaining guards. But I didn't pause or even look in his direction—my mission was Malachi, and I had eyes only for him. Malachi didn't seem aware of the noise or the fighting or the heat. His eyes stayed closed as I reached the top of the platform and pulled the key from my pants.

My heart squeezed painfully at the sight of him, so close at last, so torn up. "Malachi," I said softly, putting all my hope into that one precious word. "Malachi, it's Lela."

At the sound of my voice, his eyes flew open and landed on me. He tried to speak, but all that came out was a quiet moan. His lips were moving, but he didn't seem able to put any breath behind his words. I gently touched one of the few uninjured places on his chest. He flinched, and my fingers drew back slick with his sweat and blood. "Shhh, I'm here."

The manacle around his neck was the first to go. I jammed the key in the lock and sent a silent prayer of thanks skyward as it turned easily and allowed the heavy iron cuff to swing away from his throat. He groaned as his head fell forward. I knelt at his bleeding, blistered feet and unlocked the manacles at his ankles. I freed his right arm, which fell heavily at his side, revealing deep wounds in his wrists where he'd tried to pull himself loose. Bracing his body with mine, averting my eyes from the barely closed wound covering his reforming heart, I unlocked the manacle on his left wrist.

And then he was free. He sank onto me, and I couldn't hold him up. He was over six feet tall and outweighed me by about sixty pounds. We fell to our knees beneath the shade of the metal overhang, his sweaty face against my neck, his arms limp and twitching. To my left I heard an explosion and a scream. I couldn't tell if it was human or Mazikin, but it didn't matter. "Malachi," I whispered. "Open your eyes and look at me. Look at me, Malachi. Please."

"I wish you were really here," he said weakly.

"I *am* here," I said, the tears springing to my eyes. "And I need you. I need you to stand up and help me. We're getting out of here."

He winced as a wistful smile pulled at the raised claw marks on his face. "I miss your scent. Wind and salt. Like the sea. Wild . . ." He slumped against me. Blood trickled from the corner of his mouth.

"Oh God," I said, my voice breaking. This wasn't working. He didn't believe I was real. I took his face in my hands, as carefully as I could manage. "Malachi? Come on, open your eyes. I'm right here."

"I miss you," he mumbled, but his eyes stayed closed. "So much."

The heat at my back was nearly unbearable. My spine was being hard-boiled; I needed to move. I gazed into his face, the dark circles around his eyes, the wounds on his right cheek, the blood on his lips, and a desperate idea hit me. For the last seventy years, Malachi had been a Guard. It was who he was. It was more real to him than nearly anything else.

I swallowed hard and mustered as much volume as I could. "Get up, Lieutenant," I barked. "That's an order!"

His eyelids fluttered. "Hmm?"

"Up," I snapped, holding my face close to his. "Get. Up. That is an *order*."

He blinked slowly, like he was trying to clear his head. His gaze sharpened as he focused on my face. He grabbed my arm, holding on to me for balance. "Lela?" His hand landed on the side of my neck, and he pulled me close, until we were nose to nose. "You can't be here. They'll . . . I won't let them."

It broke my heart. He was worrying about *me*. "Then I need your help," I said as his metallic breath huffed against my face. "I'm not leaving this platform unless you're with me."

His muscles tensed beneath my palms, but his limbs wouldn't quite work right, and he couldn't rise to his feet. I slid my arms around his waist, ignoring his sharp intake of breath as my chest pressed against his, putting pressure on the wound at the center of his body. With all my strength, and a little help from him, I pushed us up to standing and held him as he raised his head.

He froze, muttering something I didn't quite catch.

I looked up into his face, terrified that I had caused him unnecessary pain in my clumsy attempts to get us moving. "Are you okay?"

He swallowed, his gaze riveted on something over my shoulder. He repeated what he'd just said, and this time I understood it: "Behind you."

I'd blocked out the rest of the world over the last few minutes, because I was so focused on Malachi and what he needed. That had been a terrible, stupid mistake. I twisted around. We were completely surrounded. Not by Mazikin. By people. Arrayed silently on the steps behind us, daggers sheathed in their belts. I searched their faces, mostly concealed beneath hoods, and didn't recognize a single one. Ana and Takeshi were nowhere among them. The dark-cloaked leader in the center took a few steps toward us, lifting her hood and showing me her face. Pale skin and white-blond hair. The one I'd seen in the city, near the factory, and in the square two nights ago.

I reached behind me, holding Malachi steady as his legs began to buckle. “Who are you?” I tried to sound braver than I felt. Were these people loyal to the Smith? And . . . had Ana and Takeshi been taken? Had they been killed?

The pale woman smiled, but it didn’t reach her ice-blue eyes. “I’m Treasa Kirwan, servant of the Tanner,” she said in a loud Irish-accented voice that cooled the temperature in the square at least ten degrees. “And you’re coming with us.”

FOURTEEN

BEFORE I COULD EVEN draw a knife, Treasa gave a quick wave of her hand, and the hooded humans rushed up the steps and tore me away from Malachi. They used my cloak against me, wrapping it around me, pinning me inside. A reeking, scratchy bag was lowered over my head and pulled tight around my neck, plunging me into suffocating darkness. I fought uselessly as I was carried down the steps and wrestled onto a hard surface that rumbled and rattled—I knew I was in the back of one of those mechanized carts.

"Malachi!" I shrieked, flexing and writhing. A hand clapped over my nose and mouth. My lungs burned. I needed air, but there was none to be found, and so I fell down a deep black hole, still calling for Malachi.

I swam through the darkness, my hands sliding over skin and cement and metal, trying to find a place to anchor myself but finding nothing . . .

I came to with a gasp, lying on damp cement. The room was dimly lit by a single candle, which sat on the floor by a steel door. I rolled to my hands and knees, drawing deep breaths, waiting for pain but feeling none. I wasn't hurt. I got up and walked to the door.

I tugged at the handle, but the door didn't even rattle in its concrete frame. I spun around and leaned against it, frantically trying to think through what could have happened. Ana had taken out one of the Mazikin guards, and then she'd run into the building where Takeshi had said the other guards were sleeping. I had no idea what had happened after that. They could have been ambushed. Killed. Taken prisoner. By the Mazikin, or by the people who had taken us. And—

I blinked, lifting the candle and focusing on a dim shape at the other end of the long, narrow room. A bed of goatskin, and on top of it . . .

"Malachi!" I ran to him, sobbing with relief. He lay sprawled on the thick pallet, and he tensed when my hands skimmed up his arms to his face. "It's me. Please wake up." I dropped to my knees. "Malachi?"

As soon as my fingers touched his chest, he lurched up with a cry. His swinging arm caught me hard in the face, and I flew backward, hitting the floor headfirst. Fireworks boomed in my skull. I gasped for air and rolled to my side, blinking.

Malachi was crouched in the corner next to the platform bed, his knees drawn to his chest and his arms over his head. Even from where I lay, I could hear the desperate whispers bursting from his throat, though I couldn't understand the words. Slowly, squinting to clear my vision, I got to my hands and knees. "Malachi?"

He went on mumbling, his shoulders trembling. Smears of his blood marked the space around him, coming from the gashes along his legs and hips and sides. I crept closer, my heart crumbling at the sight of him all balled up and terrified. I'd never seen him look scared, not really. He'd always seemed like he could handle anything, but no one could withstand the kind of torture he'd experienced.

"I came here for you." I inched closer. "Nothing could stop me."

He made a quiet, desperate sound but didn't raise his head. I reached out and touched his foot, a mere brush of my fingers, but drew back quickly when he shrank away. I looked around us. My mouth nearly dropped open when I saw the steel bucket filled with water at the foot of the bed, with a small rag hanging from it. Next to it was a set of clothing—goatskin pants and a tunic, very similar to mine, only bigger. Someone had given me the means to take care of him. And inside my heart I carried the means to heal him. Now I just had to get him back on the bed and hope he'd let me touch him.

"You know my voice," I said. "You know I'd never hurt you."

"Lela," he whispered.

"I'm here." This time, I touched his elbow, which was perched atop one of his knees, a shield for his head. He pulled more tightly into himself. He was shaking, whether from fear or pain, I didn't know.

"Where are we?" he asked, his voice breaking.

"I'm not sure. But at this exact moment, it's just you and me, and we're safe."

"Can you . . . Can you summon Raphael? I . . . I've been injured."

I squeezed my eyes shut. He sounded so young, like a little boy. "I know you're hurt," I said. "I can help with that."

"I need Raphael. Can you get me to the Station?"

He thought he was in the dark city. "I can get you what you need." I rose on my knees and gently stroked his hair, alert to any signals that he needed me to stop. But though he didn't lean toward me, he didn't move away, either.

"What's wrong with me?" he asked in that same choked voice. "I had the worst dream."

"I know." I sat down next to his legs. I didn't know how much time we had, or what was going to happen to us when it was up. So I threaded my fingers into his hair while his whole body trembled. I didn't want to tell him where we really were. I didn't want him to realize that none of it had been a dream. But I needed him to come back to himself sooner rather than later. My thoughts spun with worry and love and all the possible things I might say.

"Remember that night we were up at the top of the Station?" I finally asked. "You and I, we were up there, and I let you put your arms around me. I hadn't let anyone do that . . . ever." I laughed softly. "And it felt like I was starting to wake up from a bad dream."

"Me too," he whispered.

"Your arms felt like armor around me, and even though I was in that scary place, I felt safe."

"I'm glad."

"I know I've never really done that for you . . ."

"You're wrong." He was quiet for a few moments, as my thumb stroked along his scalp. "You're doing it right now."

I was so relieved by his response that it took me a minute to be able to speak. "I'm really here with you. We're really together."

One of his hands slid unsteadily down his shoulder to his arm, and I reached for it, tangling my fingers with his. "You feel real," he murmured.

"Come closer, then."

He let out a shaky breath. "Am I as broken as I feel?"

Tears burned my eyes. "You're a little banged up." I tugged on his fingers. "But I promise I can make it better. Come here."

Slowly, he raised his head, his dark eyes clouded with fear and hurt. I opened my arms as his face crumpled with pain, as his movements stretched and pulled at a hundred badly healed wounds and a dozen fresh ones that were still raw and bleeding. With my help, he crawled back to the bed and curled on his side, once again drawing his knees to his chest, protecting his vulnerable body in the only way he could after being chained wide open in that square for days. His back was the least damaged part of him, so I edged onto the bed behind him, propping up on my elbow so I could look down at his face, the gashes deep and horrible along his cheek and temple. "Tell me to stop if you need me to," I whispered in his ear.

Then I laid my arm over him, my fingers gently caressing his face, my chest against his back. I'd never willingly been this close to a naked man, but it was Malachi, and any fog of anxiety was blown away by my determination. I held him, touching his face, his hair, his shoulders, his back, all the while thinking of who he was to me. He thought I was strong, but he was willing to lay down his life to protect me. He thought

I was beautiful, but he treated me as a precious gift instead of something to take for his own pleasure. He thought I was worth something, and he was worth everything to me. This man had endured lifetimes of suffering, but he could still love, and give, and dream of his future. He was a leader who would sacrifice himself for the weak, who used all his gifts—his intelligence, his cunning, his strength—to protect others. It was a privilege to love him, even to have a shot at giving him the things he needed.

I closed my eyes and leaned my head against his shoulder blade, imagining my love as a living thing that wrapped itself around us, that warmed his skin and closed his wounds, that healed his heart and moved the blood through his veins, that soothed the nightmares and cleared his mind. Little by little, he uncurled his legs and stretched them out, groaning with the effort. I raised my head and looked him over, but it was hard to tell if he was healing, because he was such a mess. "Malachi?"

"I'm awake," he whispered, his lips barely moving as he rolled slowly onto his back. "Just . . . resting."

I touched my forehead to his. "How are you?"

"Ruined," he breathed.

It burned from my brain to my throat to my heart. "No, you're not."

"But this wasn't a nightmare. I'm in the Mazikin city." His black-brown eyes searched my face, begging me to disagree.

"*We* are in the Mazikin city," I told him. "You're not alone."

"How?" he asked, swallowing. "How did you get here? Did Juri—?"

"The Mazikin didn't take me," I reassured him. "I came after you. The Judge let me come. And Ana—she came, too. We found Takeshi. And rescuing you was the first step . . ."

"What do you mean 'first step'?"

I bit my lip. "To get out of here, to even have a chance, we have to destroy the portal the Mazikin use to possess people. And we have to kill the Queen."

His eyes widened, and I felt his pulse quicken.

"I'm sorry. It gets worse, too, because I'm not sure if Takeshi and Ana made it out of the fight alive."

"This is my fault."

"Are you serious?" I kissed the tip of his nose, because it seemed like the least bloody part of him. "Don't you dare. The Judge is sliding her chess pieces across the board, and if we want to get out of here, we'll play the game and keep moving."

He tried to lift his head but gave up quickly. "I don't think I can move at all."

"It's okay," I said, glad when he relaxed into the blankets. "Rest." I sat up and peered at the clear water inside the bucket. I grasped the soft rag next to it. "I'm going to clean you up."

He let out a weak bark of laughter. "I don't think that's going to help much."

I dipped the rag in the water and wrung it out. "You never know," I said, anxiety building inside me. Was my love strong enough? How quickly was this supposed to work? "Hold still."

I started at his feet, wiping gently at the raw spots, cleaning away the dirt. The water raised goose bumps and plastered the hair on his legs to his olive skin, but he didn't flinch away; he simply closed his eyes and let me work on him. "This isn't the first time I've done this, you know," I said, watching the drops trickle over his knees and remembering our time in the dark city, when I'd taken care of him after he'd been bitten by Juri, who now controlled the body Malachi had left behind.

"I know." He rewarded me with the faintest smile but kept his eyes shut tight. "I wasn't awake that time, though."

He hadn't been completely naked and exposed, either, like he was now. Aware of how he must feel—how vulnerable—I stayed very focused on the hurt places, on the blood and dirt. I didn't slow down or stop as I worked my way up his hips, pressing the cloth to the evil-looking bite marks that had turned his thighs and sides into nothing but raw meat. I kept rinsing out the rag, wringing the red-tinged water into the bucket, until the blood was washed from his skin, until every wound was as clean as I could get it. He didn't move, but I could tell by the tension on his face that the venom in those wounds was working its way through his system and forcing his body to work harder to heal. Although it wouldn't kill him here like it might have anywhere else, it had to hurt.

I relaxed a little when I reached his waist and could concentrate on his stomach and chest, parts of him I had seen before, touched before. I avoided the area below his ribs, wiping the cloth gently around the edges of the worst of it. When I was finished, I leaned to kiss his temple, and my braid fell over my shoulder and tickled the skin of his. "You look a lot better."

He slowly opened his eyes and directed his gaze to the pocked gray wall on the other side of the bed. "Don't lie to me, Lela."

"I would never lie to you," I said, carefully spreading a soft goatskin blanket over his legs and waist and sitting next to him on the pallet. I let my fingers skim over the smooth skin of his forehead. "Do you remember our plans that night, the night you got taken? I know you've been through a lot . . ."

"Do you think I'd forget something like that?" He sighed. "I was living for that moment, being back in your arms. I think I had been, for the longest time."

I wiped a tear from the corner of my eye. "Me too. It's the real reason I came here. I figured I'd drop in and we could have that talk."

His laugh was a little stronger this time, but when it shook his chest, pain flashed on his face and he arched like he was trying to get away from it. I touched his shoulders and forced myself to examine the wound on his chest, where the Queen had speared him with her steel-tipped claws, where she'd forced her hand into his body and ripped him apart. It was a livid red, ugly and tender-looking, like raw steak. I met Malachi's eyes, reading the story of agony written in their depths. "How many times did she do that to you?"

"I lost count," he said wearily. "I lost track of time. Maybe three times, maybe twenty."

My hand hovered over the wound, which was slightly depressed, like a shallow sea in the terrain of his body. My gaze slid along his stomach, over the flat plains and sculpted muscles, over the bite marks and claw marks that somehow couldn't destroy the simple beauty of him. "You are so wrong," I breathed. "They didn't ruin you at all."

I don't know why I did it. Maybe I wanted to help, to show him how much I loved him. Maybe I hoped I could fix him. Maybe I needed the warmth of his skin. Maybe I wanted to make sure he was real, that I'd found him at last and wouldn't lose him again. My hand descended and brushed over his heart.

He jerked halfway off the bed, all his muscles taut, clenching his teeth around a terrified cry. I yanked my hand back, the apologies already falling from my mouth, the tears already clouding my vision. My own hand suddenly felt like the enemy, like my fingers had somehow morphed into steel-tipped claws and dredged up all the dripping, blood-soaked memories, pulling them to the surface and forcing them on him in a moment when he'd been open and vulnerable. I wrapped my arms around myself, wanting to disappear.

He fell back, sucking in deep, panicked breaths, his eyes glittering in the light of the guttering tallow candle. His whole body was shaking. He looked like he'd been spat from the mouth of a monster. And I knew that I'd brought it all back, the last thing I wanted to do. Finally, I understood how it felt to be the demon, how it felt to awaken a terrible memory in someone you loved. I knew why he'd recoiled that day on the mat in our Guard house, when he'd felt me tense beneath him, why he'd pulled away. I'd understood it before, but not like this, not from my gut. Not the shearing, twisting pain that came from being the hands of the enemy.

"I'm so sorry," I said in a hoarse whisper. "I shouldn't have done that." Frustration and horror burned me. I'd wanted to heal him, and I'd done the opposite.

Malachi stared at the ceiling as his body slowly relaxed, and I waited, not wanting to make it harder for him. His eyes blinked open, and he held his hand out to me, still breathing hard. "Lela, give me your hand."

I did as he said, slipping my shaking hand into his. He turned my palm and brought it to his mouth, planting a tender kiss right in the center of it, making me ache. And then, before I realized what he was doing, he pressed my palm against the wound in his chest. It throbbed hot and raw against my skin as he flattened his hand over mine. Malachi tensed again, throwing his head back, the fear and pain etched deeply into his features.

"What are you doing?" I tried to pull my hand away, but he held it there, his grip surprisingly strong.

"Stop fighting me. I can't fight both of you," he said, his voice cracking. Through the wound, his heart skipped erratically, weak and frantic, like a butterfly held between the paws of a cat. He kept his gaze rooted on the spotted cement ceiling above us. The veins on the back of his hand stood out as his fingers clamped over mine, keeping my palm pressed firmly over the sunken spot on his chest.

I can't fight both of you.

The words danced in my head, their meaning just out of my reach as they tumbled with my own crazy worry for him. But as we passed the minutes, locked in that position, me trying to pull away and him refusing to allow it, his strength seemed to grow. Not like it had been, but an echo of it, swelling with every shuddering gasp, until it hit me—

He was fighting *her*. The Queen. His memories.

He was reclaiming his body.

He was refusing to let her have power over him.

He was using my touch as his weapon.

I stopped trying to pull away.

Slowly, very slowly, I rose up on my knees, leaning over him again, letting him have what he needed. My hope, my strength, but mostly, my love. His pupils were big black circles in his deep-brown eyes, and when he blinked, a tear streaked down the side of his face. He was there but not there, and I knew that feeling so well, that struggle between *now* and *then*, between the safety of *here* and the danger of *there.* I let the warmth of my skin do my talking, and I bowed my head and kissed his shoulder, drawing in the earth-and-sun scent of him, the smell that meant home to me now. His free hand rose from his side and caressed my hair, pulling me near, and in the muted silence of our prison cell, I heard him speak again, but this time it was a single word. He said my name, whispering it like a prayer, like a ward against the darkness, against all the things that had tried to destroy him.

When his voice faded to nothing, when the shaking stopped, when his breath evened out and his heart settled into a beat that only occasionally faltered, I looked up and found his gaze focused on me. And I said the only words that came to me. "I love you."

He looked down at himself, at his clean skin, at the closing wounds, at his hand over mine, protecting his heart. His eyes met mine. "I know you do."

FIFTEEN

I AWOKE TO FINGERS in my hair and discovered that Malachi had removed the tie from my braid and unraveled it. One of his hands was tangled in my curls, and the other was around my waist. Maybe minutes ago, maybe hours, I'd stretched out next to him, and he'd scooted over and let me sink onto him with a little sigh of pleasure. I'd settled into his arms and laid my head on his shoulder, and I'd let him guide my hands to the places that felt best. I'd sent my love through the connection of our bodies, hoping it would be what he needed.

Now he was asleep but holding me tightly as his eyes moved beneath his lids. I hoped his dreams were peaceful. The dwindling candle illuminated his profile, the harsh outline of his cheekbones, nose and brow, and his body . . . I raised my head. I had no idea how long I'd been asleep, but his wounds had, for the most part, healed completely. Scars, yes. Lots of scars, red-and-silver streaks and semicircles that would never allow him to forget what they'd done to him. But no open wounds, no more bleeding. I kissed his chest and laid my ear over his heart.

It didn't sound the same.

It was beating, and that should have been enough. But I felt a shock of fear as I listened to it falter. Not on every beat, not by far. But every time I started to think it might have been my imagination, it skipped a beat or stopped completely. Whenever it did, Malachi shifted restlessly until it resumed its rhythm, the drumbeat that accompanied the faint wheezing sound of his breathing. What used to be a powerful, silent rush of air with every rise and fall of his chest was now labored and halting. *It just needs time. It's only been a day. He'll be fine.*

I closed my eyes and focused on being in his arms again.

"Do you know how long we've been here?" he whispered.

"Did I wake you up?"

"I don't mind." He kissed the top of my head. "I thought I would never touch you again. I don't want to miss a minute of it."

"But you need to rest." I let out a breath as his lips brushed over my brow and tilted my head up, scratching my skin along his scraggly beard. The scars on the underside of his neck, where the chains had cut his flesh, were pink and tender. My fingers crept up, drawn to the vulnerable spots. They were hot to the touch, and he stiffened but didn't pull away.

"Am I hurting you?" I asked. I was snugged up against his bare skin, which was still mending itself.

"Not as much as you would if you pulled away," he said, giving me a sad half-smile and turning his face to mine, letting me see the vicious scarring on his right cheek, from his temple to his jaw, where the Queen had anchored her claws.

"Nothing could make me do that."

His eyes skimmed over my face. "I believe you. If you were willing to come here . . ." His skin paled as his expression fell. "Did Juri hurt you?" His gaze darted to my mouth. "Did you know it wasn't me?"

I took his hand and traced his fingers along the silver crescent scar on my neck. "Not at first," I said in a strained whisper.

Shards of hatred glinted in his eyes. "I want to destroy him."

"Maybe we can. If he's in the land of the living, his body's still here, and I'm betting it's near the portal, which Takeshi said would probably be in the Queen's palace." I turned toward the locked door of our concrete cell. "But first, we have to figure out how to get out of here. We were captured by a bunch of humans as soon as I unlocked your chains. They said they worked for someone called the Tanner."

"Humans?"

I nodded. "I'm getting the sense the Mazikin aren't in complete control. We stole the key to your chains from a guy called the Smith, and he seemed pretty masterless despite his loyalty to the Mazikin. And I don't know where we are now, but I think that if the Mazikin had us, they wouldn't have given us fresh water and clothes, or put us together."

"I've seen the woman who captured us before," Malachi said. "When I was in the square. The white-haired one with the dark cloak."

"She said she was a servant of the Tanner. And I think she'd been following Takeshi, Ana, and me."

Malachi wound one of my curls around his index finger. "I saw your mother, too, I think," he said in a hushed voice. "For a moment, I thought it was you." He closed his eyes, like it hurt him to remember.

"The Mazikin who possessed her took her as a pet. She and my mother were going to help us get you to safety."

Malachi shifted slowly until we were chest to chest. Then he laid his hand on my face. "What was it like for you to see her again?"

"Weird. I . . . she's like a stranger to me, but she looks at me like she knows me. Sometimes. Though most of the time, she seems completely lost in her own head." I thought back to the moments in her arms. "But . . . she still loves me. Somewhere in there, it's real."

His thumb stroked over my cheek. "I asked Raphael about her, after you nearly sacrificed your life to save the Mazikin that had taken her body."

"And he actually gave you an answer? That's got to be a first."

He smiled. "I suppose he thought I needed to know. He knew you wouldn't talk to me about it, because of what I'd done, how I'd pulled away from you." His eyes met mine. "And he also knew I was so distracted by it that I couldn't do my job."

I ignored the little stab of pain at the memory of those weeks we'd spent barely speaking to each other. "Because you thought your Captain was losing her mind."

"No," he said quietly, "because the girl I love was in terrible pain."

I leaned forward and he kissed my forehead. "I don't know how to feel about her," I said. "I have some memories of her, but they're really fuzzy. And even though I know it wasn't her fault, it's kind of hard to get over being abandoned like that. I'm not sure I was better off without her. It's not like there was someone else waiting to love me . . ." My throat closed at the memory of what had happened instead.

His warmth seeped through my clothes, reaching all my cold places. He didn't have to tell me it hurt him to think of what had happened to me—I *knew* it. And I trusted it. Which was nothing short of a miracle. He held me there, silently telling me he loved me now, wordlessly hoping it might be enough, and my body relaxed, letting him know it was. My hands skimmed up his back, tracing patterns that said I needed it, that it was the most precious thing in the world to me.

I raised my chin, and our lips collided. He moaned softly, a sound halfway between pain and pleasure, and as our kiss deepened, I tasted the iron-salt of his blood in his mouth. The heat of his skin burned me, and I didn't know if it was fever or desire. His scarred, naked body was so close to mine, and most of me wanted to touch all of him, and let him touch all of me. My heart hammered, eager and scared, curious but too nervous to be steady. My fingers curled into his shoulder, and he flinched.

I pulled away from his mouth. "I'm sorry," I whispered.

He brushed a light kiss over my cheek. "Are you all right?"

I nodded, and he drew me close again, tucking my head into the hollow of his neck, filling me up with the scent of his skin and the growing strength in his hands as they smoothed my hair and stroked my face.

And that's how Treasa found us when the steel door opened with a scraping clang.

I rolled off the bed and landed in a crouch in front of Malachi. My hands traveled automatically to my thighs, but, of course, they'd stripped me of my weapons and gloves before they'd thrown me in here.

Treasa watched my realization with a small smile. Her white-blond hair was in a tight ponytail secured at the base of her neck. She had a wide forehead, a narrow chin, and skin so pale that the only thing that kept me from deciding she was an albino was her blue eyes, which slipped past me and landed on Malachi. "You look better. *Much* better. Interesting." Her gaze shifted to me with sharp curiosity.

The soft pat of Malachi's bare soles on the cement floor told me he was sitting up. "Thank you. I feel better," he said evenly. "Are you our host?"

Treasa gave us a tight grin. "Only the messenger. You are wanted by the Mazikin, Malachi." When she saw me stiffen as she said his name, she said, "Don't be stupid. You were screaming his name, *Lela*."

I guessed Malachi had been shouting mine as well.

I tried to brush off the odd feeling of vulnerability that came with this woman knowing our names. "Awesome. So . . . he's wanted by the Mazikin. Can you tell us something we don't know?"

"They are like a swarming hive at the moment. Right now, pictures of Malachi's face are being painted in every district of the city. A trip through the portal is being promised to the Mazikin that turns you in—and a life of comfort is being promised to any human who does the same. We thought it would be safer to hide you here."

I stood up. From the soft rustle behind me, I could tell Malachi was sliding on the pants that had been left for him. I really didn't want Treasa to be able to look at all of him, and so I took a step to the side, blocking him from view. "And where, exactly, is here?"

Treasa shifted her weight, like she was bracing in case I attacked. She had one of those long, straight daggers tucked into the belt looped around her narrow waist, and her slender white fingers fluttered toward it. I wondered if she knew how to use it. Her eyes narrowed as she assessed me. "You are the guests of the Tanner."

"Guests or prisoners?" I asked.

"We don't take prisoners," she replied in a flat voice.

I felt a solid, warm presence at my back a second before Malachi's hands came to rest on my shoulders. "You were kind to leave clean water to tend my wounds," he said to her. "And to provide clothing for me. Please convey our gratitude to the Tanner."

"You can convey your gratitude to him yourself." She raised a pale eyebrow as she looked him up and down, and scars or no scars, it was obvious she liked what she saw. "He has granted you an audience."

Malachi's grip was steely, a warning. "Wonderful." He turned to grab the folded leather shirt from the foot of the bed, and I saw how he had to brace himself to keep from falling as he straightened again. I also heard the faintest wheeze as he inhaled, and noticed the anxiety that flashed in his eyes before he pulled the leather tunic shirt over his head, hiding that terrible scar. Protectiveness welled inside of me. I wanted to order him to lie back down. I wanted to tell Treasa where she could shove the Tanner's invitation.

But I followed Malachi's lead and even smiled at her as she held the door wide and gestured for us to follow her. I took Malachi's hand in mine, needing the connection—and the silent means of communication. She led us along a low concrete corridor, past a number of closed steel doors. The way was lit by flickering, primitive bulbs.

Treasa gave me a sidelong glance. "You are nicely recovered from your encounter with the Smith," she said in an amused voice. "I did not expect to see you walking, let alone fighting, anytime soon."

"How do you even know about that?"

"It's my job to know."

"Were you following us?" I remembered that cloak disappearing behind a corner just before the Smith's men ambushed us. Takeshi had gone after the person, and I'd never found out what happened.

"Most people stabbed through the gut aren't killing Mazikin in the square less than a day later," she said, blithely ignoring my question.

Malachi's eyes went wide, and I gave him an apologetic look. "I've always been a quick healer," I said.

She rolled her eyes. "Of course you are." She shoved open a steel door and we entered a huge cave-like chamber. Although I was sure the building, like every other in the city, was made of concrete, it felt like I'd crawled into the stenchy embrace of an animal. It smelled like pee and rotten eggs and burned meat. Bile rose in my throat.

Every surface was covered with animal hides. A furry patchwork beneath our feet. Spotted yet smooth irregular shapes covered the walls, stitched together in an unending tapestry of flesh. On either side of us were long tables, crowded with men and women whose attention was riveted to a stage where at least a dozen barely clothed humans were undulating to a low beat played by two others crouched on the floor, pounding on an assortment of drums.

Malachi tugged me a little closer to him. Treasa walked noiselessly to the front of the room, toward a raised platform upon which sat what looked every bit like a throne. It was a wide chair with a high back that extended at least six feet above the seat, upholstered with cream-colored leather. Metal and bone tools—some sort of pliers studded with wicked sharp spikes, knives with barbed tips, and something that looked like an ice pick—were arrayed around the edge of the throne in a kind of deadly frill.

On the throne sat a man. He had dark-blond hair and a beard that was brown around his mouth but lighter where it grew in matted curls around his face. His eyes were blackish brown, as fathomless as Malachi's. As he watched us approach, his lips, an intense shade of red, curled into an amused smile. "Welcome, *Captain*," he said to Malachi in a gravelly voice. His accent told me he was British, or had been at one time. "I'm the Tanner. Do you have any idea how badly the Mazikin want you back?"

"I do," said Malachi. "Are you going to let them have me?" His voice was steady, but his hand trembled in mine, and now it was my turn to squeeze.

The Tanner chuckled, a thick, phlegmy sound. "That greatly depends on whether our interests are aligned." His gaze shifted to me. "I heard you caused quite a commotion in the Smith's yard. There's buzz all over the city about it."

I shrugged. "He stabbed me. I don't like being stabbed."

The Tanner laughed raucously, and then started to cough, a deep rattle that made me wince. "I'm glad to hear that. And I was even more glad to hear that you decimated that selfish bastard. About time."

"The Smith is human, like you," I said. "I'd think you would be allies."

Next to me, Treasa shifted uncomfortably. "You would be wrong."

"Too right," said the Tanner, running one of his huge hands over his unruly beard.

I gestured at his throne. "You've certainly got a lot of nice metal tools there."

The Tanner grunted. "We were allies at one time. Many years ago. But now . . . let's say we have different visions for the future."

"Glad to hear it," I muttered.

"Glad you're glad," he said. "I think we could help one another."

I looked up at Malachi, and he gave me a small smile. "You're my Captain," he murmured. "This is your decision."

"I'm not the Captain anymore," I whispered. But Ana wasn't here to make the call.

I turned back to the Tanner to see him surveying me with interest. "Why do the Mazikin give you so much independence?" I asked. "I was told that every human here was a servant."

He gave me a rueful look. "I've been here for a very long time, and because of the way I arrived, I was more able to speak up for myself."

"The way you arrived?"

He leaned forward, letting his elbows rest on his thighs. "Did you know that the Mazikin managed to find their way to the land of the living?"

I frowned. This dude was definitely not from Rhode Island. But then I recalled Ana telling me that the Mazikin had found their way out of the Shadowlands before. Five hundred years before. "You didn't come from the dark city, then."

He shook his bushy head. "Got way too drunk one night and let the wrong people walk me home. Next thing I knew, I was tied to a table." He pointed across the room at a few men watching the dancers onstage. "Same thing happened to Bartholomew and August over there. We're from the same town."

Since the Tanner hadn't committed suicide, he would never have belonged to the dark city. He'd never have been as depressed and passive and confused as the rest of the humans around him. "So you showed up here and started skinning goats for the Mazikin?" I asked.

He gave me a darkly amused look. "Aye, girl, I've been of service to the Mazikin. Not sure I had much choice if I wanted to keep my own skin. But now they trust me, and you should be very glad of that."

I thought about Takeshi's hatred of the Smith—and of the man in front of me—for their collaboration with the monsters who controlled this city. And then I felt Malachi's hand in mine, no longer chained, safe and solid. "At the moment, I am."

He smirked. "Good. Because I want your help."

"With what?"

He grinned, revealing his rotting teeth. "I think it's time for a little rebellion."

SIXTEEN

BEFORE I COULD REPLY, the Tanner waved his arm, beckoning to someone at the back of the room. The metal door scraped open, and Takeshi and Ana were escorted into the chamber. Malachi made an anguished sound at the sight of them, and Takeshi and Ana's eyes lasered to him. Malachi let go of my hand as they walked, with guards on either side of them, toward the front of the room.

They came to a halt in front of us. "Captain," Malachi said to Takeshi, so quietly I could barely hear him.

Takeshi smiled. "Captain," he said in reply.

Then the two of them strode forward and met in the middle, grasping each other in a fierce hug. Though Malachi was taller and more muscular than his mentor, Takeshi seemed to be holding him up for a moment. They pulled apart abruptly, their emotions quickly sinking beneath smooth exteriors, but

I could see the tremors of Malachi's unsteady breaths. It was like there was too much to be said, so they'd decided to say nothing at all.

Takeshi gazed up at the Tanner. "Thank you for your hospitality."

The Tanner arched an eyebrow. "I never thought the famed and feared scourge of the city would be saying that to me."

"I never thought I'd be saying it," Takeshi muttered.

The Tanner snorted, and then gave Ana a distinctly hungry look. "And you're one of them, too. A Guard." He smiled wide again, making me shudder. "Four of you. This is an unprecedented opportunity, I'd say."

"What kind of rebellion are you considering?" I asked, casting a sidelong glance at Ana. The Tanner was creepy in the extreme, but we couldn't exactly be picky about allies right now. "Because we were considering one, too."

"I'd never have guessed," he replied drily. "Tell me what you were planning."

Ana stepped forward to stand next to me. "You want us to tell you our plans in a roomful of people who could take that information straight to the Queen?"

The Tanner looked around with surprise, at Treasa, at the dancers performing for a host of leather-clad people lounging at the tables along the side of the room, and then back at us. "Everyone here is loyal to me. Traitors are sent to the meat factory."

I barely concealed my disgust. "How about this, then—you have all the power. I think you can understand why that makes us hesitant to spill our guts."

"I could spill your guts for you," Treasa volunteered, her hand on the hilt of her dagger.

Malachi gave her a murderous look. "Try."

She stared at him like she might enjoy taking him up on the challenge, but then she shrugged.

The Tanner, who had watched the exchange with amusement, held up his hand. "Peace, Treasa. I understand their concern." His gaze landed on me. "I want to dethrone the Queen. She is the source of misery in this city. With her gone, the Mazikin will be finished."

"What do you mean?" asked Malachi. "They rule the city."

"But she is the mother of all of them."

My eyebrows shot up, but then I remembered her oddly distended belly as she appeared in front of the crowd in the square, and how Takeshi said that all the Mazikin cubs were kept in one nursery. "Wait. What? *All* of them?"

The Tanner nodded. "She's like an ant, and this is her hill. Kill the Queen, and they have no mother. None of the female Mazikin can breed."

"What about a father?" Ana asked.

"The Queen has many . . . companions. She picks the strongest to father her cubs."

"But is there a King here?"

"Who do you think built the portal and found a way through it?" The Tanner grunted. "The King was her mate, one of the original two. He disappeared many years ago. He called himself Nero. I imagine he'll return someday, but—"

"He will never return," Malachi said quietly.

"Eh? How can you be so sure?"

"Because I disposed of him." Malachi's voice was steady, like the memory of that victory was giving him strength.

The Tanner let out one of those boiling, phlegmy laughs. "Forgive me if I suggest that it would take more than—"

"Malachi is telling the truth," said Takeshi in a loud voice. "He stalked Nero, tricked him, captured him, and nearly died a few times in the process." He gazed at Malachi with a fond, exasperated sort of respect, like a big brother might look at a younger sibling who'd pulled a badass yet incredibly dangerous stunt. "Nero is imprisoned in the dark tower behind the Suicide Gates," said Takeshi. "He's not coming back."

The Tanner's eyes lit with glee. "So again I say—if we kill the Queen, that's it. We'll be able to escape this hellish place."

"That's what we want, too," Ana said, though she looked hesitant.

I didn't share her caution—I couldn't believe our luck. The Smith seemed to hate anyone who opposed the Mazikin, but the Tanner was the opposite. We'd offered the Smith a chance to be our ally, a chance to help everyone get out, and he'd flatly turned us down. But the Tanner seemed to want the same thing we did. "Why now, though?" I asked. "You said you'd been here for a long time."

His eyes slid over the four of us. "There are few strong souls in this city. Over the years, I've gathered a few and protected them well in exchange for their loyalty. But we have been so long under the oppression of the monsters that most are utterly defeated."

"You look like you're doing okay," snapped Ana. I stifled a smile. She didn't do subtle well.

The Tanner ran a hand over his broad chest. "I am old and tired. I only want to help my people be free. You are warriors, and you can be the instrument of their salvation. When the Mazikin began to stir with their plans to capture Malachi, I sent my spies to watch for the Guard here." He pointed a thick-knuckled finger at Takeshi. "I'd hoped *he* would attempt to liberate the new prisoner, and that we could help. Imagine my happiness when those fireballs exploded against the dome—I knew something was happening. And then Treasa came back with reports that two women had escaped off a meat cart and were loose in the city." He grinned again, displaying those scary black teeth. "I knew what you were immediately. I knew now was the time."

Ana crossed her arms over her chest and stared at him.

"I have weapons," he offered, as if he could see the gears turning in her mind. "I've built an arsenal. Not like the Smith's, but I can arm you. And I have people. We can take my strongest guards. We can sneak into the palace and take them by surprise." He raised his eyebrows. "I know a way. I worked on it for years, but it's been ready for a while now. I just needed the force. Help me. It won't be easy, but we can triumph over the Mazikin together."

Ana turned to us. I could read the indecision in her eyes. She didn't trust him, but she had no other plan—especially since he had us more or less at his mercy. I nodded at her. This was our chance. She looked at Malachi. He glanced at the Tanner and then nodded, too. She focused on Takeshi. He gave her a small smile. "Up to you, Captain," he said quietly.

Ana stood up a little straighter as she met the Tanner's bottomless gaze. "Okay. Let's do this."

As soon as Ana agreed to an alliance, the Tanner produced a map of the underground tunnel system he'd been working on. Takeshi and Malachi pored over it eagerly. Takeshi knew the city well, but it was clear these paths were new to him. Malachi was simply a map enthusiast, having devoted years to constructing a map of the dark city. When we'd been in the land of the living, I knew for a fact he'd spent time on Google Maps, memorizing the layout of the neighborhoods we patrolled. By the end, he knew Rhode Island as well as I did. Better, maybe. And as he eagerly stared at the Tanner's map, I had no doubt he was readily absorbing the information. It filled me with so much relief, seeing his mind sharp and focused, seeing Malachi as he should be. I was grateful to the Tanner for helping it happen.

As we all looked over the map, we saw that the Mazikin city was much smaller than the dark city, maybe ten miles square, but still vastly complicated, especially because there was an entire network of tunnels and caves belowground. We decided to take a team of twenty through a series of tunnels that led to the underground river that acted as the water supply for the entire city. It flowed under the Bone Palace, connecting to their kitchens and waste-disposal system. What that meant: because the palace was at the northern edge of the city and the river flowed to the south, the Queen and her favorites got clean water, and the rest of the city got water polluted by their waste. I actually found myself pitying the inhabitants of the southern areas.

The Tanner said he had a way for us to sneak into the palace from right below it. We'd take it over from the inside out, when they were least expecting it. It seemed like the best chance we'd ever have, so we accepted the bone-handled weapons he offered, the stiff leather armor, and the thick boots, and we followed the Tanner into the catacombs he had created beneath his fortress, where the rest of his people were assembling.

Malachi stayed close to me, though I wasn't sure if it was because he was trying to protect me—or if he needed my protection. I wasn't complaining. I was still trying to convince myself we were really here together, that I could really trust it, though the warmth in his eyes and the careful touches he gave me were bringing me closer with every passing minute. He slid his fingers down the strap of my satchel, untwisting it at my shoulder. "Ready," he said softly.

I put my hand over his, holding it to a spot next to my collarbone, where a starburst scar decorated the skin beneath my tunic. "Can you do this? You could stay, Malachi."

"Perhaps you should," said Takeshi. "You don't look like yourself."

Malachi stiffened. "With all due respect, neither do you. And yet here you are."

Takeshi grinned. "Here I am. And I suppose I'm not your Captain anymore."

Malachi rolled his eyes, but his posture loosened. "When you were, you didn't exactly go to much effort to prevent me from getting injured. I seem to remember you *causing* me injury on a few occasions."

Takeshi shrugged as Ana joined us, having acquired a few thigh sheaths and knives from the Tanner's guards. "When it served a purpose, I didn't mind sacrificing." He gave Ana an admiring look, and I was reminded that she was the reason he was here. He'd postponed his shot at getting released into the Countryside because he hadn't wanted to leave her behind. He took her hand and laced her fingers with his.

"I know," said Malachi, glancing at their joined hands. "And neither did I."

"Do you think this is going to work, Takeshi?" I asked. We were in a huddle apart from the rest of the guards, men and women who were gearing up and speaking in low, nervous tones. The Tanner had disappeared into his own private chamber with Treasa.

Takeshi gave the side-eye to the Tanner's people, who struck me as different from the walking wounded I'd seen at the Smith's stronghold. Those people had been scarred, hunched, and oppressed. These people stood straight, their faces bright with pink cheeks and red lips. They had few scars or injuries to slow them down. Somehow, the Tanner had taken care of them and kept them strong. Even Takeshi looked slight and wary when compared to them. "I had no idea he'd built his own tunnel system," he said. "Or that he'd gathered such numbers. He's been planning this for some time."

"And you trust him?" Ana asked, running her hand up his arm.

"I don't trust anyone," he replied simply. He put his hand around the back of her neck as her face fell, drawing her close and whispering something to her in Japanese.

Malachi cleared his throat. "Once we've destroyed this portal, do we have a plan for making it back to the gates of the city? We'll have to travel the length of it. Ten miles at least, north to south, according to the Tanner."

"It should be chaos," said Takeshi, releasing Ana, whose cheeks were glowing. Whatever he'd said had put her at ease . . . and apparently turned her on. "Our goal should be to sneak out and run. I have a few tunnels we can use to go part of the way, and there's a safe chamber on the east side of the city that contains a few Mazikin disguises."

Malachi's brow furrowed. "What about everyone else?"

"What do you mean?" Takeshi asked.

Malachi straightened his shoulders. "What about the other human prisoners in this city? How will we get them out?"

"We won't. It's impossible. If the angels will not intervene, there is no way to liberate the entire city. And you know they won't. Raphael and Michael made that clear, time and time again. We don't even know how long they will open the dome after we destroy the portal. For all we know, it will slam shut before we can even make it to the gates. I do not trust the Judge. She's shown that she's very willing to abandon her Guards when it suits her."

"But we have to try," said Malachi.

"You served the Judge for years, Malachi," said Ana, moving so she was halfway between Malachi and Takeshi. "Why do you still feel as if you owe her anything?"

"I don't," Malachi snapped, his clipped accent razor-edged. "But I owe the people who are imprisoned here because I went on a stupid, fanciful crusade to liberate their souls!"

I put my hand on his chest. His voice had risen, becoming loud enough to draw stares from the Tanner's guards. Worse, Treasa was standing not twenty feet away, watching us. She'd appeared out of freaking nowhere, and I had no idea how long she'd been there.

"We'll figure it out," I said to him, sliding my hand down his forearm to grasp his fingers. His determination to atone for what he saw as his responsibility in trapping countless tortured souls in the city was what had caused him to pull away from me and into himself. It was part of what had made him vulnerable to the Mazikin, the thing they'd used to ensnare him. But though I'd come to the city only for him, I couldn't help but share his desire to do something for the others. Malachi was my top priority, but he wasn't my only consideration. "We'll do everything we can. Maybe the Tanner will help. He said he wants his people to get out."

I looked to Ana for support, but she was shaking her head. "I don't see how it's possible to free everyone in the city," she said, shooting Malachi an apologetic look. "And it wasn't part of the conditions the Judge set. We need to focus on the mission—and then on getting ourselves out. I don't want to be trapped here forever."

"Let's head out!" roared the Tanner. We looked up to see that he had emerged from his chamber wearing a full set of leather armor and carrying a heavy spike-studded mace and a long knife. His cheeks and lips were flushed, like he'd been standing near a fire.

As we lined up to descend deeper into the tunnels, I edged close to Takeshi. "Do you have the grenades?" I whispered in his ear. To my knowledge, he hadn't set any off in the square as we freed Malachi, but I dearly hoped he'd found a way to conceal them before being captured.

He glanced at me. "Had to stash them in the square when the Tanner's people attacked. No one will find them."

I was in shock. "Are you seriously saying we're going in without our best weapon?"

Ana's fingers closed around my arm and squeezed hard, a warning as Treasa walked by, glaring. I didn't look away. If the skinny bitch wanted to take me on, she was welcome to. The knowledge that Takeshi had lost our grenades had put me in a really bad mood.

My violent thoughts were interrupted as we were engulfed by the claustrophobic darkness. I had to focus on not twisting my ankle. We were single file, the Tanner's well-armed people in front of and behind us. My boots slid noisily in the loose gravel of the steeply sloped tunnel, and soon Malachi had slipped his fingers around the back of my pants to keep me steady. I was embarrassed and grateful at the same time. Ahead of us I could hear muttered conversation, but it was so dark and echoing that I had no idea who was speaking, or about what. We filed downward like that for several minutes before the trail flattened out. My hands skimmed along the rough-hewn walls of the passage, which were becoming increasingly damp.

"We must be getting close to the river," Malachi said.

"Correct," replied Treasa from behind him. I jerked, unaware that she'd fallen in that close to Malachi—and that she'd managed to get at our backs. I wanted to push Malachi in front of me to get between them. Malachi gave one of my curls a little tug, like he was reading my thoughts.

Gradually, the temperature in the tunnel dropped, and soon I picked up the faint sound of rushing water that grew louder the farther we went. Finally, the tunnel opened up in a cavern. A few of the men who had been walking in front of us held up lanterns—tallow candles in crude glass jars dangling from straps of braided leather.

It suddenly occurred to me that all the leather in the city probably didn't come from goats.

At the far end of the cavern was an arched doorway, and from the other side came the roar of the river. "We face a long hike upstream," boomed the Tanner over the white noise of the water. "The rocks are slippery, so be cautious. One wrong step and you'll be carried away. It's not a good way to spend eternity."

Since drowning couldn't kill someone here, I supposed they'd suffer all the pain of that experience without escape. I had to wonder where the river led, though, and if anyone had tried to get out that way.

The Tanner gave me and Malachi a shrewd look. "If you think that's a way out, think again. The Mazikin have thoroughly explored that option. The river flows through the dome—but living creatures do not."

So much for that. We followed the small crowd through the archway and entered the underground tunnel carved by the river. Our pathway was much narrower than the trail we'd been on before. I instinctively grabbed for Malachi's hand. His voice was in my ear a moment later. "What is it?"

"I'm not much of a swimmer." And now that I knew the river wasn't an escape route, it seemed even scarier.

"You're not going to end up in the water, Lela, so it won't matter," he said.

Ahead of us, the Tanner's people were already picking their way along the rocky, wet edges of the tunnel. Treasa had pushed her way in front of me and was now between me and Takeshi. It was like she was trying to keep the Guards from having the opportunity to talk or plan without her overhearing. I didn't have the headspace to worry about it, though, because I was too busy trying not to freak out.

All we had was a narrow lip of stone, about a foot wide and obviously man-made. The pathway to the palace must have taken years to create. The spray from the rushing river soaked my hair and face as soon as I stepped onto the trail, but my cloak was waterproof, so I wasn't too soggy, for which I was pretty thankful. I concentrated on my hands and feet, copying Treasa's movements. She trod carefully, gracefully, and deliberately, never making an impulsive move. As much as I disliked her, she was a good person to have in front of me.

I had no idea how long we traveled like that, single file, one foot in front of the other, conversation impossible because of the relentless raging of the white water that flowed not two feet below our trail, but after a while I grew numb. I began to fantasize about being back in Rhode Island with Malachi, about what we could do if we ever got a chance to live. We'd never had a shot, not even close, and I wanted a future. For both of us. I wanted to take him to the beach and lie on the sand with him. I wanted to buy him a Del's frozen lemonade and watch his face as the tart sweetness hit his tongue. I wanted to kiss him in the rain. So many normal, boring, perfect moments. If only—

It happened so fast. Ana's foot slipped on a smooth rock as we reached a curve in the tunnel, and with a shriek, she splashed into the current. In half a second, her fingers were curled over the jagged rocks as the river did its best to drag her away. Treasa and I started to reach for her, but Takeshi was there first. With firm hands, he grasped hers. Ana's face was a mask of fear, her mouth open in a soundless scream. "Try to get a foothold!" Takeshi shouted.

She shook her head, but I could see flashes of movement beneath the water. She was trying. Malachi wrapped his arm around my waist to hold me steady as I grabbed her sleeve and attempted to help Takeshi drag her out of the torrent. Inch by inch, we pulled her from the water, and Takeshi smiled as she grabbed a handful of the tunic over his chest.

"You're all right," he said loudly.

Her fingers tightened on his shirt as she pulled herself onto the jagged trail. But then her knee slipped and her hand jerked downward. Takeshi lurched forward and tried to catch himself, but his palms slipped over the slimy rocks.

And then he was in the water. Malachi and I caught Ana as she tried to dive after him, and Treasa crouched low and reached for Takeshi's hands, which were clinging to the wet stone. In a moment suspended in time, he turned his face upward and looked at Ana. He opened his mouth as if to speak, but the river had other ideas. It ripped him from the rocky shore and into its white embrace.

Within a few moments, he was gone.

SEVENTEEN

FOR A MOMENT, I was stunned into stillness, but then Ana's shrieking brought me back. Treasa was holding her against the cliff wall, and one of the Tanner's stout men, who had been in front, was shouting at Ana to calm down. But her face was twisted with pain and panic. Malachi's arm was steel around my body, and I knew he wanted to get to her, but it was impossible unless we wanted to risk losing more people to the rushing water.

The hard-muscled man ahead of Ana began to drag her while Treasa wisely stripped her of the knives at her thighs. She probably saved the man's life, because Ana was reaching for them a second later, desperate to get free. She'd totally lost her mind, and I couldn't blame her. I steadied Treasa when Ana kicked her in the leg, making her falter. We all inched along, and for many tense moments, the only sounds in my head were the water and Ana's cries.

After what seemed like ages, we reached an alcove of sorts, a salt cave that was relatively dry, studded with crystals that reflected the weak lantern light as we pressed ourselves into it and collapsed. Malachi edged past me and gathered the sobbing Ana in his arms. She grasped his neck as he held her shaking body against his. The Tanner's people, men and women alike, looked genuinely regretful, if puzzled by the intensity of Ana's reaction. I was reminded of what Takeshi had said, how rare love was in this city. How cheap life was, and how common misery and suffering were. But Ana—she'd lost her Takeshi. *Again.* He'd been carried away while she watched, powerless. And one look at the river told me he didn't stand much of a chance. I tried not to picture his slender body pressed against the wall of the dome while the water flowed through it. Drowning for eternity.

I shuddered and lowered myself to the floor of the cave. I wanted to comfort Ana, but Malachi was handling it. His hand cradled her head, holding it to his chest. He gave me a sidelong glance so full of sorrow that it brought tears to my eyes. He'd lost Takeshi, too. Knowing Malachi, he was probably thinking there was something he could have done.

After a few minutes, the Tanner knelt in front of the three of us. He waited for Ana to pull herself together and notice him, which she did remarkably quickly, wiping her tears and releasing Malachi.

"We're going to rest here for a while. Bed down and gather your energy," the Tanner said. "Then we'll make a push and try to get to the palace." He held a metal object in the light of a lantern. It was a simple metal pocket watch, but not with numbers on it. There was only one hand, and only two hours were marked. Where the twelve and the six could usually be found, it said *F* and *B*.

He let us examine it for a moment. The hand had passed the *B*. "It's just after the black hour, when the Mazikin are most active. We can rest until here." He pointed to a spot where the nine should have been. "And then we'll try to arrive at the palace before the fire hour." He pointed to the *F*.

I nodded to show that I understood, trying not to make a face as his breath blew toward me. I had smelled a lot of foul things since arriving in the city, but this dude's breath? The worst thing ever. It was a strange combination of rot and sewage, and it matched his black teeth perfectly. He turned to Ana. "Shame about the Guard," he said, then retreated deeper into the cave, beckoning for Treasa to join him.

I leaned around Malachi and looked at Ana. "What can we do?"

She shook her head. Her gaze on me was dark and intense. "Follow through with the plan," she said, her voice flat. "And hope for the best. I will never give up."

I will never give up. It was what Takeshi had said to her.

"Get some sleep, you two," she continued. "And make each other strong."

"Ana . . ." Malachi began, reaching for her again.

She held up her hands to fend him off. "No. Enough of that. I'm fine."

Malachi pulled back, frowning. "You aren't alone in this."

She eyed the Tanner's people, some of whom were watching us with keen interest. "I know, guys," she said to us. "Trust me, I know. Just . . . let me be, all right?"

Malachi hesitated, then nodded.

I sighed. "Okay." I wanted to say so many things to Ana, but at this point, I was fairly sure every word would hurt her.

As Ana turned her back to us, Malachi scooted a bit closer to her, unwilling to let her go very far. Then he pulled me toward him. He'd shed his satchel, and he pushed mine off my shoulders and set it next to his. "Come here," he said quietly. "I need you."

I sank onto him as he sat against the wall of the cavern, his legs stretched out in front of him. His fingers burrowed in my wet hair, and I buried my face against his scarred throat. "I'm so sorry," I said.

"I don't want to talk about it," he replied in a strained voice. "I can't."

My arms tightened around his chest. "Whatever you need."

He kissed my forehead. "I feel stronger when you're touching me."

I tipped my head up so I could look at him. "Me too."

He stroked my hair away from my face. "I should have remembered that before I tried to let you go. Or maybe I knew it, and didn't feel that I deserved it."

"You were punishing yourself." He'd punished me, too, whether he meant to or not. Even now, it was painful to think about all those weeks we had ignored each other. I didn't regret the time I'd spent with Ian—he'd been a great friend. But if I'd had a choice, I would have been with Malachi. Ian knew it, too. I wish Malachi had.

"I was punishing myself," he said. "And I might still be if I hadn't realized it was making me weaker."

I stiffened. "So you didn't come back because you wanted me?"

He gave me a squeeze. "I always want you. It is a constant. But I have to atone, Lela. I don't feel like I can move forward unless I somehow make up for what I've done."

"Haven't you suffered enough, Malachi?"

"It's not about suffering. Or maybe it is, a little." He sighed. "I don't know. It feels so big that perhaps nothing is enough. So many people are here because of me."

"And a lot of others aren't because you stopped the Mazikin over and over again in the dark city. You never let them overrun the place." I took a breath and softened my tone. At some level, I understood and respected his sense of responsibility, his determination to make up for what he'd done. But most of me just wanted him to be able to rest, to have peace.

He closed his eyes and shifted his body so that we were touching from head to toe, until it was hard to feel where I ended and he began. He took my hand and guided it under his leather tunic, over the muscles of his abs, the welts of his scars, up to the slightly sunken mess at the center of his chest. He let out a breath and closed his eyes as he pressed my palm over it. And I didn't care that we were in a small salt cave with twenty other people. I didn't care what they thought of us, tangled together like this. I only wanted to be near him.

He leaned his cheek against the top of my head. "I'm so tired, Lela. I've never been this tired."

Fear slid down my spine like an ice cube. Every soul had its limit, and Malachi had been pushed so far that I wondered if he truly had the energy for atonement. "Rest, then. We have a few hours."

I bowed my head against his shoulder and monitored the rise and fall of his breath as he sank into sleep. As I sat there, willing him to be strong, offering him everything I had, I silently promised him—no matter what I had to give up—that I would get him through this. He deserved peace and safety more than anyone I knew, and with every ounce of fight I had in me, I would make sure it happened.

I woke with a start when someone roughly shook my shoulder. Treasa's pale face hovered before mine in the darkness. "We're leaving now," she said.

I blinked in the near dark. Malachi and I had slid down the walls of the cavern and ended up wrapped around each other, my head on his chest, and his head resting against our satchels. His arms were tight around me. I pulled my hand from under his tunic and stroked his face. "Are you awake?"

"I am now." He released me and pushed up on an elbow. We both turned toward Ana. She sat with her back against the cavern wall, staring at the ground. She looked hollow, like her heart had followed Takeshi downriver in that cold, merciless current. I wondered if I'd looked like that, right after I lost Malachi. Hesitantly, he touched her shoulder, and she didn't move. His hand fell away. I felt bad for him, because he only wanted to help. But at the same time, I knew from experience—her loss was so profound that *nothing* would help.

We got up and stretched. After hours spent in Malachi's arms, I felt renewed and rested. He'd said he loved me a few times, but now I knew it for sure. It swirled inside me like a bright white light. I glanced up at Malachi, and he smiled. "How do you feel?" I asked him.

He stepped close to me and spoke quietly. "Like I'm healing."

I put my arms around his waist. "Me too."

I let go of him and accepted the satchel as the Tanner strode past us toward the mouth of the cave. "We'll walk without stopping until we reach the area below the palace," the Tanner said, "and then we'll send a small party up to scout."

With that plan in place, we set out, enduring countless hours of hiking. The river grew wider the farther we went, but the current calmed as well and the roaring subsided. Ana walked in front of me, her steps steady and slow. She was eerily calm. And although I wondered how she could be so composed after losing Takeshi, I was glad she was, because we needed our Captain.

At long last, the narrow trail grew a bit wider, and the water flowed gently alongside us. Several yards ahead of me, a lantern bobbed up and down in a rhythmic pattern. "They've reached the palace!" said one of the men hiking in front of Treasa. "Go quick and quiet now."

We picked up our pace until we made it to a patch of land shielded by a rocky outcropping. The Tanner gestured at us to come ahead, and as we did, something brown and liquid splashed from above and landed in the river. Malachi put his arm around me and tugged me back, recoiling in disgust. The Tanner chuckled and pointed at several huge pipes descending from high in the stony ceiling, their wide openings directly over the river. "And that would be the palace's version of a sewage system."

We joined the Tanner at the wall of rock and peeked around it to see a short path leading upstream to another stretch of level ground. Sections of metal pipe had been piled at the edge of the space, right next to a large horizontal cog connected to chains and buckets that dipped into the river.

The Tanner wedged himself next to me and Ana, and nodded toward a narrow ladder that led straight upward.

"Maintenance shaft. For the ones who have to fix the pipes. Most of the buildings in this city don't have running water, but the palace does."

"Do you know where that ladder leads?" Ana asked.

"If my informants are accurate, it leads to a dishwashing room off the kitchens. If you go in at the fire hour, it should be quiet. This is when the Mazikin sleep." He held up his weird watch, and it was almost on the *F*.

"Then what are we waiting for," Ana said. One by one, we climbed around the outcropping, which shielded the trail toward the tannery from the view of any of the palace inhabitants that had to come down here.

Once all his people had made it to the cog-and-bucket system, the Tanner looked up at the ladder, which ascended into darkness. We couldn't see the top. "Go ahead," he said. "Get up there and send word about what awaits us."

Ana's eyes narrowed. "You're not coming?"

He shook his head. "I thought perhaps this was a task best left to the warriors." He gave us his black-toothed smile. "But I will send Treasa."

While the Tanner beckoned Treasa over, I edged close to Ana. "I don't trust her," I whispered.

"We'll cut off her head if she so much as twitches in the wrong direction," Ana said matter-of-factly.

We looked up the rungs of the ladder. "If we're caught, it won't be good," Ana muttered as she glanced at Malachi, who seemed to be assessing the Tanner and his men. I wondered if he was counting their weapons and watching where they sheathed them. He was the one I was worried about, too. What would the Queen do if she got ahold of him again?

Ana put her hand on my arm. "He can do his part, Lela. And you can do yours. Just follow my lead."

I nodded. "Sure thing, Captain."

"Let's go, folks," she barked. "I'm getting bored down here."

Malachi strode toward us. Seeing him from this distance reminded me of what had been done to him. He stood straight and tall, yes, in pants and a tunic that fit like they'd been made for him. But the skin of his neck was still pink with scarring, and those scars striped all the way up the right side of his face. I didn't want to see him get torn up anymore. I wanted to tell him to stay behind, but I knew he'd never accept that.

The three of us gathered at the base of the ladder, and Treasa joined us. "You go first," Ana said, flashing a poisonous smile full of warning.

Treasa regarded her with a steady stare. "I'm trying to help you," she said quietly. "And I'm sorry about Takeshi. He was a—"

"Don't say his name to me," Ana snapped. "Unless you want it to be your last word."

Treasa's expression didn't change. "Allies and enemies are hard to distinguish in this city, Captain. It's easy to mistake one for the other." With her satchel on her back and her knives at her belt, she mounted the ladder and started to climb. I got on it after her, with Ana behind me and Malachi bringing up the rear. I suspected Malachi had wanted to make sure Ana had us around her, and that he could catch her if she faltered. At the moment, though, she seemed pretty steady, like the hollowness inside her had been filled with molten steel. I wouldn't want to face Ana and her blades when she was like this.

My arms and legs began to ache by the time the cavern narrowed, becoming a vertical tunnel. When we'd started out, I'd felt strong, but it was amazing how quickly that vigor had drained away. Raphael had said that the city wouldn't sustain us, that we would gradually weaken. Maybe, even though Malachi and I could recharge each other a little, it wasn't enough to keep us strong. Biting my lip, I looked below me to see Ana, her face pale and grim, and Malachi even farther down, clinging to the ladder. I was willing to bet his heart was faltering, and I couldn't reach him. "You guys okay?" I called.

Both of them nodded, and I looked up to see Treasa glaring down at me. "Shut the bloody hell up," she hissed. "We're close."

When we reached the trapdoor, she pulled out a flat metal object the size of a ruler and slid it up between the metal door and the rock. A moment later, she'd lifted the door a few inches and was peering around. Then she swung it upward and climbed out. I followed eagerly, emerging into a dark room that smelled like shit and rotting meat. I covered my nose as I moved aside for Ana. "Ugh. What is that?"

"We're close to the kitchens," whispered Treasa.

"I don't want to know what's on the menu," I muttered, stepping over to the trapdoor and pulling Malachi up. His muscles were twitching, and he leaned on me gratefully. I swiped my hand over his sweaty face, wishing we could stop here and rest. But we couldn't waste the opportunity the fire hour had given us.

I closed the trapdoor and positioned the crude locking mechanism so it looked locked but could easily be pushed aside with jostling from below. Treasa gave me a nod of approval. She pulled a small lantern from her cloak and used what looked like a palm-sized safety pin to create a spark and light the candle inside. We were in a high-ceilinged room with a giant pipe running along one side, and a trough on the other. It was filled with metal plates and knives, all smeared with grime. The only doorway led to a primitive but huge kitchen with multiple fireplaces. Iron pots and large flat griddles were stacked in various places.

"The kitchens are supposed to be along the main corridor," whispered Treasa as we huddled in the doorway. "And the throne room is at the end of it."

"We should count how long it takes us to make it to the throne room," said Malachi, "and identify possible points of exit."

"As well as the location and number of the guards," added Ana in a flat voice. "We're kidding ourselves if we think everyone in this palace is asleep."

"Agreed," I said, drawing a knife. The others followed suit. "I'll go first."

Ana nodded. We pulled our hoods over our heads and crept through the doorway and into the quiet kitchen. Treasa held her lantern close to her body, where she could easily cover it with her cloak. Behind me, I could hear the quiet wheeze of Malachi's breathing.

We reached the main corridor and peeked out. The floor, lit with lanterns that flickered along the hallway, looked like it was made out of narrow stalks of polished white wood. My brow furrowed as I gestured at it. "I thought there weren't any trees around here."

Treasa gave me a look. "It's not wood, idiot. Why do you think they call it the Bone Palace?"

"Why do they have to be so freaking literal here?" I peered up the hallway and saw a big open room about forty yards ahead. It was lit with a blue glow. I looked over my shoulder at Ana. "What do you bet that's the portal?"

She nodded. Treasa held up a finger. "I'm going to count steps. Keep up."

I launched myself after Treasa, jogging silently, trying not to think too hard about what . . . or who, really . . . lay beneath my feet.

A soft cough of surprise came from behind us. I whirled around. Malachi and Ana were facing two Mazikin. They were dressed in leather cloaks, one red and one blue, and staring at us with their tongues lolling. The one in blue was leading a human in a matching blue cloak by a leash. If they sounded the alarm, we'd have countless Mazikin descending on us quickly. We had no clear way out unless we could make it back to the kitchens—and the Mazikin were blocking our path.

The one in red opened its mouth. Ana reached for her knives, but it wasn't going to happen fast enough. The howl pierced the silence—

And ended in a high-pitched whine as the Mazikin in blue fastened its jaws around the red-cloaked Mazikin's throat.

EIGHTEEN

IN AN INSTANT, MALACHI and Ana were standing, knives drawn, over the struggling red-cloaked Mazikin. The blue-cloaked human had been lurched to the floor as its master fought, and the human's hood fell back.

"Mom," I said in a choked voice.

Ana quickly cut through the leather strap of the leash that had been strangling her. Rita didn't back up, though. She threw herself toward the blue-cloaked Mazikin and clung to its back.

Malachi tried to lift my mom off the pile as the red-cloaked Mazikin let out a gurgling death rattle, but Rita clawed at him and he let go quickly. The blue-cloaked Mazikin raised its head. It was Zip. She wiped her bloody muzzle on her cloak and whined. Ana knelt next to her and began to speak to her in Mazikin, and Malachi quickly joined the conversation.

I clenched my teeth. Hearing him speak that ugly language reminded me forcefully of those moments after Juri had possessed Malachi's body. I'd never wanted to hear those evil sounds coming from his beautiful mouth again. I turned back to Treasa, who was scanning the halls, looking like she was about to explode.

"We'll be lucky if that one in red didn't wake the guards," she muttered. "We have to get the carcass out of this hallway."

Malachi seemed to be telling Zip the same thing, because the two of them stood up, wrapped the dead Mazikin in its red cloak, and dragged it into the kitchen while Ana and my mother followed behind, using their own cloaks to mop up the blood left on the bone floor. They disappeared into the kitchen while Treasa and I haunted the corridor. A moment later, a low growl sent us scooting into the kitchen.

"The guards are coming," Treasa whispered as Malachi and Zip emerged from the room with the trapdoor.

"Food scraps," said Ana quickly, and when she saw my look of confusion, she added, "They have excellent senses of smell. We can hide, but they'll know we're here. Come on." She followed her nose to the source of the awful smells, a huge pile of rotting food at the back of the kitchen. Without hesitating, she grabbed a handful and rubbed it on her clothes. Trying not to barf, I did the same, as did Malachi and Treasa.

Zip had cleaned off her mouth and stripped herself of her cloak. She shoved my mother toward us and motioned for us to give her the same stench treatment, then loped toward the hallway. We crouched behind a shelf of huge iron pots and listened to her having a conversation consisting of grunts and coughs with several Mazikin out in the main corridor. Malachi offered whispered translation. "She's saying that she forgot her comb in the kitchens and came to get it. She says she stubbed her paw in the darkness and cried out, and is apologizing for bothering them. She works here, apparently."

Takeshi had told me as much. "Are they buying it?"

Malachi nodded. "They don't suspect her. They're actually speaking quite affectionately to her."

I let myself sag with relief. My mother edged up close to me, covering her mouth with her hand. *"Yo quiero que vuelva Zip,"* she said in muffled tones. *"Los demás quieren robarme los dientes, pero ella no les permita."*

Ana gave her a worried look. "Lela, your mother is saying something about having her teeth stolen—"

I put my hand on her arm. "Don't tell me what she says unless it actually makes sense."

Malachi reached over and tucked a curl behind my ear. I noticed he didn't disagree with me. "Zip's coming back," he said, rising from behind the shelf.

She joined us, and my mother threw herself at the Mazikin, wrapping her arms around Zip's furry neck. Zip patted her head lovingly. My mother had probably never experienced that kind of protective caring. Somehow, here, of all places, she'd found someone . . . or some*thing* . . . that cared about her.

Zip, Malachi, and Treasa conversed for a few minutes before turning to me. "She said she can take us to the throne room," Ana translated.

Zip led us back into the main corridor, and we jogged toward the throne room. The blue glow grew brighter, and as we reached the edge of the vast room, we could see light sparkling against the salt-crystal-crusted ceiling. On one side of the room was a semicircular set of steps that led up to two thrones, everything made of bone. The curved tops of the thrones were lined with human skulls. Behind the throne platform was a huge mosaic, colored bits coming together to form one giant grinning Mazikin face. I glanced at Zip, and she pointed to my mouth. I looked back at the mosaic and squinted.

"It's made from teeth," Treasa whispered.

And suddenly the reason my mother was babbling about teeth seemed totally logical.

We slowly edged into the room. There were two sleeping Mazikin guards leaning against the wall near the source of the blue light, which looked like a giant well, framed by a waist-high circular wall made of stacked stones. Pointing to the guards, Ana touched Treasa on the shoulder, and the two of them skimmed quickly along the edge of the room, drawing their knives. They killed the guards silently within seconds. Zip skittered after them and gestured into a hallway a few yards away from the bluish well—which I could only assume was the portal—and the three of them dragged the bodies into the darkness of the corridor. Malachi, my mom, and I reached the well as they returned without the guards.

I looked down into the portal, a swirling well of sparkling liquid blue about ten feet below the edge, lapping at the rocky walls. The gelatinous substance made soft slurping sounds as it moved in its slow circle, a beautiful sapphire whirlpool. I gripped the stacked stones, feeling the cold radiating up from the portal's surface. "What is that stuff?"

Zip was hooting and coughing. Ana leaned close to me. "Apparently that's a closely guarded secret. But look." She pointed at the bottom of the well. "See them?"

Deep in the blue goo, I saw . . . Mazikin. Lying at the bottom of the well, perfectly still. "Are they dead?"

"They're probably the ones occupying bodies," said Malachi.

So a Mazikin jumped through, and its spirit flew off to displace a human soul while its body sank to the bottom of this well to wait for its return. "What happens if you jump in there without a body waiting on the other side?"

Once Ana had translated, Zip shook her head, shuddering. "Then your spirit has no home, nothing to contain it. It leaves your body and is lost forever," Malachi said in a hollow voice. "Perhaps it is like the dark tower. An end."

"So I guess a pool party is out of the question," I muttered.

Malachi chuckled, and I returned my attention to the creatures lying dormant at the bottom of the well, cocooned in blue gelatin until they returned to themselves. I tried to make out each Mazikin's features, wondering which one was Juri. I wondered if he could feel our stares, if he had any idea how badly I wanted to destroy him. I wished Takeshi were here with the grenades, because I wanted to do it right now. But just as I was imagining what that might feel like, the surface of the portal began to hum, vibrations that made the floor shudder beneath our feet.

Zip let out a yelp and shoved my mother away from the portal, gesturing for us to follow. I heard Mazikin growling coming from the main corridor. As we ran past, I glanced into the portal and was filled with horror. The surface had changed to reveal a wavering, distorted image: a man, lying on a table. We were peering down at him from above. He stared upward, looking absolutely terrified. His wrists and ankles were tied. Next to him stood a few people, stroking his arms, but I couldn't see who they were . . . until one of them leaned over the man to speak to him. I recognized the black hair, the shape of his head, the muscles of his shoulders.

It was Juri, wearing Malachi's body. And he was about to send another human to hell.

My fingers curled over the rocks. I was caught, wanting desperately to draw a knife and dive in, though I knew that would never work. Juri tilted his head and looked up, wearing a wicked smile I recognized and loved, and I froze up completely.

His eyes narrowed and his smile faltered, almost as if he could see me.

Wait. What if he *could* see me?

A steely arm wrapped around my waist and dragged me backward. "There's nothing we can do right now," Malachi said as he pulled me into the corridor where the others had hauled the bodies of the Mazikin guards. Malachi guided me into a dark room, the first doorway on the left. My heart was pounding hard enough to make breathing an effort. Had Juri seen me? It wasn't possible, right?

Zip waited inside the small chamber, where blood was smeared on the floor. This was where they'd brought the guards, but they were nowhere to be seen. Zip closed the metal door after us, and Treasa held up her lantern as the stench hit me.

We were in a Mazikin bathroom. There was a row of holes in the floor at the back of the room, and the odor made me gag—though I suddenly knew where they'd stashed the bodies. They were probably floating down the river at this very moment.

Zip edged to the front of the room, farthest from the toilet holes, and picked quietly at the wall. A beam of blue light pierced the almost dark. Ana and Treasa leaned close. "We can watch from here," Treasa said in a bemused whisper. "They'll never sense us."

"What if one of them needs to pee?" I asked.

"It will be the last thing they ever do," Malachi said, holding up a knife.

All six of us huddled around the openings in the wall. Apparently, we weren't the first people who had thought this toilet room was a great location for spying. I had a narrow view of the throne room from between cracks in the bone paneling. This wall was about five yards away from the portal, which was now humming loudly. Several Mazikin had gathered around it, but then a rumbling engine noise sent them scrambling away. Zip whimpered as the noise became louder. A moment later a huge heavy mechanized cart rolled into view, driven by a chauffeur with pointed ears poking through its leather cap. The Queen herself lounged on the wide platform at the back, on a soft-looking mattress. Her belly seemed even more distended than the last time I'd seen her.

Next to me, Malachi stiffened and pressed his hands against the wall. The last time he'd seen the Queen, she'd ripped his heart out. From the fierce tautness in his muscles, I could tell he was trying to control his terror at seeing her again. I refocused on her, those black eyes watching the portal greedily. With the help of two Mazikin in gowns, the Queen rose from her cart and waddled clumsily on her hind legs over to the portal's edge. She looked in and licked her lips. I held my breath, and not because of the smell. If Juri had seen me, would he tip her off? Was there a way he'd let her know?

But she didn't act like what she saw in the portal was anything other than what she expected. She smiled down at it, baring her razor fangs and blowing a kiss to whomever she was looking at inside, probably Juri. Then she beckoned another Mazikin forward, grunting and growling at it.

"She's congratulating it for winning the lottery and telling it to obey Juri's orders as if they were her own," Ana whispered.

Now my hands were pressed to the stone wall. The mood in the throne room was celebratory, but somewhere in my home state, in the land of the living, there lay a man desperately clinging to his life. His soul. He was about to be lost, ripped from himself. And there was nothing I could do to stop it.

The lucky Mazikin climbed up on the stone wall surrounding the portal. It wasn't wearing any clothes. It stroked its own fur with trembling clawed fingers. Its ears twitched. My eyes burned. This was so many kinds of wrong. How had this been allowed to happen once, let alone a million times? How could the Judge allow these creatures that she had created to do so much harm?

My throat tightened as the light from the portal became a column of solid blue that threw dancing sapphire prisms over the room. They were reflected in the ebony eyes of the creatures. The Queen ran her hand over her belly, then raised her arms. When she brought them down, the naked Mazikin jumped into the portal.

I pressed my forehead to the wall and bit my tongue, trying not to scream with rage. I could almost feel it—the fight, the despair, the losing battle. I turned to Malachi and wrapped my arms around his waist. His arms coiled around my back and neck as we clung to each other. The jubilant howls of the

Mazikin slithered like snakes through the cracks in our space, winding around us. It only made me hold on to him tighter.

"We have to get them all out of the city," he whispered desperately in my ear. "No one can be left behind. Not a single one."

I nodded against his chest. "I know." I had no idea if it was even possible, but we had to try. No one who had suffered the agony of being sent to hell could be abandoned here. "I *know.*"

He held me as the yowls of triumph grew quiet and the light filtering through the cracks grew dim. When I finally pulled myself away from him, it was nearly silent again. I could hear each breath from our small scouting party.

Zip and Treasa were speaking quietly near the back, though how they were tolerating the stench from the toilet holes was beyond me. Zip was pointing down one of the holes, and Treasa was nodding eagerly.

"Oh my God," said Ana in a quietly disgusted voice. "They're talking about whether the Tanner's people can climb up through the holes. The Tanner brought rope."

"I'm glad we took the ladder," I replied.

"We should probably get back," Ana said, turning to Zip and posing a question in Mazikin. After Zip answered, Ana translated. "In an hour or so, the palace workers will start to get up and prepare for the Queen to hold court. This place will be crawling with Mazikin."

Zip slowly pulled the door open, and we all crowded into the side hallway, sucking lungfuls of relatively fresh air. We hadn't taken two steps toward the throne room when the portal emitted a deep, percussive thump and filled the chamber with blinding light. Zip's black eyes went wide. Without a word, she grabbed my mother and dragged her back into the hallway, barking at us as she fled right past the bathroom and out of sight.

Malachi cursed and shoved me back into the bathroom. Treasa and Ana dove in a second later, pulling the door shut behind them. Malachi covered my mouth and squatted next to the wall, pressing his face to the cracks. "The Mazikin that was just sent into the portal has returned."

"Already?" I asked. What the heck?

I jammed my forehead against the wall next to Malachi's. The mechanized cart roared into the room, bringing the Queen back, along with about a dozen others. They surrounded the portal as the light turned white, and with an odd sucking sound, the naked Mazikin shot out of the gelatinous depths, over the edge of the wall. It hit the bone floor with a hard thunk, already howling and gibbering. The Queen growled, and Ana whispered, "No."

The naked Mazikin got to its feet. It was covered in crusty gray stuff, like the blue goo had dried instantly as the portal spat the creature out. The Mazikin grimaced as it tried to scrape the junk from its fur. And then it pointed a shaking, clawed finger.

Right at our hiding place.

NINETEEN

WE DIDN'T HAVE TIME to run. The door to the bathroom was ripped open, and the Mazikin were on us. I drew a knife and thrust it straight up into the bottom of my attacker's jaw. The creature dropped like a stone. But the space was so small that we had no room to fight. Malachi's elbow cracked against my upper arm, making me drop my weapon. Two Mazikin tackled me, burying me in suffocating, reeking fur.

My face was pressed to the floor by a clawed hand. Malachi's boots were next to my head. He was still on his feet, and the yelps and screeches of the Mazikin told me he was doing serious damage. I couldn't see Ana or Treasa anywhere. One of my captors hefted me up, one hand clamped around my throat and the other digging up under my tunic to curl its claws against the fragile skin of my belly. It snarled at Malachi, who went pale and dropped his knife.

I shook my head, wanting him to keep fighting. But Malachi merely nodded in response to the Mazikin's order and raised his arms in the air, following me as I was lugged backward into the throne room, past the glowing portal. The Mazikin released my throat and threw me to the ground. I caught myself and started to scramble up, but the thing landed on my back a moment later, angling its claws right under my chin.

"Stay still, Lela," Malachi said softly.

The Queen stood right in front of me. Her skirts swished against the bone floor near my fingertips. The creature on my back grabbed a handful of my hair and jerked my head up. The Queen's coal-black eyes met mine. "Welcome," she cooed in an oddly human voice.

She grinned, sliding her thick black tongue along her fangs as she raised her head to look at Malachi. The three of us were surrounded by Mazikin, maybe fifteen of them, those who had gathered to witness the return of the lottery winner, who was shivering and glaring at us like we'd stolen all its Christmas presents. Which I guess we had. It hadn't been in its new human body for more than two minutes.

"My Juri. He is so cunning," the Queen said. "He sent this one back to tell me he'd seen *Guards* in my throne room. Good thing he also knows where the spies like to hide." She grunted at the Mazikin on my back.

My captor wrenched me to my feet, pulling out some of my hair in the process. I couldn't scream, because the creature's steely grip was on my throat again immediately, cutting off my air supply as the tips of its claws dug into my skin. The

Queen leaned toward me until her snout nearly touched my nose. "Are you the one who stole my prize?" she said, her black canine lips shaping around the words. "Did you come to my domain just to steal him?"

I tried not to look at Malachi, but I couldn't help it. There were Mazikin on either side of him, their knives pressed to his neck, his chest, his stomach, his back. His arms were up, hands empty and helpless. And his eyes were on me. The Queen followed the direction of my gaze and smiled. "I thought I might have lost you forever," she said to him, almost lovingly. "I'm so glad you came back."

Awkwardly, her belly leading the way, she waddled over to him while the others circled us on all fours. "You couldn't stay away, could you? You can't hide. Not you."

Malachi watched her approach. "I came to seek my vengeance," he said suddenly.

She snarled. "And her?" She swished her claw through the air toward me. "Is she here for the same purpose?"

He shook his head. "She's nothing. A slave who let me inside the castle."

I closed my eyes. He was trying to protect me. And when I opened them, he was glaring at me, warning me to keep silent. I couldn't have spoken if I wanted to, though. I couldn't even swallow. If my captor didn't loosen its grip soon, I was going to black out. My ears filled with a roaring, rushing sound.

And somehow, I still managed to hear the Queen say, "Get my silver-tips."

Hatred and rage blasted through me. There was no fucking way I was going to let it happen again. I stomped on my captor's foot, then grabbed its hand with both of mine and bent sharply, throwing the creature over my shoulder to the floor. I slid its knife from the sheath at its belt but didn't bother to kill it. Instead, I leaped at the Queen. I was caught midair by at least four Mazikin, who slammed me to the floor so hard that my vision went white.

When it returned, the Queen was leaning over me. "You're one of them, too," she said quietly, her voice shaking with eagerness. "And you came for *him*."

She made a motion with her claws, and I was pulled up again. This time, blades were pressed to all my soft spots, too, like they'd done with Malachi. "I think," the Queen announced, "that we should play a little game."

Her belly shifted, making me shudder. She saw my reaction and ran her hand over the huge mound. "I don't suppose you are a mother?" she asked.

I blinked.

"I didn't think so," she continued. "You can't possibly understand."

"Explain it, then." I was willing to say almost anything to buy us some time. I glanced around, trying to see where they were keeping Ana and Treasa, but I couldn't move my head more than an inch, because there were knife blades at either side of my throat and the back of my neck.

The Queen peered at me with her glittering black eyes. "Why not? It's better that you understand. You were sent here by *my* mother, after all." When she saw the unease her words caused, she tilted her head. "You know the Judge created us? She made us to be objects of love. She favored us above all, even the angels."

"You rebelled, though." As soon as the words were out of my mouth, Malachi shook his head slightly, his eyes going wide.

The Queen blocked my view of him. "Rebelled," she said with a growl. "I suppose history is written by the victors. And yet . . . I think the Guards are in a unique position to understand what it means to be a Mazikin."

She ran a clawed finger down my cheek to my neck, where my pulse beat wildly. From a few feet away, I heard a sharp intake of breath from Malachi. I wanted to see him, but I was afraid to move. "Don't you ever want to break free of her?" the Queen murmured. "Don't you ever wish you could live your life, without the shackles of servitude?"

"Were you a servant?"

She snarled. "I was a pet. There isn't much difference."

"You called her your mother."

She pressed close to me, until her belly hit mine and her breath was rank on my face. "She was a terrible mother."

I let out a snort, trying to control my frantic heartbeat. "I know the feeling."

Her eyes widened. "Do you?"

"I was abandoned by my mom."

"And did she imprison you under a dome, at the mercy of the elements?"

"No, she tossed me into the foster care system, at the mercy of anyone and everyone."

Her round ears twitched. "You're pretending that you know what it's like, but you don't. All we wanted to do was rule." She began to turn back to Malachi.

"You wanted to rule?" I said, unwilling to let her get close to him. "That's why you're here?"

She pivoted back to me, her wet nose quivering. "We were punished for who we were."

"You were created by someone just so she could love you. I heard you had the run of the Sanctum, too. And you must have. I mean, look at you, wearing dresses and speaking English and walking on two legs. You even figured out that portal. It doesn't exactly look like she locked you out in the yard on a short chain."

The Queen's ears angled sharply forward, and she growled.

I was getting to her. "You were created to be loved, and you were given freedom. And you basically took a huge shit on all of that because you wanted to be in charge. Then you turned around and started to imprison other living beings. You know, because you're so much better than the Judge. From where I sit, you're not exactly a good mother, either."

"Lela," snapped Malachi. "Shut up."

The Queen sighed. "You're not very interesting." But it was clear from the agitated twitching of her ears and nose that she was mightily pissed. The crowd parted, and to my horror, a small Mazikin came forward, carrying a cushion—upon which rested five steel-tipped razor-sharp blades. The Mazikin held me tighter as the Queen calmly began to slide them onto the claws of her right hand.

She held her hand up when she was finished, and the group around us began to hoot and snarl. "I'm feeling hungry," she purred. "Time to play."

She took a step toward Malachi. I lunged again, but this time, the Mazikin holding me was ready. Steel bit into my flesh, and clawed hands held me tight. The Queen smiled. "You love him, don't you? This Guard who made my children suffer, who left them in fear, who murdered so many of us. You love him."

Tears stung my eyes. "I love him. Please don't hurt him again."

Her claws glinted as she looked down at them. "You'd take his place?"

Fear writhed inside my belly. But my love for Malachi was stronger. "Yes."

"No!" roared Malachi. "She will not."

The Queen's tongue lolled with amusement. "No?"

"She was tricked into the service of the Judge, and she hasn't been a Guard for even a hundred days. She hasn't had time to hurt your children. But I have."

A tall Mazikin with a scar across its ugly snout stepped forward. It had been hovering quietly at the edge of the group, but now it put its arm around the Queen and hooted softly in her ear. Her black lips curled into a smirk. "My beloved Sil tells me this girl strangled the life out of his last body. He says she bashed Juri's head in. Tell me again she hasn't hurt my children."

"Not like I have," said Malachi in a loud voice. He looked pale but strong as she approached him. "I've done terrible things to them. I've slit their throats. I've imprisoned them in the dark tower. I've—" His words ended in a sharp groan as she sank her claws into the side of his face.

I struggled helplessly against the Mazikin who were keeping me immobile. I wracked my brain to find words that would get her away from him. But Malachi looked triumphant as blood ran down his face. "I killed your mate *decades* ago," he whispered. "Nero. He will never return to you."

She let out a vicious growl and grasped his face in both her hands. Malachi closed his eyes, drawing deep breaths through his nose. He knew what was about to happen.

And it was what he wanted.

I threw myself backward against my captors, kicking desperately, ignoring the stabbing pains in my back as their blades sank in a few inches. Sil stepped forward and grasped the Queen's shoulder, talking to her again. Whatever he'd said made her squint at Malachi, who remained perfectly still as she scored his face with her claws.

Then her hands fell away from him.

His eyes popped open, and it was easy to read the anxiety there. Especially when she said, "You are right, Sil. This is better."

She stepped toward me. Malachi shouted, "I pushed Nero through the doors of the tower myself. I watched the horror take him over! He knew he would never escape!"

She bared her fangs at him. "Then this is exactly what you deserve, Captain. You took my mate . . . and I take yours."

The sound that came from Malachi was pure pain. He twisted abruptly and gained control of one of his captor's daggers, which he plunged through its heart. But he was impaled with three other blades before he could draw it out again. He sank to his knees, his eyes round, blood soaking his tunic. His eyes met mine, and my heart broke as I read the apology and horror there.

"Hold him," said the Queen. "Make him watch as I eat her heart."

I closed my eyes. I couldn't stand his pain on top of my own. *You'll survive,* a tiny voice inside me said. *You can survive anything.* I knew it. I believed it. But I also knew this was going to go so far beyond any previous understanding of pain I'd had. I nearly gagged as I felt her rotten breath huff across my face.

"Please," Malachi said hoarsely. "Please don't."

She didn't answer him. Her claws stroked down my face, almost lovingly. I prepared for what would happen next, for the pressure and tearing as those claws ripped through me, for the agony of steel piercing my heart. A sudden peace came over me.

"Now!" a human voice roared.

The Queen yelped and spun away from me, and I opened my eyes to see the Tanner and his fighters charging up the main corridor, weapons raised and ready for battle.

TWENTY

I FELL TO THE floor as the Mazikin guards who'd been holding me leaped forward to defend the Queen. The Tanner, looking like a demonic Viking with his mace and his beard and his horrible black teeth, took out two Mazikin with a single swing of that heavy spiked club. Treasa was with him, and it struck me—she'd escaped. When the Mazikin had come after us, she must have slipped down those toilet holes and gone for help. But where was Ana? They'd been together, hadn't they? I scanned the horde of humans trying to fight their way into the throne room, but she was nowhere in sight.

Our Captain was gone.

The sounds of war surrounded us: roars and snarls and yelps and screams, human and animal, male and female. I looked around and saw Malachi, curled in on himself only a few feet away. One of the creatures had left its dagger embedded in his chest. As a guard hustled the Queen onto her mechanized cart and the rest of the Mazikin tried to keep the human invaders at the entrance to the throne room, I scrambled over and covered Malachi with my body. I pressed my face to his shoulder as my knees slipped in a growing pool of his blood. “Hey. I’m here.”

He didn’t seem able to speak, but his red-soaked fingers closed over mine and held them to his arm. As much as I wanted to protect him from the battle raging all around us, I couldn’t, not if I wanted to complete this mission. This was my responsibility now. I had to go after the Queen. I glanced down at the handle of the dagger embedded in his chest. “Malachi . . .”

“Take it,” he wheezed. He gave me a sidelong glance and a weak, pained smile. “You’d be doing me a favor.”

With shaking hands, I touched the quivering hilt. Malachi bowed his head and squeezed his eyes shut. With a huge pull, I wrenched it from his body, and he couldn’t fully contain his cry of pain. Praying that I hadn’t damaged him even more, I got to my feet. A flash of blue off to my right caught my attention. My mother and Zip were huddled at the entrance to the side hallway where we’d hidden earlier. I hoped they stayed put. Neither one of them was armed.

The Queen’s guards, including Sil, had gotten her situated on her cart. One of them shoved the chauffeur, who’d already been impaled by someone’s hurled dagger, to the bone floor. The engine roared. Staying low, I ran toward the cart, but a Mazikin leaped for my throat right as I was about to jump on. Its claws scrabbled at the sleeves of my tunic. I kneed it in the chest, then drove my blade down through its shoulder, into the center of its body. It dropped at my feet, and I yanked the blade from the carcass as the cart lurched into motion.

There were three guards on the cart with the Queen. I raced after the vehicle as it ran over one of the Tanner's men, leaving him with a caved-in rib cage, staring glassy-eyed at the ceiling. I hurdled over him and sprinted after the cart, which was heading for a corridor opposite the entrance to the main hallway, where the Tanner, Treasa, and most of the fighters were battling a dozen Mazikin.

It was up to me.

Two Mazikin guards were crouched on the rear of the cart, knives drawn. One of them hurled himself off as I got close, but I dodged to the side as he hit the floor and rolled away. Another guard held on to the Queen's mattress, bracing himself as I lunged for the cart. I blocked his blade with my bloody dagger and heaved my body onto the back. Claws slashed down but didn't penetrate my tunic. I sliced at the guard's blade arm, and he yelped, nearly losing his balance.

I began to crawl toward the Queen, whose focus was riveted on her escape route. The cart lurched suddenly. I peered at the driver—Sil—who was now under attack by a Mazikin in a blue dress. Zip and my mother had jumped onto the cart and were fighting him for control. Zip had her claws around his neck and her teeth clamped over his already-scarred snout as he tried to keep the cart moving. My mother was smacking at his hands and trying to grab the wheel.

My momentary distraction turned out to be a huge mistake. I flipped onto my back when I heard the growl behind me, but I couldn't block the strike. The Mazikin guard, blood soaking his right arm, stabbed me, piercing my shoulder all the way through with his blade. I screamed, drawing the attention of the Queen. The cart was slowing, but I couldn't roll off, because I was pinned to her mattress. The Queen snarled and began to crawl toward me, her silver-tips flashing.

I jerked my blade up, catching the guard in the throat as he began to pull his dagger from my body. His eyes rolled back as he tumbled off the cart—taking my weapon with him. I reached up in time to block the Queen's descending claws, but her jaws clamped down on my forearm and she began to shake her head. Her black eyes caught mine, and I saw the anger there . . . along with a hint of amusement. I yanked my arm down as I jerked up and head-butted her across the bridge of her short, wrinkled snout. She roared and let go of me, but my arms were too injured to allow me to fend her off again. I brought my knee up, but she threw herself on top of my legs and smirked.

Then she plunged her silver-tipped claws into my body.

Everything slowed down as my chest filled with the most unimaginable pressure, like it was about to explode. My vision turned red. My ears filled with shrieks, but I was pretty sure they weren't coming from me.

The pressure disappeared as a wild creature with curly black hair and flashing amber-brown eyes landed square on the Queen's back, pulling her away from me. Clumsy with her enormous belly, the Queen flailed and howled as my mother ripped off one of her silver claws and jammed it into the Queen's neck. *"Nadie puede robarle a mi bebé los dientes!"* my mother shouted.

I stared, unable to breathe or move, as the Queen's clawed hands scrabbled at the narrow blade now wedged in her neck. In the driver's seat, Zip was still wrestling with Sil. She was bleeding badly—it looked like he'd torn her throat open, and her grasp on his neck seemed weak. The Queen's writhing caught Sil's attention, and with a roar, he let go of Zip and lunged for my mother.

Zip wrenched the wheel before he landed, and Sil went flying off the cart. He hit a wall and landed in a heap. The engine sputtered as Zip swerved away from the exit and back into the throne room. My mother reached me as we bumped along. With soft hands that smelled like wet dog, she stroked my face. Still unable to speak, I looked up at her. Everything else was a blur. Only her face was real. I saw clarity in her eyes, and tears that fell hot on my cheeks like rain. She stroked my hair. *"Te amo, Lela,"* she whispered. *"Siempre."*

She pulled the blade from my shoulder and pushed me off the cart.

I hit hard, my head cracking against the bone floor. Nerveless, paralyzed, and slowly losing consciousness, I watched as Zip, her head lolling, her throat torn, gunned the engine. My mother gazed at me with a peaceful smile that lasted until the cart collided with the stone wall around the portal. With a crunching explosion, the back rose into the air, tossing Zip, my mother, and the Queen straight into the blue depths.

The first thing I became aware of was a warm hand pressed high on my stomach. I tensed.

"It's me, Lela," Malachi whispered, and I relaxed a little, drifting, letting my senses feed me information. His earthy scent was all around me. His arm held my back to his front, and his palm was right over the spot where the Queen had forced her claws into my flesh. I tugged my tunic up, noticing it was new and clean. Malachi moved his hand from my skin to reveal five curved pink scars.

"It was the worst of your wounds." He laid his hand on my stomach again.

I put my hand over his. "We're still in the palace?"

"The Tanner's people brought us in here to recover."

I shifted onto my back, every muscle aching. We were on a soft leather pallet in a cool, windowless room, lit by a single guttering lantern next to the bed. "My mom and Zip . . . they're gone."

He sighed. "I know. I'm sorry."

"Do you think it hurt?" I whispered as I remembered my mother's wide eyes as she flew into the portal.

"I'm not sure we can know."

I closed my eyes. "She saved me."

Malachi kissed the tip of my nose. "And you will carry that knowledge with you forever. Your mother loved you, and in the end, she gave her life for yours. You were the opposite of worthless to her."

A quiet sob escaped from me as he bowed his head, his arms tightening around me. I pressed my face into his chest and took a few deep breaths to steady myself. I couldn't afford to break down or dwell in it, not now. I touched Malachi's face where the Queen had clawed him. The wounds were merely scars now, healing well. "I'm glad they let us be in here together."

His eyes met mine. "I think they know what we are to each other."

"Is that a good thing or a bad thing?"

"Right now it's good." His nose grazed my ear. "When Zip crashed the cart into the portal, it stopped the battle. The

Mazikin were devastated by the loss of their mother. They were easily defeated after that. The Tanner has control of the palace now. We should rejoin them as soon as we can."

"Did you see Ana anywhere?"

He frowned. "Not after the Mazikin found us in the bathroom. I'd assumed she was with Treasa."

"What if Treasa got rid of her?"

"Do you really think that's possible?"

"Ana's been through a lot, and Treasa knows this realm better than she does. Or"—I paused—"do you think she might have gone after Takeshi, to try to rescue him?"

"I'm sure she's missing Takeshi, and she would definitely want to save him. But she wouldn't abandon us." He sounded so tired.

"How are you?" I asked quietly.

He was stripped to the waist, so I could see that his stab wounds were closed. I ran my fingers over the new scar tissue. At this point, there was more of it than healthy unbroken skin on his torso. I kissed one of the spots where his flesh was smooth, warm. Mine.

"Better now," he whispered. "Do that again." His hand slid into my hair, and I whimpered as his fingertips touched a huge knot at the back of my head. "I'm sorry."

"It's okay. I guess I'm not quite recovered."

He cupped my face, his thumb stroking my cheek. "Then maybe I need to work harder." He grazed my lips with his. "I like this. I like being able to give you what you need."

I smiled against his mouth. "You've done that since the moment we met."

He wound one of my curls around his finger. "No, I haven't. But I'd like to make up for my failures."

"I guess that would be okay," I said with a chuckle, thinking I'd like nothing more.

He propped himself on an elbow. "Let me start now?" His eyes, full of warmth, roamed my face. Slowly, he leaned over and kissed my temple. "She scratched you here," he murmured, his lips lingering on a spot high on my cheek. His breath was hot on my skin as he trailed tiny kisses down to my neck. "And a guard's claws pierced your skin right here."

I gasped as I felt his tongue on my throat, the heat of that touch sending tingles of pleasure streaking down my spine. I wove my fingers into his black hair as my heart beat faster. "How does it look now?" I asked, my voice barely there.

"Scarred," he whispered against my skin. "But no less beautiful."

"The same goes for you," I said. "Remember that."

He raised his head, and his dark eyes met mine. "I do, every time you look at me." And then he was kissing me, his lips firm and sure as he took possession of my mouth. I responded eagerly, welcoming his tongue and the taste of him. My hand skimmed up his side and over his back, across the places where the Mazikin blades and claws had pierced him. He groaned as my fingertips slid over the welts and shallow depressions, but not with pain.

"This feels so much better than when Raphael heals us," he said.

"I was thinking the same thing. I wish this worked everywhere, and not just in this city."

"Tell me where to touch you." His fingers gently made their way toward the knot on the back of my head, leaving a trail of cool comfort. It was the opposite of Mazikin venom, spreading strength instead of weakness.

"*There* is good," I said in a strained voice. It hurt, but the discomfort was lessening with every second. "And . . . my back. My shoulder, too."

He laid his forehead against mine. "Show me."

I reached up to the strings that held my tunic shut at my neck, undoing them with fumbling fingers. I tugged at the material, moving it away from the itchy, achy place on my left shoulder. I was still mostly covered, but I felt like I was baring myself to him.

Malachi brushed his fingers over the spot where the guard had stabbed me. "You're shaking."

"I know."

"Because you're scared?"

"I don't know." I closed my eyes. "I am, but I'm not. I don't know how to explain it."

"I don't like to think that I'm reminding you of things you'd rather forget, just by being close to you."

I tucked my face against his chest. "I don't know how to do this. Any of it. It feels good. You feel good. But it also terrifies me."

"Hey," he said softly. "Look at me."

I slowly raised my head, melting inside at the sight of his harshly beautiful face. "I'm sorry for making this so complicated."

"Isn't being this close to another person always complicated?" He gave me a shy smile. "Then again, I wouldn't know."

Juri's cruel words right after he'd taken over Malachi's body came back to me. *Did you know he died a virgin, Lela? Twice!* Malachi was feeling his way through the dark with this whole relationship thing, and he was trying really hard—for me. I drew his face to mine, kissing him with all the tenderness I had. "I wouldn't really know, either. But I know that I trust you."

"And that is precious to me." He lowered his head and gently pressed his lips above the spot where the Mazikin had stabbed me straight through. It was a movement so full of adoration that a tear leaked from my eye. No one had ever made me feel this treasured. I wrapped my arms around him, never wanting to let him go. We stayed like that, shutting out the rest of the world, letting our fingertips and mouths linger softly over the broken places, healing each other the best we knew how. His hands skimmed over my bare skin, reverently, like he was mapping every inch. It wasn't about sex, though I couldn't help the desire I felt as I looked at his body, as I saw the heat in his gaze whenever his skin touched mine. That only made it sweeter, because I knew I wanted that at some point, someday, but neither of us would push it now, because this was about more than that.

The aching in my muscles subsided, the throbbing in my head faded, and the scars on my body went from pink to silver. One look at Malachi told me it was the same for him. And with every moment that passed, I knew he loved me, knew it was real. The things that were invisible in the land of the living, the quiet concern, the silent longing, all of it was tangible here, as good as stitches and antibiotics—the most powerful kind of medicine.

When we felt strong enough, we forced ourselves to get up, knowing the mission was not over. The Queen was dead. She'd been destroyed by her own portal, sent into nothingness by the swirling blue. My mother and Zip had made it happen. A gnawing sense of loss made my gut feel empty. My mother, who'd abandoned me and lost herself, had gathered enough strength in hell to save me. And now I would never see her again.

"How are we going to destroy the portal?" Malachi asked as I climbed off the bed. We were in an ivory-hued room, a beautiful tomb of bone built from the remains of humans who had suffered and died, again and again. It gave me the creeps. I wanted this palace to crumble.

"The plan had been to use one of the grenades. We had six left." I tucked a loose curl behind my ear. "But Takeshi said he left them in the square when the Tanner's people captured us. Do you think the Tanner would send a few people with us to go get them?"

I strode toward the door with purpose. As soon as we destroyed the portal, we could leave. I had no idea how we'd manage it, but I knew there would be an opening in the dome, and I was determined to get us all through it.

I yanked on the door. It was locked. "What the hell?"

Malachi joined me and pounded on it. A second later, it was opened by an armed guard, a burly guy with only one eye, his other merely an empty socket covered by a sagging lid. "You look better," he grunted, then licked his lips with his bright-red tongue.

"Why were we locked in?" I asked.

He shrugged, his daggers clinking dully at his belt. "For your own safety."

Malachi cleared his throat. "We need to see the Tanner now, please."

"Of course. He told me to bring you." He turned on his heel and stalked down the hall.

Malachi took my hand. There was a tension in his grip that increased my own alertness. The guard led us down a set of steps that opened up to the corridor, which the Queen had been trying to escape down. We passed an opening to another hallway, from which echoed sharp, mewling yelps and animal shrieks. The one-eyed guard grunted. "They're killing the cubs. Too many Mazikin in this city already."

The shift in power was startling but clear. The humans controlled the palace now. I wrinkled my nose. The whole place smelled like roasting, burning meat, which was strange, since the humans here didn't eat. We entered the throne room, which was full of activity. People everywhere. And the Tanner was sitting on one of the skull thrones, watching the show while the grisly tooth mosaic loomed behind him. The guard walked us over to the base of the wide steps.

The Tanner gave us a huge black-toothed grin. "Here you are! Treasa was correct when she said you'd heal each other." His eyes glinted. "How nice."

I glanced around. "Is Ana here?"

His smile didn't fade. "Treasa was the last to see her."

"What does that mean?"

He arched an eyebrow. "It means exactly that."

I crossed my arms over my chest. "I need to know what happened to her."

"You need to know?" He chuckled. "Are you in charge, little girl?"

"Not of you, but I am the ranking Guard now, and we have a mission—we need to destroy the portal as soon as possible so all of us can leave the city."

He stared at me for a moment, and then that phlegmy laugh boiled up from his throat. He slapped his thigh and stomped his foot, drawing questioning gazes from the humans who had been mopping the floors and sweeping up rubble from our earlier battle. "Oh, we're not going to destroy the portal," he said between wheezing chortles.

Icy fear sluiced through my veins. "What? You said you wanted your people to be free. Destroying the portal is the way to do it. The dome will open."

He shook his head, and his smile turned nasty. "No, my girl. The portal itself is the way to escape."

"You . . . can't get out that way," I said, confusion making me stammer. "You're . . . human."

"Am I?" He ran his creepy red tongue over his black teeth. "I've been here for so long that I've forgotten what that means." He patted his belly as it growled.

That sound was the key I needed to unlock a new, horrible understanding.

The city won't nourish you, Raphael had said. But the Tanner . . . he'd grown hungry.

He *belonged* here.

"How long have you been like this?" I asked, hating the tremors in my voice.

"So long," he said with a sigh. "And my best men, they're like me. Good thing we have an endless supply of meat." He gestured at the main corridor as a cowed-looking Mazikin, its ears pressed back against its head, wheeled in a huge cart, atop which lay what appeared to be a roasted carcass . . . and it definitely did not look like a goat.

This was why the Tanner's people looked so strong, so hardy in a city that sapped the strength out of its human inhabitants. They'd let the city own their souls, and then they'd eaten what it had to offer.

"You've turned into one of them," Malachi said, his voice cold with hatred. "You might not look like an animal, but that's exactly what you are."

"I suppose so," the Tanner said, though he didn't look sad about it. "But I think it's time for a fresh start." His eyes lit on the portal. "I plan to make that start in the land of the living. It's high time I returned. Thank you for helping me."

Malachi and I flinched as steel pressed to our necks and chests. Guards surrounded us as the Tanner slowly descended the steps, looking every inch the malicious predator, his ruby lips moist and gleaming. "And thank you in advance for providing our entertainment as we wait for our ticket out of this place."

TWENTY-ONE

MALACHI AND I CURLED against each other within a heavy metal cage in a corner of the throne room, where we'd been brought to wait as the Tanner and his people chowed down on their feast. Malachi held me snug between his legs, his arms wrapped firmly around me, my hands over his. It was partly because there was barely room for the two of us in here and partly because we felt stronger this way.

As the minutes and hours passed, humans arrived in a steady stream. The Tanner must have sent word, because they were crowding in from the main corridor, probably having hiked along the underground trail near the river from the tannery. Many of them had the same weirdly crimson lips, men and women who eagerly eyed the meat and leaped at scraps thrown from the Tanner's carts.

Chained outside our enclosure was Sil, his thick, hairy wrists and ankles bound, his snout still oozing blood from Zip's earlier attack. He glared at us with a hatred so intense I could almost feel the burn. Malachi ignored Sil, one of his oldest enemies; he was too busy watching his new enemies.

The Tanner sat on his throne, tearing his way through a platter of meat, and several of his men sat around him, gnawing at bones he tossed away. I squeezed Malachi's hand. "I feel so stupid for thinking he was an ally."

"We had no idea it was possible for a human to actually turn into a Mazikin, Lela." He drew me closer. "Focus on what's next, not what came before." He kissed my temple. It didn't make me feel any better. We were in a terrible situation that was obviously about to get worse, and I had no idea how to get out of it—or how to protect him.

Treasa stood next to the Tanner's throne, wiping his mouth between bites. She saw Malachi staring and nudged the Tanner with her elbow. He smirked. "Don't look so impatient, Captain," he called. "I'm nearly finished with my meal, and then you can put on a show."

He gestured to his guards, who grabbed Sil by the ankles and dragged him away from the pen, to the center of the throne-room floor. The Tanner looked down at him fondly. "I've dreamed of meeting you like this, old friend," he said to the Mazikin. "Every time you lorded it over me, delivering your orders from the Queen. I've wanted you on a leash for the longest time."

"The Mazikin will never let you keep the Bone Palace," Sil snarled in guttural English. "Ibram will come, and he will bring his enforcement squad."

The Tanner laughed. “You’ve been blinded by your position of power, so close to the Queen,” he said. “I’ve already sent word to the Mazikin enforcers in the city that she’s dead, that I control the portal. They’re perfectly willing to work with me. Ibram was quick to pledge his loyalty in exchange for another trip to the land of the living.”

“But you will not fool Juri,” Sil roared. “You may be able to possess a live body, but Juri will not let you keep it for long. He can see who enters the portal. He’ll know.”

The Tanner nodded. “So imagine how eager he’ll be to cooperate when he knows how easily I can destroy *his* body. I’ve got the tools. I could fish him out of the well and drive a dagger right through his heart.” He grinned when he saw the realization in Sil’s eyes. “You Mazikin live such incredibly long lives. Far longer than humans in the land of the living. Juri might enjoy being human, but he won’t want to spend the rest of his existence in the same body as it grows old and sick. He’ll need to trade up, and in the meantime, he’ll give a lot in exchange for the safety of his hairy hide.”

Sil struggled against his bonds, baring his fangs. The Tanner leaned forward. “What would you give for a chance to enter the land of the living again, my friend? I can offer it to you.”

Sil became quite still, blinking at the Tanner. “In exchange for what?” he growled.

“Defeat the Guards and you can have your pick of bodies. I promise you.” The Tanner waved a broad hand at us, and Malachi cursed under his breath.

“You want me to fight both of them?” Sil asked, his ears twitching.

"One at a time." The Tanner's gaze flicked between me and Malachi. "So they can watch each other die."

"I'll go first," I whispered. "I—"

"Stop it." Malachi gave me a sharp squeeze. "One of us should stay whole for as long as possible, and that's you."

I pressed my face into his neck, feeling the pulse there, steady thumps followed by a few weak skips.

"They're coming," Malachi murmured.

Tears welled in my eyes as the crowd parted to form a path between our cage and the spot in front of the throne where Sil lay. I couldn't let this happen. I couldn't watch Malachi be hurt again. "I know this seems stupid and all that, but I need you to let me fight first," I babbled, putting my fingers over his lips when he started to argue. "See if you can get free. See if you can make it back to—"

"The Captain will go first!" called Treasa in a loud, clear voice.

Even though both Malachi and I had been given that title at various times, I knew exactly who she was referring to.

The Tanner frowned. "I think the girl should—"

"She wouldn't last two seconds." Treasa smirked. "It wouldn't be that entertaining. Let her watch Sil disembowel her love."

The Tanner stroked his hand down her arm and gave her an admiring look. "Feeling hungry yet, dear?"

She smiled, something cold glittering in her eyes. "I'm getting there."

I shuddered and held Malachi tight, all my systems switching into panic mode. "Can you beat him?" I whispered.

"I don't know," he said as he bowed his head into my hair. "But I'll try."

"Remove them from the cage," said the Tanner.

Treasa brushed her fingers against his face. "Allow me." She stalked toward us.

"Don't watch." Malachi tipped my face up to his. "And no matter what they do to me, remind yourself that I will survive." He smiled, like this was nothing, like everything was simple, but I could see the exhaustion that shadowed his face. "Then you can fix me up."

Before I could reply, his lips descended on mine, desperate and hard. His words might have been light, but his kiss told me he didn't want to let go. His fingers clutched at my skin, a bruising pressure that I welcomed and returned. Our cage door swung open, and Treasa stood before us. "Your opponent awaits, Captain."

Malachi kissed my forehead and released me. "Will I have a weapon?" he asked as he crawled from the cage and stood up.

Treasa shook her head.

I followed him out of the cage, using all my energy to hold myself together. I didn't want to make this even harder by losing my shit while he fought. I would *not* distract him. The other guards surrounded Malachi and led him to the spot where Sil was bound. They formed a large circle around the two enemies. Treasa took me by the shoulders and began to guide me toward them. I flinched away from her, but she wrenched one of my arms behind my back and forced me across the floor until we came to a stop in the middle of the crowd, halfway between the portal and the throne. Behind it, the giant Mazikin grinned down from its mosaic, and I realized how naive I'd been; to think the Mazikin were the only evil creatures in this city.

The Tanner and his men pressed in closer. Looking over the crowd, the Tanner's face lit up when he spotted Treasa. He waved her forward, but she merely nodded at him and grabbed my chin, forcing it up so I could see Malachi facing off with Sil from between the shoulders of the men in front of us. A guard was unlocking the shackles on the creature's feet. Sil's hands were already free and scrabbling at the bone floor, his razor-sharp claws leaving long divots. Malachi stood watching, his pink and silver scars standing out on his olive skin. His expression was one I'd seen him wear so many times before. Utter calm, total concentration. The spider waiting for the vibration in its web.

And then Sil's feet were free. He leaped at Malachi, who quickly sidestepped him, sending him barreling into the Tanner's men, who pounded on the beast and shoved him back into the circle. Their attention was entirely riveted on the action, their eyes alight with bloodlust. It made me want to scream. Or stab someone. I glanced over my shoulder at Treasa. Her gaze didn't leave the fight as she pressed something small and cold into my palm.

My heart stopped as my fingers closed around it.

"Eyes front," she hissed.

I obeyed her and nearly cried out as Sil swiped at Malachi, leaving four red gashes across his forearm. Malachi grimaced in pain before blocking another slash and kneeing Sil in the bottom of his jaw, then driving his elbow into the top of the beast's head. But as Sil fell, he raked his claws along Malachi's thigh. Malachi's pants were instantly soaked with blood, and he fell to one knee, within reach of Sil's snapping teeth. They closed around Malachi's wrist and jerked him toward the floor, where the two opponents became a blur of blood and hatred.

Malachi was going to get ripped to shreds.

I lunged forward, only to be pulled back almost instantly by Treasa. "No, you little idiot. Go now. Ana said you'd know what to do with it."

I whirled all the way around, gaping at her as she released my arm. "What did you say? Where's Ana?"

"She was injured when she fell through the toilet hole, but she's alive."

"Why should I believe you?"

"Believe me or not. I really don't care." Her gaze flicked over my shoulder at the fight. "This is your chance," she hissed, nodding toward the grenade I now clutched against my chest. "Takeshi said it was powerful, and Ana said you could use it to get us all out of here." She raised a pale eyebrow. "Were they lying?"

A million questions flew through my mind, about Ana and Takeshi, about Treasa. But then Malachi shouted with agony from behind me, and I knew I had a choice. Try to save him . . . or take this chance to destroy the portal. I shoved past Treasa, away from the fight and toward the swirling, shimmering blue. There were so many humans gathered to watch the carnage that everyone was pressed back to front and shoulder to shoulder, but they seemed too distracted by the brawl to pay attention to me. I could see glimpses of the portal's wall not ten yards away. The crowd was sparser there—no one wanted to risk falling in and losing their soul.

I knew that once I pushed the button on the grenade, I had about ten seconds to get clear, or else I'd probably be destroyed by the explosion. That might not be a bad thing—if

I was blown up, I'd appear at the city gates as Raphael opened the dome. It would be easy to get out.

The problem? It would mean leaving Malachi to fend for himself. And there was no way I was going to do that. Which meant I had to wait until the last possible second to push the button. And then I had to run—and to try to get Malachi to safety. From the ravenous cheers behind me, I knew he was suffering. I knew he was hurt. It only made me more determined.

So determined that I didn't see the looming shape that blocked my way until I ran into it, face-first.

The Tanner leaned down, his hot, rank breath right in my face. "What are you doing, little girl?" His huge hand clamped itself around my neck as he scanned the crowd. "What have you done with Treasa? How did you get away from her?"

He squeezed, turning my world red. I focused everything I had on keeping my fingers closed tight around the tiny globe in my fist. He didn't seem to know I had it, which was my only advantage at the moment. Well . . . not the *only* one. I opened my mouth like I was trying to say something, and his grip loosened.

"Thanks," I said, sucking in a huge breath. And then I kneed him in the balls. His eyes went round, the veins at his temples bulging. As the crowd shrieked and Sil roared, I threw myself to the floor and skidded along the smooth surface, dodging the red-faced Tanner as he grabbed for me. I scrambled along on all fours, keeping low as he shouted for someone to stop me, his words lost in the snarls and cheers from the mob. His heavy footsteps shook the ground as he chased me. I reached the wall of the portal just as the Tanner plowed into me, crunching me against the stones. Searing pain zapped through my ribs, and my fingers tingled and went numb.

The grenade rolled to the floor. The Tanner grabbed a fistful of my tunic and dragged me off the wall. I went limp, pitching forward, my head lolling as I frantically searched for the small black sphere. Finally, I found it, right next to the portal wall. I kicked at the Tanner, forcing him to pay attention to my feet, while I swiped it off the floor.

With a grunt, he lifted me in the air. My body felt like it was being broken in half as he hefted me over his head. I heard someone calling my name, but it sounded so far away, like a voice from a dream. I stared up at the bluish salt crystals on the distant ceiling.

"You wanted to get to this portal so badly, little girl. Well, here you are," said the Tanner between rattling breaths. "I'll let *it* deal with you."

I craned my neck, trying to get one last view of Malachi, but the crowd was too thick. A few people were now facing us, watching with fascination. The Tanner took a step toward the whirlpool, bracing as he prepared to toss me in.

And I was overcome by the same impulse I'd had so many times in my life. *Survive.* Fight back. It was the same feeling I'd had that night I'd retaken control of my body and myself after months of abuse from Rick. It was the same thing that drove me to slam a rock into Juri's head in the dark city. I had never surrendered, and I wouldn't let this evil bastard be the first one to make me. I reached back and grabbed two handfuls of the Tanner's tunic right as he hurled me forward. My fingers curled tight, securing the grenade between my palm and his sleeve. He staggered against the wall as my body flew over his head and crashed against the inside of the portal, a few feet above the deadly gelatinous goo. Beneath me, the lifeless, soulless bodies of my mother, Zip, and the Queen swirled slowly. My mother's hair billowed around her like a cloud. Her eyes were wide open.

The Tanner grimaced, trying to pry my white-knuckled fingers from his tunic as all my weight pulled him down. He was a huge, burly man, but I wasn't a waif. I slammed my toes against the stone wall, digging them into the cracks and using my leverage to drag him toward me. My eyes met his. "If I'm going in, you are too," I said, a grim sense of victory filling me like a raging flood. I didn't care if I was about to lose my soul forever—as long as he went down with me.

"Guards!" he called out, but from somewhere above and beyond me, I heard the sound of cheering and a high-pitched yelp.

I pushed all worries for Malachi away and yanked on the Tanner, succeeding in pulling him a few inches farther over the edge. "Come on," I huffed. "You wanted to escape through the portal. This is your chance."

But he was loosening my grip. With a crack, he broke one of my fingers. Pain blazed along the top of my hand. He broke a second finger with a crunching twist, and my hand fell limp. My other hand, the one still holding on to him and to the grenade, began to slip. He gave a pained chuckle as he reached for it. "What do you have here, little girl?"

He grinned, showing me all his black teeth. But then that smile vanished, replaced by a grimace of fear. Malachi landed on the portal wall like some kind of avenging demon, covered in blood, his eyes dark with fury. His muscles stood out in sharp relief as he raised his arm and hurled one, two, three blades into the Tanner's body, each movement sending ruby droplets raining down on me. The knives hit with deep thumps, penetrating the man's tunic and his flesh. The Tanner let out a strangled groan as his muscles went slack. Malachi's gaze locked with mine.

And then I was falling.

TWENTY-TWO

INSTINCTIVELY, I CLUTCHED AT the grenade as I slipped, and one of my fingers sank down on the button.

Instead of plunging into the blue goo, though, I slammed into the portal wall, arms and legs flailing just inches above certain death. Together, Malachi and Treasa yanked me out. I had only a moment to see the wide-eyed faces in the throne room, the blood, the Tanner's body sliding forward into the whirlpool, and then I tossed the grenade into the portal. "It's activated," I gasped.

"This way," snapped Treasa as the Tanner's people stared in shock, unsure of what to do.

Completely unaware that the whole place was going to blow.

We lunged for the back hallway and bolted for the bathroom as Malachi counted down. “Six,” he said in a strained voice as we dove into the tiny, stinky space. Shouts in the hallway told us the Tanner’s men were in pursuit.

Treasa moved viper-quick, lifting the wooden frame over the toilet holes. “Only way,” she said—right as Malachi said, “five.” He swayed on his feet, and his shoulder hit the wall, which was when I realized that most of the blood he was wearing was his own. Sil had torn him open, and his strength was fading fast.

Treasa touched my shoulder. “Trust me.” Then she jumped.

I looked down with a flash of worry, wondering if Malachi’s shoulders would fit, but then he shoved me toward the black pit as he said, “Three! I’ll be right behind you!”

I plunged downward, sliding and falling and drowning in stench, my head and hips and shoulders and knees bumping against the slimy surface. From above came a massive bone-rattling explosion, and then the whole world began to shake. I fell forever, dimly aware of a flash of red fire, wondering if I was imagining the screams that rolled over me in a wave, and praying Malachi had made it.

I broke into the open air for a bare moment before hitting the water. It filled my lungs as I gasped. I spread my limbs and kicked frantically, unsure which way was up. Something splashed into the murky river next to me. I opened my eyes.

Malachi. Blood swirled in crimson ribbons around his body as huge chunks of rock landed all around him. The palace appeared to be collapsing on top of us. Forgetting my own panic for a moment and the fact that I was still underwater, I reached for him. Someone yanked at the neck of my tunic, and I glanced over to see slender fingers clutching my shirt. My head emerged, and my body heaved, water flowing from my mouth as my stomach clenched. Ana was kneeling on the rocky shore, trying to help me onto the bank. I jerked myself away from her and forced one word from my mouth. "Malachi."

I thrust myself back underwater, relying on sheer instinct. Malachi had lost a lot of blood, and I wondered if he'd hit his head on the way down. His arms floated at his sides, his head bobbing, his eyes closed. With my unbroken fingers, I grabbed the waist of his pants and pulled with all my strength. White-blond strands of hair on my periphery told me Treasa was also there, and she wrapped her arms around his torso and kicked upward. Together, we wrestled him to the bank, Treasa's sure strokes keeping both me and Malachi moving. With Ana's help, we pushed him onto the stone ledge. The cavern shook, and slabs of rock pelted the water only a few feet away.

"We'll be buried if we don't move!" shouted Ana.

"I'll take his chest. One of you take his feet," I yelled, barely able to process my own relief at seeing Ana here, alive and unharmed.

I locked my arms around Malachi's chest. His head lolled on my shoulder. Ana grabbed Malachi's lower legs and looped her left arm around them; her right arm stuck out at an unnatural angle from her body. We heaved him up, both of us groaning at his staggering dead weight. His sides, back, stomach, chest, and arms were a mess of deep claw marks, revealing torn muscle underneath. His left arm had been shredded by Sil's fangs. I could see his ribs through the torn flesh on his left side.

Treasa led the way, and we made surprisingly rapid progress along the path to the tannery. I was grateful for the physical effort and clear goal, which left no room for worry or indecision. While the whole world roiled and trembled, we carried Malachi until our arms twitched and the path became too narrow to risk going on. The water beside us turned white and frothy, and we looked back at where we'd been, where we'd jumped through the primitive plumbing system and into the river. It was a wall of rock now, as if the entire Bone Palace had caved in on itself and sunk into the ground.

"There's a cavern here," said Treasa from up ahead. "We'll need Malachi awake and mobile if we want to make it much farther."

Seeing as I was about to collapse under his weight and my own exhaustion, I gratefully helped Ana get Malachi into the shallow cave only a few steps from the trail. We set him down, and I pulled him close, holding his face against my neck. Treasa squatted at the mouth of the cavern and produced a small lantern from behind a pile of stones. She lit it with a flint lighter and set it on the pile. Ana scooted near me and laid her left hand over Malachi's shin. We gazed at each other. "We can both help him," she said.

I smiled. She loved him, too. He'd been her brother-in-arms for decades.

I smoothed his hair and pressed my other palm over the flayed skin at his ribs. My broken fingers throbbed but were already healing. "Sil did this to him. The Tanner made them fight."

Treasa looked grim. "If I had tried to stop it, or even delay the spectacle, the Tanner would have known."

"Known what?" I asked sharply.

Her eyes were focused on her slender white fingers. "That I am not his, and I never have been. That I have been working for a long time to bring about his doom."

"You knew what he was, didn't you?"

She wrapped her arms around her knees and nodded. "He had become very hungry," she said. "And he brought many men and women around to his way of thinking."

"Which was?" Ana asked.

"That there was no way to grow strong with mercy, or kindness, or patience, or sacrifice. That the only way to thrive was to become as brutal as the Mazikin." She met my gaze. "I believe in a different kind of strength."

I glanced at Ana, who shrugged. "I believe her," she told me. "She could have taken me out after she shoved me down that toilet hole. I broke my arm on the way down and might have drowned."

"I've never been your enemy," said Treasa. "Although I couldn't reveal my true allegiance, I have always been on your side."

"And your true allegiance is to . . . ?"

"I serve the Smith."

"Great," I said. "The guy who wanted to publicly torture us."

"He lives to protect his people," snapped Treasa.

Malachi moaned, and I held him tighter as I said in frustration, "We asked him to help us! I told him we could get his people out, and he stabbed me for my trouble."

Treasa's eyes narrowed. "You can't dig out of here or break the dome. He has tried all those things, determined to save the innocent condemned to this hell. But he realized that unless he wanted to give up his soul and become evil like the Tanner, there was no way out. He gave up on finding one a long time ago. When you showed up making those claims in exchange for his help, surely you realize what that must have sounded like to him. You wanted him to risk the people he protects for what he knows to be impossible?" She scoffed. "He has done everything within his power to preserve their souls and spare them pain—but also to spare their goodness. This is why he sent me to spy on the Tanner, to gain his trust and find a way to stop him."

"Were you in the alley the night he captured us?" I asked. "If you're on our side and you knew what he would do, why didn't you stop the ambush?"

She gave me a puzzled look. "I suspected you were here to free him," she said, nodding at Malachi, "but I hadn't seen anything to indicate you were here for more than that. I helped you because I learned of your desire to destroy the portal, but I still don't have any evidence that you're willing to help the rest of us escape this city."

Ana ignored Treasa's implied question about our intentions and turned to me. "That night near the Smith's, Takeshi caught her a few blocks away. By that time, you and I had already been captured. She told Takeshi she was loyal to the Smith, and he offered her a grenade in exchange for information on how to get into the metalworks compound to save us."

Treasa nodded. "I told him about the master key and made him vow not to kill my master."

Ana held up her right arm, and I could see the odd dent and the swelling. "When Treasa pulled me out of the water, I was in so much pain and so angry that I was ready to cut her head off. But then she pulled the grenade out of her pocket."

Treasa looked slightly peeved. "The Guard said it was powerful, and that I could use it to destroy the Tanner, but he said he wouldn't tell me how until after the two of you were safe."

Ana snorted. "He figured that if you were stupid or lying about being on our side, you'd end up blowing yourself up. I didn't know you'd still have it with you." She looked over at me. "After I broke my arm, I couldn't make it up the ladder, so I told Treasa to get the grenade to you, that you'd know what to do. She said she'd take care of it, told me where to find a cache of supplies, and said she'd bring you and Malachi back if she could." She winced. "And I was left to wait down here." She looked downriver, toward the place Takeshi had been carried away.

She hadn't had him to help her heal, and it probably reminded her of how she'd lost him as she sat down here alone, healing badly. I ached for her. Where was Takeshi now? Was he suffering?

"He was supposed to come back," Ana said in a small voice. "He should be here right now."

"What?"

She closed her eyes. "Nothing. It doesn't matter now."

I didn't know what to say, so instead I looked upriver at the wall of rock, now acting as a dam. The water level had already dropped well below the stony shore outside our cave, only a trickle where a raging current had once been. The avalanche of stones had completely cut it off—for now. "We're going to have to leave soon. The river's eventually going to bust through the dam, and I don't want to be sitting here when it explodes."

Ana gave me a smile full of sorrow and nodded at Malachi. "Then focus on how much you love him."

I ran my tender, healing fingers through his hair and pressed my cheek to his, letting my thoughts float to that dream I had of him in the sunlight, of him turning his face to the light and enjoying its warmth on his skin. In that dream, there were no circles under his eyes, no scars on his body, no echoing memory of pain and fighting. He'd laid his weapons down, and he was able to rest. Malachi was a warrior, but in his heart, he wanted peace. He didn't enjoy the battle, even though he'd always done his duty. He wanted a simple, happy, ordinary life, a dream he'd never had a chance to pursue. I wanted it for him. I'd never met anyone who needed it more. Whether I was part of it or not, he deserved that.

I laid my palms over his wounds, my thoughts turning those images over—wishing hard, but not for myself. Not for what I wanted from Malachi, only what I wanted for him. I smiled as I felt heat return to his skin, as I watched open wounds stop bleeding and knit themselves together.

He was starting to stir when Treasa cocked her head. "Do you hear that?" she whispered.

"What is it?" I asked.

Ana jumped to her feet, holding her right arm. "Someone's coming."

I held Malachi tightly to me. "Can you tell if it's Mazikin or human?"

She released her arm and drew her knife. Next to her, Treasa did the same. Hesitantly, Ana peeked out of our cavern.

Then she gasped and let out a sound halfway between a sob and a shout. She was out of the cave before I could say a word. I carefully laid Malachi down and grabbed a sharp rock, preparing to fight yet again. I stepped out of the cave, rock held high. Takeshi was standing in the slippery empty riverbed. Ana was in his arms, shaking as she clung to him.

He looked over her shoulder and saw me standing on the shore. "You've accomplished your mission. The dome is open. Let's get out of here."

Malachi was sitting up when we returned to the tiny cavern, running his fingers over his new, gruesome scars. Before he turned away to sling a cloak over himself, I saw a flash of despair in his eyes. I could tell that he was losing himself, wound by wound. My voice loud and overly cheery, I said, "Up for another hike?"

He leaned out of the cave and sighed as he saw Takeshi. "I should have had some faith," he said.

"When I saw the Tanner's map and how the tunnels connected to the river, I knew what I had to do," Takeshi said, releasing Ana but keeping his fingers wrapped over her badly healed arm.

Ana put her hand over his. "I agreed to let him go try to retrieve the grenades. I thought we'd need them to kill the Queen and destroy the portal." She looked at me. "I didn't count on you, Zip, and your mother taking care of the Queen without them."

"But I have them now," Takeshi said, lifting his tunic and revealing five grenades, slung diagonally across his belly, nearly covering the grisly scar. "And we can use them to escape."

Malachi accepted Takeshi and Ana's help in rising to his feet, then walked by my side as we ducked out of the cavern and descended into the riverbed with Treasa in the lead.

"Did you know the Tanner was evil?" I asked.

Takeshi nodded at Treasa. "I suspected, but Treasa confirmed what he really was. I knew you were probably trapped, and I'd been prepared to blast you all out of there grenade by grenade—but just as I got to the square, the palace began to collapse. I also heard a sound, like fabric tearing, that nearly brought me to my knees. From the southeast, there was a blinding light."

"Raphael opening the dome," I said quietly.

We were able to hike much more rapidly in the riverbed than we had on our way to the palace, when we'd been edging along the narrow rock ledge. Malachi draped his arm around my shoulders. His steps were steady enough, but he was leaning on me as if he was trying to save his strength—or maybe gather it. After a while, we passed the narrow arch that marked the beginning of the catacombs beneath the tannery. "Shouldn't we go up that way?" I asked.

Takeshi shook his head. "We can follow the riverbed all the way to the southern edge of the city, and it will be a straight run from there. It's chaos on the streets, I'm sure. We can take advantage of that and sneak to the gate. We scale it, and we'll be out of here."

Treasa stopped and turned on her heel, looking at each of us. I'm sure she was thinking the Smith had been right when he said we were only out for ourselves.

Malachi shook his head. "It isn't as simple as that, Takeshi."

"He's right," I said. "We can't just sneak out. We have to get the humans out of here. There's never going to be a better opportunity."

Takeshi's grip on Ana tightened. "There are perhaps a million people spread throughout this city. In every den, in the meat factory, in the streets. Most of them are weak and broken, and the ones who aren't seem more interested in dominating here than being free anywhere else."

Ana leaned on him. "We've completed the mission, guys. This is our chance for freedom, and you're willing to give it up? Because that's what you'd be doing if you try to liberate all these people. Think about how many there are. And what happens to them beyond the dome?"

I frowned. "You're willing to abandon these people here, just for a chance to save your own hide, *Captain*?"

"I'm saying we served the Judge for decades," Ana said quietly. "All of us. Except for you, Lela. You can't possibly know what it's like to work that hard, to sacrifice that much—and to still be treated like a pawn. We're not responsible for these people. The Judge is."

"Fine. I haven't suffered as much as you have. But I know what it's like to be abandoned." I pointed at Takeshi. "So do you. You know how much it hurts, to have your hope drain away day by day. How can you leave, knowing you've abandoned the people here?"

"I've done my time!" Takeshi shouted. "I survived only to have Ana back in my arms, and to get the peace I was so close to all those years ago."

"And what about everyone else?" I yelled back. "They haven't done their time? They don't deserve peace?"

Takeshi's expression twisted with frustration. "You say that you love Malachi. If you do, I'm your best hope. I can get him out."

He was right. I could keep fighting. I was willing to try. But Malachi was falling apart. He couldn't take much more punishment. I grimaced and put my hand over his, holding it against my shoulder.

Malachi cleared his throat. "Do you know how I spent my time while I was chained in that square, waiting for the Queen to do her worst?" He raised his head and met Takeshi's eyes. "I looked at the faces of the people. Each and every one of them, scars on their bodies, their backs bent, collars around their necks." He swallowed and squeezed my shoulder. "And I recognized so many of them. I remember cutting their throats in the dark city. I remember saying prayers over their lifeless bodies and believing I was freeing them. It was a beautiful lie, one I clung to instead of facing the reality. All I was doing was condemning more innocents to this fate." He stood up a little straighter. "I have to do something about that now. *We* can do something about it."

Takeshi stared at the ground. His hand was still curled over Ana's forearm, like he wanted to make sure she was completely healed. I turned to Ana. "You're my Captain. And I respect you. But if you tell me to leave this city without even trying to free everyone else, I won't. I can't."

"Neither can I," Malachi said quietly. He released me and slowly stepped forward, putting his hand on Takeshi's arm. "I believe we were chosen as Guards for a reason. We are stronger than most. We fight harder." He leaned in. "And we have never done any of it for ourselves."

"When is it enough?" Takeshi whispered. "Why must I fight for a master who has not fought for me?"

"We will not fight for a master," Malachi said. "We will fight for the ones who have been abandoned."

I laid my palm on Malachi's back, loving him more in that moment than I'd ever thought possible.

Ana looked conflicted. "Takeshi . . ."

"This is an impossible task," he muttered.

Malachi grinned, the scars on his face silvery white. "How many times have you said that to me?"

"Of course you'd remind me."

"And how many times has it been possible only because we were in it together?" Malachi asked, more serious this time.

Takeshi bowed his head. "This is a lot to ask."

Ana kissed him. "You know who you are," she murmured in his ear. "And I know who I fell in love with."

He closed his eyes and touched his forehead to Ana's. "Well. That settles it, then." He kissed her.

"We have to go back to the Smith," Treasa said, clearly pleased.

Malachi looked down at me. "The one who stabbed you?"

I nodded. "But Treasa trusts him and was working against the Tanner on his orders. He also happens to have more weapons and vehicles than anyone else."

"He'll have the best handle on what's going on in the rest of the city," said Takeshi as the ground rumbled again beneath our feet. "And we'd better hurry." He looked upstream, toward the temporary dam that held back the powerful waters of the river. How long would it hold?

We began to jog, following Treasa down the main riverbed and through a well-disguised crevice that connected to another tunnel system. Lit only by Treasa's tiny lantern, our way was jagged and slippery, and we hit at least one cave-in that required us to backtrack. Takeshi knew another way, though, and led us easily, his palms sliding along the rock walls as he translated every vibration. "A lot of people moving up there. It's going to be absolute mayhem."

"That might be a good thing," said Malachi as we began to climb a set of rough steps.

"We'll see," huffed Takeshi, pulling open a steel door at the top of the stairs.

The cool night air of the city wafted over my face, bringing with it the stench of blood and fear. Screams and explosions echoed in the darkness, along with a deep rumbling that coursed up through the soles of my feet. A sharp crack came from above us, and I looked up to see fissures snaking along the surface of the dome. It brought a smile to my face, especially as a bright light caught my eye. Over the rooftops of the buildings, in the direction of the city gates, there was a glow, and the cracks in the dome seemed to be emanating from it.

"We need to—" Ana began.

"Welcome back, Guards," boomed the Smith through his PA system.

I spun around. We were standing at the edge of the Smith's vast yard, right at the rear corner of the factory nearest the city wall and the dome. He stood on his platform, where he'd obviously been addressing his people, who were armed and at attention. And now all of them were staring at us.

"Seize them!" the Smith roared.

TWENTY-THREE

TREASA STEPPED IN FRONT of us, and as soon as the Smith saw her, he shouted, "Stop!"

The guards who had been about to grab us froze. The Smith came forward, yelling, "What have you done?" He glared at each of us, livid. "The Bone Palace is destroyed. The Mazikin are in a frenzy. It is only a matter of time before we are overrun. It will take everything we have to defend the factory."

"We've done it!" Treasa cried, a jittery excitement in her voice. "We killed the Queen and the Tanner, and the portal has been destroyed!"

The Smith swayed on his stumpy legs as the ground shifted beneath us, followed by more deep rumbling. "These damn earthquakes are getting worse," he replied. "I suppose you're responsible for that, too?"

Treasa looked stricken. She'd obviously expected him to be thrilled by what she'd helped accomplish, but he was so concerned with maintaining the status quo that he couldn't think past it. "We need to get inside and lock this place tight," he said.

"The river is dammed," Malachi said. "The Bone Palace collapsed in on itself and blocked it."

The Smith's ruddy face paled. "That river runs like an unstoppable force beneath this city. If it breaks loose . . ." We all knew what he was thinking. We were trapped under the dome. If the river burst free, would it flood the city? Where would all that water go?

"There's a way out," I said. "For everyone. We can leave now. There's an opening in the dome."

The Smith's bushy eyebrows drew together. "A way out? How can you be sure?"

I couldn't. All I had was the faint hope inside me and the light in the distance. I pointed to it, and he looked in that direction, squinting. "Because we destroyed the portal and killed the Queen, and because the Judge keeps her promises."

"Yes. The Judge is so benevolent." He laughed—a bitter, awful sound. "There is no telling what awaits us if we try to leave the city."

"You're right," I said. "But what future do you have here?"

He once again looked at the humans gathered around him, at those scarred faces and broken bodies. Within each of them resided a soul he'd deemed worth saving. "I don't know how to protect them if we leave the compound."

"You have vehicles and weapons. We can make a charge to the south," Ana said.

He crossed his arms over his thick chest. "The Mazikin will try to stop us. They're massing down there already. I've gotten word that Ibram and his enforcement squad are at the gates. You say there is a way out, but apparently there is some force stopping *them* from leaving, so it seems the Mazikin have turned their efforts toward keeping humans imprisoned alongside them—and punishing any who would try to escape."

"Maybe the opening in the dome is only for people," I said. "That's a good thing."

Ana nodded. "The Wasteland doesn't need any more predators."

"All the predators are in the city with us!" the Smith said in a strangled shout. "And they know we have the means to make it to the gates. The only reason they're not at the metalworks already is that we've put up barricades and traps, and they know we're ready for them. But if we leave . . ." He ran his hand over the top of his head and gestured at his people. "They could be torn apart. Look at them. They're not warriors. They're not strong."

Takeshi leaned toward him. "We can scatter the Mazikin," he said. "You've seen me do it." His eyes met Ana's, and he touched his tunic, beneath which the grenades hung. "We can clear a path. We'll help everyone get out."

"They can do it, master," said Treasa, moving forward to clutch at his sleeve. "We could get out. *You* could get out."

"I don't care about myself," the Smith said, and I knew he was telling the truth. The Tanner had been out for himself, but the Smith only wanted to protect his makeshift family. He rubbed his jaw and peered up at Treasa, a glimmer of hope in his eyes that flickered as the ground beneath us shook again, powerfully enough that the facade of a building across the street cracked. Heavy chunks of cement crashed to the pavement.

"All right. We could try," he finally said, nodding to his guards. "Nazir! Take a group to the garages and fuel the carts. Holloran! Gather everyone in the yard."

He turned to us. "You can take the lead vehicle. We must leave at dawn, well before the fire hour. We don't have much time." He glanced toward the east, where the cruel sun would rise, then back to us. "I'm trusting you with the souls of these people."

"Then we need to borrow a vehicle and make a little side trip first," I said, looking at Ana.

The Smith scowled. "For what purpose?"

"We need to get to the square." I laced my fingers with Malachi's and squeezed, a plan forming in my mind. "Everyone in this city needs to hear the good news."

I stared at the hulking beast, pulling my cloak a little tighter. "The biggest thing I've ever driven is a Corolla."

The looming vehicle the Smith had provided was the size and shape of a front loader, or maybe an industrial-grade snowplow. It had a massive scoop on the front and crudely fashioned rubber tires that were as tall as I was. It was the largest and most powerful in the Smith's fleet, and we would need it, because we had to crash through the barricades and possibly hundreds of Mazikin to get to the main square.

"Good thing Treasa's driving then," called Ana as she strode over to us from the direction of the Smith's armory, fingering the new blades at her thighs. Treasa was with her, and she scaled the side of the vehicle and dropped into the driver's seat behind a steering wheel as big as she was.

I craned my neck. "Are your feet even touching the pedals?" I asked as I climbed up the ladder on the side of the thing.

"You're funny," she said, and though her tone was flat, she wore a smile.

My grip tightened as the ground shook again. The earthquakes were brief but getting stronger and more frequent. At some point, the river would break free, and we'd either ride out on a wave—or maybe end up pressed against the dome, caught within a giant hellish snow globe.

The Smith's people were all around us, bustling in their preparations for the mad dash they were about to make. Everyone had a job—some were gathering the oldest and weakest and gently placing them on raised platforms atop the twenty or so wheeled vehicles that lined the block. Each vehicle was different, some with huge exposed engines, some with thick metal bumpers and shielded drivers' compartments, a few with plow blades like ours, and several wide flatbeds, onto which most of the Smith's people were climbing. Others were shouting orders and tucking weapons into their belts as they clung to the sides of the vehicles—these were the guards, the ones who would defend the vulnerable if any Mazikin tried to attack. A small group of men and women huddled near the destroyed fence around the yard, each holding a wickedly curved blade. The Smith had told us they were supposed to take care of those who couldn't make it to the wall. A quick decapitation would ensure that those too weak or injured would not be left to the mercy of the Mazikin. It wasn't an ideal solution, since those who died inside the city were much weaker when they came back, but it still gave them a chance.

He'd given us the use of his most powerful vehicle for one purpose—to make it to the city's central PA system. When I'd told Malachi what I wanted to do, he'd rewarded me with a kiss that I'd felt all the way down to my toes.

Someone banged against the side of the vehicle, and I looked down to see the Smith, a row of knives arrayed down his arms and around his belt. "We leave as soon as you return." His dark eyes met mine. "I'm entrusting these people to you, Guards."

"We will not fail," said Malachi, who had been given a new set of clothes and equipped with a holster for knives that crisscrossed his chest. He climbed up next to me, followed by Takeshi and Ana, who was still favoring her right arm.

The engine growled as Treasa put it in gear. The Smith grinned at her. "Bring it back in one piece," he shouted.

She saluted him, then gestured at us to hold on. Without giving us much of a chance, she floored it, and we went shooting forward. She swerved around the other vehicles in line, and I caught a glimpse of blurred faces, eyes wide and hopeful. The glowing light in the south tugged at me, but in the distance, I could hear the roar of a Mazikin horde. Treasa took a sharp right at the end of the block. Malachi's knuckles were white as he clung to the bar and laid himself flat next to me on the roof of the vehicle. Ana and Takeshi were on his other side, squinting up ahead.

A massive barricade, made of metal scraps and bones, blocked the road in front of us. Treasa pushed a lever forward, and the heavy plow blade hit the street. Sparks flew from the road as it scraped the surface, and Malachi threw himself on top of me, holding my head against his chest as we collided with the barricade, sending debris flying up and over us. We crunched over what remained and roared onto a street past the Smith's domain.

It was crowded with Mazikin and their slaves. Many of the humans were weighed down like pack mules with the Mazikin's possessions. They were fleeing south, away from the rumbling ruin of the Bone Palace, and they scattered as we motored up the road. Treasa hadn't bothered to raise the plow blade, preferring to mow through anything or anyone caught in our way. She'd been given one mission—get to the square and get out again—and she seemed determined to make it happen. Her head was low over the wheel as we collided with a mechanized cart that had broken down in an intersection. Metal shrieked as the vehicle scraped and skidded along the road ahead of us, finally careening onto the sidewalk as we barreled forward.

Through the windows and spaces between buildings, I could see that the ruins of the palace were giving off an eerie sapphire light. "Do you think the portal is still intact?" I yelled.

"Not if you dropped a grenade in it," shouted Ana as we crashed into a smaller car and went up on one wheel as another flattened the car's hood.

"The blue substance might not have been destroyed, though," said Malachi close to my ear. "We don't know what it was."

I stared at it, new fear riding down my spine. Then I reminded myself that the dome was open, for now, at least, and that meant we had to have destroyed the portal. It meant Juri couldn't possess anyone else. He might, in fact, be dead. The fight could be over.

If we got out of the city. Ahead of us, the stadium lights of the square were blinding. Mazikin scrambled from points west and north. A few humans wandered aimlessly, still wearing collars, while others lay destroyed on the street and sidewalk. It looked like a war zone.

"The Mazikin sought to punish all humans when the Tanner declared he had killed the Queen," Takeshi said, his face grim.

Treasa slowed as she entered the square, where bodies lay thick on the ground, and blood was smeared across the cement. She ground to a halt in front of the platform where Malachi had been tortured. As we stood up on the flat part of the vehicle's roof, the creatures spotted us. Some shrieked and dropped to all fours, scattering, but most ran forward.

"We have to keep them off of us," I shouted to Takeshi and Ana. "And we'll have to take turns." I pointed to the steps that led up to the platform. Malachi's blood still darkened its silvery surface. Malachi shuddered against me but didn't say a word.

"We'll keep them off you," Takeshi said as he and Ana leaped off the loader and began to carve their way through any Mazikin stupid enough to approach. Treasa hunched at the wheel, knife at the ready, while Malachi and I jumped from the back and onto the steps.

The PA system the Queen had used to address the entire city was only a few yards away. "Watch my back," I said to Malachi as three Mazikin rushed the steps from the opposite side, out of Ana and Takeshi's reach. "Then we'll trade."

He nodded and drew two knives, and he looked so fierce that the beasts slowed and began to circle him. I sprinted for the podium, stopping only to slam my blade into the chest of a torn-eared Mazikin who tried to get in my way. I grabbed for the microphone and pressed a button on the side, causing feedback to ring through the speakers.

I gazed up at the bright-white glow, the cracking dome, the carnage all around me. And I began to speak. "Attention, everybody. There's a way out of this city. Go to the gates in the south, where the light is. Help whoever you see. Every human needs to go to the city gates. There's a way out."

I lowered the mic to find several of the humans in the square staring at me, dumbfounded. I looked right at them and repeated the instructions, pointing toward the south. "Malachi," I called when I was finished. "Get up here and repeat that in every language you know!"

He finished off the last Mazikin opponent with a brutal twist of his blade and ran toward me, flinging a knife at an oncoming creature along the way and hitting it square between the eyes. He took the microphone from me and began speaking in a language I couldn't identify. I left him to it and headed down the steps, searching the chaos for Takeshi and Ana, who were nowhere in sight.

"They need help!" called Treasa, waving her arm toward the first floor of a building at the edge of the square. "The Mazikin took them that way!"

I glanced back at Malachi, who was speaking in a different language now, and he frantically gestured at the building, telling me to go.

I ran down the steps, leaping over bodies and debris, and saw a cluster of Mazikin, all wearing cloaks with black triangles on the back. Ana was on the ground, blood splattered around her, and Takeshi was in front of her. He had a grenade in his hand.

"No!" I shouted, throwing myself forward and landing on a cloaked Mazikin's back. I drew my blade across its throat and kicked another as it tried to stop me. "Get her to the vehicle!"

Takeshi had been seconds from blowing them both up—along with all of our grenades. It would have gotten us all to the gates, but not the way I wanted. While the Mazikin descended on me, all claws and jaws, Takeshi carried the unconscious Ana toward the vehicle. I stabbed and punched with all my might, taking out another and wounding one more, all while listening to Malachi's steady voice, now speaking Spanish, repeating my message to the people of the city. I only hoped they listened.

Fangs clamped over my arm, sending a shock of pain screaming up to my shoulder. I opened my mouth to cry out, but a clawed hand closed around my throat. I kicked my captor, but he deflected and gestured to two others. They grabbed my arms between their teeth and pulled, a grisly game of tug-of-war. A rending agony knifed down the center of my body as the Mazikin in front of me raised his claws, preparing to tear me to shreds.

Suddenly, the world heaved and shook, knocking us all to the ground. Rocks rained down, and the Mazikin who'd had my arms let go, yelping. I began to crawl toward the open square, stones hitting my back and legs. Then one hit me hard in the head. The cement beneath me was churning like ocean waves, making it impossible to get to my feet.

Arms closed around my chest and dragged me forward. My feet skimmed along the ground as Takeshi said, "I think our work here is done, Lela."

We were both thrown to the roiling ground as a fissure opened below the archway next to the platform and streaked its way across the square, creating a five-foot-wide chasm separating us from our vehicle. Malachi and Ana were already on top of the loader, though Malachi looked like he was about to leap off again to get to me.

"Get up!" shouted Takeshi as I felt a strange sensation.

Water. It gushed up out of the fissure at an incredible rate, flowing over my hands and soaking my knees. I shoved myself up and held Takeshi's hand as we jumped over the widening fissure, splashing onto the cement and stumbling against the side of the front loader. The engine coughed and roared as Treasa began to back it up. Takeshi pushed me up the ladder, and Malachi grabbed my outstretched hand and pulled, wincing as he saw the torn places on my forearms. He laid me down on top of the loader and helped Takeshi up as a massive explosion sent a shock wave over the square. I raised my head to see a huge geyser of water rocket up from the ruins of the Bone Palace and hit the dome.

"Go!" I screamed to Treasa.

She slammed her foot against the pedal. We shot out of the square and headed west as the river rained down.

TWENTY-FOUR

TREASA WAS A TOTAL badass behind the wheel, crashing through anything that got in our way as we raced back to the Smith's compound. Malachi held me close, doing what he could to heal my arms as we huddled on the top of the front loader. Takeshi was doing the same for Ana, but her wound was much worse—she'd nearly been disemboweled by Mazikin claws. She was pale, and so was he. He'd buried his face against her neck as he murmured to her, his desperation palpable. We'd have to fight to get to the gates, and she was barely conscious. The grenade belt was coiled around his arm, and I tugged it away from him and counted—we still had five left.

Malachi watched my shaking hands as I stroked the little spheres. "Do you think it worked? Do you think the people will head south?" he asked, bowing his head over mine as the deflected river water poured down.

"If our words didn't do it, the river will." It was a few inches deep on the roads now, flowing south. The force of the water hadn't overcome the thick dam—instead, it had found another route, bubbling up and into the city. With nowhere else for the water to go, the place would fill up. We might have to swim to the gates.

Treasa motored back through the barricade and hit the horn as she shot along the road where the rest of the vehicles were parked. We were to be the lead, and the rest of the drivers shifted into gear, the fighters holding on to the sides, weapons at the ready.

The Smith's voice boomed over us—he had a bullhorn pressed to his lips as his vehicle, another one with a plow attached, pulled away from the courtyard fence. "Help anyone who needs a ride. Kill any Mazikin who attempt to stop us. We only get out of this if we're together!" He took a noisy breath and then repeated his message in two other languages before handing the bullhorn to Nazir, who repeated it in a few others. Already, other humans were flocking to the vehicles, which were sagging toward the flooded streets as their loads grew heavier. We'd never be able to take everyone. I could only hope the rest would follow after.

Malachi pulled his hands away from my arms. "They're a little better," he said as water dripped from his hair and into my eyes.

"They're a lot better," I said, flexing my fingers.

He ran a finger down my cheek. "You know why."

I nodded, leaning in for a quick, devastatingly sweet kiss. I trusted his love completely. All I wanted was a future where

I could explore that with him, and now it felt within reach. "How are you feeling?"

"Strong enough for one more fight," he said as we lurched forward again.

I hung on while Treasa plowed through yet another barrier. The Mazikin were scarce here, but the humans were swarming. The Smith's people grabbed the injured and heaved them onto the carts, calling to the others in at least a dozen languages, urging them to follow. The direction was hardly necessary; the water was rolling in waves over ankles and lapping at cloaks, threatening to weigh people down. One man sprinted toward us from the south, away from the gates. He waved his arms, and Treasa slowed enough for him to grab our ladder. He had a cloak over his head and grimy hands that grasped the rungs. "English?" he yelped as Malachi heaved him up to join us. The man pushed his hood back. He was covered in mud and soot, maybe having come up from the mines, and immediately threw himself down on his belly to keep from sliding off the side. "Name's Keller," he said. "Heard someone tellin' everyone to run south!"

"That was us. What's going on up there?" I couldn't see more than a few blocks ahead. The light at the gates was so bright that it was blinding.

"The beasts have put up roadblocks and barricades. They're not letting anyone through," Keller replied, his head low over the bar we were clinging to. "No humans allowed beyond the edge of the mining zone. You might want to turn back."

"Not a chance," Treasa yelled.

"The mining zone ends about ten blocks north of the gates," Takeshi shouted over the belching of the engines. He was stroking Ana's hair. She was starting to come around, but she still didn't look good.

Takeshi looked at the grenades in the belt, which I'd slung over my shoulder, and raised his eyebrows. "You're the ranking officer. What do you want to do?"

I exhaled slowly, reminding myself that I had been Captain once before. I could do this. "We have to get as close as we can before we use the grenades," I said. "We only have five, and we're going to need at least one to blow the gates." We were streaking by the jagged rock formations that marked the mining zone, heading for a light so bright it was now impossible to look at directly.

Treasa crossed an intersection where the water was only an inch or so deep. "There they are," she shouted, pointing over the wheel at a brown mass of bodies on the other side of a roadblock.

"One block to the end of the mining zone!" Takeshi yelled back. "Get ready!"

We all drew weapons, and I handed one of mine to Keller. Treasa accelerated. "Hold on tight!" she called, looking over her shoulder. She did a double take when she saw Keller.

He grinned at her—then lunged forward and plunged his knife into her neck.

Treasa arched back helplessly as Keller bared his teeth, revealing his bright-red tongue. He shoved Treasa's lifeless body off the edge of the truck before any of us could stop him. She disappeared beneath our wheels even as we called her name. The loader immediately slowed, then lurched forward as the vehicle behind us crashed into our rear, followed by echoing crashes all the way down the line. I threw myself at Keller as he tried to wrench the wheel and take us off the road.

He'd been too covered in soot for us to see the truth until it was too late—he was one of the Tanner's people and belonged to the city. He didn't want to be freed.

I wrapped my arm around his neck in a stranglehold, but he jammed his blade back, forcing me to let go or lose an eye. Distantly, I was aware of Takeshi and Malachi shouting at each other about getting Treasa back on the vehicle, and of loping brown figures emerging from the buildings on either side of us and hanging out of the windows. This was an ambush, but since we were the lead vehicle, we had to get through or everyone else would be stuck. I jerked my knee up and hit Keller in the belly, then nailed him with an elbow strike to the jaw as he bent double. I tried to shove him over the side, but the asshole hung on, kicking at me.

I drew a knife and stabbed him in the leg. He toppled over the front of the loader, his arms waving.

Behind me, Takeshi shouted a warning as Mazikin jumped from the windows and onto our front loader. Ana was blinking and starting to stir, but she was still vulnerable. I wanted to protect her, but I had to get us moving again. With my shoulders hunched, protecting my neck against the claws I expected any second, I forced my way into the driver's seat and glanced behind me. Malachi was clinging to the side of the loader, and Takeshi was on board, Treasa lying at his feet next to Ana. Somehow, Takeshi had unscrewed the bar we'd been holding on to and was swinging it like a staff. It took only a few seconds for him to clear the top of the loader, sending Mazikin flying in all directions. As he knelt to grab Malachi, I pressed the gas and moved us forward, crunching over Keller's body. If we stayed still any longer, it was clear we were going to be overrun.

The Smith was bellowing into his bullhorn, telling everyone to go south, away from the water, but there were Mazikin crowded at a barrier a block in front of us. Their cloaks bore black triangles, and they were wielding blades. I slipped the grenade belt over my head and handed it back to Malachi. "Throw one to clear the way," I said to him.

He pulled a grenade from its pouch, then got to his knees, trying to stay balanced as I bumped forward on the potholed road. He stared at a spot beyond the barrier and, with a smooth arcing motion, hurled the grenade into the air.

It landed quietly in the churning crowd, and Malachi began to count. "Slow down, Lela!" he shouted between numbers. "You'll get there too—"

The explosion rattled my teeth. Screeches and shrieks and angry roars came from the smoky haze up ahead, but I merely squinted and hit the gas, bumping over Mazikin bodies toward the bright light ahead. The water below our tires was rising again, and far behind us, the deep booms of buildings collapsing continued to shake the ground. The whole city was caving in on itself, falling into the maze of caverns belowground, and our trailing vehicles could get caught in the destruction if I didn't find a way through it fast.

I ran over dozens of Mazikin before they got smart and began to dodge out of the way. We were within five or six blocks of the gates now. Takeshi and Malachi were fighting off Mazikin who kept leaping onto the sides of the front loader. Ana was up, too, lying on her stomach and hurling knives at the charging beasts. But Treasa was completely lifeless, her body destroyed. One look at her told me there was nothing of her left to protect. Malachi had positioned himself near my back to prevent any of the Mazikin from climbing up the side and taking me down. At block four, I had him toss another grenade to clear the way again. I stomped on the gas pedal before the smoke had even cleared.

Hugely stupid move. The explosion had hit a weak spot in the road and created a deep crater, and before I could swerve, we hit it at top speed. The impact crunched me against the steering wheel and threw all my passengers to the ground as the loader flipped on its side. My shoulder hit the cement. I couldn't draw breath, and by the time I managed to get to my feet, I was behind a wall of people. Ana, Takeshi, and Malachi, plus several of the Smith's men, were all trying to push forward through the vicious Mazikin to get to the gates. Over the noise of battle, I could hear a growling voice over a bullhorn.

"It's Ibram," shouted Malachi. "He says to give up or we'll all be gutted and stashed in a cavern to rot."

The Smith shouted back, standing high on his vehicle as his people circled him, desperately trying to hold back the Mazikin who had climbed the sides of his loader. He was yelling encouragement in as many languages as he knew, but the Mazikin were closing in. We were only two blocks from the gates, and now I could see the rows of cloaked Mazikin barring the way. Ibram stood in front of them with his bullhorn, snarling in Mazikin. His fanged smile was visible, even from a distance.

"Keep pushing forward," Ana screamed, her voice cracking as Mazikin overwhelmed the Smith's loader. They tore the bullhorn from his hands, and horror filled his eyes as one of the monsters locked its jaws onto his throat. He toppled backward, even as his people fought to save him and themselves. His voice fell silent, and Ibram filled the gap with his hateful growling. Frightened faces turned to me, to us, to the Guards, searching for a signal. I spun and looked toward the light, so close but out of reach.

"We can't win," I whispered to myself. We had no choice but to try, though. The people behind us had to keep moving or they'd be caught by the water, crushed by the collapsing buildings, maybe trapped for eternity. We couldn't surrender.

Ana must have agreed. Clutching at her barely healed stomach, she shouted, "Malachi, throw another grenade!"

"We're too far," he called out as he jammed his knife through the skull of an oncoming Mazikin. "We only have two left, and if I miss—" He stopped abruptly and looked over his shoulder at me, then fell back. The human fighters in front closed the gap to keep trying to push ahead. Takeshi was still swinging his staff, holding the creatures off while Ana slashed weakly with her knives. But there were so many Mazikin in front of us that we'd reached our limit. We couldn't move forward. And now that the Smith had been overwhelmed, more were closing in from behind. Malachi's hand closed over my shoulder, and then he swung me close. "I can get us out."

"What? You said it was too far, too much of a risk—"

He pulled my face to his, his kiss hard and searching. It was over quickly, and when I looked down, he had our last two grenades in his hands. "Malachi—"

"I love you," he said, pressing his forehead to mine, so close our noses touched. "I'm in love with your strength, your determination, the way you never *ever* give up. These people need those things from you now." He closed his eyes for the barest second, then kissed me again and smiled—a beautiful smile. "And they need this from me. This is my atonement, Lela. This is what I was meant for."

He let me go and tossed one of the grenades high in the air, landing it halfway between where we stood and the gate. Then he plunged forward into the Mazikin horde, and never in all the times I'd seen him fight had he been more deadly. With his short, sharp, devastating movements, he downed Mazikin after Mazikin, breaking bones, slashing with brutal accuracy and decisive strength, moving so quickly that none of them could stop him.

I started to follow, but the explosion knocked me back, and I landed on Nazir. He blinked at the sky for a moment before his hands closed around my arms. We shoved up to our feet. My ears were ringing, but my vision was clear.

Within the haze, a single figure ran toward the locked gates, into the knot of elite Mazikin defenders tasked with keeping that metal barrier closed at all costs. Malachi was nearly there, having cleared away most of the horde within a one-block radius, but the Mazikin he'd passed were chasing him. He was surrounded by at least thirty of them. Ibram had tossed his bullhorn aside and charged forward.

He landed on Malachi's back, taking him down only feet from the gates. Takeshi, Ana, and I surged toward the Mazikin who were piling onto Malachi. A horrible sense of certainty washed over me as one of them raised its curving razor claws and slashed them down.

I don't know if they ever hit home. The explosion ripped sound from my mind. Heat enveloped me as I watched in silent, terrible realization. Bodies tumbled through the air, and smoke billowed. My voice broke as I tried to call Malachi's name. He'd set off the last grenade. Right there at the gates. In the midst of all the Mazikin. He had been right there. I crawled forward. All around me, people sprinted past. And when the smoke cleared, I saw smiles, eyes filled with hope. Ahead of me, beyond a smoking black crater, there was nothing but open space.

The gates were open. And Malachi was gone.

TWENTY-FIVE

PEOPLE POURED THROUGH THE open gates like the river that was chasing us, headed for the light on the other side. Arms lifted me to my feet. Ana and Takeshi's lips formed words I couldn't hear.

Malachi, I mouthed. *Where is he?*

They shook their heads.

I stumbled forward, supported by my fellow Guards. My footsteps shuffled into the shallow black crater and out the other side, smearing ash on my toes as tendrils of smoke spiraled into the air. If he were killed, wouldn't he be right here, beyond the gates? Shouldn't he be waiting for me?

I scanned the crowd, all the faces blurring as they scrambled out of the Mazikin city. So many faces streaked by—some of them strangers, some vaguely familiar. I dug in my heels, trying to slow down, but Ana and Takeshi kept pulling me toward the light. Finally, I yanked my arms from their grip, needing to find Malachi before I did anything else. I knew he'd be waiting there. Maybe he needed me.

I stood in the sandy space where I'd first entered the dome. People and vehicles swarmed around the black crater. Faraway screams and cries filled the air as broken, wounded people ran, stumbled, crawled toward freedom. Some of them carried others on their backs or dragged the injured through the sand.

Malachi wasn't among them. He wasn't there. I looked back at the opening in the dome, which had been torn like a curtain, ragged edges flapping in the desert wind. A massive crowd stood in the sand outside, bathed in white light, and still more were coming as the Mazikin tried to stop anyone they could. A few yards away, one Mazikin leaped on top of a woman and angrily twisted her neck, then tore her head off. I blinked, expecting her to appear in the space where I was standing, but all I felt was a breeze streaking by my cheek.

The dome was *open*. She wasn't trapped in the city anymore. Her soul was free to go wherever she belonged, be it the Countryside or whatever realm she needed or deserved. And that meant it was the same for Malachi, who had set off that grenade intentionally, knowing he'd be reduced to ash.

Malachi had killed himself.

"Oh God," I whispered. Was he in the dark city now? Rage twisted inside me as tears burned my eyes. I swayed in place, watching the Mazikin go after the stragglers.

I'm in love with your strength, your determination, the way you never ever *give up. These people need those things from you now.*

Those were his last words to me. Not *Help me, find me, weep for me.* Not *Love me, save me, remember me.* Help *them,* he'd said. It was what he'd sacrificed himself for, why he'd suffered. He'd dreamed of seeing these people freed. This was why he'd fought for so long, and so hard, and at such a high price. He had atoned.

But there was still work to be done.

No matter where he was now, I knew what he'd want. He would never abandon these souls, would never fall to his knees and grieve, would never surrender. And neither would I.

I drew the one remaining knife I had and ran back toward the city. Only a few blocks away, buildings shook and crumbled as pieces of the dome cracked and tore, like some kind of stiff fabric. Most of the Mazikin had fled, but a few who wore the black triangle remained, tearing through the humans as they tried to get through the open gate. "Ana, Takeshi!" I shouted. "Help!"

I didn't wait to see if they were coming to my aid. I charged up to one of the Mazikin guards and threw myself onto its back, plunging my knife into its ear and riding it to the ground. Before I could get to my feet, another landed on me, and I got my hands in front of my neck a split second before it slashed at my throat. I lunged to the side, twisting to ram my knife between its ribs. Its eyes bugged and its tongue lolled as it hit the cement, and my fingers were wet with its blood as I reclaimed my blade.

I have no idea how many Mazikin I killed or how many people I helped escape. While the city collapsed around me, I became a machine, ignoring the pain in my body and the knot of despair in my heart, focusing only on getting every single living soul through the gates. Takeshi and Ana ran past me a few times, helping stragglers limp toward freedom, protecting them from desperate, ravaging Mazikin. I felt the faint warmth of gratitude, knowing they were making Malachi's sacrifice count.

I ventured in another block, to the blood-splashed overturned vehicles that had piled up within sight of freedom. Water lapped at my ankles as I marched along, searching for anyone left alive who might need help getting out. Few Mazikin remained, and those who did skulked in the open first floors of the buildings that were still standing. Their ears were flat to their heads, their tongues hanging out as they panted their anxiety. The city was doomed, and they could probably smell death in the air.

Eventually, I reached the loader where the Smith had been perched, shouting to his people through his bullhorn. Just as I was wondering if he'd gotten out, I spotted him, lying crumpled and gasping against a tire. I knelt next to him, trying to pull him up, only to discover that one of his legs was hanging by a thread and he had a terrible wound in his throat. The creatures had torn him open and abandoned him to suffer, and in the chaos, he'd been left behind.

"Come on," I huffed, trying to pull him to a stand.

He let out a hoarse groan. "No. I'm too heavy."

"We have to *go*, dude," I said, getting behind him and sliding an arm under his shoulders.

"Are there others?" he asked between wheezes. "Get the others."

I looked around, but not a single live human remained. Plenty of headless, destroyed bodies, but no living people. Except for him. "No one else. Come with me. I'll help you."

His dark eyes met mine. "You would be doing me a favor, you know."

I shook my head. "No. You can make it. Your people are waiting for you."

He gave a pained chuckle. "And you think I could lead them through the desert beyond this dome?" He glanced down at his leg. "No, Guard. You will lead them for me. Let me go. Help me go."

"But you don't know where you'll end up," I said. "Really, you don't—"

"Wherever the Judge decides I go, I'm sure I've earned it." He nailed me with a piercing gaze. "Don't fail me." His short, thick fingers closed over my right hand, the one that held the knife. "And make it quick, if you don't mind."

I placed my hand on the side of his face, letting my thumb stroke down his homely, weathered cheek. I closed my eyes. And when I opened them, I didn't hesitate or let myself think about it. I used every ounce of merciless strength I possessed, and I cut decisively, and when I was sure it was enough, I didn't look down. I got to my feet and walked. Past the overturned loader, past the place where Malachi had kissed me good-bye, past the spot where he'd sacrificed himself so everyone else could be free, and through the gates. Beyond the dome, the masses of people churned, so many that the desert seemed full. The world behind me was breaking, tearing, collapsing in on itself. Like my heart.

I stalked through the tear in the dome, not bothering to look up at the source of the bright light that covered the endless crowd of people. Ana and Takeshi were standing with a few men with rag-wrapped feet, wearing stained, worn leather armor. One of them, a muscular blond with harsh features, looked up as I came toward them.

"Lela," said Ana, gesturing to the man and his comrades, "these are the Guards of the Wasteland. They've been tasked with helping us get these folks to the Countryside. And this"—she put her arm around the blond guy—"is Sascha. He helped me when I came here before, and he gathered the others to guide everyone through the desert."

Sascha. The name was familiar, but I was too dazed and destroyed to find a connection. "Good," was all I could say. "That's good."

Sascha stood up a little taller. He towered over the rest of us. "We need to get these people moving," he said in thickly accented English. "It's not an easy journey."

He strode forward, followed by the other Guards. Ana stayed behind.

"Don't ask me how I am," I said quietly.

"I won't. But Lela, listen to me: what Malachi did?" She gestured at the enormous throng of people spread across the desert in front of us. "This is what he wanted. It's what he's needed. For *so* long."

"I know."

She remained in front of me for another second, then released my shoulder and turned on her heel. She reached Takeshi and took his hand, smiling up at him with hard-won happiness on her face. The crowd parted for them, needing to be led, and then swallowed them up as everyone began to follow.

I knew she expected me to do the same, but I couldn't get my feet to take another step.

"You don't have to. The others will take care of it now," said a voice from behind me. One I recognized well. I turned to see the Mazikin city sinking and crumbling into the sand as the dome sealed itself up again. And Raphael, standing in front of it like he saw this kind of thing every day. His face was glowing, too bright for me to look at for long.

"Did we get everyone?" I asked.

"Everyone who didn't belong in that city is no longer in the city," he replied, inclining his head toward the crowd, which was plodding away from us. "The Guards will lead them through the Wasteland. Those who belong elsewhere will get there. They will see where they're supposed to go."

"That easy?"

"That easy and that hard."

"And me?"

The brightness around him faded, like he was pulling it back inside himself. "You are not finished."

I shook my head, tears stinging my eyes. "Yes, I am."

He said nothing. Just stood there, waiting.

I pressed my lips together and rubbed my eyes. "Fine. But before you take me anywhere, I need to know. And don't tell me I don't. Where's Malachi? If he's in the dark city, I'm going to—"

He held up his hands and chuckled. "As much as I enjoyed our last dramatic encounter, I have no wish to repeat it. Malachi is not in the dark city."

The breath rushed out of me, and I sank to my knees. Raphael caught me, putting his incredibly warm arm around my back. "He had no wish to die," he said softly. "He didn't feel despair. He wasn't trying to escape. In fact, I think he very much would have liked to stay. In other words, the dark city was not what he needed."

A tear slid from my eye. "So can I see him now? Is he at the Sanctum? Is he okay?"

Raphael squeezed my arm. "He's absolutely fine, Lela. Much better than fine."

I swiped my sleeve across my face. "Awesome." I needed to see him. To talk to him. I needed him to hold me, and whatever I had to do next would be bearable. As long as he was with me.

"Lela, you must understand something," Raphael said gently, like he could hear my thoughts, as I'd long suspected he could. He moved in front of me and made sure I was looking at him. "Malachi has done everything he needed to do."

"What are you saying?" I whispered.

He smiled his beautiful, dazzling, painful smile. "Malachi is no longer a Guard of the Shadowlands. He's been released into the Countryside, to enjoy his forever."

I stalked up the pristine white aisle toward the dark figure waiting at the front. This time, the inhuman Guards on either side of me all stared at me with respect. But I didn't care. I'd been hollowed out and burned. I was empty. I reached the front of the courtroom and waited for the Judge to acknowledge me. I should have been scared or awed, but I just felt numb.

She raised her head, and this time, her eyes were amber brown, like mine, like my mother's. Her gaze held me still while she glided forward. She looked like this weird melding of Diane and my mom, and it made my stomach churn. Not with nausea. With want. I wanted her to hug me, and I hated it. I wanted her to put her arms around me and tell me it was going to be okay, even though it was the cruelest thing she could have done. I stepped back as she drew near. "Why?"

"That's a huge question for a little girl," she said, but not in a mocking way. She halted in front of me. "I know you're tired, baby."

"Don't call me that. And I'm not *tired*—I'm done. Important difference."

"But you're not. Juri is a threat in the land of the living, and he has ten other Mazikin with him."

"Wasn't his Mazikin body destroyed when we blew up the portal? Shouldn't that have killed him—including the part of him that's in the land of the living?"

She shook her head. "The substance in the portal is pure life. It can't be destroyed; only the passageway can. Juri's Mazikin body, and those of the others, is preserved. Deep underground, most likely, but still there. And as long as it is, he can occupy that human body—"

"Malachi's body," I snapped.

"Kill Juri and the remaining Mazikin in the land of the living. If they've been buried, their animal bodies will die as soon as their spirits return. End the Mazikin threat forever. That is your mission."

"No." But even as I said it, I thought of Diane. And Tegan. And Ian. And Henry. The ones I'd left behind. The ones Juri could so easily hurt. "Send someone else." Someone better. Stronger. Whole. That was what they needed.

The Judge touched my chin, sending painful, deep tingles coursing across my skin. "You're so angry."

"Am I supposed to be happy?"

"You feel how you feel. I understand it."

"Well, maybe you can help me out, then," I snarled. "I thought you might be some kind of God person, you know? I thought you knew everything. But then I found out that you created the Mazikin. You let them do this. And now you're using me to clean up your mess."

She tilted her head. "If I am some kind of 'God person,' do you really think you're capable of understanding me?"

"I'm capable of understanding that a million people were sent to hell because you couldn't control your pets," I shouted, right in her face, knowing she could zap me out of existence with a twitch of her eyebrow, and almost hoping she would.

She merely stared at me with her new, fathomless Rita Santos eyes, and I had to look away. "You abandoned all those people," I said in a choked voice. "You left them at the mercy of evil creatures that *you* created."

"But I didn't abandon anyone," she replied. "I sent Takeshi, Malachi, Ana, and you."

I grimaced. "How does that make up for hundreds of years of suffering? How could you create those things? How could you allow them to take over like that?"

"I loved them, and so I gave them one thing," she said quietly. "The one thing I give to creatures I love. Do you know what it is?"

"A massive dome so they could create a hell that outdoes any kind of hell I'd ever imagined? Did you gift wrap it, too?"

"No," she said patiently. "I gave them free will."

I looked up at the ceiling, a swirling, living mosaic of crystals, shifting and roiling like an ocean. "Well. How nice of you."

She chuckled, sending vibrations through the floor that rattled my bones. "I wouldn't say that. Free will makes every kind of evil possible, baby. Every single kind. But . . ."

My eyes were drawn to hers, like they were magnetic. "But . . ."

She smiled, and it was both joyful and sad. "Free will is also the thing that makes love real."

She loved the Mazikin, and she'd wanted them to love her back. But they'd chosen something else—a shot at power, the chance to shed her authority and make their own rules. All because she'd loved them enough to give them a choice.

"Do *I* have a choice?" I asked.

"There's always a choice," she replied. "But that doesn't mean you get to determine which options you have."

"In other words, all the options are shitty." I was smart enough not to ask for the Countryside, for Malachi, for freedom.

"You can apply any term you like."

"And you already know what I'll choose."

She raised an eyebrow. "Does that really matter?"

Did it? I was too tired to think, but I knew I couldn't just curl up in a ball and abandon every person in the land of the living who was in danger because Juri and his Mazikin were still on the loose. I didn't have it in me to walk away from them. "Send me now," I said. *Before I fall apart.*

She leaned in, filling me with this jittery sense of unease, like I was about to be struck by lightning. "Fight hard," she whispered.

I always do, I was about to say, but I was jarred into silence as my vision turned black.

When it returned, I was in the living room of the Guard house in Warwick. Henry lay crumpled on the carpet in front of me, sleeping or maybe unconscious. I rubbed my stinging eyes, took a breath, and immediately began to cough as a wave of heat rolled over me.

The curtains, the furniture, the walls . . . everything was on fire.

TWENTY-SIX

I CROUCHED, GATHERING HENRY'S lean body in my arms, and squinted out the front windows. A group of people stood on the front lawn, lit by the glow of the fire, making them easy to see even though it was dark out. And as one of them dropped to all fours and loped across the grass, I knew exactly who they were and what they'd done. With all of Malachi's knowledge in his head, Juri had known where and when to strike.

"Henry," I said between coughs, shaking him. "Come on, *please*!"

He stirred weakly as the flames crawled toward the ceiling. I hooked my arms beneath his and drew him along the hallway toward the rear of the house, which opened onto a wooded area, behind which was another neighborhood. The smoke was thick, making it nearly impossible to breathe. I was unarmed, and all our weapons were in the basement. And I knew what waited for us outside. Juri wanted to lure us out and end us for good.

I paused in the hallway outside the kitchen as a crash near the front door told me the house was starting to come down. If I tried to get to the basement, it might collapse on my head. Instead, I darted into the kitchen and grabbed two steak knives. I was still wearing my stained leather clothes, so I jammed the knives into two empty sheaths and lunged for Henry as the ceiling began to rain bits of ash and debris. As the cinders burned holes in our clothes, I heaved his arm over my shoulder and wrenched him up, putting my arm around his waist and limping down the hall toward the back door. Henry's feet were moving, but he was pretty out of it. He wouldn't be much help once we got outside, and that meant I was about to have a knife fight on the lawn. In the middle of Warwick, Rhode Island, where my probation officer would love nothing more than to see me brought up on a murder charge. Killing Mazikin had completely different and very serious consequences in the land of the living.

I never thought I'd miss the Shadowlands, but there I was.

My lungs burning, I reached the cramped mudroom and peered through one of the cloudy glass panes in the back door. I didn't see anyone. My fingertips skimmed over the handle of the steak knife at my belt. "You and me, Henry. It's up to us," I said in his ear.

"Captain?" he wheezed.

"Yeah. I'm back."

"Didn't expect that," he said, his voice so weak that I clutched him tighter, my fingers against his bony chest.

"We're going out the back, and we may have to fight."

He tried to raise his head, but it seemed too heavy for him. "Can't."

His voice was saturated with exhaustion and pain, and I understood it well—so I wracked my brain for how to motivate him. And it hit me: Sascha. I remembered who he was. That Guard from the Wasteland was Henry's soul mate. "I saw Sascha, Henry. Outside the Mazikin city."

He started to lift his head. "Sascha?"

"Earn your way back to him, Henry. We have a mission, and I need you."

His fingers tightened over mine. "Give me a weapon."

I handed him one of the steak knives. "All I have at the moment."

"More than enough." He leaned on me, still wheezing.

I shoved open the back door. "Through the woods. Then we get onto the street, where people can see us." Fear of getting caught worked both ways. Juri was too smart to get himself thrown in jail.

We limped rapidly down the steps as a siren howled in the distance. My ears alert for any sound of footsteps behind us, I half dragged Henry onto the back lawn and headed for the woods beyond it—the thick late-spring foliage that would help us to hide.

A low chuckle reached me, even over the wail of the fire engines as they rumbled up the street. I looked over my shoulder.

Juri stood in the backyard, leaning against a tree, gorgeous in the firelight. His face was unscarred, his back straight, his arms crossed over his chest. He looked completely relaxed. His black-brown gaze was so familiar, so intent. "I missed you, Lela," he said, his eyes lingering on my body.

Rage exploded through me—not just because of who he was, but because he'd reopened the deepest wound I had by looking and sounding so much like Malachi. "Fuck you, Juri," I yelled as the red lights of the fire trucks flashed at the front of the house. Shouts from the firefighters didn't sound scared, so that told me the Mazikin in the yard had probably fled already. "If you came for a fight, let's go."

Henry leaned away and braced his hands on his thighs, giving me freedom of movement in case Juri charged. I drew my knife.

Juri smirked. "Not yet. I'm not ready for this to end." He took a few lazy steps away from the tree, his gaze never leaving my face. "See you at school, my love." In a scary-quick move, he sank into the billowing smoke of the side yard.

"The rest could be anywhere." Henry pulled on the back of my tunic, and it was enough to get me moving again. Juri's words rang in my mind as we staggered into the stretch of woods and out the other side, into a neighborhood that was nice enough for the residents to call the police if they saw two homeless-looking folks stumbling around in their gardens.

"Where to?" Henry asked.

I had no idea. We scrambled between two fences. I tripped over a recycling bin, sending bottles and cans clinking and rolling. A light in the house next door came on. "Anywhere but here."

Henry's breath was labored, and his face was blackened with soot, but his steps were a bit steadier as he sucked in the clean air. "My phone is in my pocket," he rasped, then doubled over, coughing and retching as his lungs worked hard to get rid of all the smoke he'd inhaled.

I led him along a driveway and onto the street, knowing we needed to get out of here or risk getting questioned by police. Security lights clicked on as we walked up the road. I fished Henry's phone from his pants pocket.

With my eyes closed, I visualized the number that had popped up several times on my own phone, one I'd rarely called. I punched it in and hoped for the best.

"Hello?" said a sleepy voice.

"Tegan. It's Lela."

"What the hell? Where have you been? And why are you—?"

"Can you come get me? I'm near your house." I read off the street name, knowing that her parents' huge property was less than half a mile away, down near the bay.

She groaned. "Fine. But where the hell have you been? I mean, I know you have stuff going on, but skipping town for a week isn't exactly—"

"A week?" When I'd been to the dark city, I'd come back only a few hours later, even though it had felt like I'd been gone for a month. "Are you sure?"

"Are you drunk?"

"Can you just come get me?" I pleaded as another set of lights came on and someone stepped onto their front porch. From the silhouette, it looked like the person was holding a phone to his ear. Shit.

"Yeah, yeah. Hang on. I'll be there in a few minutes."

I closed my eyes in relief. The last time I'd been with Tegan, she'd seen Juri kill Jim right in front of her. Raphael had taken those memories from her, promising it would spare her the pain, but mostly to keep her from talking about what she'd seen and blowing our mission. I'd wondered what

Raphael had left her with. But whatever she knew, it wasn't stopping her from coming to the rescue.

I told her the intersection where we'd be waiting and prayed that no one would try to stop us. My muscles were screaming with fatigue. The last time I'd had a moment of rest had been before we'd destroyed the portal. Those few hours of healing, in that bed with Malachi. His hands on my skin. His mouth on mine. His arms around me. The weight and scent of him. All of it rose up and threatened to drag me under. Only Henry's scarecrow body leaning against me kept me in the now.

We moved slowly along the sidewalk, no longer running but still alert. "So. I've been gone a week?"

Henry nodded. "I lay low. Guarded your friends. Then Juri showed up at the house."

I had to wonder if Juri had done it because of what he'd seen in the portal. He'd known I was in the Mazikin realm, and he might even know the portal had been destroyed. Had he guessed I would return?

"You came back alone," Henry said hoarsely.

Alone. My chest ached, the empty space filling up with hurt. "Yeah. He's okay, though." Henry and Malachi had become friends, and I knew Henry admired him. He also understood what Malachi meant to me. "I got him out of there, Henry. He's in the Countryside, where he belongs."

It was all I'd wanted for him. I'd been willing to become a Guard because I thought it meant he'd be free, and now he was. Sure, he wouldn't get his ordinary human life, but he'd have something better. He'd have heaven. Maybe he'd find his family. Maybe he'd be with his brother. No more fighting. No more dying or killing. Only sunlight and rest. It should have made me happy, but instead I had to blink back tears. It should have given me hope, but all I wanted to do was lie down on the ground and sleep forever.

Now Henry was almost holding *me* up. "So we're back to trying to stop them here. Just the two of us." A hint of bitterness had crept into his raspy voice.

I nodded. "But they can't multiply anymore. We destroyed their portal, so the ones here are the last ones, and they're stuck. They can't get back without risking permanent death, and they can't bring any more in."

He chuckled. "That is a fairly significant development, Captain."

I looked up the road as we reached the intersection. "The Judge said there are still eleven of them here, including Juri. Once we terminate them, that's it."

His eyes met mine. "That's it. I wonder what happens after that."

I was saved from answering as Tegan's little BMW pulled up at the curb. Her window slid down, and she recoiled at the sight of us.

"I am the best friend ever," she said, popping the locks.

Against my will, I smiled. Tegan was annoying and ignorant, but I kind of liked her. I opened the back door and helped Henry inside, then got in the front seat. Her nose wrinkled. "Jeez. You stink. Like you've been at a barbecue hosted by skunks."

"Or in a house fire," I muttered, glancing over at her.

Tegan's short brown hair was sticking up, like she'd rolled out of bed. She looked in the backseat. "Hey, Henry. You look like shit."

He laughed and then coughed a few times. "I know. Thanks for picking us up."

I looked back and forth between them, and Tegan patted my leg. "Henry's my stalker." She didn't say it in a freaked-out way, though.

Henry rubbed a grimy hand over his face, which only made it more evenly filthy. "She's more perceptive than I figured. She also . . ."

"Henry drove me home after Jim ditched me," Tegan said, her voice changing, becoming tight and strained. "I was too messed up to realize Henry was probably a serial killer. But he hasn't slaughtered me yet."

I gave Henry a tight-lipped glare. In his ordinary human life, he pretty much *had* been a serial killer. The only difference was he'd gotten paid.

Henry smiled, and I realized he kind of liked Tegan, too.

"Anyway," she continued, "when a few creeps cornered me outside the mall a few days ago, Henry ran them off. We have an understanding."

"As Jim's *uncle*," Henry said, "it was the least I could do after my nephew took off. He ran with a rough crowd, and I felt responsible."

Tegan pulled up to her property and punched in the security code. As the metal gates swung open, I looked across the rolling lawn. Malachi had been here the night we went to prom. That meant Juri knew it was her house.

"How much security do you have around this place?" I asked.

Tegan snorted. "Considering that my dad defends some of the most unsavory characters in the state, I'd say . . . a lot. He's kind of paranoid."

Perfect.

She followed a narrow roadway around the back of the mansion. "You can spend the night in the carriage house," she said. "If you don't want to go home to Diane, that is."

Diane. Before I could ask, Henry leaned forward and said, "She's fine, Lela. She's okay."

"Pretty upset, though," added Tegan. "She's called me several times, wanting to know if I've seen you. She's afraid yours might be one of the bodies in that club that burned. I was, too, until Henry told me you were just hiding out for a while. I had no idea you were trying to escape from a gang, Lela. You could have told me."

I hadn't known myself, but it seemed a pretty good cover. "Um. Yeah. My past is sort of . . . yeah. But now I don't want anything to do with them." I rubbed my eyes. I needed to rise from the dead and let Diane know I was okay. But I knew that was going to be a pretty intense experience, and right now, all I wanted to do was sleep. "I'll go see Diane tomorrow. She's probably at work right now." Ironically, she might be safer down at the medium-security prison than she was in her own home.

We got out of the car, and Tegan unlocked the carriage house, which was about the size of Diane's regular house. She flicked on the lights in the entryway and pointed up the stairs. "There are three bedrooms up there. I'll bring you guys some clothes. Lela . . ." She seemed to notice my outfit for the first time. "What the hell are you wearing?"

She narrowed her eyes and came toward me, reaching out to touch my goatskin tunic. I stepped back into the shadows as she said, "Is that a knife? Is this a costume, or have you lost your mind?"

"Ah, Tegan, I would love some regular clothes, though I don't think your pants would fit me." Tegan was built like a pixie, and I was a bit more . . . *more.*

She waved her hand. "I'll bet my mom has stuff. I'll bring it over tomorrow. I'm going back to bed."

She walked toward the door and then turned to me again. "Lela, are you okay?" she asked quietly. "You look . . . different."

Because I'm done, I wanted to say. *I'm running on empty and I'm afraid it's not going to be enough.* "I'm all right." I forced the words out. "It's just been a hard week."

Her brow furrowed. "See you tomorrow?" She didn't sound sure at all.

I nodded. "I'll be here. Thanks again, Tegan. I'm sorry for all this."

Her fingers ran down the doorframe, and she watched their motion, like her thoughts were far away. "It's okay." Then she left us alone.

Henry had sunk onto a stool at the breakfast bar. "I've spun a lot of lies in the last week. Raphael didn't take much from her. Just the memory of the club. But she remembers the ambush. And she thinks she remembers a fight with Jim."

Jim. I wished he was here right now. He'd become a really dependable Guard, and we needed all the help we could get. "Where do you think he is now?" I asked as we trudged toward the stairs.

Henry shrugged. "That kid had a lot of stuff to work out. He did well at the end, though."

"It would have been nice if he'd had a chance to live. I know it's what he wanted. I think it's what he was missing." Jim had spent his entire existence in the Countryside, a perfect sort of paradise, and somehow, it hadn't been what he'd needed. Or maybe it had been, but only after he'd had a chance to make his own mistakes and experience the consequences.

"Everyone's heaven is different, I think," Henry said, and I suspected he was thinking of Sascha, of what they'd shared in the desolate Wasteland. I knew what he meant, too, because Malachi and I had that. In the worst place in the universe, we'd been together, and at moments, we'd had happiness and safety and contentment. I hadn't wanted anything else.

Sadness flooded me, and I waved my hand at one of the bedrooms as we reached the top of the stairs. "Get some rest," I said to Henry, my throat tight with sorrow. "I need to take a shower and sleep."

I'd reached my limit. One more word or reminder or demand and I'd crack. Henry retreated silently into one of the bedrooms, and I limped into the bathroom. I laid my knife on the counter and stripped myself down. The mirror told me all I needed to know. Grimy face, scarred body, greasy hair. I looked as broken as I felt.

I turned on the shower and stepped in, welcoming the spray of hot water on my face. Wishing I could melt and flow down the drain. Wishing someone would lift this stuff off my shoulders. The creatures I had to kill, the people I had to protect.

The boy I had to miss.

A sob came out of me before I could stop it. "I miss you," I whispered. "I didn't want to do this without you." And I wasn't sure I could.

I sank to the tile and wrapped my arms around my knees, letting the water wash away the dirt, leaving only the wounds. If I succeeded in this mission, what then? Succeeding probably meant staying alive, and staying alive meant staying here.

Growing up and getting old. All while Malachi roamed the Countryside, forever young and strong and perfect.

If I died, though, it would mean I'd failed. And if I did, what would happen? Juri would be free to live and to kill. Who knows where I'd go next. Hell, the Judge might even send me right back into action. By the end of it all, I'd be a zombie girl held together with scar tissue.

I let out a miserable laugh. "Who am I kidding? I already am."

If Malachi were here, he'd be thinking about his mission. But I couldn't. I was too tired, too sad. So I let the water run until it turned cold, and then I scrubbed myself shiny clean and tiptoed into an empty bedroom, where I crawled naked between the sheets and cried myself to sleep.

TWENTY-SEVEN

"Ready for this?"

"No." I held on to the strap of my seat belt and stared at the front of Diane's house. Her car was in the drive, but the shutters were closed, which was unusual for her. She liked the light.

Tegan poked my shoulder. "Maybe she'll understand. She's always seemed pretty cool, if a little scary."

I stared at the house. "She's both those things."

"Will you be at school?"

I rubbed at the ache in my temple and looked down at my clothes, designer workout gear that Tegan had stolen from her mom. "I think I have to be, unless she drives me straight to the RITS. But I'll try to get there." Juri had said he'd be at school, and who knew what damage he'd do to get to me. "Hey. If you see Malachi . . ."

"He hasn't been at school since prom, either. I figured you were together."

"We're not. *Definitely* not."

She shrugged. "There were a lot of post-prom breakups. It's been a big drama fest. Greg is still in the hospital, Alexis is hobbling around on crutches, and we had two assemblies about gang stuff last week. Ian has hardly said a word to anyone. He just looks shell-shocked." She gave me a sidelong glance. "I told him you were alive, but I'm not sure he believed me."

Another intense encounter I wasn't looking forward to. My fingers closed over the door handle. "I'll talk to him later, assuming Diane doesn't kill me first."

"Good plan. Do you want me to wait?"

"No, go ahead and get to school. I'll catch up with you later." I got out of her car and trudged up the steps. My eyes skated over the tulips in her flower beds. Lovely and normal. It was a painful sort of illusion. In the dark city and the Mazikin realm, things looked exactly as horrible as they were. Here, there were birds chirping in the trees, and little kids shrieking and giggling at a nearby playground, and the sweet scent of honeysuckle in the air. All of it seemed safe, and clean, and right. But none of it was. Not for me, and not for anyone close to me. I sniffed as the breeze lifted my curls. Would the Mazikin still smell like incense now that they weren't doing their possession ritual to bring more of their family to the land of the living? Had we lost that advantage, too?

I reached the front door and knocked. I didn't have my key. Heavy footsteps caused my stomach to tighten, and then the door swung open. My foster mother's usually smooth face was creased with worry and grief, and her silver hair was a dry, broken mess. Her deep-brown skin had a grayish cast; her eyes were puffy and bloodshot. She stared at my face and then looked me up and down. In that moment of stillness, my heart beat so hard that I couldn't breathe. She was the only one who hadn't abandoned me. Yet.

"I'm sorry, Diane," I whispered.

Her eyes widened as tears spilled over, so fast that they were flooding down her cheeks. Then her hands shot out and grabbed my arms, and in a raw second I was pressed against her chest as she sobbed. Her grip on me was steely yet soft as she held me close. "Are you hurt? Do we need to go to the hospital? Do you need to eat?"

Before I could answer, she shook me by the shoulders, hard enough to rattle my teeth. "Where the hell have you been? Do you have any idea what the last week has been like for me?" she yelled, her voice rising with every word. "No one had any clue where you were! I thought they'd either find you dead or tell me you were gone for good! What got into you?"

I tried to twist myself out of her grip before she snapped my neck with her frantic shaking. "I'm sorry! Let go! Diane!"

She stepped back, her chest heaving. "Explain, baby. Right now. Because a lot of people have been looking for you. And me—" She put her hand to her mouth to hold in another sob, all the while waving her finger at me.

I reached forward and grabbed that finger, giving it a little shake that made her upper arms wobble. "If you'd give me a chance, I'll explain!" It hurt to see her so upset. "I'm so sorry, Diane. I had to lie low for a few days after that prom gang-fight thing. I didn't want anyone I cared about to be hurt."

"It's my job to make sure you're safe!" she shouted. "You could have come to me."

"But you *are* one of the people I care about. I didn't want you to get hurt, either."

She put her hands on her ample hips. "They can come at me. Who are they—just baby thugs? You think I haven't dealt with worse every workday for the past twenty years?"

I rubbed my hand over my face. Sleep hadn't restored my strength or energy. In fact, I felt emptier. Every word made me more tired. "More than baby thugs, Diane. Look, I know you can handle a lot, but I didn't want to . . . I don't know . . . bring it here." Not that I had a choice in that. If Juri wanted to destroy me, he'd come here sooner or later, right when he thought it would hurt the most. And as tough as Diane was, few people could last more than a second against him. I wasn't sure I could, either. "They could still come around."

She sighed. "What did you get yourself into?"

"Uh, if I said 'hell,' could we leave it at that?"

She seemed to swell before my eyes, like an angry rooster. "What do you think?"

"How about you help me get back on track? Can we do that? I turn eighteen in less than two months. The state won't have to worry about me after that, but I'm sure Nancy would love to put me up in the RITS until then." My probation officer dogged my every move, waiting for me to screw up.

Diane *mm-mm-mm*-ed her disapproval. "One of the conditions of your probation is staying in school, baby. What did you think she would do?"

"She's already put in the violation order, hasn't she?"

"She said she would if you turned out to be alive."

"How sensitive of her. What did you say?"

Diane looked away. "I had to be escorted out of the Department of Children, Youth and Families by a security guard. She's not pressing charges, though."

I fought a smile. "You're awesome. You know that, right?"

"I don't like anyone threatening my kids, baby."

And I didn't want anyone threatening Diane. I needed this to be over, quickly. Once I had terminated every single remaining Mazikin, then they could put me in jail or whatever. It wouldn't matter. I felt so numb that I didn't think I'd care. The future I'd wanted felt like a distant daydream. I couldn't believe I'd ever thought it could be real. "If I show up at school, will Nancy send cops to pick me up?"

She smoothed her hair down. "I'll call your social worker and tell her what's going on. Maybe Jen and I can settle Nancy down. But you have to go back to school, baby. If you miss another day before graduation, you'll only be handing her ammo."

I glanced toward the kitchen, at the microwave clock. "I'd better get ready, then. Can you drive me today?"

She nodded, a sad smile pulling at her lips. "I'm glad you're okay," she said hoarsely. Then she put her hand over her mouth again and trundled back to her room. I went to my own bedroom and paused in the doorway. My backpack was propped against my desk. My bed was messy—like no one had touched it since I'd left. A pile of shoes lay at the foot of my bed. My usual clutter.

I walked toward my chest of drawers to pull out a more Lela-like outfit than what I had on, but I froze when something glinted in my periphery. Slowly, I turned to look more closely at the pile of shoes.

Under my sneakers, partially obscured by a pair of boots, was a pair of high-heeled sandals. Silvery, strappy, deadly. The heel of one of them was smeared with blood. These were the shoes I'd worn to prom and left in the Guard house.

I knelt near the pile, cold sweat prickling the back of my neck, and pulled one of the sandals from beneath the other shoes. As I did, it snagged on a shimmery piece of material that had also been tossed—or placed—in the pile. It was one of my thigh sheaths, specially made to hold my knives against my skin beneath the fluttery skirt of my prom dress. It had been ripped off me when the Mazikin had ambushed our prom limo. A small curled piece of paper, the size of a sticky note, slid from the sheath. My fingers shook as I unfolded it.

The only way to keep them safe is to come back to me.
Don't make me wait.
~M

I sat in my first three classes, barely registering the stares and whispers from my classmates. The note from Juri was tucked in my pocket—and so was a knife. I was risking getting in major trouble, but we were tucked into suburbia, free of metal detectors. So unless someone patted me down, no one would know as long as I didn't have to whip it out and stab someone. If I saw Juri, that was more or less my plan. I'd frantically checked all the doors and windows at Diane's house—and found that the basement lock had been broken. As much as I hated to scare her, I showed it to Diane before she drove me to school. I wanted her to be vigilant, and sometime last night, someone had broken in.

I knew exactly who. And I was sure he'd taken a sick pleasure in the note, in being able to write in Malachi's neat, precise script, in signing it using Malachi's initial. I figured he'd show up at school, thinking he could taunt me, but he wasn't in the morning class Malachi and I had shared. As I walked to fourth period, though, hands closed over my shoulders from behind. I reacted instantly, throwing back my elbow and spinning around to slam a knee strike into any available body part.

My victim let out a moan and crumpled to the floor. I yelped and knelt beside him. "Ian! God, I'm so sorry!"

He was on his hands and knees in the middle of the hallway, and people were glaring at me like I'd tried to murder the Easter Bunny. Or, in actuality, their prom king. I looped my arm under his and helped him to his feet, only to have him push me against the lockers. This time I didn't fight, because I knew one false move would have teachers scrambling—and someone calling 911. I braced my palms on his chest and looked away from his green eyes. His fingers dug into my shoulders, his thumb pressing into the spot where one of the Mazikin guards had driven a blade right through me. I winced.

His grip loosened. "Tegan told me you were alive, but I didn't know—" His hands fell away, and his voice shook as he said, "The last time I saw you, I thought it really would be the last time."

I rubbed my shoulder and forced myself to look at him. "I'm fine."

His eyes searched my face. "You don't look like yourself. At all. What happened to you?"

It was similar to what Tegan had said. *You look . . . different.* Like the defeat was written across my forehead. "Rough week. But I'm all right."

"Bullshit," he said softly, then ran a hand through his chestnut-brown hair. "But I've sort of given up on trying to understand. I just didn't want you to be dead, and I got my wish."

"Are you okay?" I looked up and down the hall. If any of my classmates were Mazikin, or if Juri was watching, talking to Ian would only put him in more danger.

He followed my gaze and narrowed his eyes in understanding. "It's not over, is it?"

"It is for you. You need to stay away from me," I said in a low voice, sidestepping him and heading up the hall.

"What the fuck, Lela? Are you kidding me?" He caught up and hooked his fingers around my arm. "I care about you. A bunch of my friends are dead or hurt, and you're obviously still wrapped up in something. And I thought we—"

"You thought what?" asked a painfully familiar voice. Juri stepped from a side hallway and put an arm around me, tugging me away from Ian. I froze at the feel of Malachi's hands on my body. He even smelled like Malachi, earth and leather. He was wearing jeans and a T-shirt, revealing a few of the scars along his forearms, as well as the number tattoo on his left arm. His hand slid down to my waist, and words escaped me, especially when I looked up into his eyes, so dark they were almost black. "Hi," he said, and it was so gentle and so *Malachi* that it made my eyes sting with tears.

"You're back too, then," Ian said in a flat voice.

"I am," Juri replied, "and I would be interested in hearing why you put your hands on my girlfriend a minute ago."

"I'm not your girlfriend," I tried to say, but I only mouthed it. I couldn't get any sound to come out. Too much. It was way too much.

Juri looped one of my curls around his finger as he held me close.

"Lela, if you don't want him to—" Ian began, then flinched as Juri leaned forward.

"She is *mine*," Juri said, almost a growl.

He sounded nothing like Malachi, and I wrenched myself away from him, my heart hammering, my tears barely contained. He didn't try to keep ahold of me. He merely chuckled and put his hands up in surrender. "Even when we're disagreeing," he added.

"Lela, are you really okay?" Ian asked as the bell rang.

I wanted to tell him the truth. I was the furthest thing from okay anyone had ever been. But if I did, he'd only want to help. He'd want to be my friend. Ian was one of the nicest guys I'd ever met. He was good. And if I let him in, Juri would slaughter him. I sucked in a breath. "I'm fine. You'd better get to class."

Ian's jaw clenched, and he shook his head. "Whatever."

As soon as he disappeared around a corner, I shoved Juri hard enough to send any normal person crashing into the lockers. But he wasn't a normal person, and he absorbed the blow without even stepping back.

"Leave Ian alone," I snapped.

Juri snorted. "I don't like him. Malachi didn't like him, either. If he touches you again, I'm going to peel his skin off while he's still alive. And if you *let* him touch you, I'll make you watch."

"Why are you even here?"

He raised his arms, his eyes growing wider. "Where else should I be?"

"I'm going to kill you," I said in a low voice.

His fingers were in my pocket before I could move, and I felt them close around the hilt of my knife. "No, you're not," he said softly.

I tensed, preparing to feel that blade in my stomach, but instead his fingertips stroked at the hollow of my hipbone beneath the fabric of my clothes. I tried to step away, but his other hand curved around the back of my neck. He set his forehead on mine. "No, you're not," he repeated, still stroking, making my stomach churn. "Come to me tonight."

"No fucking way." I jerked my fist up to slam it into his throat.

He caught it easily in a firm grip, then ran his thumb over my knuckles. "Your heart's not in this, Lela. It was a terrible thing for the Judge to do, to send one girl to stop me and mine."

"I've done all right so far. At least, that's what your Queen probably thought, right before she died." I hadn't actually killed her, but I was willing to take credit just to get him to let me go.

He only held me tighter. "I don't know exactly what you've done, but I'm going to make you pay for all of it." His words were at odds with his voice, which was low and caressing, a seductive version of Malachi I'd only seen a few times.

"By talking me to death?"

He laughed. "Maybe. I'm never myself when I'm around you."

I put my hands on his waist, trying to push him away. But not trying very hard, because it felt so good. And so horrible. He was reminding me of everything I'd lost.

"Really, I should kill you slowly," he continued, "and I should allow all my family to participate. I should eat your heart and send you back to the Judge, broken and useless."

"You can try," I whispered, but they were only words. I knew the truth: I was already broken and useless.

"Oh, I think I will. But not yet."

"Why?" A terrible, shameful part of me wanted him to kill me now, to have it over with.

Juri tapped the side of his head. "Maybe it's him. All that passion." He closed his eyes, savoring. "Maybe I want what he never got to have. Maybe I want the satisfaction of knowing how much it would hurt him to know that I'd claimed you." His fingers slid down my cheek. "Or maybe, when you add him and me, this is what you get. Come to me tonight, or else I will kill the ones you care about, one by one. You know I can do it. And you know that a new basement lock will do nothing to protect Diane. Just like you know that Mr. Murray's advanced perimeter security system could never keep Tegan truly safe. Don't test me, Lela."

He pressed me up against a locker and bowed his head, grazing his nose along my throat, whispering an address while chills rolled over me. "I want you there alone," he murmured against my ear. "If I so much as smell anyone else, Diane will be dead by morning." My hands pushed against his chest. I gritted my teeth to hold in the sob.

"Hey, guys, cut it out unless you want in-school suspension," called one of the hall monitors as she turned the corner. "Get to class or I'm making the call."

Juri chuckled. "I'll see you later, then," he said. He kissed my cheek and walked quickly down the hall, leaving me to stagger to my next class.

TWENTY-EIGHT

JURI DIDN'T SHOW UP at lunch. I stuck around long enough to register his absence and then spent the rest of the break in a bathroom stall, trying to pull myself together. I'd known it would be hard to face him again, but I'd had no idea what it would actually feel like. I'd thought I would see only the monster inside.

But that wasn't what had happened. Instead, I saw the boy I missed more than anything else, the one I wanted by my side, the one I'd journeyed into hell to get back. And as much as I hated it, when Juri touched me gently, when he moved close and spoke softly, it felt like an echo of Malachi.

I knew it wasn't him. Juri couldn't fool me.

But I could fool myself.

It was the most deadly, destructive kind of pretend, and I knew that giving in to it was as good as surrendering. "He's gone. For good," I whispered to myself. "Stop wanting him." I said it over and over again, as if the repetition would make it happen.

I zombie-walked through my afternoon classes, silently chanting. When I walked out of school, Raphael was waiting at the curb in his nondescript gray sedan. My eyes were drawn straight to it like he'd called my name. The door opened as I approached. I sank onto the seat. "I thought I'd see you before now."

He pulled away from the curb. "Though it may seem like it, I actually can't be in more than one place at the same time."

"Why has a week passed?" I asked. "Last time, it was only a few hours or something, wasn't it?"

He tilted his head. "But this time, the Mazikin are here, making connections with other realms that should never be made, and tying their timelines to each other as well. While you were in the Mazikin realm and before you destroyed the portal, Juri brought several of his family into the land of the living."

A hard chill went through me. Who had he gotten ahold of? I tried to think back, remembering the sea of frightened faces as the humans swarmed out of the Mazikin city, but none of them stood out. I'd been so focused on looking for one face in particular that I hadn't seen much else. "The Judge said there were eleven in total."

"Then that is what's true."

I rolled my eyes. Eleven didn't seem like much, but it was a pretty high body count if I thought about what the headlines might say. Especially considering the number of casualties so far. Homeless killings, vigilante turf wars, an explosion at an abandoned club . . . Rhode Island had itself a deadly crime wave. "Okay, so what now? We have no house, no weapons, and only two Guards, one of whom is suffering from some major smoke inhalation." *And one of whom would love to curl into a little ball and disappear.*

He gave me a sharp sidelong glance. "I've already healed Henry. I also brought weapons from Michael. He sends his regards. I have acquired you a small house to use as a base. Henry is settled in now and awaiting orders."

I watched the scenery go by for a few minutes, once again struck by the deceptive ordinariness of each house, each car, each lady pushing a stroller down the sidewalk. None of it seemed real to me now. "So, was the Mazikin city destroyed for good?"

"The city disappeared into the sand, but the dome is still in place. Some of them may have survived, of course. They have proven themselves to be hardy creatures."

I sat up a little straighter. "Hang on. So some of them might have survived, and the blue goo stuff can't be destroyed. What's stopping them from digging up the Mazikin who were inside the portal? What's stopping them rebuilding it?"

"You are."

"I have to go back there?" It felt like someone had stuffed my stomach full of splinters.

"There is no reason for you to go back. But there is every reason for you to eliminate all the Mazikin here. Even if the Mazikin in the city could rebuild the portal, it wouldn't matter as long as there was no one on the other side."

"It's happened at least once before," I said in a flat voice. "How did they get out in the first place?"

"If I am to believe Ana and Takeshi, who gave us a full report before they were released into the Countryside, Sil is dead, Ibram is dead, and so is the Queen. Nero, the father of nearly all the Mazikin and the one who escaped initially, was imprisoned in the tower many years ago. That leaves only one Mazikin capable of masterminding reconstruction of the portal."

"Juri."

"Correct. He only needs assistants on the other side."

I covered my face with my hands, my fingers curling into my hair. "He can see them. He can communicate with them using that blue goo stuff. I've seen it happen."

"But if you kill him here before they rescue his body there, he might never have the chance. I suggest you complete your mission as efficiently as possible," he said as he pulled into the driveway of a plain white cottage at the very end of a cul-de-sac, set apart from the other houses and surrounded by high hedges.

I looked at his freckled face. *Can you hear my thoughts? Do you know what this is like for me?*

And did he know how messed up I was inside?

"As I said, perhaps you should complete your mission efficiently," he said gently, "for the benefit of all." His gray eyes were full of too much knowledge, and it did nothing to ease the pain in my stomach. Would he think I was a traitor because I let Juri touch me, because I let him walk away without even trying to fight? Would he tell the Judge how pathetic and tired I was? What would—? "Lela, maybe you should get out of the car now."

I blinked. "Right. Yes. Right." I threw open the door and lunged for the driveway, stumbling as my toe caught on a fissure in the crumbling blacktop. "Thanks for the ride," I called without turning around, making as quickly as I could for the house.

Henry was inside, sitting at a white-painted wooden table in the eat-in kitchen. Lace curtains fluttered at the window. Like someone's grandma had done the decorating. Henry's crossbow lay disassembled across the tabletop, and he was using some kind of stone to sharpen the tips. "We going hunting tonight?" he asked casually.

"I am."

He set the bolt down and met my eyes. "Alone?"

I nodded. I knew that Juri would unleash hell if Henry picked off his Mazikin while I was with him. "We need to figure out exactly who the other ten are. I know two by sight—Juri and the one who possessed Evan Crociere."

Henry looked thoughtful. "You want to make sure we know all the players."

I sat down at the table. "Yeah. Then we'll know when we've gotten all of them. We can track their movements even if they try to run."

"What about the ones we do know?" He ran his thumb over the edge of one of his bolts.

"If we kill Juri first, the rest will probably scatter. Who knows where they'd go. The Judge said she wanted them dead."

His eyes narrowed. "But Juri's the one giving orders. He's the most dangerous."

Especially because he was the one with knowledge of how to rebuild the portal. My heart beat faster. "He is, and we'll take him on. But I'm going to do reconnaissance tonight. I want you to protect my friends. And if I'm not back by morning, I want you to stake out Diane's and make sure she's okay. Can you do that?"

We stared at each other for a few seconds. "You're the Captain," he finally muttered, gathering the pieces of his bow and stashing them in a satchel at his feet. I kept my eyes on the tabletop as he packed the rest of his gear, slung his pack over his shoulder, and headed for the door. He paused at the threshold. "Be careful tonight. He's more dangerous to you than anyone."

I bit the inside of my cheek and did not look up. A moment later, the door clicked shut, and he was gone.

I went home and ate dinner with Diane. She'd talked to one of her cop friends, who'd promised to do a few extra patrols in the neighborhood. She'd also replaced the basement lock, though I knew full well it didn't mean much. I watched the news with her, my stomach tight as the reporters showed images of the suspected arson in Warwick, the charred ruin of our Victorian Guard house, though the anchor said it had been abandoned for some time. Authorities were speculating that the incident was evidence that the crime wave might be spreading to our town, since the accelerant had been the same as that used in the club fire. Then the news anchor listed the people identified as having been in the abandoned club when it burned to the ground, and stated that a significant number of them had lived in Warwick before disappearing.

With relief and dread, I waved good-bye to Diane as she pulled down the drive, heading for her job at the prison. It was time for me to go, too.

My old Corolla was parked at the curb, but Raphael had left us his gray sedan, and I decided to take that to Juri's. The last thing I needed was to have my car traced to a crime scene.

The address Juri had given me was in Coventry, past the Flat River Reservoir. Rhode Island might be a small state, but it was capable of serious boonies. It took me nearly an hour to get there, and every minute that went by left me more nervous. What the hell was Juri doing out here, and how stupid was I to come alone? As I tooled along the narrow road, woods on either side, I called Henry and described where I was. I told him that if he didn't hear from me in two hours, he should come with his bow and do his worst.

He was happy enough to make that promise. He let me know that Ian was in for the night and said he was headed to Tegan's property. Once again, he lingered at the end of the call, told me to be careful, then hung up. In the silence afterward, I promised myself I wouldn't let him down. I'd show him I could do this—I'd go there, look around, identify the Mazikin so we could go after them later, and fight my way out if I had to.

I was still trying to psych myself up when I reached a long, winding drive with a mailbox that matched the number Juri had given me. At the end of it was a rickety old ranch house in a clearing, with several cars parked out front. One of them had a "Warwick High Honor Student" bumper sticker. I made sure my knives were securely strapped to all my favorite places and got out of the car. My head spun as I inhaled the scent that hung in the yard like a heavy curtain—it wasn't incense. It was acrid and subtly sweet. Chemical fumes burned my nose.

A house in the middle of nowhere. A chemical stench. A horrible certainty welled up inside me.

Juri appeared in the doorway and sauntered onto the porch, looking unfairly gorgeous in Malachi's skin. He gave me a wicked smile as he descended the creaking wooden steps to the yard. "I was starting to get worried that I might have to come after you. Although . . . that might have been fun." His hungry eyes slid from my toes to my face, taking in every inch.

My hands crept toward the knives strapped to my waist. "Did you buy yourself a house in the last week, Juri?"

He looked back at the peeling siding, the dingy windows, the gutters packed with rotting leaves. "Oh, no. It turns out I'm related to the owners." His grin was so sinister it made me shiver. But so did the realization of what he'd done—it was so calculated. He'd come out here, found the place he wanted, and . . .

"Were they cooking meth before or after you possessed them?"

"I had to have a nice source of income, Lela. Sil was more interested in not getting caught. He possessed people no one would miss. He has always been a cautious little animal."

"He *was*, yeah."

"I am less timid," Juri said in a voice that was almost a growl. "The people I chose actually had something to offer me."

I looked at all the cars parked on the weedy lawn, then at the house. Who was in there? I pulled my gaze away from the yellow glow behind the dirty windows to find Juri watching me. "Look at your little mind whirling," he said in a bemused voice, but then he grew serious. And when he did, he looked so much like Malachi that it made my knees weak. "You look so tired, my love. Come here."

I didn't want to. But I did want to.

"I won't hurt you. You can come closer." He held out his arms. A spider welcoming me to his web.

My hands curled into fists. "I can't make the same promise."

"I'd expect nothing less." He reached me in two steps and grabbed my hand. I tried to yank it from his grip, but he was too strong. He placed my palm flat on his chest so I could feel his heart—Malachi's heart. Strong. Steady. No faltering, weak skips. As it should be. "Where is he now, Lela?" he asked softly.

I glared at the woods over his shoulder. "None of your freaking business."

"Did my Queen entertain him well?"

"Yeah, until she was thrown face-first into the portal without a body waiting on the other side."

His hand tightened over mine, squeezing until I jerked my knee up. He blocked the strike easily. "I knew she was gone. I knew the portal was damaged, too." He leaned down. "But I'm going to fix it."

"Really, how? Did you know your city is in ruins?" I snapped. "The Bone Palace is nothing but a pile of femurs." I shouldn't have been riling him up, but I needed him to back off and stop acting like Malachi. It was draining away my will. "The river flooded the streets and brought every building down. I watched the whole city sink into the sand."

His eyes glittered with violence. "You're lying."

"How about you let me cut your throat, and then you can go find out for yourself?"

His arm snaked around my waist, and he pulled me against him, bringing back memories I needed to push away.

"If that's true, Lela, then where's Malachi? If he's not still imprisoned in my city, why isn't he here?" His steely fingers closed around my chin and forced my head up. "What could keep the esteemed Captain from his wayward, stubborn girl? After promising her that his heart—*this* heart—beat for her and her alone, what could stop him from remaining by her side?"

I glared at him, trying to summon some energy and focus my hatred, trying to ignore the feel of Malachi's body against me, trying to forget him completely. But then Juri's eyes widened, and he gave me an amused, sympathetic look. "He's been released, hasn't he?" he said. "He left you."

He *tsk*ed as I once again tried to shake him off, but his touch was gentle as he rubbed my back. "No, it's all right. I know it must hurt." He smoothed my curls and tucked me against his chest. It destroyed me. Even though part of me knew I should fight, the rest of me was so tired. Worn all the way through. Needing to be held close.

"I remember the first time I saw you," he said, his voice a caress. "A ghost like so many others—abandoned, alone, damaged. But so fierce. *Not* like the others. You wouldn't let me touch you, and every time you told me to get away, I wanted you more. Even now, every time I see you—"

I pushed against him, needing distance, but he wouldn't give it to me. It was like he knew his body was the drug that could keep me still. Like I was the fly, and the spider's fangs had sunk deep. No escape.

"Malachi and I are not so different," he murmured. "When it comes to you, at least. So here we are again. You have been abandoned so many times, Lela. By your mother, by your friend, and now . . . by him."

"Stop," I whispered.

"I can be Malachi for you. You can pretend. Just let yourself believe."

My fingers curled into his shirt. My body felt heavy and loose. I didn't want to struggle anymore. All I wanted was comfort.

Juri's breath tickled my ear as he spoke words that shattered me. "I love you, Lela. I'd sacrifice my own soul to save you. I'd give up my freedom to be with you. I'd kill a million times to protect you."

Tears streaked down my cheeks, wetting his shirt. My arms skimmed around his waist, and I gave in. The illusion crashed over me like a wave.

"In all my years of dreaming," Juri continued, speaking with my love's voice, "I dreamed of you, even before I knew you were real. In all my years of wishing, I wished for you. The moment I saw you, I felt it. My whole world shifted. My whole existence grew brighter."

I turned my face and pressed my forehead to his throat. Malachi was all around me, the only thing I craved. His pulse pounded against my skin. His warmth spread through me, flowing through my veins.

"I'll never leave you, Lela. I'll never abandon you."

I let out a sob as he said what I most wanted to hear. There was the slightest tremble in his hands as he ran them down my spine, the barest shake in his voice as he spoke. *This isn't real, Lela. Wake up,* a voice in my head screamed. But the rest of me was lulled by the quiet, by his arms around me. Dimly, I thought of the dark tower, of the temptation I'd felt to lie down and let it have me. Like then, I could give up. Right now. I could let the illusion take me. Or I could keep fighting.

"But I don't want to fight anymore," I whispered.

"Of course you don't," he murmured. "Of course you don't. And you shouldn't have to. Stay with me, and I'll take care of you."

This isn't real, and you're not done yet. This time it was Malachi's voice whispering deep inside my mind, like it had during my darkest moments in the tower. The words pricked inside my mind, and I shrank away.

Juri held me tighter. "Nothing could keep me away from you. No one will get between us. Because I am yours. And you. Are. *Mine.*"

The deep growl rumbled in his chest, jerking me back to reality, as potent as a shot of pure adrenaline. In a flash, I'd dropped all my weight to the ground, slipping out of his grip and rolling away before I jumped to my feet again—six feet away.

"Nice try," I panted, my knife already in my grip, my skin tingling.

He ran his knuckles along his jaw. "You seemed to be enjoying it."

My fingers tightened over the hilt of the blade. Malachi was gone. *Gone.* He'd never said any of those things to me, and they weren't real. He was in the Countryside, where he belonged. And here I was, playing make-believe with his worst enemy. "Don't do that again. I'll freaking stab you if you try."

His eyes flashed. "No, you won't." He took a step toward me and licked his lips as I took an unsteady step back. "Come inside. You came here to scope the place out, didn't you? I'm sure you told Henry you were doing reconnaissance." He chuckled. "Don't disappoint him."

He beckoned to me and headed up the porch steps. I shoved my hands in my pockets. One closed around my phone, and the other around the handle of my knife. I was ready . . .

But *so* not ready for what awaited me inside the house.

I frantically began to count. There were five people in the kitchen—no, six—which was filled with large canisters and pots and what looked like an oversized chemistry set. Evan Crociere stood near the stove with his arm around a girl I recognized. She was in my pre-calculus class. The stench wafting out of that room burned the inside of my nose and throat.

The dank living room was lined with couches and chairs, which held over a dozen people, a few of them with little glass pipes at their lips. Others were watching them, eyes vacant, and others were entertaining themselves in ways that made my stomach roil. Sweat and vomit mixed with the chemical fumes, making my head pound. Doorways at the other side of the living room opened onto what were probably bedrooms. I was betting there were people in there, too.

More than eleven. The place was packed.

Juri chuckled as he traced his finger down my cheek, making me stagger to the side and nearly step on a dude who'd passed out against the wall. "If you're wondering," he said softly, "not all of them are Mazikin. And not all my Mazikin are here."

I inched backward toward the door as Evan eyed me warily from the kitchen. Juri threw his arm around my shoulder. "It's awful not knowing who the enemy is, isn't it?"

"No," I whispered as the girl from my pre-calc class sauntered out of the kitchen with eyes only for Juri. Had she been possessed? Or was she still herself, just really captivated by the guy she thought was Malachi?

Juri gave her a gentle shove toward one of the bedrooms. "I'll be right there."

My head spun as I ran through my options. I could call the police—I had no doubt they'd be very interested in this place, judging by the telltale smell. But Juri and his Mazikin would scatter, and I still had no idea who they were. I needed them together and thinking they were safe. Thinking they had us, that their threats and their cleverness had neutralized the Guards. If Juri thought he had won, he'd stay put. And I could find a way to destroy them.

But I couldn't destroy *all* of them. Not everyone in this house was Mazikin. And some of them, judging by the Warwick High T-shirt on one of the drugged-out guys on the couch and the WHS Quahogs cap lying on the floor next to a chair, were my classmates. They might have been possessed . . . or they might have just been looking for a high. That didn't mean they deserved to die.

Juri's arm coiled around my waist, and he pulled me back against him, so hard that I gasped. "What are you going to do, my love?"

"Let me go." I hated the weakness in my voice.

His hands stroked my waist. "You can't win, Lela. Not if you want the already decimated senior class of Warwick High to make it to graduation with all its remaining members. I have a few already, and I could kill a lot more before you could stop us. And I chose carefully. You won't be able to tell who's who. They're at your school. You sat in class with them this morning. They're out tonight, at parties, on Facebook. They were at Ian's baseball practice today. They watched you get in the car with the angel after school. How will you fight us?"

My heart nearly stopped. I didn't know who to fight. I didn't know what to do.

He played with the hem of my shirt, his fingertips brushing the bare skin above my jeans. "I'll hold back. For you. As long as you give me what I want."

I clenched my teeth. "And that is?"

He spread his fingers across my side, stroking my ribs. "I want what he wanted. I want you to give yourself to me. And I think you want to do exactly that."

"You're wrong. You're an evil fucking psycho—"

"Shhh. You know who I am. And who I can be, if you let yourself believe it. Really, what loyalty do you have to the Judge? She's hurt you, just like she hurt my family. And at her bidding, you destroyed them all. For what? Only to be sent back to do more killing. She's using you, Lela."

He spun me in his arms and tilted my head up. "You said you didn't want to fight, and you don't have to."

My phone interrupted and chimed with a text. Juri let me go and stepped back as I pulled it out.

If you don't reply in the next sixty seconds, I'm on my way.

Juri gave me a half smile. "Maybe we're done here tonight."

Never taking my eyes off him, I backed to the door and spun toward the porch, skipping the steps and jumping onto the lawn. My vision was blurred with tears, and my thoughts were blurred with the craziness of everything. I jogged to my car and got in as Juri's lean silhouette darkened the doorway to the house.

I punched in a text telling Henry I was on my way, and then drove away from the new Mazikin nest. I'd been through a lot in my life, and I'd faced plenty of enemies. I'd survived over and over again. I'd never surrendered. I'd believed I never would. But as I sped down the gravelly road toward Warwick, it felt a little like I already had.

TWENTY-NINE

I DROVE TO THE Guard house, hoping we'd have a training room in the basement where I could spend a few hours punching the hell out of cloth dummies. Every moment and every mile brought replays of what had just happened. Juri had sounded exactly like Malachi. He'd touched me like Malachi had. And I'd let him. I'd clung to an illusion and let it flow through my veins like a drug.

I shook my head, trying to clear it. The lights in the Guard house were on, but there was no car in the driveway. When I walked in, though, Henry was sitting at the white wooden table. His dust-colored stare was heavy as I trudged over and sat down across from him. "Everybody's locked up tight for the night," he said, crossing his arms over his bony chest. "And Diane won't be home for several hours."

"Good. I got a look at some of the Mazikin. Sort of."

His eyebrows rose.

"They're cooking meth—"

"What's 'meth'?"

"They've got a house out in the woods, and they're making drugs and selling them. The owners of the house are definitely Mazikin. But he's got other people out there, too." I put my head down on the table, resting it on my folded arms. "Honestly, I don't know how many of them were Mazikin and how many were human."

"Did you try to find out?"

"I'll go back tomorrow night," I said quietly. I didn't know what else to do. And a small but terrible part of me wanted to feel those hands on my skin. Wanted to hear his voice in my ear. Wanted another hit, something that would numb the pain for a few minutes.

"You got inside the house. They didn't try to stop you?"

I shook my head. "I think Juri wanted me to see what he'd done."

"And he didn't try to capture you or kill you?"

I peered up at Henry. "Got something on your mind?"

He let out a hollow, dry bark of a laugh. "Plenty. What did he say, Captain? What's his angle?"

I shrugged and looked away.

"What's *your* angle, then?" he asked, his voice taking on an edge. "How many nights are you going to play this game?"

"I'm doing my best, Henry. Sorry I'm not making things happen fast enough for you."

Henry's eyes flitted over me. "Did he try to act like Malachi? That would be a mighty hard lure to resist."

I ran my tongue over my teeth. "He can't fool me."

"It's not him I'm worried about."

"I better get home." I sat back in my chair.

Henry leaned forward, resting his elbows on the table. "It feels good, doesn't it? Makes you want to forget everything. Forget who you are and what you're supposed to do. I know what that's like." He scratched at a spot on his stubbly cheek. "It's what got me killed in the first place."

I'd had my palms braced on the table, ready to run back to Diane's and hide for a few hours, but his words froze me in place. Henry had never talked about himself, not much, at least. "What do you mean?"

"I'd been taking people out for years. All contract work. For the mob, mostly, but a few independent gigs. I was always alone. Didn't have any friends. Couldn't afford to let anyone close." He looked at a spot on the wall while he talked, like all the memories were right there in front of him. "I was in Chicago for a job. Some midlevel associate who was ratting to the feds. I spent the weekend stalking the guy." He chuckled. "Didn't realize someone was stalking me."

I took my palms off the table and placed them in my lap. Waiting.

"In those days, men like me . . . we couldn't exactly be ourselves. But there were places we could go. I needed that sometimes, you know? Just needed to touch another person and have that person touch me. Made me feel real. Less like a ghost." The color rose in his cheeks as he met my eyes, then he looked away, clearing his throat. "Anyway, I found one of those places that night, right near the main drag where my target was staying with his mistress. I figured a few hours wouldn't make a difference. And as I walked up to the place, a man stepped out of the shadows and offered me a cigarette. Marvin Riccio." Henry shook his head as his lips shaped themselves around the name. "He was like me. A killer, through and through. And we'd been together before. Love and hate could be wrapped so tightly around each other . . . That's how I felt about him. There he was, right when I needed someone, and even though I knew it wasn't quite right—I mean, why was he there? *Right* there, when I was in town for a job?—I knew what I wanted. He made me weak."

"You let him get close to you."

"It happened so fast. One minute I was lighting up, and the next, we were in the alley, and he had his hands on me, and I never wanted anything so bad. Never felt so wanted, either. Always felt that way when I was with him." He stopped there, still staring at the wall. "It felt good to be wanted," he said, so quietly that it was hard to hear him. "It felt good, in those seconds, to think he couldn't stay away from me."

"Seconds."

He nodded. "I was on the ground with a knife in my gut after that. And you know what he said to me as I lay there dying? He said, 'It was never real.'"

I closed my eyes. "I'm sorry, Henry."

"That wasn't the worst part, Captain. What made it burn was that I already knew. I'd known it all along. I'd just chosen to pretend. So I died knowing that I'd done it to myself. And when I got to the Wasteland, I knew I belonged there. I didn't even fight it."

I backed my chair away from the table, nearly falling over backward because I was so eager to get away from him. "I'll see you tomorrow, Henry. I have to go." I felt for my keys in my pocket as I strode toward the door.

"It's not real, Captain," he called after me. "Pretending will only get us all killed. Sometimes all you can do is face what's in front of you and see it for what it is—and what it's not."

The door slammed hard behind me, and I ran for my car. I drove past the turnoff for Diane's and got on the highway as Henry's words rang in my head. My head felt like a time bomb as I went over the bridges to Newport and drove all the way to the spot that always drew me at times like this. I followed the rocky trail of the Cliff Walk through the dark, listening to the ocean licking at the shore several yards below me.

I sat down on the boulder where I'd stood months ago, demanding to know if Nadia was all right, shouting at the sky to tell me where she'd gone. One gust of wind was all it had taken to push me over the edge.

One gust of wind was all it would take now.

I couldn't stay here. I couldn't do this. I wasn't strong enough, not anymore. Everything had been taken away, and Henry was right: my mistakes were not only going to get me killed—they were going to be the death of others as well. I was a liability.

It was never real. That's what Henry's lover—his killer—had said to him. Shivering as the wind blew my hair around my face, I had to wonder if any of this was real. What made something real? I'd been in a city where people could grow whatever they wanted out of nothing—were those things real? I'd been in a hell world where existing meant endless horror, but love could heal with a touch. Was that real? Now that I was here, in the land of the living, what I'd always assumed was reality didn't feel like it anymore. I didn't feel connected to any of it.

I put my hand out, looking for the edges of my reality, wondering if I could pierce it like a soap bubble. What would happen if I got up and started walking, right over the edge? Or what if I simply lay down and didn't get up?

"I've had enough," I said to the sky, addressing the Judge, wherever she was. "I give up."

The quiet hiss of waves was the only reply.

I rose to my feet and held out my arms. "I give up," I shouted. "Do you hear me? I can't do this!"

I threw back my head, waiting for the wind to carry me over, not caring where it took me as long as I didn't have to feel this miserable loneliness anymore. "Come on," I screamed at the Judge. "What are you waiting for?" I swayed in place, the toes of my boots right at the edge of the rocks. "Please," I whispered. "I'm done."

I'm in love with your strength, Malachi whispered back, an echo in my memory. *I'm in love with your determination, the way you never* ever *give up.*

The sob forced its way from my throat before I knew I was crying. I stumbled over a rock, landing hard on the gravel trail. I rolled to my back and looked up at the moon. "You'd be so disappointed if you could see me now," I mumbled, though I knew full well Malachi couldn't hear me.

These people need those things from you now.

I let out another shuddering sob. He'd said that to me at the gates of the Mazikin city, trusting me to do everything I could to usher all those human souls to safety. I'd thought I had, but there were more people in danger right now. *Right now.*

While I was here, wishing. Pretending. Doing exactly what all the people in the dark city did—instead of going in search of what I needed, instead of facing reality and dealing with it, no matter how painful, I'd grown myself a shabby imitation of what I most wanted, and then buried myself in false comfort. And in doing so, I'd turned away from everything I thought I was and everyone I cared about.

Ian. Tegan. Diane. Henry. So many others who could still be saved—unless pretending was more important to me than their lives. Unless my desire for a few minutes of illusion was worth more than their safety. Unless my craving for escape outweighed my sense of duty.

"I don't abandon my friends," I said, my voice cracking. I slowly stood up and dusted off my pants. I was the disposable abandoned girl . . . I had been, at least. But I didn't abandon people. I didn't turn away. And I didn't give up. "I will *never* give up," I whispered.

I was still exhausted. Still grieving. Still feeling like all my insides had been smashed up and stomped on. But I wouldn't stop until I had done the job I'd been sent here to do. It wasn't about loyalty to the Judge. Not at all.

It was about me choosing who I wanted to be.

I took deep breaths of sea air and got into my car, drove back across the bridges, and headed for Diane's. I needed to get a few hours of sleep before I faced tomorrow. I'd have to be a lot sharper and more focused if I was going to succeed. If I was going to look at Juri and face the reality. He was just a corrupted copy of Malachi, and he could only fool me if I let him. And by allowing him close to me, I wasn't honoring the memory of what Malachi and I had together. I was spitting on it. Malachi deserved so much more from me than that.

The only thing I could do was accept that he was gone, hold on to the memories of what we had together, and stop trying not to miss him—I would never stop missing him.

I parked my car and tromped up the steps, then swung the front door open and tossed my keys in the basket in the entryway.

Midtoss, it hit me. The door hadn't been locked.

I pressed myself against the door. He was leaning against the wall. Only ten feet away.

"Diane keeps her spare key under the ladybug stone in the flower bed," Juri said quietly. "It's a bit of an obvious choice."

I drew my knife, rage flaring inside me. "If you've done anything to her—"

"She's at work, as far as I know." He took a slow, cautious step toward me. "I couldn't stay away, Lela."

My fingers tightened over the grip of my knife. "Your mistake."

His brow furrowed. "You don't look happy to see me."

"Oh, I'm happy. You picked the perfect time to show up."

I lunged for him, my knife hand darting out like a viper. He raised his arms and jumped back, his eyes wide as he shook his head in disbelief. "You're serious?"

"Deadly serious." And even more determined because he didn't think I'd actually do it. He thought I was weak. And he was wrong. I struck again, nearly slicing one of his fingers as he skipped to one side and put a chair between us. As I moved forward again, he tossed it at my feet, forcing me to jump to avoid getting tripped up by its legs. He caught my wrist as I flailed, but I slammed my knee into his gut.

He groaned. "I don't want to hurt you," he said through clenched teeth as my fingers dug into his neck. His arm was wrapped around my waist, his other hand clamped over my wrist to keep me from slamming my blade between his ribs.

"I *do* want to hurt *you*," I huffed, then slammed my forehead against his cheekbone. He dropped me abruptly, and I rolled away, getting to my feet immediately.

He let out a hoarse laugh as he touched his fingertips to his already-swollen cheek. "That was very good."

"Shut up." He was trying to sound like Malachi again. It wouldn't work this time. "You've got balls, coming here like this. You really must have thought you had me." I circled to the left, trying to get him into the open space of the living room, where he couldn't toss furniture at me.

I was wary; Malachi had been a master at improvising, and Juri would know all his tricks. Which of Diane's possessions would he use as a weapon against me? The vase on the coffee table? The metal lamp next to the couch? Juri smiled as he saw me assessing the possibilities. "Fighting here isn't a good idea," he said. "Diane has such a lovely home."

"Then maybe you shouldn't have broken in again."

He frowned, and I took that moment to go for his legs. It had worked once before, on the practice mat in the basement of the old Guard house. Malachi hadn't been expecting that kind of attack, and it was the only time I'd ever beaten him.

He let out a startled grunt and bent his knees as I plowed into him, knocking him backward over the coffee table, which collapsed with a rending crunch under our weight. He gasped with pain as I drew the knife up his calf, but the fabric of his jeans was too thick to allow me to cut deep. In an instant, his fingers were around my wrist again, squeezing so hard that I cried out. He threw himself forward, grabbing my other wrist as I put my hand out to stop him.

Then he was on top of me, the relentless weight of his body pinning me to the floor. I jerked my head up to smash it into his, but he ducked to the side and used his shoulder to hold me down.

Until I bit that shoulder, sinking my teeth into his muscle.

He roared in pain, then pressed his body so hard onto mine that my jaws were forced open. I couldn't breathe. I couldn't move.

"Stop it now, Lela," he said sharply. "This is getting ridiculous."

Having him mock me was like pouring acid over the wounds. With a wrenching cry, I struggled, trying desperately to get out from under him. But he held both my wrists in one hand and grabbed a fistful of my hair, using it to hold me down. "Stop, Lela. Stop."

"Fuck you," I yelled, tears leaking from the corners of my eyes. It couldn't be over so soon. This couldn't be how it happened. I felt so stupid. I couldn't even protect myself, let alone anyone else. But I still wouldn't give up. "You're going to have to kill me, Juri. I won't stop."

He gently kissed my forehead. "You've got it all wrong, and I should have thought of this. Look at me."

His weight on me lessened, just a bit, and my mind started to work, waiting for the exact moment to throw him off or knee him hard. To keep him from getting suspicious, I looked into his eyes like he'd asked.

"It's me," he said softly.

"You've fooled me with that line before. I'm not playing this game again."

Fury flashed in his eyes. "You shouldn't ever have had to play it."

"Stop. No more pretending."

He nodded. "No more pretending. Look at my neck, Lela. Really look."

I did. At the smooth olive skin of his throat. He had none of the terrible scarring Malachi had been left with after his time in the Mazikin city. My gaze moved automatically to the scar where Juri had bitten Malachi's neck.

It wasn't there. "What the—"

Keeping my wrists imprisoned in his iron grip, he reached down with his other hand to untuck his shirt and pull it up. Terror streaked through me.

"Shhh. Lela, I'm just showing you. Look."

I glanced down to see his abs, unscarred and perfect, not marred by the huge hollow spot where the Queen had rammed her claws into Malachi's chest. But of course this body wouldn't have any of that. It would only have the scars Malachi had brought with him to the land of the living. This was the body Malachi had been forced to leave behind when Juri possessed him. Slowly, he took one of my hands in his, still keeping the other secure. His eyes lingered on mine as he guided my palm to the place where four deep claw marks had scarred Malachi's back.

They were gone, too. All that lay beneath my hand was warm skin.

"Say my name," he said quietly.

"You're not him," I said in a choked whimper. "He's gone. I don't know what you've done, but you can't fool me. He was nothing but scars after the Mazikin realm. He would have those—"

"All of them had disappeared by the time I reached the Countryside." Cautiously, like he was trying not to spook me, he released my hand and left it on his back. I couldn't have moved it even if I wanted to. I was paralyzed with shock.

"You *know* me. Say my name," he said again, bowing his head so his nose grazed along my cheek, making me shiver. "Please, say my name. I fought my way out of heaven just so I could hear it again."

"Malachi?" I said, my voice trembling.

His eyes shone with relief and love. "Yes."

THIRTY

I BLINKED UP AT him, taking in every inch of his beautiful face. "What did you do?"

He looked a little sheepish. "The same thing I've done on two other occasions."

"You stormed the Sanctum." When he nodded, I said, "How is that even possible? You were in the Countryside!"

He let go of the arm he'd been holding above my head and propped himself on an elbow so he could look down at me. "When you were in the Countryside, how did you see the dark city?"

I thought back. "I saw Nadia's face on my arm and started thinking about her, and it sort of . . . appeared." Other remembered conversations struck me. "And Jim was in the Countryside, too, and he saw the Blinding City. He said he'd been feeling restless and wanting more, and then it became visible to him. And Ana told me that the moment she understood that Takeshi wasn't in the Countryside, the Wasteland appeared to her, and the Mazikin city is at the very edge of it, in the desert."

Malachi nodded. "Then you know how it happened."

I tentatively touched his face. "But didn't you find your family?"

He closed his eyes. "I did." He smiled. "It was good to see them. To know how happy they were. And they hadn't forgotten me. My mother cried."

"How could you leave all that?" I asked as his head dropped into the space between my shoulder and neck. I wrapped my arms around him, my fingers in his inky-black hair. "You'd wanted it for so long."

"Because I wanted something else even more." His breath was hot against my collarbone. "And when the Sanctum appeared in front of me, it was not a hard decision. Or, it was one I'd already made, at least. The Judge was rather exasperated when I showed up again."

I pressed my lips together, trying not to laugh. "You are too much," I whispered, holding him tight. "I can't believe you did this. Why would you let yourself get sentenced to be a Guard again? I mean—"

"I think we should clean up a bit before Diane comes home," he said abruptly, raising his head. He stood up, leaving me flat on my back, still reeling. After a few seconds, I sat up to find him gathering pieces of the splintered coffee table. "I'll take these to the garbage."

He walked out to the front, and when he came back, I was running the vacuum, trying to get bits of shattered glass up from the carpet. We cleaned silently. It didn't take long.

When we were done, her living room looked a bit emptier and I knew I'd have a lot of explaining to do. Malachi tied off a garbage bag and set it by the door, then came over to me. His cheek was red and puffy where I'd head-butted him, and his jeans had a bloody slash across the calf, but he wasn't limping.

"You could get Raphael to heal that when you get back to the Guard house," I said.

He shrugged and took one of my hands, then placed it on his chest. Just like Juri had done last night—and I stiffened. Malachi let go of me, frowning. "What did he do to you, Lela?" he asked, his voice quiet and deadly.

"The worst thing he could have done. He pretended to be you." *Worse, I pretended, too.*

He looked down at his hands. "And now you don't want me to touch you."

I shook my head. "I . . . I just feel like . . ." I didn't know how to say it. I felt like I'd cheated on him somehow. It didn't seem fair for him not to know. "I let him touch me," I explained. "I knew it wasn't real, but I let him put his hands on me."

His eyes were so dark. Fathomless. I couldn't read them as he said, "Why?"

"Because I missed you. And I was so tired. I just wanted a few minutes of comfort." I swallowed back the memory of it, the defeat. "I wanted it so badly," I said in a choked voice.

"Did it help?"

"No," I said, grimacing. "It was confusing and awful."

"And if I touch you now?" He was still, waiting for my answer.

"It might still be confusing."

"I'm going to make it unconfusing, then." Again, he reached for my hand, and I let him take it and lay it on his cheek. He turned his head and kissed my palm. "No matter what he did, or what he said, he could never pretend well enough." He tipped my chin up. "Because he hasn't felt himself grow stronger simply because you were touching him. He hasn't healed your body with his hands on your skin. He will never understand the power of that. And that means he could never make you feel what I can."

Then his lips were on mine, warm and delicious, as his fingertips trailed down my cheek to my throat. He traced them along my collarbone as he deepened the kiss, sliding his tongue into my mouth and making me moan at the taste of him. I coiled my arms around his neck, our connection stealing my breath, his hard body up against mine, his arm around my waist, crushing me to his chest. My hands skimmed over his shoulders, down his back, all the way to his waist. Everything was smooth, no bumpy scars beneath his shirt, and suddenly, I wanted to see what this kind of miracle looked like. I pushed up his shirt, and he pulled it over his head and let it fall to the floor.

My heart beat like a jackhammer as I touched the spot where the terrible scar had been, right in the center of his chest. Now it was perfect, muscles knitted together beneath skin that goose-bumped wherever I touched. He shivered, then laughed to himself. "I was surprised, too."

"I love you, no matter what you look like."

"I know." He drew in a sharp breath when I stroked my fingers down the center of his stomach. "Lela—"

I didn't know how to explain. Mostly because this was the biggest feeling I'd ever had. I stood on my tiptoes and kissed him again, my fingers curling into the lean muscles of his back, trying to translate the powerful, shaky need twisting inside of me. After a few minutes, with that need drawing tighter with every second, Malachi groaned and lifted me off my feet. My legs wrapped around his waist. "Where?" he said against my mouth.

"My bed," I mumbled.

He carried me down the hall and into my room, then sank with me onto my single bed, never lifting his mouth from mine. I couldn't steady my breathing, couldn't catch up with myself. I could feel the tension in his muscles, the firm lines of him, the urgency as his hand gripped my hip.

He's here and he's real. I said it to myself over and over. *You have him now.* But how long would it last before we were separated again? My fingers clutched at his back, and I pulled my mouth from his to taste his skin, my teeth scraping against his neck and drawing a broken sigh from him. He'd settled himself next to me, not on top of me, so I turned to him, hooking my ankle over his calf. His hand was just beneath my ribs now, and I kept expecting it to venture up, to maybe try to pull my shirt off like I'd done to him, but it stayed where it was.

I wasn't sure if I was glad or upset about that.

I nipped at the bony hollow at the base of his throat, and he curled his fingers around the back of my neck, holding me there. His pulse was beating furiously, steady and fierce. But when I drew my tongue down the center of his chest, he abruptly rolled onto his back—and nearly off the bed. I grabbed on to him and scooted back toward the wall so he could have room. "Sorry," I said as he chuckled. "Did I do something wrong?"

His eyes were closed, and the smile on his face was so sweet that I couldn't keep myself from kissing him. "No, nothing wrong," he said breathlessly when I lifted my head. "But you can't keep doing that."

"Why?"

"Because, Lela, it's a little . . ." He sighed. "I just want to go slow. I don't want to relive what happened between us on the training mat that day. You were scared, and I didn't even notice."

"You did."

He stroked the hair away from my face. "Not quickly enough."

I looked down at my hand, my fingers splayed across his chest. "But you do . . . you want this, right?" I certainly did. I just didn't know how to get there. It was a little like looking at this beautiful oasis in the distance, but the desert around it was strewn with land mines, all these things that had happened to me, memories that ambushed me at the worst times.

Malachi captured my mouth with his, nibbling at my bottom lip before releasing it. "You know how much I want you," he said, kissing my jaw, my neck.

I knew. Juri had made sure of that. He'd used it as a weapon against me. Malachi must have felt me tense. "Do I want to know what he said to you, when he was pretending to be me?"

I shook my head.

Malachi looked me over, his gaze walking itself up my legs, over my stomach and breasts, up to my eyes. "Did he tell you that I can't get you out of my mind? Did he tell you that I imagine kissing and touching you when I really should be thinking about other things? Did he tell you that sometimes it scares me—how much I desire you, and how deep it goes?"

I had to work hard to hold his gaze as I nodded, waiting for his anger and frustration. These were all things I should have been hearing for the first time, but Juri had already beaten him to the punch. I would have been pissed if it were me, if a monster went to Malachi, wearing my skin, and told him all my secrets. But Malachi didn't look upset.

"All of that is true," he said. "I won't lie." He touched his forehead to mine. "But did he tell you how much I care about you?"

I blinked up at him. Malachi kissed the tip of my nose. "Did he tell you how absolutely precious you are to me?" When he saw my puzzled look, he smiled. "Did he say *any* of the things that mattered?"

"He only said you, um . . ."

Malachi rolled his eyes. "I'm sure what he said was as crass as possible. You don't have to repeat it. But maybe you'll let me translate." His hand skimmed over my stomach to my side. "What I want is everything. If you gave me your body but not the rest of you, it would be a fairly crushing disappointment. I don't want to do anything unless all of you is there and wanting it, too."

I touched his chest. "I don't know how to do that. Things sneak up on me. I never know when a touch or some other sensation will trigger a memory."

He kissed the top of my head. "I know," he whispered. "Which is why I want to take things slow. So that when we finally are together, it will be because you're ready, and I'm ready, and neither of us can wait another minute. I can wait for that. It's worth waiting for."

I gave a sniffly laugh as he pulled me into another kiss, our teeth clacking together before we sank into each other, arms wrapped tight, me halfway on top of him and not nearly close enough. It was everything I ever could have wanted—free of fear, free of expectation and worry, free of the past. It was just me and him, happy and whole and hopeful. Like we had in the Mazikin city, we guided each other's hands to the places that felt best. But this time, it wasn't about healing. It was about pleasure. We moved slowly, translating every breath, every tensing muscle, until Malachi had me wound so tight I thought I might catch fire.

After several ecstatic, frantic minutes, Malachi chuckled as I kissed his chest. His hands closed over my hips. "Forgive me for saying it, but . . ."

I nipped at his skin. "What?"

"I think we're going to be very good at this." The low timbre of his voice sent delicious shivers across my skin. And as he rolled to his side, his fingers hooking behind my knee and sliding my leg along his hip, as his mouth collided with mine and I welcomed it, I couldn't have agreed more.

Of course, that was the moment the front door slammed and Diane yelled, "What the heck? Lela!"

I jumped off of Malachi, and he went crashing to the floor. He shot to his feet—just in time for Diane to come down the hall and see him standing there, awkwardly adjusting his pants. His shirt was dangling from her fist.

She arched an eyebrow as she glared at him. "Baby?"

I cleared my throat. "Yeah?"

"You invited this boy here?"

"Er. Yes. Yes, I did."

Malachi stepped forward to take his shirt from her, but she held it up and gave him a warning look that froze him where he stood. He cleared his throat. "Ms. Jeffries, I—"

"Mm-mm-mm," she said, and his mouth snapped shut. "This is not how we do things in this house."

"Well, technically," I said, scooting off my bed and straightening my shirt, "you never said I couldn't have a boy here."

She fixed me with a stare. "How about I say it now?"

I held up my hands. "That's okay. I'm sorry. We weren't really doing much—"

She eyed the bite mark on Malachi's shoulder and waved his shirt like a flag. "I found this in my living room. Any other clothing items lying around here?"

"I will be happy to put it on again," Malachi offered, his cheeks flushed. "In fact, I'd be grateful if you would . . ."

She was fighting a smile as she tossed it at him, and in less than two seconds he was tugging it down over his front. Diane snorted. "I'm going to give you a few minutes to *compose* yourselves," she said, "and then you can see Malachi to the door, baby." She began to walk back down the hall. "After that, I want to know what happened to my coffee table!"

Malachi and I stared at each other for a moment, and then both of us started to giggle. I'd never heard that kind of sound come from him, and it made me laugh even harder. He covered his face with his hands and sank onto my bed, then seemed to decide it was inappropriate and jumped to his feet again.

"I should go," he said, wiping a tear from the corner of his eye. "That could have been a lot worse, and I don't want to push my luck."

I walked into his arms and hugged him tight. "We have a new Guard house."

"I know. It's where I arrived. Henry seemed glad to see me."

"I'll bet he was. What did he tell you?"

Malachi looked down at me. "Only that it's bad, and he's been protecting Ian and Tegan. He said I needed to find you as soon as possible."

"Juri has gotten to a bunch of our classmates, Malachi. He had a whole crowd on this property he's taken over, and I couldn't tell who was Mazikin and who was human."

Malachi's expression darkened. "Then it's good I returned."

"You think you can figure it out?"

"I have an advantage that neither you nor Henry has." He smiled, and it was cold as mid-January. "I'm wearing Juri's skin."

THIRTY-ONE

I WALKED INTO SCHOOL a few hours later with a grim sense of purpose. I'd spent the earliest hours of the morning planning our strategy with Malachi and Henry at the Guard house, and another few stolen minutes kissing Malachi while Henry went off to take advantage of his chance to rest.

Malachi and Henry had left early to watch the school, to see if Juri showed up, but Evan Crociere had driven into the parking lot alone. When the first bell rang and there was no sign of Juri, we put our plan into action. I'd expected to see Malachi at lunch, but when I walked into pre-calc, he was already there, looking confident and gorgeous with his arm around the girl who'd been with Juri at the meth house last night. She had long, straight brown hair and a beaky nose. Her clothes were clean—she looked better groomed than most Mazikin I'd seen. But then again, so did Juri. Her nails were long but painted blue. Her eyes were full of hunger and hatred as she raised her head and looked at me. "What are you looking at?" she snapped.

Malachi's grip on the girl tightened, and she smiled.

As I sank into my seat, he gave me a cold smirk that sent a chill down my spine. When I heard him murmur something to the girl and her soft, delighted intake of breath behind me, I forced myself not to turn around and stab her with my pencil—and I promised myself I'd make this up to him later. But when I heard her low odd purring—a sound no human would make—my jealousy went away.

He'd gotten her to reveal what she was.

I sat through that class, trusting that he wouldn't allow the Mazikin sitting right behind me to hurt me. He had my back, even if he was masquerading as the enemy. I spent more time listening to his movements and breath than I did to the teacher. When the bell rang, I got up quickly and turned to the two of them. She was already standing next to his desk, her hands in his hair, his resting on her hips. He gave me a sidelong glance and raised an eyebrow. "I'll see you at lunch," he said to me, then slid his fingers down the girl's leg. At the back of the classroom, Laney, who he'd broken up with on prom night, looked like she was about to cry.

I felt a bit like doing the same, but I channeled that hurt into stalking out of the classroom. Putting on a good show for whoever happened to be interested. Two hours later, I made my way to the packed cafeteria. Ian, Tegan, Laney, Jillian, Levi, and Alexis—her leg in a cast—were sitting at their usual table, which looked a lot bigger since so many of our friends had been killed or injured. Ian stared at me, maybe wondering if I was going to join them, maybe wondering if I'd head out to the parking lot and eat in the spot where we'd shared several impromptu picnics when both of us were trying to escape our grief.

Tegan was less subtle, waving me over, but I made for a table at the back of the room. Malachi was there, surrounded. Seven kids were sitting either on or around the table. Pre-Calc Girl was sitting on his lap, and Evan Crociere was lounging next to them, running his fingers up and down her back. His long, skinny legs were stretched out in front of him, clad in baggy jeans with plenty of pockets where I'd always assumed he stashed his weed. But even though he looked like the jerk he'd been, his movements were pure animal now, and it reminded me of some of the things I'd witnessed on the streets of the Mazikin city. I recognized four of the guys at the table as having been at the meth house last night, and two looked extremely strung out—bloodshot eyes, greasy hair. Were *all* of them Mazikin? Did we really have seven of the remaining eleven right here? Hope quickened my steps.

"Lela," Tegan called, right as Malachi shoved Pre-Calc Girl off of him and stood up, his eyes focused on me. His lip curled as he beckoned me forward, the gesture so commanding that I swear half the cafeteria was staring at him. Probably most of the girls were wishing he was looking at them instead of me.

I approached his table, my heart pounding. "What do you want?" I barked, putting my irritation at Pre-Calc Girl and her wandering hands into my voice.

Malachi gave me a once-over, letting his gaze linger on my chest in a way that made my cheeks burn. He sank back onto his seat. "Join us for lunch." He flashed a mischievous smile. "I'm quite hungry."

Everyone else at the table, including Pre-Calc Girl, snickered. Evan gave me a satisfied smile and made room for me. "Yeah, Lela," he said, showing his teeth. "Sit right here. I want you close."

Evan might be Mazikin now, but the thing inside him had all Evan's memories, and that included his intense hatred of me.

"Not sure I want to sit with you," I said, wrinkling my nose as I made eye contact with each of them. "You guys kind of stink."

The guy sitting closest to me growled, deep in his chest. Malachi chuckled. "If you don't sit with me," he said, "I might get bored. I wonder if Diane is still sleeping, or if she's gotten up for the afternoon?"

Even though we'd agreed he would make this threat, it still sent rage all the way through me. He said it so coldly, with a glint of eagerness in his eye, and horror suddenly struck me. What if this was actually Juri? My eyes darted to his neck, but Pre-Calc Girl had her hand over the spot as she stood behind him, her other arm stroking his chest.

"Sit down, Lela," he said firmly.

A stocky guy with an underbite and bad skin grabbed my wrist and twisted, but before I had a chance to punch him, Malachi nailed him in the forehead with a pen, hitting him hard enough to leave a swollen bump tipped with blue. The guy howled and smacked his hands over his face, while most of the others at the table cringed, their posture wary, all eyes fixed on Malachi. He glared at each of them in turn.

"She's mine," he hissed as a vein pulsed at his temple. He coughed out something in Mazikin that had all but the two strung-out guys crossing their arms protectively over their chests.

He'd probably threatened to eat their hearts.

His eyes met mine. "They won't bother you . . . unless I tell them to." He held out his arm, inviting me to sit. "I'm getting tired of waiting for you to come to me, Lela," he said softly.

I shivered. He sounded *exactly* like Juri. Again I glanced at his neck, but Pre-Calc Girl's hand was still there. I walked around the table and sat down next to him, Evan on my right. Evan's fingernails had grown long, and he'd filed them to points.

"I can't wait to watch what he does to you," Evan whispered, leaning close.

I can't wait to watch what he does to you, I thought. "So, shall we go around the table and introduce ourselves?" I suggested. "Because I don't know all of your names."

Malachi stroked his hand down my hair, letting his fingers sink into my curls. "You make me laugh, Lela. It makes me so sad about what happens next."

He didn't sound sad.

"I think we've outgrown our need for school," he said breezily. "We're leaving now."

"What?" That had not been part of the plan.

"We'll have more fun elsewhere."

The excitement from the others was palpable. They shifted in their seats, their long fingernails scraping at the surface of the table. "But I . . ." I closed my mouth. My probation officer would love to hear that I'd skipped the last half of the day.

Malachi—or was it Juri?—stood up and turned his back before I could get a look at his neck to confirm. He peered over his shoulder at the stocky guy with the red bump on his forehead. "You drive."

"I thought she was driving," the guy replied, looking at Pre-Calc Girl.

"I have other uses for her," Malachi said smoothly, his fingers twisting into her hair and jerking her near. "Help Lela out of her chair, please. Lela, please remember that I won't hesitate to skin Diane and make you watch if you don't behave."

Two guys, one of them wearing a Quahogs cap to cover his scruffy blond hair, came at me, and I was too stunned to fight. Our plan had been to wait, to go after school, but here we were, marching out of Warwick High at noon, surrounded by seven kids who had been tied to a table and possessed. Seven dead kids. We passed through the double doors that led to the student lot. Malachi was improvising, right? But if that was true, why was I the only one who was surprised? I fought the urge to tear myself away from them and start running.

But then again, this was the best chance I'd have to take out most of the Mazikin.

We were heading toward the corner of the lot when someone shouted my name. I craned my neck to see Ian jogging toward us, with Tegan several paces behind. Her face was pale with worry. Malachi peeled himself away from Pre-Calc Girl and strode past Evan, growling something in Mazikin that made Evan wrap his fingers around my upper arm.

"Lela," Ian called. "Hey. Wait!"

I shook my head, my eyes wide as Malachi strode forward to meet him. Dread choked me. I knew that walk. I knew the coiled tension in every muscle.

Ian didn't slow down. As Malachi stepped into his path, Ian drew back his fist. But as it rocketed forward, Malachi sidestepped him and rammed his elbow into Ian's back, sending him to the ground with a crunch. Tegan screamed. I nearly did, too, but Evan chose that moment to yank me toward the car. I struggled as Malachi planted his foot on the side of Ian's face and leaned over to say something to him. Ian's fingers were twitching. His eyes were open. He didn't try to get up.

Malachi stepped back and walked toward us, unhurried and predatory, Tegan shrieking in the background.

Evan wrapped his arm around my throat. "Come on, Lela. Time to die," he said, grunting to the others as we approached an old Bronco. Malachi caught up with us as I was being hauled into the backseat. He gestured to four of the Mazikin to get in, then shoved the two strung-out guys, making them fall to the pavement. It confirmed what I had started to suspect—those two weren't Mazikin.

Evan laughed as they collided with the blacktop. His arm was still around my neck as Malachi got into the backseat and sat next to me, with Pre-Calc Girl crammed in on his other side. Evan said something in Mazikin, and all of them let out animal chuckles, including Malachi. I leaned so I could see Ian. Tegan was helping him to his feet. His face was bleeding, and it looked like every breath caused him pain, but he was up and watching us drive away.

As Stocky Guy pulled out of the parking spot, I turned to Malachi and felt pure relief as I caught a glimpse of his neck—smooth skin, no scars. It was really him.

And we were in a vehicle with five Mazikin. This was a dangerous game, but now I had proof I wasn't playing alone. Still . . .

"Did you enjoy that?" I snapped at him. "You didn't need to hurt him."

Malachi chuckled, his dark eyes on mine. "Yes, I did," he said softly, even as Pre-Calc Girl's hand crept onto his thigh. "Don't worry about him now. Worry more about what's waiting for you."

I nearly smiled—it reminded me of what he'd said when we were trapped in a cage in the Bone Palace—*Focus on what's next, not what came before.* He was reminding me of where my thoughts should be. But before I could relax too much, he leaned his head back and allowed Pre-Calc Girl to nuzzle his neck. I looked away and found myself staring into Evan's bloodshot eyes. They narrowed, and he poked Malachi in the shoulder. With a growl, Malachi shoved Pre-Calc Girl away. Evan began speaking in Mazikin to him, and the conversation got intense quickly. Something wasn't quite right, but Malachi was so forceful that Evan was cringing against his window by the time Stocky Guy pulled onto Cedar Swamp Road, right by the airport. We motored onto a gravel road, all the way to an abandoned construction site. Malachi gestured to the site with an I-told-you-so kind of expression. "See? It's perfect," he said to Evan.

As soon as we were out of the car, Malachi grabbed Evan by the scruff of the neck and slammed him against the hood. "And don't question me again." He raised his eyebrows and waited until Evan nodded his head in defeat.

Malachi gestured for me to walk beside him as we hiked across loose gravel to an old trailer. The others looked confused, their eyes darting to the road, crouching any time an airplane roared overhead, which was pretty much every few minutes or so. I kept my attention on Evan, who skulked behind us, his eyes on Malachi like he expected him to attack again.

"I stashed him in here," Malachi said. "And I thought it was time for a reunion."

We entered the trailer to see Henry, his hands tied behind his back, his head down. Though I was relieved that he was in position well ahead of time, I choked out his name and lunged for him. Pre-Calc Girl and Stocky Guy dragged me backward and shoved me down so I was on my knees next to Henry, whose eyes were closed. I could tell from the tension in his body that he was alert, though. We'd chosen this spot because it was so loud no one would hear the chaos as we slaughtered however many Mazikin we'd been able to ensnare. Our new Guard house was nearby, reachable by car or by a quick sprint through the woods. My fingers twitched with eagerness and a bit of fear. I was about to kill kids I'd gone to school with, or, at least, it felt a little like that. If we succeeded, though, we'd have rid Warwick High of the Mazikin, and all we'd have to do was get Juri and the other five who were left.

And then we'd be done. The possibility shot adrenaline through my body.

The Mazikin circled us, making no pretense at humanity now. They poked at Henry, who stayed limp and unresponsive, and tugged at my hair. Evan was watching me as Malachi knelt behind us and made a show of tightening the ropes around Henry's wrists.

"How did you capture him?" Evan asked. "He's been hard to track."

Malachi's head jerked up. "I told you I would."

Evan laughed and nodded. "You did." He scratched his head. "But you also said he'd burn to death in the fire."

Malachi growled at him, the sound coming from deep in his chest, making me shudder. I hadn't known he was capable of making those noises. Evan shuffled his feet and glared at Malachi before turning his attention to me.

"You don't look that nervous," he said, sniffing at my hair before standing up straight again. His hand slid along his waist and behind his back. Henry moaned softly. Malachi went still.

"I've been through stuff like this before," I said to Evan, itching to grab for my knives. "Did you expect me to cry and beg for my life?"

He was quiet for a few moments, looking back and forth between me and Malachi.

"No, Lela," he finally said with a faint, evil smile on his lips. "I expected you to beg for his."

He pulled a handgun from his waistband, swinging it around so quickly that I barely had a chance to register what was happening. Malachi jumped to his feet as Evan aimed.

And pulled the trigger.

THIRTY-TWO

CRACK.

Malachi staggered sideways, leaving a long smear of red against the back wall of the trailer. Evan growled and took aim again. I lunged for him.

But Henry got there first. He jumped to his feet—and took the second bullet in the chest. His eyes went wide, and he fell back. I plowed into Evan, my fingers wrapping around his wrist, rage coloring my world red. He might have been taller than me, but he was also skinnier and not as strong. I shoved him against the wall of the trailer. Pushed beyond my awareness of anything outside the two of us, I stripped the gun from Evan and slammed it against his head over and over again. As his eyes rolled back, I whipped my knife from my pocket and gave him a permanent kind of rest.

As I ripped the blade from Evan's throat, another Mazikin landed on my back. His fingernails raked across my collarbone, leaving fiery streaks of agony. I pivoted around and jammed my knife upward into his gut, leaving him doubled over and whimpering. Knowing there were three left and that we couldn't let them escape, I leaped to my feet and nearly fainted with relief as Malachi, his left shoulder soaked with blood, locked Pre-Calc Girl in a stranglehold while he downed the baseball-cap guy with a vicious side kick. I crunched the butt of Evan's gun into the now-capless Mazikin's head, then drew my blade across his throat.

"One of them got out." Malachi slammed his knee into Pre-Calc Girl's face, sending her to the ground like a bag of rocks, her nose gushing. "Stay with Henry," he added in a faltering voice, then sprinted out of the trailer, presumably to chase Stocky Guy, who'd escaped.

I finished off Pre-Calc Girl, and then I turned toward a wheezy gurgling sound that filled me with dread. "Raphael, I need you," I shouted to the air, then dropped to my knees beside Henry, who was on his back next to the chair where he'd been "tied." One of the ropes still dangled from his wrist. Blood trickled from his nose and mouth. "It's okay, Henry," I said softly, sliding my arm under his neck and gently lifting his head.

His gurgling turned into a choked laugh. "Not a chance," he mumbled.

I pressed my hand over the wound on the left side of his chest, trying to stem the horrible flow of red. "Raphael," I yelled again, my voice breaking.

"No," he whispered. "'s okay. But you have to do the rest without me."

"Shut up." I squeezed my eyes shut. He'd sacrificed himself to save Malachi. And even though I knew Raphael had probably heard me summon him from wherever he was, I also knew with terrible certainty that he wouldn't get here in time. Henry's blood seeped between my fingers, a merciless flood. My Guard was going to die before our mission was completed, and I had no idea what that meant for him. Still . . .

"Sascha's waiting for you," I said, my mouth close to Henry's ear. "He'll be so proud of you." I tightened my grip on Henry as he shuddered, his fingers scrabbling at his neck like he couldn't get enough air. "No matter where you go next, you'll find each other. But for what it's worth, I think you deserve the Countryside."

His eyes met mine, and the tears welled up fast. "Captain . . ."

"You've been the best Guard, Henry. I know it wasn't what you wanted. But you've been loyal and badass. And wise. You totally set me straight. We wouldn't be here if you hadn't been with us."

A tear slid from his eye and wet my fingers. For a moment, he simply gazed at me, his body becoming still and loose, relaxing in my arms. And then: "Thank you, Lela."

I knew the moment he left, the second he moved on. And with everything inside me, I prayed that he and Sascha would find one another again. I had no idea if that prayer was worth a thing, but I'd take the chance. Because their heaven was in each other, and with every cell in my body, I wanted that for Henry.

A hand closed around my shoulder, and I snapped my head up to see Malachi leaning against the doorframe behind me. “I caught the one who escaped,” he said in a weary voice. “But he made some noise. We have to leave.”

“Henry . . .”

“I know, Lela,” Malachi said, his voice catching.

“Say that prayer? Can you do that for him?”

Malachi nodded, his expression creased with grief. I let Henry go, closing his eyes and getting to my feet. I put my arm around Malachi’s waist and let him lean on me as he bowed his head. With halting, whispered words, he spoke the prayer: the desperate wishes of our hearts, our gratitude to Henry for being our ally, our grief that he was gone, our hope that he was in a better place now.

When Malachi finished, he raised his head. “I can hear sirens.”

“We can’t leave him here.”

“I can’t carry him,” he replied. “I’m sorry . . . I . . .” He looked down at his left arm, blood dripping from his fingertips. He shivered against me. We needed to get back to the Guard house so Raphael could heal him.

“I’ll take care of Henry,” said Raphael, appearing next to me.

I blinked at him, my eyes burning, tears staining my cheeks. “You’re too late.”

Raphael gazed down at Henry, who looked more peaceful in death than he ever had been in life. “He accomplished what he was sent here to do.” He glanced around the trailer, at the bodies crumpled on the floor, the blood everywhere. “I’ll take care of this and meet you at the Guard house.”

Malachi’s hand slipped into mine. “Come on,” he said softly. After a gentle tug and one last look at Henry, I followed my Lieutenant out of the trailer and broke into a jog behind him. Even though he’d only been to the new Guard house a few times, Malachi's steps were sure as he picked up speed and headed for the woods. He held his left arm against his body, and I heard bursts of pained breath every time he leaped over a fallen tree trunk or a divot in the path. My chest was screaming, too, and I knew the Mazikin claw marks would require healing, but apart from that, I was uninjured.

We scrambled through the woods as flashing lights from the distant highway told us that cops would soon be swarming over the construction site, wondering where the hell all the blood had come from. There wouldn't be a body in sight. Though we hadn't told Raphael about Stocky Guy, I trusted him to handle that, too, opening a door to a different realm and tossing the empty shells through, making them disappear forever.

When we reached the Guard house, we were out of breath and on the verge of collapse. Malachi fell onto a couch, his grimace telling me how much pain he was in. I rushed over to him, wincing at the neat hole through the crest of his left shoulder. A few inches and he would have been in the same predicament as Henry, but this was bad enough. He had movement in his arm and fingers, but it had bled a lot and was obviously painful.

"Raphael will be here soon," I told him, smoothing my hand over his sweaty black hair. "We'll have you fixed up in no time."

He closed his eyes. "I'm sorry for what I had to do as Juri. You understand?"

"I think so."

"I had to stop Ian from following us," he said, his voice strained. "And I had to make it look convincing." His eyes opened. "They had something planned, for after school. I know you were supposed to stay until the end of the day, but if we hadn't left, they would have known immediately that something wasn't right."

"How do you think Evan figured it out?"

"He became suspicious as soon as I changed the plan. I never found out what they were going to do."

I took his hand. "It's all right. You did everything you could. We'll figure it out."

He groaned. "Lela, could you get me some water? Maybe a cloth, too?"

"Of course." I got up quickly, my heart skipping at how weak his voice sounded. I went into the bathroom and grabbed a towel, then got him a glass of water. When I returned, he took the towel and flattened his palm over it, pressing it to his wound and trying to stop the bleeding. I sank next to him, and he scooted over to make room on the couch. "*I* can do that."

He sipped the water as I put pressure on the wound. "We only have six left to kill, including Juri," I said, trying to sound reassuring. "We can do this."

He nodded toward my chest, at the bleeding ragged claw marks. "Raphael will need to tend to you."

"You're going first," I told him. And then I laughed. "And that's an order."

But he didn't smile. Instead, he sighed. "Lela, I have to tell you something."

Raphael chose that moment to appear in our living room. "All the bodies have been disappeared," he said to me. "You will not be linked to the scene. Do you want to be healed asleep or awake?"

"Malachi is worse than I am. He has to go first."

Raphael gave Malachi a speculative look. "You didn't tell her. Interesting choice."

"Tell me what?" I said, my stomach knotting.

"I will not heal him, Lela. That would be interfering with the natural course of events, beyond what is necessary to allow you to complete your mission."

"I have no idea what kind of joke this is," I snapped, glaring at him, "but it isn't funny."

Malachi set his water glass down. "When I went before the Judge, he agreed to let me return to the land of the living one last time." He laced his fingers with mine. "But not as a Guard. I am, for all intents and purposes, a civilian."

After demanding that Malachi let me take him to the hospital—and getting flatly turned down—I asked Raphael to put me under, because I was too short-circuited to manage the pain. Malachi had known this might happen. He'd known that if he was wounded, he'd be on his own, but he'd kept it from me. The frustration twisted inside me, even as everything went black and silent.

I woke up long before I was ready, jolted into awareness by Raphael's blazing hands. "You need to see this," he said, pulling me up still aching and half-fixed. He held out my phone.

On the screen was a text:

I've taken something of yours.

It had come with a picture. Tegan, Ian, and Diane, hands behind them, sitting in the dingy living room of the meth house.

Even as I cried out, unable to process the terror that came with that image, the phone vibrated with another text:

If you aren't here in an hour, I will skin them alive.

I jumped to my feet and staggered as a wave of dizziness crashed over me. I hit the wall and managed to grab the doorframe to keep myself from sliding to the floor. "I have to go."

"Yes, you do," said Raphael. He flattened his palm against my chest. The jolt of fire from his hand made me scream and fall to my knees, tears streaking from the corners of my eyes. "Sorry."

He stepped away, and I fell forward, catching myself with my hands.

"Lela?" Malachi was still in the living room. He sounded weary and weak, and it reminded me of what he'd done.

"I'm going," I growled, pushing myself to my feet and striding into the living room. He was on the couch, the bloodstained towel on his shoulder, but he sat up when he saw the look on my face.

"What's happened?"

"Now we know what they had planned for after school. Juri has Diane, Tegan, and Ian. And if I'm not there in an hour, he's going to kill them in the worst way possible." I walked to the kitchen table, where Henry's weapons had been laid out, waiting for his return. My jaw clenched as I looked them over and grabbed his knives.

"I'm going with you," Malachi said from right behind me.

I bowed my head, anger boiling just beneath my surface. "No, you're not."

"Lela, you can't stop me."

I whirled around and shoved him, my hands colliding with his chest and making him stagger back. "I bet I can. What the hell, Malachi? Why didn't you tell me?"

He leaned against the wall, wincing as he moved his left arm. "Because I suspected you would react like this."

That only made me angrier. "Can you blame me?"

"No," he said gently. "But obviously, I was hoping this wouldn't happen, and that we could avoid the whole discussion."

"Is that how you operate? Avoiding things until they bite you in the ass?"

Raphael chuckled from his position on the living room couch, where he was lounging as if he'd come over for tea or something.

"Shut up," Malachi and I said at the same time.

He chuckled one more time and disappeared.

Malachi flexed the fingers of his left hand. "If Juri has Diane and the others, you need my help."

I glared at him. "I'll figure it out on my own." Because if he went like this, Juri would eat him for breakfast, and that was one thing I couldn't take.

"You're not being logical," he said, his voice quiet.

"I'm not being *logical*?" I yelled, waving a knife between us. "When has any of this ever involved logic? If I'd been logical, you'd still be chained in the square, having your vital organs torn out of you! If I'd been logical, we never would have met! I've always done what felt right. I do what I can to protect the people I love, and even though I don't like you very much right now, I love the shit out of you. If anything happened to you, it might take me out for good."

"You love Diane, too," he murmured.

"Shut. Up!" My hands shook as I picked up Henry's belt and slid the knife into one of the sheaths, then added three more.

"Lela, I know you're scared." Malachi's voice was so calm that it made me want to kick him. "And I'm sorry I didn't tell you. I thought you wouldn't let me help if you knew."

"You were right."

He moved a little closer. "I didn't want you to see me as weak. I saw how you looked at me in the Mazikin city. I liked how you looked at me this morning a lot better. And I needed you to let me help you. It's why I came."

I wrenched the belt around my waist but struggled with the buckle because my hands were so unsteady. Malachi stepped forward, and before I had a chance to push him away, he fastened it for me, tucking the end into the belt loop. Pain was etched into lines around his mouth, but he was using both hands. His eyes met mine.

He had me—I loved Diane. She was my family in this life, the only person who had really protected me like a parent should. She had made a place for me in her heart and hadn't demanded that I do the same, but it had happened, anyway. I had a mom, and I'd always be grateful for what she'd done for me in the end, but Diane was also my mom, in a different way. A real way, a true way, and as much as it terrified me to let Malachi walk into danger one more time, it gave me the best chance of getting her, Tegan, and Ian away from Juri.

"Don't you dare die," I whispered, my fear for him choking me.

"I don't plan to." His fingers stroked down my cheek and lifted my chin. "I'll go into this knowing that you need me to stay alive."

I clamped my lips shut over the sob that was trying to break free. “What if it’s not enough?”

“Lela,” he said tenderly. “You walked into hell for me. I fought my way out of heaven for you. No matter what happens, there is one thing I don’t doubt at all: we will find each other again.”

THIRTY-THREE

I PULLED OVER ABOUT half a mile from the meth house and stared out the windshield. The sun was setting over the forest ahead of me, a ball of orange fire licking at the treetops. "Are you sure you can do this?"

"Henry and I practiced in the evenings when we were both home," Malachi replied, hefting Henry's old crossbow and leaning it on the dash. His wound had stopped bleeding and we'd bandaged it tightly, but he still didn't have full movement of his left arm. He'd lost a lot of blood, and his olive skin was paler than it should have been. I knew he was in pain—and trying to appear stronger than he felt.

"Get them into the clearing and I'll take them out," he continued, arching an eyebrow and giving me an unfairly sexy smile. "I'm actually quite a good shot."

That didn't surprise me at all.

"Okay." I bit my lip. "I'd better go."

He drew me toward him and gave me a deep kiss that left me aching. "Be careful. He'll be looking for all your weak spots."

"He already knows what they are." Because Malachi did.

"But he overestimates his own strength. He always has."

"He's pretty damn strong."

"So are you," he said, his lips brushing mine as he spoke. "And I have your back."

"But your priority is to get Diane and the others out of the house." I slid a grenade from the pack between us and pressed it into his hand. "And blow it to hell."

His eyes flickered with concern. "You'll be on your own."

"Only for a little while." I was determined to hold out that long.

His hands wrapped around either side of my neck, and we leaned our foreheads together, noses touching. Finally, he opened the door and got out, carrying the crossbow against his right shoulder, his own belt studded with throwing knives. He didn't look back as he disappeared into the woods, heading for the little house I'd showed him on Google Maps. One look had been all he needed to orient himself and fix the location in his head. "Be safe," I whispered at his retreating back.

I put the car in gear and pulled onto the road. If all went as planned, we'd take out Juri and his five remaining family members, and then I'd be done. I had no idea what would happen after that, but I was eager to find out. As upset as I'd been at the news that Malachi no longer had access to Raphael because he wasn't a Guard anymore, it also meant he was already free. He could live his life. He could have the future he'd craved, and make it whatever he wanted. But I was still a

Guard, so I could only hope the Judge would let me be a part of it.

I was cranked pretty tight by the time I turned into the driveway. I wasn't sure how long it would take Malachi to approach on foot, but I knew he'd be moving as fast as he could. The chemical stench was overpowering as I got out of the car; it burned my nose, making my eyes water. A few cars were parked in front of the rambling meth house, including Ian's cherry-red SUV.

Knowing I'd arrived with only minutes to spare, I stepped in front of my car, onto the overgrown lawn. "I'm here, Juri!" I called.

He appeared in the doorway of the house a moment later, a wicked smile on his face. He looked gorgeous in an evil kind of way, his black hair messy, his stride loose as he descended the porch steps. "Lela," he said in an amused voice that carried a cruel undercurrent. "What have you been up to?"

"I have no idea what you mean," I said, putting every ounce of dumb I could manage into my voice.

That muscle in his jaw began to tick. "Where is Evan? I expected him to help me this afternoon."

"Sucks to lose track of family." My eyes were hard on his. "Where's Diane?"

He crossed his arms over his chest. "Five of my Mazikin are missing, and your friends were kind enough to tell me they left school with you in tow." His dark eyes flared with a spark of rage. "Oh. And apparently I was there, too."

My heart stuttered.

"He's come back, hasn't he?" he asked. "I'll take as much pleasure in killing him this time as I did before. Is that what you want?"

"I want my foster mother and my friends."

He took a step closer to me. "And I want Malachi, bleeding out in front of me as I do unspeakable things to you. Does that sound like a fair trade?"

"Sure. It sounds fair." I drew a knife. "But life isn't fair, asshole."

The whisper of the bolt slicing through the air was the only warning Juri had, and yet somehow it was enough. He dropped into a crouch—but Malachi's aim had been good. Juri roared as he yanked the bolt from his left shoulder. He lunged at my legs, catching me by surprise as he drove the bolt through my calf before ripping it out again. He grabbed my wrist and slammed my hand to the ground, causing me to drop my knife. Then he rolled with me until we were against my car, shielded from the woods and Malachi's bolts.

"I didn't want to hurt you," Juri shouted into my face. He clamped his eyes shut but held me tight as I struggled. He shook his head back and forth, like he was trying to jar something loose.

When he opened his eyes, hatred glittered in their dark depths. "No, that's not right," he said with an unhinged chuckle. "I do want to hurt you. I've *always* wanted to hurt you. I've always wanted to be the only one to hurt you."

Then his mouth crashed down on mine. I gagged as his tongue invaded me, as he kissed me so hard I thought my jaw would break, as his bitter venom poured into my system. My head spinning, my hands scrabbling, I bucked my hips and lunged for my knife.

Juri buried his head against my neck, his teeth scraping my skin. "How do you want to die, Lela?"

"I don't." I wrenched back his head and spit in his face, then head-butted him hard, still reaching for my blade.

He snarled and punched me in the stomach. "Can he hit a moving target?" He rose to a crouch as I struggled to draw breath. "Because I've got guests waiting for me, and I'd better go take care of them."

I caught his ankle as he surged to his feet, and he fell forward, his boot narrowly missing my face. I finally got ahold of the knife and tried to stab him, but my arms weren't quite working the way they were supposed to. Juri growled and grunted, calling to his family, maybe to hurt Diane and Ian and Tegan. I drew the knife along his leg, barely cutting through fabric, but it was enough to get his attention.

He let out an animal howl and twisted around, leaping for me again. I rolled out of the way and staggered to my feet as two Mazikin burst onto the porch. Juri barked some order at them, but before he finished, one of them pitched forward with a bolt buried deep in his throat.

It had come from behind him. Malachi had gotten into the house.

The surviving Mazikin spun around and barreled back inside. Could Malachi handle four Mazikin and save three hostages? Anything could happen. If he blew himself up again, that was it.

But Juri was all I could handle at the moment.

His elbow cracked down on my ankle, instantly numbing my foot. "We've been here before, haven't we?" he said in a harsh voice. "It won't end the same way."

I kicked at him, using my elbows to drag myself back onto the grass, into the open. From the house, there came a long terrified scream, and for the life of me I couldn't figure out if it was Tegan or Diane or someone else. I flopped onto my back, trying to push myself up to sitting, but I couldn't get my arms beneath me. Juri was stalking after me, his dark eyes riveted on my face as I tried to focus my vision. My stomach turned, threatening to rebel completely.

Juri chuckled. "All it took was a kiss to have you on your back. Why didn't I try that before?"

"Oh my God, you talk way too much," I muttered. "Just come at me." I couldn't let him go into the house. I needed to give Malachi the best chance I could.

As Juri crouched next to me, there was a muffled explosion and a flash. The kitchen windows blew outward, showering us with glass. I rolled, and Juri collapsed backward, his hands over his face. When I raised my head, Ian was stumbling onto the porch, his face bloody and swollen, his wrists raw, carrying Tegan, whose ankle was bent unnaturally. Diane followed, coughing, her silver hair wild, holding on to the back of Ian's shirt. Her mouth dropped open when she saw me in the grass. Before I could shout at her to run, Juri pitched forward on all fours and charged.

All my desperate love for her brought me to my feet to stagger after him. But I wasn't going to get there in time. His four-legged lope ate up the distance, and Diane looked so startled and horrified that all she could do was flatten herself against the wall next to the door, her hands up to shield herself.

"Diane," I screamed as Juri reached the porch steps and launched himself at her. I'd never felt so helpless.

But just before he made contact, Malachi barreled out of the house and caught Juri midair. They flew backward off the porch, landing with a hard thunk in the grass a few feet from me. Malachi had a few cuts on his arms and face, but what worried me most was his left shoulder, which had bled through the bandages. I was trying to summon the coordination to help him with Juri when he shouted, "Get them away from the house! Eight!"

Eight seconds until detonation. A Mazikin, its face black and its clothes on fire, stumbled through the doorway and onto the porch. A second one, more agile, used its pal as a springboard to leap past us and charge after Ian, Tegan, and Diane. I looked down at Malachi, struggling with Juri, both of them sporting bloody shoulders and throwing brutal, sharp punches. And then I looked at my defenseless friends.

I couldn't abandon them. Clutching my knife as tightly as I could, I limped after the Mazikin. "Hey! Did you know I killed your mom? Your Queen is dead because of me."

The Mazikin stopped short and whirled around, its nose twitching. Then it jumped at me, and I got my knife up in time to deal it a glancing blow that knocked me off balance. Juri's venom was doing its thing, sending waves of buzzing numbness coursing through me in slow, lazy surges. But I wasn't out of commission yet. As the Mazikin, a middle-aged guy with tattoos all over his neck and arms, descended on me, I jammed my foot into his knee. He fell on top of me as the house gave off a deep, percussive thump and then exploded, fire shooting into the sky.

"I'm not going back," the man huffed. He snapped at me, trying to close his teeth over my neck as I clumsily punched and stabbed at him. Finally, he grabbed my wrists and pinned me to the ground. "Never going back!" he roared, his jaws wide as he struck.

But he never reached me. A tree branch cracked down over his back, and Diane appeared over his shoulder, her eyes blazing. "Get the hell off her!" she shouted, raising the branch and smacking it down again. The Mazikin snarled and caught the branch with Diane's next blow, but then Ian tackled him, slamming the guy to the ground. After a quick glance told me that Malachi and Juri were still going at it in the middle of the clearing, their silhouettes dark in the light of the fire, I once again rolled to my knees, forcing myself to concentrate on keeping my fingers wrapped around the knife. Ian was punching at the guy, pouring all his hatred into every blow, his bloody face vacant but tense.

"Ian, stop," I said, crawling forward.

"No."

"Yes. Just for a minute. Please."

He looked up at me, awareness returning to his eyes. "Why?"

I dragged myself forward and fell on top of the tattooed Mazikin, then abruptly slashed my knife across his throat. "Have a good trip." I slowly got to my feet.

Ian stared at me. "You killed him."

I glanced at Diane, who I had expected to react with horror, but she merely crossed her arms over her chest and glared at the Mazikin's body. I returned my attention to Ian. "I'll explain later. Please get Tegan and Diane into the woods."

"You're not coming?"

"I have to help Malachi."

Ian's eyebrows shot up as he looked toward the two struggling figures on the lawn. "Which one?" he said, his voice made of pure WTF.

"Just go," I said, already moving toward them. The last remaining Mazikin besides Juri had somehow gotten far enough away to survive the explosion and was running toward the two men fighting on the lawn. I broke into a hitching jog, even though my feet each felt like they weighed one hundred pounds.

The Mazikin tackled Malachi, dragging him away from Juri but holding him down, leaving my Lieutenant at the mercy of the creature wearing his skin. Wiping at his face and rolling his wounded shoulder, Juri stalked toward Malachi, who was fighting to get his arms free. His shirt had ridden up, revealing beautiful, smooth skin. Vulnerable. Easy to destroy.

Adrenaline exploded through me, temporarily pushing back the numbness. I slammed into Juri, stabbing down as hard as I could, slicing along his ribs but not penetrating the bone. He snarled and arched back. Our legs got twisted on the way down, and he landed on me with a crunch. I didn't have time to get the knife up again before he ripped it from my hand. "You stupid little bitch," he roared, sounding more animal than human. "Go tell your Judge she will never be rid of me!"

He slammed the blade through my stomach. The pain was like an explosion inside me, setting fire to my mind.

Through the blaze, I heard Malachi call my name. Juri yanked the knife from my body and lunged forward to meet him in the middle. Panting, trying to stay focused despite the agony, I squinted and saw the Mazikin that had grabbed Malachi lying in a bloody heap on the grass. Juri and Malachi were locked in brutal combat again, but Malachi was barely keeping the razor-sharp blade away, fighting in pure defense as Juri attacked with a vicious smile.

I put my hand on my stomach, my fingers sliding over my bloody skin. My legs were like blocks of cement, and I shivered violently as I pulled another knife from its sheath. Malachi's voice was in my head, from the first training session we'd ever had. The first time he'd ever taught me to throw a knife.

Only as a last resort.

I had nothing else. I couldn't move my legs.

Not everyone throws well enough to do anything but give the enemy a weapon.

It wasn't my enemy I wanted to give it to. I cocked my arm as the strangest sensation crept up my chest and into my throat. Burning and wet. I coughed, and blood splattered onto my hand. "Shit," I whispered, managing to prop myself up on an elbow. I spat a mouthful of blood into the grass and concentrated on my target. With a silent prayer, I threw that knife with all my remaining strength as Juri delivered a brutal elbow strike that doubled Malachi over. He brought his knee up sharply, catching Malachi in the chest. Juri kicked him away just as my knife sliced along his upper arm and landed in the grass between him and Malachi. Juri looked down at his bicep and back at me, and then began to laugh. A mocking animal laugh. A laugh that said he knew he had won.

Darkness licked at the edges of my vision. Even the fire from the house wasn't enough to light the night. But it was enough to allow me to see Malachi scoop up my knife and descend on his enemy, the fire reflecting in his black-brown eyes, rage consuming his features, looking for all the world like a lion pouncing on its prey.

I never saw him land.

THIRTY-FOUR

"OPEN YOUR EYES, BABY. You're all right now."

"Diane?" I said, my eyes popping open.

No. I was in the Judge's chambers, a place I hadn't wanted to see again. Ever. I looked down at myself. My clothes were bloody, but my body was intact. Nothing hurt. *No.*

"Yes, I'm afraid so," she said softly, her voice telling me she was close. But I couldn't raise my head. I didn't want it to be real. "It's real, baby. You have to face it."

Her fiery-orange fingernails nudged my chin up, and I found myself looking into her amber-brown eyes. "You're strong enough to face it," she said gently.

I looked around. The inhuman Guards were arrayed on either side of the aisle that led out of her chambers, as usual, but all of them were facing the front, and their eyes were on me. A few of them had their hands over their hearts, in a kind of salute.

I'd been hunched over on the white marble floor, and I sat back on my knees. "Malachi," I said to the Judge. "Did he get Juri?"

"I can show you," she said to me, "but only if you're sure you want to see."

My stomach tightened, like there was still a wound there, even though it felt fine. No numbness, no pain. "Show me."

She pointed at the white wall of her chambers, and the burning meth house appeared before us. There, on the grass, lay Juri, his head canted at an awful angle, his throat cut to the bone. And a few feet away, Malachi was bent over, on his knees.

He was cradling my body. His broad back shook as he sobbed silently.

The image disappeared, and the Judge looked down at me. "You completed your mission, baby. You did a good job. I'm proud of you."

I couldn't say thank you. I didn't feel proud. I felt tired. She stroked my hair and pointed at the wall again. There lay the Countryside, emerald grass and rolling hills, wildflowers blooming, sun shining.

"You're free to go," she said.

I remembered what it felt like, to sink my toes into those soft green blades, the sweet fragrances on the air, the warmth. Nothing would ever hurt me again. And the more I stared, the more I saw people, their faces coming to me even though they were at a distance, like a camera with a powerful zoom lens. Takeshi and Ana swam in a crystal lake, water beading on their brown skin, their faces lit with happiness. Nadia lay on her back in a meadow with a group of other teenagers, pointing up at the clouds like she saw something beautiful there. Treasa and the Smith sat on a rock overlooking a field of wheat. And Henry and Sascha walked hand in hand through a forest. As I watched, Sascha put his arms around Henry's narrow shoulders and pulled him close. Their kiss was pure relief and tenderness. Home after so many years at war.

My attention shifted back to Nadia, and as though she sensed me, she sat up. She looked right at me. And she smiled. She got to her feet and opened her arms, inviting me to join her.

But instead of moving toward her, I collapsed in on myself, pulling my legs to my chest and bowing my head against my knees. Through my arms I said, "I have a question."

"Go ahead."

I swiped tears from my face. "Did you know all this would happen from the very beginning?"

The Judge gazed down at me, her eyes filled with a cold that hit me bone-deep. "Does it really matter if I did?"

"Did you choose me? I mean, from that night on the cliff, that night I fell. A gust of wind pushed me over the edge and started this whole thing. Was that you? Can't you just tell me?"

"Would it really help you to know?"

My fingers curled into my pant legs. "I want to know if you picked me to go through this. If I somehow got lucky." I spat the last word, my resentment making it hard to draw breath.

"Baby, I chose you," she said, her voice full of amusement. "But I chose *a lot* of people."

I stared at her, and she sighed. "You can't see things the way I do," she said. "You're not made that way. But you can understand this. Say you're walking down a road, and a big brick wall drops down in front of you. What would you do?"

"Are you serious?" I snapped. "Are you really giving me some inspirational proverb right now?"

She chuckled. "Just go with it."

I gritted my teeth to keep from screaming at her. "I don't know. Maybe I'd climb over it."

"Choice. What if it's too high?"

"I'd try to go around it."

"Another choice. But it's too big to get around. Then what?"

I threw my hands up. "I don't know. I'd try to dig my way under it. Or chip my way through it."

She started to laugh. "Choice and choice. But you could have sat down in the road and stayed where you were. You could have turned around and gone back the way you came." She put her hands on my shoulders and lifted me to my feet as if I weighed nothing. "But that's not who you are."

"And your point is?"

"You're the only one who made the sequence of choices that led you to this place. Yes, there were things you didn't control, obstacles that landed in your path. But each and every time, you decided what to do. You entered the dark city. You found Nadia. And when given your chance to enter the Countryside, you gave that up for her. You chose to go after Malachi when he was lost to the Mazikin. You chose to liberate the city. You chose to stay and fight in the land of the living, even when you were tempted to give up. Each and every time, you took the steps. You made the choices. So maybe I chose you, but more importantly, *you* chose you."

"And Malachi?"

Her eyes flashed with humor. "He is exactly the same. He made his choices. He knew the risks and accepted them."

And now he was broken and grieving in the land of the living, and I was here, about to be released into the Countryside. But maybe . . .

"Can I have a reward for my loyal service?" I asked, squaring my shoulders. "I think I've earned it."

"What do you want, baby?"

I turned to her, meeting her eyes. "One more choice."

She gazed out on the Countryside, where Nadia was waiting. "I'm offering you an eternity of peace."

"But what I want is a choice," I repeated.

"I won't make promises," she said. "If I give you a choice, it doesn't come with guarantees. Not happiness, not freedom from tragedy, not protection from illness or injury or grief or failure."

"That's life, right?" I murmured.

A slight smile curved her red lips. "That's life. It can be hell, baby."

"But sometimes it's the opposite."

"Only sometimes. You could have the opposite all the time."

I looked at the wall, at the Countryside, but it had disappeared. What I saw there now was Malachi, still cradling my body as the fire raged. Diane was on her knees next to him, tears rolling down her face as she spoke into her cell phone, probably calling an ambulance I was way past needing.

"Do you really want all that pain? You're so tired. You've been through so much. Every soul has its limit."

My eyes traced over Malachi as he kissed my forehead, as his tears fell on my face, as his hands threaded through my hair. "And every soul has its haven. Its heaven, too."

She put her hand on my shoulder as we watched paramedics arrive and try to pull him away from me. Weak and bleeding, he still fought, hunched over my body like he was my only chance at survival, my only protector. Then Diane's hands were on his back, gentle and insistent, and he let her pull him into her arms. He'd never looked so young or helpless. She held him against her as they both sobbed. I'd hurt them so much.

"Only because they love you," the Judge said softly.

I turned my attention to my body—my blood-soaked, defeated body. Broken so many times, unable to take any more punishment. One of the paramedics squatted next to me, placing his fingers on my neck and searching for my nonexistent pulse.

He raised his head and looked right at me, gray eyes inquisitive. Raphael.

"Now's the time, then," said the Judge. "Make your choice."

Raphael raised his eyebrows, waiting.

"It's made," I said.

She took my face in her hands. "Be brave, baby. Your days of fighting aren't quite over."

My heart skipped a beat, but then I saw her smile. "Because that's life," I said.

She nodded. "That's life. Do it well. When I see you again, I want to be able to tell you that you did a good job."

"I'll try. And thanks."

She grinned as the charge built in her hands, making me feel like I was about to be struck by lightning. "You're welcome."

My world became darkness again.

I lay back, feeling the sun on my face, the sound of the waves lulling me. A breeze ruffled my curls, and I pushed them away from my forehead.

Laughter reached me from a few yards away, and I turned my head to see Ian throw a bikini-clad Laney over his shoulders and charge with her into the water. Her shrieks weren't as annoying as they used to be, probably because she was making Ian happy, and that made me happy.

"If I did that to you, would you throat-punch me?" Malachi asked as he sank onto the towel next to mine.

The summer had darkened his skin, turning it a delicious brown. The silver indentation on his shoulder was the only battle scar he carried, and the rest of him was perfect—muscle and smooth flesh. I propped myself up on an elbow, taking in the view as he stretched out his long legs and sat back, his board shorts low on his lean hips. Heaven. Help. Me.

"Are you sure you could manage it? I'm heavier than I look."

He arched an eyebrow. "Is that a challenge?"

And just like that, he was on me, strong arms pulling me up and lifting me high, holding me tight as he bounded toward the water. "I'm not a good swimmer," I yelped. It was why I'd spent the entire day on the sand.

"Then you should practice more," he called back as he reached the water and kept running, waves splashing my face until he pitched forward into the ocean, plunging me into the cold.

I flailed, scared for a moment, but then I wrapped my arms around his neck as he planted his feet in the sand. He crouched low, so the water was up to my neck. He pushed my wet hair out of my face and gave me a saltwater kiss. "See?" he said. "Nothing to be afraid of."

"It's hard to be afraid when you're with me." I laid my head on his shoulder as he walked into deeper water. My fingers found the spot on his back where the bullet had exited, and I stroked it. "Does it still bother you?"

The night we'd defeated Juri, Malachi had been rushed to the hospital in an ambulance, too, but he hadn't been tended by Raphael on the way. I'd made a miraculous recovery, but Malachi had to have surgery to repair the damage to his shoulder. It hadn't slowed him down much, though.

"I feel it," he said mildly, his arms around my waist, his fingers caressing my ribs. I still had scars of my own, but they'd faded, and people only tended to notice them if they looked very closely. Malachi, who knew where each one was and where it had come from, seemed drawn to them, his fingertips tracing those places with tenderness. As if we were still in the Mazikin realm and his love could heal the broken spots.

Come to think of it, maybe that's why they were so faded.

A wave hit us, lifting us in the swell and carrying us a few feet. When we landed, Malachi said, "It's like being in the jaws of a big friendly animal."

I snorted. "A little like the dark city. Except nicer."

"This is so strange," he murmured. "Sometimes I wake at night convinced that all of it has been a dream. I'm always surprised that I'm not in my cot, back in my quarters, my map on the wall, my weapons around me."

I touched his cheek. "But you're glad, right?" He was living in the Guard house, the little cottage near the airport. I was pretty sure Raphael had bent the rules when he set stuff up for Malachi, but I was grateful. While Malachi was in the hospital, we'd discovered he had a social security number, a bank account, and the deed to the Guard house. Not enough to be wealthy, but enough to give him a chance to figure out what to do next.

Malachi leaned his forehead on mine. "So glad," he whispered. His kiss was deeper this time. My legs locked around his waist as our mouths melded.

"Get a room, you two," Ian said as he swam past, splashing us. We broke apart as Malachi splashed back, laughing.

"Sometimes I wish we had Raphael around to mess with people's memories on a regular basis," I said quietly as Ian reached the shore. "It's so helpful."

Tegan, Ian, and Diane all remembered most of what had happened. But they didn't remember Juri. And they *did* remember that Malachi and I had been with them the whole time, victims alongside them, almost falling prey to the vicious drug ring responsible for the fires and the crime wave. Sure, there had been an investigation, but we were all cleared.

"Now we have to be crafty all on our own," Malachi said, drawing his hand up my leg. "But I think we can manage."

"Yeah?" I asked, breathless at the sensation.

"Mmm," he murmured against my skin. "After all, you did walk into hell for me."

I kissed his jaw, weaving my fingers into the thick black hair on the back of his head. "And you fought your way out of heaven for me."

He touched his nose to mine, and our eyes locked. "I think that means we can do anything."

We stayed like that, waves lapping our bodies, wrapped tightly, unwilling to let go, as the sun warmed our skin. I knew every moment couldn't be like this. There were no guarantees. There would be pain, and fighting, and struggles, and tears, because that was life. It was dangerous and unpredictable. Malachi and I would make our choices, and other people would make theirs, and it was impossible to know what would come of them. But as I heard his voice in my ear, as I felt the safety of his arms, as I sensed the adoration in his touch, I knew that, for a moment at least, I had found my heaven.

ACKNOWLEDGMENTS

Wow. The end of a series. There are so many people who helped make this happen, and I am grateful to all of you! Courtney Miller, my acquiring editor: thank you a million times for believing in this series from the start. The wonderful team at Amazon Publishing, including Timoney Korbar, Deborah Bass, and Erick Pullen: thank you for working so hard to give these books the visibility they needed. I'd like to thank copyeditor Elizabeth Johnson for nitpicking in the most delightful way. Additional thanks goes to my proofreader, Janice Lee. To my cover designer, Tony Sahara: thank you for designing a brutal, beautiful cover for Lela's final round. And to my developmental editor, Leslie "Lam" Miller: you are an absolute gift and will always be welcome in my margins (and in my parlor).

Thank you to the team at New Leaf Literary & Media, especially Joanna Volpe, Danielle Barthel, Jaida Temperly, and Lauren Wohl. And to Kathleen Ortiz, my agent: you are so many things—patient, empathic, fearsome when necessary, kind and strategic at all times. I am so glad we chose each other.

A special thank you goes to Petra Ippendorf (Safari Poet) for giving Treasa Kirwan her name.

I am blessed with fabulous writing friends. Lydia Kang: your name in my in-box is all it takes to make my day. And to Brigid, Jaime, Virginia, Justine, Stina, and Lori, thank you for cheering me on and lifting me up. I am also endlessly lucky to have a boss who not only helped me design my "day job" but has also helped me keep doing it despite all the competing demands of these two intense professions: Paul, I am forever in your debt. Thank you also to my team—Catherine, Anne-Marie, Chris, Casey, Kim, and Erica, as well as the entire staff of CCBS. You guys make it worth the juggling act. I'm so proud to be associated with you.

Thank you to my parents, Jerry and Julie; my sisters, Cathryn and Robin; my husband, John; and, of course, my kiddos, Alma and Asher. You hold me together.

I am grateful to all the bloggers who have helped spread the word, and to the librarians and teachers who took the time to share my books with their students. Thank you for helping this series and this book find its audience. And finally, thank you to my readers. Thanks for giving Lela a chance, for understanding her, and for rooting for her. Thanks for hanging with her and Malachi for three books. Thank you for laughing and crying with these characters, for letting them into your heart. It's hard for me to let them go, but knowing that you care about them eases the pain of this good-bye.

© Rebecca Skinner

SARAH FINE WAS BORN on the West Coast, raised in the Midwest, and is now firmly entrenched on the East Coast, where she lives with her husband and two children. When she's not writing, she's working as a child psychologist. No, she is not psychoanalyzing you right now. She is the author of the young adult novels *Sanctum*, *Fractured*, *Of Metal and Wishes*, and *Scan*. Her first adult fantasy novel, *Marked*, releases in early 2015 from 47North.

Find Sarah online at www.sarahfinebooks.com or on Twitter @FineSarah.

For more information about the Guards of the Shadowlands series, and to read excerpts from Malachi's personal journals, visit www.GuardsOfTheShadowlands.tumblr.com.

PRAISE FOR *SANCTUM*

Guards of the Shadowlands, Book 1

"As a modern-day 'Orpheus and Eurydice,' *Sanctum* will be a hit with urban fantasy readers, who will love its top-notch world-building, page-turning action, and slow-developing romance." —*School Library Journal*

"This is one of my favorite books of this year! . . . Smart and sexy." —*Reading Teen* blog

"In this well-developed concept of the afterlife, details are well-executed and the setting is described flawlessly. Without a doubt, readers will look forward to the next installment of the Guards of the Shadowlands series." —*Library Media Connection*

"Many original, interesting ideas create this complex world and creatures lurking through the afterlife. [Readers] will be excited to find this is [the] first of a trilogy." —*Voice of Youth Advocates* (*VOYA*)

"Dark, gripping, and impossible to put down. *Sanctum* is smart, original, and pulls no punches—just like Lela, one of the strongest heroines I've ever met." —Erica O'Rourke, author of *Torn*

"Theology be damned, though: Lela and Malachi are both likable protagonists, and readers will be happy (though not surprised) to find them drawn together; the supporting cast among the Guards is also strong . . . [T]his trilogy opener has a lot going for it." —*Kirkus Reviews*

PRAISE FOR *FRACTURED*

Guards of the Shadowlands, Book 2

"Between the expanded worldbuilding and well-paced suspense, Fine presents a . . . bridge to carry readers to Book 3." —*Kirkus Reviews*

"High stakes and heart-pounding action continue in this satisfying sequel." —*Booklist Online*

"Fans of the series will swoon over the make-out scenes and bite their nails during the gory fights, yearning impatiently for the next volume." —*Voice of Youth Advocates (VOYA)*